CODE RED

N.R. WALKER

COPYRIGHT

Cover Artist: N.R. Walker & Sam York
Editor: Boho Edits
Publisher: BlueHeart Press
Code Red © 2021 N.R. Walker

BLURB

Maddox Kershaw is the main vocalist of the world's biggest boy band. He's at the top of every music chart, every award show, every social media platform, and every sexiest-man-alive list. He's the bad boy, the enigma, the man everyone on the planet wants a piece of.

He's also burned out and exhausted, isolated and lonely. Not in a good headspace at the start of a tour.

Roscoe Hall is Maddox's personal manager. His job is high-flying, high-demand, high-profile, and he loves it. Maddox has consumed his entire life for the past four years. Roscoe *knows* him. He sees the real Maddox no one else gets to see.

He's also in love with him.

When the tour and stress become too much, when the world begins to close in, Roscoe becomes Maddox's lifeline. But as Maddox knows already, and as Roscoe is about to learn, the brighter the spotlight, the darker the shadow.

CAUTION WARNINGS

Code Red deals with mental health issues, including anxiety and panic disorder.

Reader discretion is advised.

CODE RED

N.R. WALKER

ATROUS

CHAPTER ONE

"ROSCOE HALL," I answered my phone, out of time and patience. It didn't dawn on me that it was Ryan's number until after I'd said my name. It was my twentieth call this morning already.

"Just confirming ETA for 9:00 am."

I checked my watch. It was 7:30 now and I'd already been up for far too long. It was a big day, and I could take a moment to breathe once we were all together.

"Yeah, Ryan. Will be there, thanks."

There was a brief pause. "Is Maddox with you?"

"On my way to get him now."

"See you there."

I pocketed my phone and did one last check. Phone, wallet, passport, tickets, keys. I grabbed my carry-on, locked my front door, and wheeled my suitcase down to the waiting car. I hadn't even greeted the driver when my phone rang again, and it beeped *again* on my way to collect Maddox.

I was organized and efficient, aggressively so.

It's what made me good at my job. Being the personal

manager for one of the world's biggest boy bands was every minute of my life.

These boys didn't accept second best for anything, and neither did I.

And I should clarify that while they were classified as a boy band, they were men. They might have started out as boys—they were just kids in high school when they formed their first band. But they were twenty-three now. They'd done the small local gigs, needing their parents' permission to play in bars and clubs around LA when they were underage.

The story of how the band called Atrous made it to the big time was well-known.

The five boys came from nothing. A garage band that crossed pop with rock and rap, playing small gigs wherever they could, when a well-known radio DJ saw them and uploaded footage to his social media. Platinum Entertainment, one of America's biggest entertainment management companies, signed them, and they'd been on the top of the world music stage for the last four years.

To the outside world, these guys were the ultimate success story.

They had no idea what went on when the lights went out.

Saying I was *the* personal manager of the whole band wasn't true either. Personal assistant, handler, manager. It was all the same. But it wasn't just me. I was one of three. Ryan Morten, Amber Seratt, and I were the personal managers of Atrous, as a whole. While the three managers looked after the five band members, I was, however, the unstated personal manager of one of them in particular.

Lead vocalist and rapper, main dancer, bad boy, Maddox Kershaw.

Ryan and Amber took care of Jeremy, Wes, Luke, and Blake. But Maddox was mine.

Well, not *mine*. But mine.

God, how I wished he were mine . . .

Over the last four years, Maddox and I'd just gelled. He didn't trust easily, and for some reason he'd put his trust in me. And the truth was, he needed his own personal manager more than the other four guys.

Maddox was the face of Atrous. Unwilling, but the face, nonetheless.

He carried the weight of their reputation, their brand. He was the one they hounded, the one they chased, the one they followed, the one that made headlines every other day.

He wore black, he had a full sleeve of tattoos, perfect skin, and he had attitude to spare. His motto was to burn down the institutions, to stand tall for those who had to kneel, and to speak for those who had been silenced.

He resonated with the youth around the world.

He was also incredibly good-looking.

When I say good-looking, I mean hot. Sexy, enigmatic, ethereal, even.

His heritage had been talked about a million times. So much of his life was public. His grandparents on his mother's side were Japanese, and his grandparents on his father's side were Dutch. He was a second generation American, a very talented musician, and he was incredibly smart.

He sang like an angel and danced like the devil.

And he answered the door looking like a mix of both. His hair was wet from the shower, he smelled warm and clean, he wore black cargo pants, a black T-shirt, and combat boots. It was his standard attire. Seeing him like that made my heart feel far too big for my chest. "Forget your key?" he asked. He even almost smiled.

It had been so long since I'd seen him smile . . .

Yes, I had a key to his house. But that was for emergencies only. I followed him inside. "You ready? The others are meeting us there."

He grumbled something that sounded like assent. His house was still dark, open and vast, mind-bogglingly expensive, and it felt empty. It was in Beverly Hills, worth a reported twelve million with incredible views of the canyon and the city, but Maddox had the blinds drawn.

He plucked a black hoodie off the back of his sofa and pulled it on. I ignored how his T-shirt lifted a little, exposing a sliver of pale skin above his waistband. I'd seen him shirtless a thousand times. Hell, I'd even seen him in his underwear. It was nothing new, but it still managed to warm my blood.

I grabbed his two suitcases, wheeling them toward the door. He picked up his black backpack. "Got my passport?"

"Yep," I replied. "We're all good. Your mom's got her key and security numbers?"

"Yeah," he said with a shrug.

His mother was going to come look after his place while we were gone. We'd be gone for almost seven weeks. Seven long, grueling weeks.

"Come on, I have an iced coffee waiting for you in the car."

He pulled up his hood, but I swear there was the beginning of a smile before the shadow stole it.

My phone buzzed again, and I pulled it out of my pocket and groaned at the screen. Another message that could wait until we were in the car. I pulled the door shut behind us, made sure it was locked, and wheeled the luggage to the waiting car. I opened the car door for him, I closed the door for him, I loaded the bags into the trunk—it was my job to do these things for him—and finally I got into the back of the car with Maddox.

My phone buzzed again, and I thumbed out a quick reply. We'd been driving for about ten minutes when I realized Maddox hadn't said a word. He'd sipped his coffee but not much else. I looked at him then, really looked at him, and underneath the killer good looks was a tired man.

"You sleep okay?" I asked.

He scoffed as his answer, then glanced pointedly at my phone. "Did you? Has your phone stopped yet?"

I didn't need to reply because we both knew the answer.

He nodded because he knew he was right and proving his point, I replied to some more emails and messages on the drive downtown. Yes, we all lived in LA, and yes, we were staying at a hotel in LA because when the tour began, the band and the whole crew would stay together. Mostly for logistical and security reasons, but also for bonding. We were one unit from day one, regardless of location.

As the car pulled into the hotel's underground parking lot, Maddox's eyes trained on the people rushing about. "The guys are already here?" he asked.

"Yep. Arrived five minutes ago."

His shoulders relaxed a little, and for that I was glad. He and his bandmates were like brothers; they'd been through everything together. He was closer to Jeremy than the others, but the bond between the five of them was clear. I was relieved that he'd be with them again. I was pretty sure he'd spent the last few days by himself, holed up in his house. I'd spoken to him on the phone, even came to see him a few times, but getting ready for a tour was a busy time for me.

Before we came to a complete stop, he was quiet and chewed on his bottom lip. I wanted to ask him if he was okay, but there wasn't time. I doubted he'd even answer that question, or answer it honestly, anyway.

"You excited?" I asked instead. "Sellout stadium tour, twenty-three concerts. You ready for that?"

He met my gaze and didn't look away. His smile was as brief as it was beautiful. "Yeah. Of course."

I didn't believe him, and it was devastating how he could look right at me with those dark, dark eyes and speak so sincerely while he lied.

I spent almost every day with him. I knew him. I knew the real Maddox Kershaw, not the Maddox he showed the world. I knew the private one, the quiet one, the intellectual one . . .

The miserable one.

The Maddox I'd been secretly in love with for years . . . the Maddox I could never have.

"Maddox," I said, but his door opened from the outside, and people were getting luggage from our car and giving directions, and there was no time.

The commotion had begun. These seven weeks were going to be brutal.

He lowered his head, pulled up his hood to hide his face, and got out of the car.

CHAPTER TWO

AS SOON AS Maddox and I walked into the common room, he was greeted by his bandmates with hugs and warm smiles. It relaxed me in ways I wasn't sure I understood. It was like seeing the lone wolf return to the pack. There was safety in that circle of boys, and selfishly, the pressure was off me.

Even if just for a moment.

"My favorite dickbag," Jeremy cried, hugging him the hardest, and Maddox's smile was genuine. His laugh made me smile. I noticed a camera crew of three in the corner filming the boys as I walked up to Ryan and Amber. "Morning," I said. I nodded toward the cameras. "Who are they?"

Ryan made a low growl sound, and Amber's expression was pissed. "Ambrose dropped them on us this morning. Apparently Platinum wants this trip filmed for a documentary."

The fuck?

The thing about band management was there were a lot of people behind the scenes, including a chain of command, or pyramid hierarchy. The management company, Platinum

Entertainment, was owned by a man named Arlo Kim. He was the big boss. In my four years in the job, I could count the times I'd seen him on my fingers. He was clearly a masterclass in business management because he'd launched Atrous into the stratosphere. That couldn't be denied.

Next link in the chain was Neil Ambrose. He was the actual band manager and who we three personal band managers answered to. We acted as the liaison between top management and the band. Ambrose was a good man, though he sometimes found himself in between a rock and a hard place trying to please everyone. Management usually won out every time.

Whatever Arlo said went. Like all management companies and their "boy bands," he basically owned Atrous. And apparently Arlo Kim had thought filming every minute of the boys on tour was a good idea.

Like a tour wasn't stressful on its own without worrying about having additional eyes backstage, in dressing rooms, and meetings.

Goddammit.

"And we're just hearing about it now?"

"For what it's worth, Ambrose was apologetic," Amber said. She was obviously about as happy with this development as I was. But there was little we could do about it now.

"Where's Ambrose?" I asked. He would be on the trip, obviously.

Ryan shrugged. "He was with the sound equipment guys and the stage team last I saw."

I repressed a sigh. It was hard to be pissed when the guy literally had 120 people to organize for a national tour, plus a string of concerts in three other countries. He didn't just have to worry about the band, but also wardrobe, the stage production team, the choreography team, the make-up and hair people, all the assistants and runners, and that didn't include the medical crew.

This was a huge undertaking.

We'd done a world tour for the last album a year ago, so at least this time we knew what we were getting ourselves into. This tour was twenty-three concerts in sixteen cities across the US, Canada, Brazil, and Argentina. There was a lot of travel and a lot of expectations. A world-class stadium tour was no small feat.

There were always small windows of time for unexpected things on these tours, and of course the boys would need some downtime between concerts, press conferences, photoshoots, interviews, and guest appearances on TV shows.

But the schedule was tight.

We were starting in LA, for three sold-out concerts and a steady stream of interviews and appearances, and so would begin the security mayhem. Overzealous fans and paparazzi were a constant pressure. We had our own personal security team that was always with us, but we were using local security teams in every city as well. It made sense; they were already on the ground, they were familiar with the lay of the land. They'd been prepped and vetted, and the added layer of protection was a comfort to me.

And flying by private charter plane took the usual airport terminal chaos and customs out of the safety-hazard equation. We were basically bypassing every busy airport terminal and the risk of overwhelming fans in huge crowds. But getting to the hotels, to venues, to late-night talk shows, to interviews—doing anything outside of a hotel room, basically—came with risks.

I hated that part.

And of course, Maddox was the center of attention, the

target for fans and photos; he was the money-shot for the papzz to exploit.

I hated that part the most.

Ambrose walked into the common room. No matter which hotel we stayed at, we always used a large conference room as our common meeting room, usually on the same floor as our rooms. It was used like our personal living room, giving us extra space, but also great for meetings, rehearsals, a dressing room if needed, and it was usually where we ate all our meals together.

"Morning!" Ambrose said brightly. "Welcome to day one."

He gave a brief rundown of the next few days, starting with a tour jacket photoshoot today, photos that would be used on the special release tour album cover. It was an easy introduction to the busy schedule, and the boys had an hour to get settled in their rooms before we'd be leaving for the location.

Amber, Ryan, Ambrose, and I sat in the meeting room and went through our itineraries, making notes and going through the finer points we'd discussed ten times already. Soon enough we were on our way down to the underground parking garage. There were three black SUV-style vans that looked like they were out of a presidential motorcade, our security standing guard at each one. Each van was the luxury kind most celebs used these days. Three seats across the back, two seats near the door, all leather of course. It resembled the interior of a private jet more than a van. There was plenty of room, and most importantly, we could see out but no one could see in. These windows weren't just tinted. They were some high-tech security feature that the record company had paid a fortune for. Bulletproof *and* paparazzi proof.

Amber, Blake, and Luke took the first, Ryan, with Wes and Jeremy, in the second, and Maddox and I climbed into the third.

We drove to the photoshoot location, which was down past Laguna. Hair and make-up met us there, along with wardrobe, and the photoshoot went well. The boys were in good spirits, laughing and joking as usual, and while the photographer, set designer, and lighting crew worked to get the best shots, Arlo's camera crew filmed everything that went on.

The racks of clothes, the table of jewelry, the behind-the-scenes people who were just trying to do their jobs. They didn't get in the way at all, but even having them there felt like an invasion of privacy.

I didn't like it at all.

And apparently neither did Maddox. When we were done and headed back to the hotel, he took his seat, and as soon as the door slid closed, he said, "And the film crew? What the fuck is up with that?"

I groaned, trying to take the middle ground. "Arlo's orders, apparently. It's for some behind-the-scenes documentary. Which, in all fairness, I can see why he wants to show that. People will be very interested in seeing the hard work you guys put in, and how it's not just what they see on stage."

"But?"

"Why is there a but?"

His lips twitched. "Because I know when you're not saying something."

I relented a smile at that. "But," I said, "I think tours are stressful enough on you guys. And make no mistake, if they get too close to you or if they get in the way or impose in any way I deem inappropriate, I will launch them and all their cameras into the fucking sun."

Maddox chuckled, the eye-crinkling kind, and went back to staring out the tinted windows for a while. "Can we get some food? I'm starving."

"Absolutely," I replied. I pulled up the group chat with Amber and Ryan. *Maddox wants food. I'm ordering burgers to be delivered to the hotel. What does everyone want?*

WE DROVE into the underground parking garage at the hotel, still incognito. I would expect it would be the last time, given people must have seen our big black vans, but it was good to see the guys relaxed and smiling as they went inside. It was only us staying at this hotel; the rest of the crew were staying at different places. Given there were so many of them—the soundies, the stage production, wardrobe and make-up, and dancers—they'd take up an entire hotel. As it was, "just us" took up half a floor.

As soon as the food was delivered, the guys ate in Luke's room, and Amber, Ryan, and I ate in the common room. "They're all psyched," Amber said. *They*, meaning the band.

"How's your boy?" Ryan asked. "He seems happier now that we're here."

My boy . . . I liked that a little too much.

"Yeah, he's okay," I replied, then sipped my water. Maddox had been quiet in the weeks leading up to now. Actually, he'd been quiet for months, and everyone knew it. "I'm sure he's just nervous and worried about this trip. Once they start performing, he'll be fine."

I didn't exactly believe that, and I was pretty sure they could tell.

"New albums and tours are always stressful," Amber added. "Just keep an eye on him and let us know if you need anything."

I gave her a smile. "I will, thanks." I picked at a few fries. "He just . . . he feels distant. I'm sure he'll find his feet once the concerts and press shit starts."

"He thinks he carries the world. He doesn't need to shoulder everything," Ryan said.

"We know that," I replied. It was almost comical. Of course he didn't *have to*. He just did.

Amber shrugged. "It's how he is. How he's always been."

I conceded a nod. "True. But it's more now. It's different. Before he thrived on it. The harder it all was, the better he did. Now he's . . . tired."

"We've got twenty-three shows," Ryan pointed out. "He can't be tired before he starts."

Amber finished her burger. "He won't let those boys down," she said. "He'll give 200 percent until it kills him."

That's what I'm afraid of.

I didn't need to say that out loud.

None of us did.

I KNOCKED on Maddox's door at 7:00 am. I heard him grumble something before the door swung inward. He was showered, dressed, and ready to go, and when I held up an iced coffee, he smiled. "You ready?" I asked, walking in. His bed was unmade, and I tried not to think about how he slept on the left side . . . how perfect it was because I slept on the right.

He sat on the bed, put his drink down, and pulled on a boot. "Yep."

"Busy day. We leave in five."

The next two days were full-on final choreography on stage, full dress rehearsals, sound checks, and roundtable talks about last minute changes and suggestions before the first concert. Tonight was their first television appearance on a well-known talk show where they would perform their newest song, "Fly."

Maddox and Jeremy had composed the score, Wes and Luke wrote the lyrics, Blake worked in the bluesy rap line. They moved it around like a jigsaw puzzle until it all fit together, and the song went to number one, on day one, in twenty-six different countries.

I picked up his black jacket. Not that it was jacket weather, but it had a hood, and he'd obviously left it over the back of the chair for a reason. "Got your phone?"

"Yes, Dad," he said with a smirk.

"I'm barely seven years older than you, so shut it."

He chuckled, that low throaty sound that rumbled through me in ways it shouldn't. He fixed his other boot, then collected his iced coffee and sipped it through the straw. "Thanks for this," he said. "Have the others eaten yet?"

"Yep. You know, you could try actually eating breakfast some time."

He put on a black baseball cap, pulled it down low, and smiled. "No, thanks."

I went to the door and held it open for him. "Move it or we'll be late."

"Yes, Mom."

I raised an eyebrow. "You wanna fucking walk?"

He laughed as he walked past me. "I'm gonna tell my mom you swore at me."

"Your mom likes me." I pulled the door closed and met him at the elevator. It was true. His parents did like me. I'd come to know them quite well over the last few years. Considering I spent almost every day with Maddox, it was only natural that I'd become familiar with them as well.

"Yes, she does."

"She promised to make me some of those almond cookie things." The elevator doors opened and we stepped inside. "I still want them, if you could ask her for me, that'd be great."

"She speaks to you more than she speaks to me," he replied.

I snorted. "That's not true. She knows you're busy, so it's just more efficient."

"Oh," he said. "Speaking of family. You still leaving me after New York to go see your folks?"

"I'm not leaving you," I said, liking that a whole lot more than I should. "It's just for a week. It makes sense while I'm on that side of the country. I'll see you through the last concert of the tour. You'll come back here to LA and sleep for a week. You won't even have time to miss me."

He was about to say something when the elevator stopped at a lower floor and the doors opened. Two people got in, both female, mid-twenties, maybe. They didn't pay much attention to us, too busy looking at their phones. But Maddox backed up against the wall, kept his head down, his cap covering his face.

Instinctively, I stepped in front of him, putting myself between them and him. They got out at the lobby, and when the doors closed again, leaving us alone, I heard him sigh. Those two girls were harmless, but the risk was always there.

That brief moment of levity, of smiles and joking around, was gone. Security met us in the parking garage, we filed into our van, and drove to the Rose Bowl stadium for a full day of rehearsals, sound checks, and dance routines for this stage set-up. Maddox never said much at all, and I didn't want to push him. He had enough to worry about without me nagging him.

Once we were there, with the guys and our team and all the familiar faces of the crew, Maddox relaxed and we all got down to business.

Watching them practice on stage never got old. They joked around together, getting their mics and earpieces all sorted. The LA morning sun was warm with not a cloud in the sky. The stadium was empty, of course, so the five of them goofed around on stage while the sound guys got ready.

They danced, they twerked, they laughed. Maddox did this slow squat and grind move that was so fucking hot, it should have been illegal. Jeremy called it a slut-drop, and everyone laughed some more as they all tried it. Then they did silly dances, and when they got the nod from the sound guy, Maddox strutted down the center stage, stripping out of his jacket like a hooker while singing the first verse, a cappella, of Joe Cocker's "You Can Leave Your Hat On."

It was sexy and sultry and I'm not gonna lie . . . it was hot.

The others laughed, and Maddox and Jeremy did some impromptu duet dance break. But once the music started, they were all serious. In key, in sync, and so beautiful to watch.

The documentary film crew caught it all, of course, and

I tried not to let it bother me that this private moment between the boys would be given to the public. Would their fans love it? Hell yes. Was any part of their lives not up for public consumption? Not so much.

"They're pumped for the tour, huh?" Amber said from beside me. I hadn't heard her come up, and I wondered just how much of my watching she saw.

"Yeah. They won't be like this by show twenty-three."

She nodded slowly. "No, they won't be."

"It's good to see them all so happy," I admitted.

Amber nodded to Arlo's documentary crew. "You know, letting the fans see them like this is a good idea. They'll eat this shit up. It's good for publicity."

"True." But I was a little sad that such a fun, private thing between the boys was going to be used to sell them. And I knew there would be quiet times after this tour before the next album where adding snippets of this footage to their social media channels would keep fans happy.

I knew it made sense. But still . . .

I left Amber in charge of watching them to go make myself useful elsewhere. We had director meetings—security, wardrobe, transport, catering—and by the time we called the boys off the stage, they were a sweaty, tired mess. But there were a lot of smiles, and with a promise of a late lunch, we made our way back to the hotel.

Maddox's shirt clung to him, sweat-drenched down his chest and back, his wet hair stuck to his forehead, his cheeks flushed pink. He all but fell into the back of the van.

His smile was contagious. "Feel good?" I asked.

"Yeah. We're ready."

"You are."

"What time are we leaving for the talk show?"

"Six."

He met my gaze. "Can we do something?"

"Like what?"

"I dunno. Anything. Just drive around, see where we end up. Maybe get ice cream at the beach?" He shrugged. "It's kinda our last day of anonymity."

I wasn't sure that was a great idea, but he wasn't a prisoner. "Sure. Let me get it organized. Who wants to go?"

"Oh." He blinked. "Um. Lemme ask," he replied, pulling out his phone and thumbing out a quick text.

They had a group chat, and within a few seconds, he looked up at me with a funny grimace. "Uh, that'd be everyone."

I sighed. That meant it was a full convoy: the band, managers, security. "Ambrose is gonna have a stroke."

Maddox laughed. "He should come."

"He should. I'll tell him to bring his credit card."

Maddox's smile widened. "Then he *would* have a stroke."

Ryan's number flashed on my screen. He was in the second car with Jeremy and Wes. They were a good ten minutes ahead of us. "Have you heard? The boys want to do something before the show tonight."

"Yep, but I hate to break it to you," Ryan said. "I don't think we'll be going anywhere. There's an issue at the hotel."

"What kind of issue?" I asked. Maddox's gaze shot to mine.

"Crowds, paparazzi. The police are trying to redirect traffic."

I sighed. That meant it was bad. "Fuck."

"Some asshole papzz are following us from the stadium. Drivers are being instructed right now," he said, and sure enough, our driver was talking into his earpiece while checking his rearview mirror.

"Be safe," Ryan said.

"You too."

The call disconnected and I let my hand fall to my lap with a shake of my head. "Fucking papzz."

Maddox sighed, his face a resigned frown. "It was good while it lasted."

And sure enough, the front of the hotel was a shitshow. Our driver zipped into the underground parking lot and security quickly blocked the access after our car. We pulled up at the elevator entrance, and Maddox squeezed into his jacket and pulled his hood up, hiding his face.

I got out first, to the sound of camera clicks and people shouting his name, even through the hotel parking garage security. I stood between Maddox and the fray, blocking their chance of any decent photo. He kept his head down, and we dashed inside.

A hotel staff member was holding an elevator door for us, and with a swipe of their fob hit our floor number. "No stops until your floor," he said.

"Thank you."

When the doors were closed and it was just us, Maddox let his head fall back. "I guess going to the beach and getting ice cream is out of the question."

I nodded. "Yeah."

He tried to smile. "And so the fun begins."

God, the look on his face just killed me. When we stepped out of the elevator, the hallway was clear, and he went straight to his door, two rooms up from mine. "Maddox," I said before he went inside. "If you want ice cream, I'll get you ice cream. Berry swirl, right?"

He smiled then, that gentle half a smile that he was famous for. "You don't need to do that."

"It's no problem."

He seemed to consider it for a long moment, but in the end, he shook his head. "Nah. Thanks anyway. I'm gonna go shower."

He disappeared through his door, and I stood there for a second like an idiot, until I remembered what I was supposed to be doing. I dialed Amber's number and put my phone to my ear. "Everyone okay?" I asked.

"Yeah, and you?"

"Yeah, we're fine."

"Good."

We now had a whole string of issues to sort out before the talk show appearance tonight. "Where are we meeting?"

CHAPTER THREE

LATE NIGHTS in LA was an iconic talk show that had been around for decades. It would be the band's first TV appearance, their first interview, for this tour. It was important. We implemented a few security modifications and briefings with hotel security and police traffic control, but nothing extraordinary.

For a little while at least we had flown under the radar. But this appearance and performance on TV would change all that.

At the end of the day, it was what we were here for.

When I returned from the security meeting, Wes, Luke, and Blake were in Jeremy's room. Room service trays with mostly eaten food were on the table, and they were watching and laughing at something on YouTube. "Where's Maddox?" I asked.

"In his room," Jeremy replied. "We asked him to join us but he had his head in his notebook. You know how he is."

I nodded. Yes, I knew. Blake burst out laughing at the laptop screen. "Here it is, here it is, watch this."

We all turned our attention to the video. It was them, on YouTube, in some clip where they couldn't have been any older than sixteen years old. They were at their high school by the looks of it, just a group of baby-faced, weedy adolescents with bad skin and braces.

Jeremy roared laughing. "Holy fuck, look at our hair!"

Luke and Blake fell back on the bed, cry-laughing. "Look at Maddox! Oh my god, this is gold."

Wes was half-covering his eyes, horrified but still laughing at the screen. "What is he wearing?"

I couldn't help but chuckle. More at them laughing so hard than what they looked like in the video. "Just as well he's not here," I said. "So he can't hear you laughing at him." I went to the door and tapped my watch. "Hair and make-up in one hour."

They waved me off and I could still hear them laughing as I knocked on Maddox's door. "It's me," I said, and his door opened a few seconds later.

He was dressed in gray sweatpants and a black T-shirt. His hair had been washed, though it was almost dry. His feet were bare. He looked annoyed. "Hey," he said gruffly.

"Everything okay?" I asked.

He stood aside, a silent invitation, and I went into his room. The curtains were drawn; the room was dark, despite the afternoon sun outside. The bed was rumpled, a notebook and a pen lay atop the covers.

Maddox went back to sit on the bed, leaning against the headboard. He picked up his notebook, though he never opened it. He seemed . . . nervous.

I sat down, trying to look natural and reduce my size in his space. "Are you okay?"

He paused for the briefest moment before his eyes met mine. "Yeah, yeah of course. Why, wassup?"

"The others are in Jeremy's room."

"Yeah, I know."

"They're watching old videos of the band and they're laughing at your hair."

A smile almost pulled at Maddox's lips but he never said anything.

"I didn't mean to interrupt. Were you writing?"

He held the notepad a little tighter but still didn't open it. "Uh, yeah."

"Music or lyrics?"

He shrugged. "A bit of both."

"Always writing," I murmured.

"Always."

"Another Billboard hit?"

He smiled, embarrassed. "Did you want a drink of something? There's water or a soda in my fridge."

He wanted me to stay?

Before I could answer, he was up and at the small fridge. "I know you don't like Coke, but there's a Sprite or some sparkling mineral shit." He turned around and handed me a bottle of mineral water.

"Uh, thanks." I don't recall ever making a point of preferring mineral water, but I guess after a few years, he noticed.

He went back to sitting on the bed. "Does it taste like fifty-dollar water?"

I almost choked on my first sip, making him laugh. "Fifty bucks?" I sputtered, wiping my mouth with the back of my hand while I read the label. "Did Jesus convert it from wine or something?"

Maddox laughed, a genuine one that wrinkled the corner of his eyes and showed off his perfect teeth. *God, he's beautiful when he laughs . . .*

That thought stopped me and I cleared my throat, giving my attention back to the bottle. "No bottle of water is worth fifty bucks."

He picked up the remote control from his bedside and offered it to me. "Did you want to watch something on TV?"

He really did want me to stay.

"To be honest, I prefer the quiet," I admitted.

"Same," he said, tossing the remote on the bed. "If there were people around, I'd have music playing, but when it's just me . . ."

I knew he preferred silence. There wasn't much I didn't know about him. When he was with the boys, it was usually chaos and noise, and he loved that while he was with them. But when he was by himself, he needed quiet. He needed to recharge, and I think that was why we paired together so well. Or ended up together, gravitating to each other because . . . well, introverts were comfortable with each other. If he had his headphones on, I never pushed for conversation. I just let him be and did my thing, and he appreciated that.

"When you've got your headphones on," I asked, "what do you listen to?"

He smiled right at me, bringing one bare foot up on the bed, and rested his elbow on his knee. It gave me a great view of his tattoos, a montage of black ink pieces that made one sleeve. He didn't wear T-shirts too often—his usual hoodies hid his artwork. "Depends," he replied, and I almost forgot I'd asked him a question. "Sometimes it's whatever's new in the music world; sometimes it's the sound of the ocean or rainforests. Sometimes it's white noise, just to drown out the sound of the world, ya know? Sometimes it's an audiobook. Just about anything to clear my head, really."

"It helps, right?"

He gave a small nod and chewed on his lip. Something he only did when he was nervous. "Can I ask you a favor?"

"Sure."

"There's a guy I wanna see. He's here in LA," he said.

My heart rate took off, thundered in my chest like bats in a cage. My stomach twisted, and I was sure my surprise was clear. "Uh, okay."

Maddox's eyes shot to mine. "No, no, not like that. He's a . . . he makes guitars. It's a store." He laughed, embarrassed. "God, Roscoe."

I chuckled, and the relief spread through me like a warm chill. "Oh, a guitar. Yeah, that shouldn't be a problem." I ignored how my face felt hot. "Guitars are fine . . . I mean, if you wanted me to call a guy for you for something else, I can do that too."

He barked out a laugh. "Uh, no. I'm good, thanks." He picked up his notepad and held it to his belly. He was clearly embarrassed and nervous. "I was kinda hoping we could go at night, but that's not looking likely. We've got concerts the next three nights. So it'll have to be during the day."

"Which means a full escort."

He frowned. "Well, I . . ."

"You what?"

He met my gaze. "I thought maybe just you and I could go."

Oh.

I stared at him. "Maddox, I . . ." I sighed. "I don't know."

He picked at the fabric at his knee. "I could go by myself."

"But you won't." Fucking hell.

"Half the time it's security that gets us noticed. If I

didn't turn up with a freaking swat team, no one would probably look twice at me."

I raised an eyebrow. "Okay, one, that's bullshit. People would recognize you. And two, even if they didn't recognize you, they'll look twice at you anyway. You've been on every sexiest-man-alive list, best-dressed, hottest-everything list for the last three years, Maddox. People might not recognize you, but they notice you."

He rolled his eyes.

"And three, the freaking swat team saves you from the unhinged fans who think you're going to marry them."

He met my eyes, determined. "Compromise with me."

I tried not to smile. "We'll go during the day."

"With no security."

"With Steve." Steve was the head of security. He didn't look intimidating, but holy fuck, he was lethal.

He huffed. "And we take an Uber. No van that people notice."

"An Uber? Are you insane?"

He laughed. "Or we leave in the laundry van or the catering truck, I don't care. But if we try and leave in our usual van, it'll be a circus. His store isn't too far from the stadium so we could go one day before the show."

I sighed. "I have to tell Ryan and Amber."

"But—"

"But nothing. I'm not compromising on that. And I'm not lying to them."

He glared at me and pouted. It was kinda cute, and he knew it. "Fine."

I smiled. "Fine."

He took out his phone, scrolled for a second, then put his phone to his ear. "Hello," he began. "I'd like to make an appointment for tomorrow morning. Yes, I know it's short notice . . . Oh, I'm calling on behalf of Maddox Kershaw."

I rolled my eyes. He *was* Maddox Kershaw.

But sure enough, five minutes later we had a private meeting tomorrow morning at ten o'clock with the man who was, in Maddox's opinion, an instrument-making genius.

He was excited and happy, and I'd do *anything* to see him smile like that.

It was hard to be mad. Even though the others probably wouldn't feel the same. "We'll have to be done by eleven to be at the stadium by twelve."

Maddox nodded. "Easy. And thank you."

"For what?"

"For letting it happen."

I gave him a sad smile. "I'll always do what I can. Without getting myself fired. I know it's hard, but you're not a prisoner."

"Except I am," he murmured. "Kind of."

"Feels like it some days, huh?"

His gaze met mine, intense and honest, and he nodded. "And they wouldn't dare fire you. I wouldn't let them."

The way he stared at me, the truth in his eyes, it was as if the air was sucked out of the room. I wasn't blind and I wasn't stupid . . . that was a look. He looked at me like he wanted me.

He shook his head and smiled to himself, though it looked almost painful. "Roscoe, I—"

A knock at his door interrupted him. "Open up, dick-head, it's me."

Jeremy.

Maddox made a face and went to the door. Jeremy walked right in and stopped dead when he saw me. "Oh,

I . . ." He shot Maddox a look I couldn't quite decipher before he tried to cover it with a smile. "Roscoe! I didn't know you were here."

I stood up. "I was just leaving." I checked my watch. "We've got about twenty minutes before hair and make-up. Wardrobe will deal with your clothes."

"I was going to wear this," Maddox said jokingly, looking down at his sweatpants and tee.

"It wouldn't matter what you wore," Jeremy grumbled. "We could be there all decked out in some designer fits, and you'd still look better than me in your old sweats."

Maddox shoved his arm. "Shut up. These are not old."

I took it as my cue to leave. "I'll see you guys in there. Don't be late."

I left them to it, happy to pretend the weirdness that just happened hadn't happened at all. Maddox looking at me like he did, that holding eye contact, heated stare. He had the fake sultry look for photoshoots or press conferences, but this was . . . this was different.

It was real. And it was aimed at me.

Or maybe I imagined it. Maybe I read it wrong, maybe he was joking. Maybe it was my wishful thinking.

But then Jeremy was weird too. Wasn't he? There was definitely something unsaid between them when Jeremy saw me in Maddox's room.

Or maybe I was just imagining things.

I shouldn't be thinking of Maddox in that way anyway. He trusted me to keep him organized, he trusted me to keep him safe and performing well. Not to be thinking of him like *that*.

Let it go, Roscoe. Concentrate on your job.

I found Amber and Ryan in the common room, where

make-up and hair were setting up. A rack of clothes was put to one side with a privacy divider for the boys to get changed, a long table with water bottles and bags of pretzels and chips and fruit. Staff were milling around getting stuff ready but none of the guys were there yet. The film crew hovered in the background.

"Hey," I said as I approached Amber and Ryan. "Got a sec?"

They both looked up from their phones. "Sure," Amber replied.

"So, Maddox has an appointment at a guitar store tomorrow morning at ten," I explained. "I'll be taking him alone."

Ryan did a double take. "Alone?"

"Well, he wanted to go by himself. I compromised and said Steve and I would go with him."

Amber smirked and shook her head. "Great compromise. At least you got Steve into the equation."

"I know," I agreed. "But I told him we *have* to be at the stadium by twelve. No exceptions."

"I think Blake was hoping to hit Rodeo Drive tomorrow morning," Ryan added. "Said it was good publicity to be seen out in public before the show."

Amber nodded. "I guess if we split up, the paparazzi won't know who to follow."

"Well, Maddox wants to take an Uber," I said. They both stared, wide-eyed. "He said, if he left in a security van, they'd follow him."

"An Uber?" Amber repeated.

"Well, either that or a laundry truck. He didn't care."

Ryan made a thoughtful face. "Can we get a laundry truck?"

I snorted out a laugh. "Highly doubtful. I'm going to find Steve before he gets too busy."

Steve was giving the security team a last minute run-through, and I called him aside. He was fine on coming with me and Maddox tomorrow, and when I told him it was just us, no one else, no anything, he simply gave a nod and adapted.

There was a reason he was the best.

By the time I got back to the common room, everyone was in go-mode. Hair, make-up, wardrobe, and there was chatter, laughs. Wes was practicing his dance moves and Luke was filming him with his phone. That would end up on Twitter, no doubt.

The film crew stayed in the corner, out of the way, thankfully. It was kind of scary how they blended into the background. I was starting not to notice them, which was a bit concerning.

It took me a second to realize Maddox wasn't there. I scanned the room—

"Getting changed," Amber called out, pointing to the room divider.

And sure enough, Maddox came walking out, wearing the tightest pair of black jeans I'd ever seen, buttoning his shirt. I got a brief glance of his chest before the fabric stole it from me. He saw me looking and he raised an eyebrow. Amused? Shocked? Pleased? But he was soon swamped by the wardrobe people fixing his collar, his jeans, his sleeves.

I pretended to be distracted by everything else —*anything* else—going on. God, I'd seen him get dressed a thousand times. Why was this different?

Because things between you are different now . . .

Were they, though? Maddox and I had always been

close. The last few months closer still, but things weren't that different.

The way he looked at you earlier was different . . .

Thankfully, a few seconds later, Ambrose came in to give us a rundown on vehicles and what to expect when we arrived at the TV studio.

Jeremy was done with hair, Wes was told to get his ass in the chair, Blake's make-up was done, and it was Maddox's turn. If there'd ever been a more redundant job, that was it. His face was fucking perfect. All Bibi had to do was gloss over him, and even she joked that he made her feel useless. His skin, his eyes, his lips . . . what could she improve?

But I still envied these staff. The way they got close to him, pulled at his clothes, fixed his hair, the way they got to touch him . . .

Christ, Roscoe.

"Roscoe?" Ambrose said, obviously not for the first time.

I blinked into focus. "Yes, sorry."

"You here?" he asked.

"Absolutely."

"We leave in ten minutes. Be ready."

When Ambrose was gone, Ryan nudged me. "You good?" he whispered.

I nodded quickly. "Yeah, all good."

His gaze flickered over to Maddox, who was now having his hair done, and back to me. "Okay then."

I ignored that and instead focused on Jeremy and Blake who were warming up their voices, singing the song they'd be performing tonight.

Beacon was their fifth studio album, and the first release off the album was "Fly." "Fly" was a huge hit in America, and this was the song's debut delivery for the tour. It needed to be perfect.

And I had no doubt it would be nothing short of perfect tonight.

Once these guys were on stage, they were like fish in water.

The thousands of hours in the recording studio and dance rehearsal studio weren't for nothing.

"How do I look?" Maddox asked, pulling on his boot.

He was in those goddamned tight black jeans, a crisp white button-down shirt that had a red stripe around one half of his waist. It was a new Versace line, and they each wore something similar but not the same. Enough to match but not overdone. "Perfect," I answered. "You all look perfect. We ready?"

There were a few cheers as they hyped themselves up, but soon enough we were walking out of the basement elevator to the line of waiting vans. Security opened Maddox's door, he climbed in, and I followed in after him.

He smelled so good.

"How are you feeling?" I asked.

"Good. Nervous, I guess."

Singing and dancing in front of eighty thousand people was nothing. In a small studio with an intimate audience and a talk show host prone to ask personal questions was a different beast altogether. I understood that.

"Well, Jeremy and Luke are center now. They'll be running lead."

The plan was for Maddox to sit on the end at the back, taking himself out of the spotlight. Most bands had a person who spoke the most, and up until now, that'd always been Maddox, whether he wanted it or not. All interviewers would redirect questions back to him, almost pushing him to say controversial things for ratings.

Don't get me wrong. Maddox said controversial things all the time. He wouldn't hold back and he didn't mince words, and that made him edgy, apparently.

It also made him bait for ratings and publicity.

And Maddox was sick of it. There were five in the band, not just him. It hadn't worked too well during the press cons on the last tour—reporters would always circle back to Maddox— but we knew it would be a learning curve for everyone.

"You'll be fine," I reassured him. "And Luke and Jeremy will be fine too."

He smiled, his face a warm glow by the fading sunlight through the car windows. "We never got to finish our conversation in my room," he murmured.

My stomach swooped; my heart came to a screeching halt before stuttering against my ribs. "What conversation was that?"

His smile became a smirky pout. "Oh, I can't remember now. But I do remember the look on your face when you thought I was gonna ask you to put in a booty call for me."

Were we dancing into flirt-territory here? I had the feeling we were . . .

Maddox leaned a little closer to me and nudged me with his elbow. "You were stunned, shocked, a little horri-fied, and if I can guess correctly, I'm gonna go with even a little hurt?"

"Hurt? Why would I be hurt? I wasn't hurt."

He raised his eyebrows—his perfectly shaped, face-defining eyebrows—before that smirky pout was back.

Yep, this was definitely him being flirty.

"Just so you know," I added. "I would do that for you. If

that was what you wanted." Then I realized how that sounded. "I mean, I would call them for you. I wouldn't *be* the booty call for you."

He burst out laughing and put his hand to his heart. "You wait till Ambrose finds out you refused one of my requests."

I snorted. "Until you tell him that your request was for me to . . . go above and beyond."

"Is that some kind of position I haven't heard of? Because I'm trying to picture it."

Jesus fucking Christ.

I lightly tapped his chest with the back of my hand and nodded pointedly to the driver and Steve in the front seat who could probably hear every word. "Are you trying to get me fired?" I whispered.

He looked out his window. "I told you before, I won't let that happen."

"Yeah, well, some things are even out of your control," I murmured.

"I'd just hire you back as my own personal manager without Arlo or Ambrose. Then they can't say shit."

"No can do. States in my contract that if I'm fired for any reason, I cannot be rehired by anyone within the company."

He glared at me. "That's fucked."

"That's the entertainment business."

He flinched, the tiniest movement, but I saw it on the profile of his face. Something was definitely going on. He was acting so . . . strange.

"Hey, Maddox," I whispered, and he finally turned to face me. "You okay?"

I expected him to smile, fake or not, and say something

like, 'Sure, why wouldn't I be?' like he usually did. But he
didn't. Those beautiful dark eyes met mine.

"I don't know," he whispered. Then he wiped his hands
on his thighs and let out a breath, and his eyes searched
mine. "I dunno, Roscoe. I'm just . . . I don't know."

Oh hell, this was not the time or place for this conversation. It needed to happen but we were just a few minutes
out from the studio.

So I did something really brave and really stupid.

I held out my hand, palm up, and he looked from my
eyes to my hand. Then he slowly slipped his hand onto
mine and he sighed at the touch, weaving our fingers. His
skin was warm, his hand fit against mine perfectly, and
when I glanced up, he had his eyes closed.

I wanted to tell him we would talk after the show. I
wanted to tell him a lot of things. I wanted—

"ETA, two minutes," Steve called out.

Maddox slowly opened his eyes, but his hold on my
hand tightened. This was new. This, his hand in mine, his
touch, had my heart hammering, my mouth dry. He didn't
let go, but neither did I.

I could say that it was because he obviously needed
some kind of reassurance, but it was for my own selfish
reasons too.

I wanted to hold his hand.

I wanted to cup his face, caress my thumb along his
jaw . . .

It hadn't always been that way. I'd been his manager for
four years. For the first year, my thoughts toward him were
strictly professional. But the more time I spent with him,
hearing him sing, laugh, watching him dance, practice,
perform, the more I got to know him . . .

The last twelve months had been a measure of self-control, to put it nicely.

I thought of him in ways I shouldn't.

It certainly didn't hurt that he smiled when he saw me, that he always made his way to me, that he always stood close.

So if he wanted to hold my hand, I wasn't going to deny him.

The car pulled into the line, and reality dawned. Lights, crowds, yelling, screaming, security, paparazzi, flashing cameras, but in the back of the van there was silence. It was so muted, it felt surreal, almost like being underwater.

Until the doors opened and the noise barreled in. Maddox let go of my hand and he stepped out, waving, smiling, ever professional. I followed him out and went to his side as the crowd pushed in. Security held them, not without effort. The noise, yelling and screaming, was deafening.

The five band members stood together, grinning and posing, while Amber, Ryan, and I stood aside. And my god, they just shone.

The photographers called out, "Maddox, Maddox, Maddox," trying to get his attention like he was the only one there. As soon as they broke apart and began to move inside, the crowd got louder, closer, and he turned, scanning . . . until he saw me. I was quickly at his side, my hand on his lower back, and security led us inside.

We were ushered through, the boys were led to the green room, and we were given a brief from the production and stage managers. It was all fairly standard and we'd all done this plenty of times, and before we knew it, it was time.

"Please welcome to the stage, worldwide super band, Atrous!"

The crowd was on their feet, screaming and cheering, and the boys filed out, waving and grinning as they took their seats. Just as practiced, with Maddox on the far end at the back, Jeremy and Luke in the front middle.

He looked relaxed and happy and incredibly gorgeous. All of them did. It took a long few seconds for the crowd to quiet down, but eventually the host could speak. He introduced them by name, and of course Maddox got the loudest cheer. He just waved it off with that killer grin, but he said nothing and the host went on. "Kicking off a huge tour of your latest album, *Beacon.*" He held up a placard with the album cover. "Tell us what this album means."

And just as practiced, Jeremy took the lead. "'Beacon' is the title track," he began. "It's been a year of growth for us, and we wanted to reflect that in our music. No matter how far we are from home or from each other, we know a beacon will bring us back."

"You've come a long way," the host said. "Since you were all in high school, practicing in Maddox's parents' garage, is that right?"

The cameras and attention trained in on Maddox. "Yep," he replied. "And Blake's dad's place. And Wes's folks' place." Maddox looked right down the camera and waved. "Hello, Mr. Acosta, and Mr. and Mrs. Holland watching back home. We love you, and Mrs. Holland, especially that spaghetti and meatballs you make for us. We'll be around for dinner when we get home in two months."

That was good. He was funny, he completely offloaded the question, made other people the focus, and gave the host a lead-in for another line of questioning. "Two months away from home, that's a long time," he said. "It's back-to-back with your last album, you did a world tour last year, you've been in the studio with the new album. You guys haven't had much time off."

"Nah," Jeremy replied. "But we don't consider this work. It's like we get up each day and get to do the very thing we love. It even makes putting up with these guys twenty-four seven for two months bearable."

The audience laughed and the host lapped it up. "Just how much time do you spend together?"

"A lot," Luke said. "Like, a *lot*. Even when we're not touring, we're with each other most days. We don't all live together anymore, which is probably a good thing, considering the five of us lived in a three-bedroom house for two years. But Maddox wasn't joking about going to Wes's parents' place for dinner. We will totally do that."

"They will," Wes added. "My mom used to say it was like she had five sons."

"You guys all lived together as well? In a three-bedroom house?"

"Yep," Jeremy answered. "But it's just what we had to do. We were young and broke."

Blake laughed. "We'd all go around to one of our parents' place every other night for a home-cooked meal so we didn't starve to death."

They all laughed, a fond memory, obviously. But a stage director signaled for time. The host pulled a white square of cardboard out from behind his desk. "I was hoping I could interest you guys for a quick game of . . ." He turned the square around. "Twister!"

The audience cheered and the Twister mat was laid on the floor. The host brought the spinner around from his desk and Maddox was quick to jump up and take it. Jeremy,

Wes, Luke, and Blake all got ready, pushing and shoving each other, laughing and goading each other.

This was going to look great. Their fans were gonna love it.

These boys were fun; no matter where they went, there was always a laugh to be had.

Until Wes sat down on the floor and took his boots off, then Luke did too, and of course he had on odd socks, which was funny enough, but then he threw Wes's boot under the host's desk, and Jeremy rolled his sleeves up, and Blake had the common sense to tuck his shirt in. They cracked knuckles and rolled their necks and pushed and shoved each other. It was two minutes of chaos. Everyone in the audience laughed, and the host found them funny too. This was going to be social media gold.

"They remind me of growing up with my brothers," the host said to Maddox.

Maddox was holding the spinner thing, smiling at the boys. "They are brothers. In a lot of ways, that's what we are."

"But they're competitive, right?"

Maddox laughed. "They would take a bullet for one another. Literally, lay down their life and sacrifice themselves. No questions, no problem. But any kind of game or challenge, and it's last man standing, no mercy." He grinned at the host. "I hope you've got insurance."

The host blinked. "Uh . . ."

Maddox laughed again and spun the board. "Right hand, blue!"

And the typical Atrous pandemonium ensued. It was like Maddox was choreographing a slow-motion brawl. They were all over each other, fighting and shoving for the best spot, yelling and whining and laughing, and it was hilariously funny.

Wes went down first, only because Jeremy kneed him. Jeremy went out next because he was laughing too hard, and Blake and Luke were human pretzels, bodies entangled in ways to keep the Bluke shippers happy forever.

No one ended up winning because Luke fell on top of Blake and they went to the mat in a heap. Maddox jumped down to inspect who might have had a hand or foot on the yellow circle. "Wait." He got down real close, looking between them. "No winner, but I now pronounce you husband and husband!"

Everyone burst out laughing, and Jeremy crash-hugged Maddox in a way that made my heart warm. It felt so good to see him laugh. The audience roared, and this was going to be on every social media outlet for weeks.

It was perfect.

They were so funny and charming, the song almost seemed secondary. It was the debut live performance for "Fly," and they sang and danced with the precision they were famous for. It was faultless. Each of them a part of the whole, a complete and concise team, though I was biased to think Maddox shone a little brighter.

When it was all over, the boys went backstage and they were on a high. They had their arms around each other's shoulders, almost dancing their way back to the waiting van. The crowd was bigger, the shouts and calls for Maddox's attention seemed louder, to which he gave a quick wave before he climbed into the waiting van.

I followed him in, the door slid shut behind us, blocking out the noise, and our world fell silent.

"You guys were so good tonight," I said. "How do you feel?"

He was a little sweaty, his face was flushed, his smile was genuine. "That felt good. Our timing was tight."

"You looked great, sounded amazing."

He only rolled his eyes a little bit, but he nodded. "The seat arrangement worked, mostly."

"It did. Jeremy and Luke were great."

He smirked. "Twister was fun."

I chuckled. "Your fans are gonna love that."

He smiled and let out a big sigh. "I'm glad it's over."

"Relieved?"

Maddox nodded and let his head fall back onto the headrest. "I never used to get so nervous." He closed his eyes. "I'm sorry about before. On the way here. I was kinda freaking out."

"It's fine," I replied. "If you ever need to hold my hand, you can."

I'd meant that as a bit of a joke, even though it wasn't, but then he opened his eyes and stared at me. His eyes on mine, dark and so brutally imploring. He didn't speak. He just stared at me, and I couldn't have said another word, even if I'd wanted to.

It was dark outside, and inside the van the only lights were passing streetlights and traffic. His gorgeous face flashed into neon view in time with my thundering heart. He lifted his hand, palm up, an offering for me to hold it.

Oh man . . .

I skimmed my fingertips up his palm before I wove his fingers with mine. His lips parted; his eyes burned into me.

This was . . . this was a bad idea, diving headfirst into dangerous waters. It had trouble written all over it. But it was exhilarating and wonderful, and it felt so, so right.

And so help me fucking god, he smiled.

We didn't speak, not another word, not even when the

car pulled up at the hotel. He squeezed my hand as the door was opened, and he let go. I followed him inside and we rode the elevator with Jeremy and Luke, and they were still buzzed about the show, so Maddox and I couldn't talk.

We were going to have to talk.

They ordered Chinese food and sat around the common room eating and talking shit. Maddox was a bit quiet but he seemed okay. Amber, Ryan, and I sat separate from them and discussed our plans for the next day, though my attention was sitting across the room with his Versace shirt half-unbuttoned—

"Everything okay?" Ryan asked.

I shook my head, more at myself for getting caught out. "Yeah, yeah, sure."

"He was brilliant tonight," Amber murmured.

I nodded. "They all were."

Amber went straight back to the itinerary, but Ryan studied me for a moment. I ignored him and pretended the list in front of me was the most fascinating thing I'd seen and that Ryan was trying to put together dots that didn't exist.

"I'm calling it a night," Maddox said, standing up. "Big day tomorrow, and we're gonna kick ass." He held his hand out and the four others covered his hand with theirs.

"Atrous," they said together.

It was their thing. Their name, their catch-cry, their brother song.

It made everyone in the room smile.

Maddox threw his takeout container and empty water bottle in the trash and got halfway to the door. He looked over to us, to me. "Roscoe," he said, nodding to the door.

What the hell?

Okay, maybe we were going to talk about what happened in the car? Maybe we weren't.

I gave Ryan and Amber a nod, took my itinerary list—ignored the film crew panning the camera to me—and followed Maddox out the door. We walked in silence to his room, my heart thumping louder with every step. He swiped his card, stepped inside, and held the door open for me.

I knew it was wrong. I should have said no.

But I looked him right in the eye and went into his room.

CHAPTER FOUR

"IS EVERYTHING OKAY?" I asked, trying to play it cool. If he noticed my voice was deeper, rougher, he never let on. I stood beside the table and he walked past me, close enough for me to smell him . . . or maybe it was just because I was in his room.

"Yeah," he replied, collecting the TV remote and turning it on to some movie, the volume on mute. "Did you just wanna hang out?"

Hang out?

What the . . . ?

"I know you've probably got a thousand things you need to do," he continued. "And that's cool. I just . . ." He made a face and pulled a shirt out of his suitcase.

"You just what?" I prompted.

He undid another button on his shirt. And another, and it took every ounce of self-control to keep eye contact and not look at the skin he was revealing. "I just . . . I don't want to be around people right now. I'm kinda all peopled out," he replied. He took a measured breath and whispered, "But I don't want to be alone."

I nodded slowly. "Okay, sure."

I didn't know what that meant—that he chose me, that he felt comfortable enough with me and not one of the boys —but I wasn't going to say no to him.

He disappeared into his en suite bathroom, keeping the door open. "Did you have enough to eat?" he called out.

That made me almost laugh. "Uh, yeah."

He came out wearing his sweatpants and his T-shirt. "What's so funny?"

"Normally that's a me-question to you, not a you-question to me."

He chuckled and took a black toiletry bag out of his suitcase. "If you're still hungry, just call room service. Or there's more mineral water in the fridge."

"Not at fifty bucks a pop, I'm good thanks."

He laughed as he went back into the bathroom. The door stayed open again, and I heard the water run. I began to wonder what the hell he was doing when he appeared with a face full of soap and a towel over his shoulder. He was rubbing circles on his cheeks, removing his make-up. "Have the mineral water, Roscoe. I'll have a water, thanks."

He disappeared again so I went to the fridge, got two drinks, and went back to the table. Maddox came back out, fresh-faced, the front of his hair wet. He ran his fingers through it, looking fine as hell, and took the bottle of water I offered him. Then he sat on the bed, resting against the headboard, his legs stretched out. He watched me as he took a sip of his water, as if he was trying to choose his next words carefully. "So what does Roscoe Hall do in his downtime?"

I smiled. Christ, we were doing small talk. "You assume I have downtime?"

He nodded, like he either understood or should have

known better than to ask that question. "Your job's just as demanding as mine, huh?"

I shrugged with a sigh. "I highly doubt that."

"But you don't have a life outside of . . . this?"

"Not really. But this isn't exactly a chore. I get to travel the world and see and do a lot of things not many people get to see or do."

"When was the last time you saw your family?"

"Uh, I speak to them often enough."

"Is that the same?"

"They live in Vermont," I said. He knew that much. "I moved to LA years before I began working with you, so I'd see them no more if I worked a desk job somewhere."

He pouted and chewed the inside of his lip. "Why did you move to LA?"

"Because rural Vermont wasn't gay enough for me. I considered New York City but I wanted sunshine and winters without snow."

He scrunched his nose up. "Snow . . . Oh, did you play hockey? I can totally picture you wearing all that gear." His eyebrow quirked upward. "Not exactly a terrible visual."

I rolled my eyes. "Yes, I played hockey."

"Nice." He nodded slowly. "But you call LA home now?"

I nodded. "Yep."

"You know, I've never seen your apartment. You know everything about me, mostly. Hell, I don't even know if you live in an apartment or a house."

Well, shit. He wasn't dipping his toe into personal territory, he was just diving right in.

"I have an apartment," I replied. "In West Hollywood."

"Nice," he said casually.

"If by nice you mean small and old, then yes."

He smiled at me. "Kinda close to mine."

It may as well be a million miles apart. "Kinda."

He scratched at the label on the water bottle. "Do you . . . do you have a roommate? Or a . . . shared living arrangement?"

"A shared living arrangement?" I repeated, because fucking hell, he wasn't just asking me if I lived with someone. He was asking if I was seeing anyone. "Uh, no. I don't live with anyone. And I'm not seeing anyone."

His eyes flashed to mine, and I knew I was right. "You were though, right? In the beginning? There was a guy. I can't remember his name. Adam, Matthew, Peter, Paul, something biblical."

I was surprised he remembered that, considering it was so long ago. He'd never mentioned it to me before. "His name was Mark."

He looked me right in the eye. "What happened?"

"I didn't have the time." Which was a nice way to put that my job—that he, Maddox—took up my every waking minute.

"Ouch. Sorry."

"Don't apologize." I shrugged. "I had a houseplant once. I couldn't even keep that alive."

He smirked. "The poor plant." He studied me for a long moment. "Do you miss it?"

"Miss what? The fern? We weren't that close."

He laughed. "No. Having someone."

I took a long sip of my drink while I contemplated my answer. I shook my head. "No. I have five men that keep me busy enough. One more so than the other four."

The corner of his lip twitched in an almost-smile, but it didn't last long. "Do you get lonely?"

Jesus, he just kept on with the hard questions.

"Sometimes," I admitted. "Do you?"

He was quiet, and I wondered if he was going to answer at all. Eventually he nodded. "Yeah. I do." He turned the water bottle around in his hand, frowning at it. "The nights are the worst."

"I'm normally checking itineraries or schedules, ordering stuff, or confirming appointments till all hours," I said. I didn't want to say outright that I didn't have time to be lonely, even if it was partially the truth.

Maddox's frown deepened. "I usually write lyrics or music, or I play around with compositions or mix tapes. Play guitar or hit the piano for a bit. But . . ." He shrugged again. "I spend most of my nights alone."

"Is that why you asked me to come back with you tonight?"

His gaze shot to mine. "Is it weird? If you think it's weird—"

"No, I don't think it's weird," I said quickly. "I like that you asked me."

A faint color tinted his cheeks.

Holy freaking hell. Maddox Kershaw just blushed.

"I trust you," he whispered, focusing on the water bottle.

"You can trust Jeremy. And Blake, and Luke, and Wes."

"Yeah, I know. Of course, I can." He shook his head, frowning again. "But this is different."

"Different?"

"Well, yeah."

"How?"

"Because it's different with you. It's quieter, for a start, and I know you're here but it's just . . . comfortable. Which probably sounds weird, but you just let me be. I don't feel like I need to be on when I'm with you. I don't need to be funny, or ready to perform, or practice, or talk about routines or songs, or if we should change the set or a dance line." He let out a long breath. "It's nothing against the guys. I love them, I love being with them. But it's like I either have noise and chaos with them, or if I need time out it means being isolated, which wears me down." Maddox gave me a small smile. "You're like an in-between."

I smiled at him. That was the most honest thing he'd said to me about how he was feeling in months. "Well, I'm glad. I like being your in-between. And just so you know, if you want to vent or bitch about anything, whatever you tell me stays between us."

"I know," he murmured. "Thank you."

"Things haven't been easy these last few months," I added. "I know your feet have barely hit the ground, and here we are kicking off a tour and these next six or seven weeks are going to be rough, especially toward the end. But Maddox, if you ever need a second to relax, just say the word. Just let me know, and I'll do whatever I can to make it easier for you."

"So I just have to say the word? Like a magic word or a secret service code word?"

I chuckled. "Any word you want."

He gave me a cheeky smirk. "And you'll do anything?"

God, the way he raised that eyebrow . . .

Now it was me who blushed. "I said I'll do whatever I can. Not anything you want. Certainly nothing illegal. It'll be a bit hard for me to do my job if I'm in prison."

He grinned. "Just what do you think I'm going to ask you to do?"

"I don't know. I don't really care. As long as it's not illegal."

"Have a beer with me."

"A beer? I thought you made it a point not to drink on tours?"

"No, I made it a point not to drink alone in a hotel room. Because that's a slippery slope that leads to a whole range of bad decisions." He swung his legs over the edge of the bed and stood up. "But I'm not alone. You're here."

It still sounded like a bad decision . . .

He went to the bar fridge, pulled out two green bottles, and handed one to me. "And you said you'd do anything as long as it's not illegal, and having a beer isn't illegal."

I took the bottle. "I'll have one. Just one."

Maddox grinned victoriously and plonked himself back on the bed, leaning against the headboard. He took a swig of his beer, found the remote control, and aimed it at the TV. "Let's see what movies are on."

"MORNING," I said to Amber as I carried two takeout carriers of coffees into the meeting room. I put them down and handed her hers.

"Thanks," she said. "You're up early today."

"I've already done an hour of cardio in the gym. Figured some caffeine would be appreciated."

"I'm sure it will be. So," she hedged. "Late night?"

I shot her a look. "Not really. And I know what you're thinking. But you can stop it right there."

"I'm not saying anything," she countered, sipping her coffee with a smile. "And I would never question your professionalism. But . . ."

"But what?"

"But I've seen the way he looks at you."

My blood ran hot and cold at the same time. It made me light-headed. "The way he looks at me?"

"Come on, Roscoe. You have to have noticed the change in him."

Of course I had.

"The last six months have been . . . tough on him." I shrugged. "You know he gets treated different. The pressure, the scrutiny, the criticism, it's all aimed at him."

She nodded. This had been discussed many times before. "He looks for you. On the very few brief moments you're not glued to his side, he looks for you."

"Because I'm his manager. I keep him organized."

She shook her head. "It's different now."

"How different?"

"I think he likes you." She leveled a knowing smirk at me. "I think he's developed romantic feelings for you."

I stared at her and my mouth fell open. When I'd resumed the ability to speak, all that came out was, "No."

She shrugged. "I know you wouldn't do anything, so don't stress. Just be careful with him. It could get ugly if it gets complicated."

My head was spinning a little, my mind was racing and my heart felt as though it was about to gallop out of my chest. "Has Ryan said anything?" I realized then how that sounded. "I mean, has he noticed anything? Have any of the boys said anything?"

"No," she answered. "Relax. It's just me. I notice these things. And when he called you over to leave with him last night, I just wondered . . ."

"He doesn't want to be alone," I admitted quietly. "He likes me being there because I don't hassle him for anything. It's like he has downtime away from everyone without being alone. And I'm telling you this in confidence, Amber. Please don't repeat it."

Her eyes cut to mine, filled with nothing but concern. "He doesn't want to be alone? He's always pushed for alone time."

"And now he's not. I think the pressure of everything is getting to him; the last album and tour, then going straight back into the studio for this album, and now this tour. I can't tell you when he last had a real day off. Even when he's at home, he's working on something. So yeah, I'm being cautious with him. If he wants me to sit in his room and do some paperwork while he remixes tracks or practices his vocals, then I will."

Or watch movies, or have a beer . . .

"Okay," she relented. "I just worry. About all of them. But I have noticed how he is around you lately. He has eyes for you. And if you weren't aware of it, then now you are. And if Ambrose catches wind of it, then . . ." She shrugged. "I don't want to see Maddox hurt and you reassigned. Our contracts with Platinum are pretty clear on that. Tread carefully, Roscoe, that's all I'm saying."

Reassigned . . .

The doors opened and the five boys walked in, still bleary-eyed and messy-haired. Ryan followed them in like he'd herded five grumpy puppies. It was hard not to smile. "Coffee, boys," I said. I held Ryan's out to him and he took it gratefully.

The band took theirs and made their way over to the breakfast bar. There were cereals and toast, eggs and bacon, and juices all laid out. It was concert day, after all. That meant a big breakfast. Then they'd eat about two hours before the concert and eat again afterwards.

They knew the routine.

But this morning, directly after breakfast and before a full dress rehearsal at the stadium, I was taking Maddox to a guitar shop. Without our security team, without the whole convoy.

I watched the boys gather their breakfast and saw that Maddox did attempt to eat some bacon and toast, but as usual, he mostly stuck to coffee. He chatted a bit, even managed to smile once or twice. He never was much of a morning person.

Until I felt Amber's eyes on me and I turned to find her watching me watch him. Christ. *How long was I staring at him for?* "Tread carefully," she repeated.

Knowing Ryan was out of earshot, I said, "Now I'm waiting for him to search for me like you said he did. Which he hasn't. So, just how sure are you about that? Because I don't think—"

She gave a pointed glance in his direction, and sure as hell, Maddox was now watching me. When my eyes met his, he smiled and didn't look away.

"Pretty sure," Amber answered. "Every time, Roscoe."

Fuck.

My heart was knocking in my chest. Figuring it was best to pretend it wasn't true, I shook my head at her and collected my clipboard on my way to where the boys were seated. "Morning," I said, brightly. "Big day ahead of us. But first, some details . . ."

THE PLAN WAS for the four others to go with Amber and Ryan in the full van convoy. To the crowd outside and to the papzz, it would look like the whole team was on the move together. Maddox and I, with Steve, would leave a few minutes later in a delivery van, heading in the opposite direction.

Steve got in the front passenger seat and Maddox and I climbed into the back, sitting opposite each other like in those army trucks in a war movie. He grinned at me as if this was the most exciting thing he'd ever done. He was dressed head to toe in his usual black: military-style cargo pants and boots, long-sleeve shirt, and a cap.

He looked good. He always looked so damned good.

After we'd driven for a while in silence, he said, "This is fun," his smile wide.

I chuckled at him. "You can thank the boys for agreeing to run interference for you."

Maddox's smile was warm. "I can't believe they're going to Rodeo Drive. Of all places. They could go any day they wanted."

I didn't mention the publicity stunt. "Luke wanted some jeans from Saint Laurent."

He sighed. "I asked them to get me a coat."

"Let me guess," I joked. "In black."

His smile was perfect pink lips and white teeth. "As a matter of fact, yes."

I rolled my eyes but couldn't help but smile. "Are the nerves starting to kick in for tonight?" The day of the first concert was always the worst for nerves.

He scrunched his nose up a little. "A bit."

Which meant he was a lot nervous. Going to this guitar store was probably a good distraction. Because in a few hours, they'd be at the stadium going through a full rehearsal before the concert. And once the tour officially kicked off, it didn't stop for seven weeks.

"So," he said. "What were you and Amber talking about this morning?"

"When?"

"At breakfast. You looked none too pleased."

Crap.

"Oh, nothing. Just trying to figure out schedules for today. We can't be late back to the stadium."

Maddox nodded slowly. "You need to work on your bullshit face. Because that was bullshit and you're a terrible liar."

"My bullshit face. Thanks, I'll keep that in mind."

He held my gaze. Those dark eyes would be the death of me. "Don't get me wrong, I like that you can't lie. You've never been good at it. But I don't know if it's admirable that you keep trying or if it's a lost cause. I can give you lessons if you like?"

"Lessons on how to lie?"

"Yep."

"Do you lie often?"

"Every day."

I squinted at him. "How so? What do you— Do you lie to me?"

"Sometimes. Though you know when I lie to you too, so we're about even."

"Do I?"

"Sure. You flinch when you know I'm lying." He studied my face. "Well, it's not so much a full flinch, but you do this thing with your eyes. They tighten or something. I'd call that a flinch."

I could not believe this conversation. "When do you lie to me?"

"Roscoe," he chided. "You know when."

"I'm not sure I do."

"When you ask me if I'm okay."

"You say yes or yeah. Or you nod."

"And you flinch. I lie, and you pretend you don't know it's a lie. It's the game we play every day, Roscoe."

What the actual fuck?

I kicked his boot with mine, maybe a little harder than I meant to. "Hey."

He smiled. "What?"

"This isn't a game we play. If you're not okay, you need to tell me. Be honest with me."

Those imploring onyx eyes were alight with daring. "How honest do you want me to be?" he whispered.

My stomach swooped and I was suddenly very nervous. "Completely," I replied, not much louder than him. "One hundred percent."

He licked his lips, and that peek of pink tongue nearly ended me. He clearly noticed me looking at his mouth because his smile became a little smug, and he tapped my boot with his. "Only if you're completely honest with me."

"ETA, one minute," Steve called out from the front seat. "The address is coming up now."

Maddox sighed, and I was honestly not sure what to say. Things were getting weird between us, the ground was shifting beneath my feet, and I knew it was a bad idea. But I also knew I wasn't going to stop it.

Because if he wanted to look at me like that, if he wanted to hold my hand, if he wanted to spend time with me, I certainly wasn't going to say no.

"Looks clear," Steve added. The van slowed and came to a stop. Steve jumped out and opened the van door for us. He stood aside, Maddox went out first, and I followed him, slipping inside the front doors of the store seemingly unnoticed.

The store itself looked like most guitar stores I'd been in, and I'd seen the inside of a few over the years. Maddox played the keyboard and piano as well. Mostly for composing and mixing with his software, but he loved his guitars.

However, this store was a tad smaller, and while guitars lined the walls, they didn't appear to be for sale. They were mostly signed, that I could see, anyway. A young woman greeted us, aiming straight for Maddox. She held out her hand, which he shook. "Dana-Rae," she said, red cheeks and a little giggly. Seeing women and men flustered around him was nothing new.

Still, I tried not to be annoyed.

Then an older man walked out, who I sincerely thought was Willie Nelson until he spoke and I realized he wasn't. He grinned as he came to us, and he also went straight for Maddox. "Good morning," he said. "Iver Rigby."

Maddox shook his hand, bright-eyed and grinning. It was weird to see him so excited, as if he were the one meeting a celebrity. "Maddox Kershaw," Maddox said. Then he put his hand on my lower back. "This is my guy, Roscoe."

My guy.

He'd just called me that. Not my manager, not my assistant, not his babysitter, as he'd sometimes joked.

My guy.

With his hand on my back.

Like he was introducing a personal friend?

Reeling from whatever the hell that meant, I shook the man's outstretched hand. "Roscoe Hall. Nice to meet you."

Steve, I realized, was standing a few meters away with his back to us, between us and the front door. There were two other customers in the store, who hadn't really paid us much attention, looking at a guitar on the far wall.

"Come this way," Iver said. He led us toward the rear of

the store, through a door, and down a short hall into what appeared to be a low-key recording studio. The walls were of a wooden acoustic design. There was a range of instruments and a mixing desk with a few different screens.

Maddox looked like a kid in a candy store.

He sampled a few guitars, discussing specifics with Iver and terminology and muso-speak that went over my head. Maddox clearly favored one kind of guitar in particular because he kept going back to it. I assumed he liked it because it was sleeker than the others until he strummed a few bars of "Fly," singing slow and smooth.

He sounded like an angel.

Iver sat back in his seat and sighed. "That's some magic right there," he said. "I think we've found ourselves a winner."

Maddox blushed a little. "Can you make me one? I'll be out of town for a couple of months though."

"I can do you one better," he replied. "You can take this one if you want."

Maddox's face looked like he'd just won the lottery. "For real? I can take it today?"

Iver nodded. "I made it a few months back. It's even numbered like the rest of them. I just had it here as a demo because you said on the phone you wanted a cutaway electric-acoustic. I like to see what kind fits the person, but I bet we can stop looking."

Maddox grinned at me, and it struck my insides much the same way he plucked the strings. He played a few riffs and it sounded so good.

I could have watched him play all day.

But we were running out of time. Maddox was expected at the stadium soon, so he asked for it to be delivered to the hotel, and after he'd handed over his card and everything was settled, he slid onto the seat at the keyboard and proceeded to play some of his songs. Familiar melodies with his incredible vocals . . .

It was stripped bare and genuine, and all Iver could do was smile and shake his head. "Guess no one can accuse him of using Auto-Tune," he said to me.

I almost snorted. "Ah, no."

There was a light knock on the door, and Steve poked his head in. "We're getting some attention."

Which was his way of saying it was time to go, and it was time to go *now*.

Maddox posed with Iver for a quick photo or two, he signed a guitar on the wall—alongside Slash, Dave Grohl, Robbie Williams, and a few others—and we said our good-byes. There was a bit of a crowd growing, though they were outside. The driver had the van pulled up out front, so Steve took the lead and I stayed by Maddox's side, between him and the curious crowd.

People called his name, but thankfully they kept a respectful distance, and he waved for their photos before he darted into the back of the van. I followed him, the door slid closed behind us, Steve got in the front, and we were gone.

Maddox was beaming. He was so happy it was contagious. "I can't believe I get it today. You know some people have to wait weeks or months, and I get it today. A freaking Iver Rigby original. I get to take it on tour with me."

I loved that he was so happy, thrilled even. But it meant he made no attempt to hold my hand, and that was disappointing. But was he sitting a little closer than necessary? Or was that wishful thinking on my part? His knee bumped mine, his shoulder, his thigh . . . and suddenly holding his hand seemed irrelevant.

Focus, Roscoe.

Needing a distraction, I pulled out my phone and let Amber and Ryan know we were on schedule and on route to Pasadena. Maddox pushed his side against mine to read my phone screen. "They're on their way now too," I said, desperately trying not to think about his body against mine.

"You have thirty-four unread messages," he noted.

"Most of those will be from Ambrose." I opened Messages, and yes, Ambrose's name appeared a lot.

"Christ."

"Well, we're on tour, it's concert day, our first concert, mind you, and we're off on our own," I explained. "With one security guard."

Maddox's eyes met mine, his face so, so close. "Is he bitching at you? Because this was my idea."

"Not really. He'll just be stressing out until you're all at the stadium. You know how he is." I opened the first message and held the phone so Maddox and I could read it together.

He slid his hand up my wrist, tender and scorching hot, until he half-held the phone, and half-held my hand. "Do you mind if I read this?"

"I don't hide anything from you, Maddox," I replied, my voice rougher than I'd intended.

He looked at me, our faces just a few inches apart. He was devastatingly handsome. Ridiculously beautiful. His flawless skin, dark eyelashes, and it was hard to tell where his pupils ended and his irises began.

He was a work of art.

His lips were pink and slightly parted, perfect for kissing.

All the magazines and websites that had voted him sexiest man alive had no freaking idea just how hot and sexy he was up this close.

"You have the cutest freckles across your nose," he whispered, blush tinting his cheeks. "They're kinda faded, but those are definitely freckles."

Oh god.

"And your eyes are so blue," he whispered, and I was almost certain I wasn't supposed to hear it. His gaze went from my eyes to my lips and back up to my eyes.

Fucking hell, was he about to kiss me?

I realized, somehow, that his hand was now on my thigh. It was burning through my jeans.

"You shouldn't look at me like that," he murmured, barely audible.

"Like what?"

He smiled, smug and beautiful. "Like you want to kiss me."

My heart banged against my ribs so hard it almost hurt. I tried to tell him no, he was wrong. I wasn't looking at him like that. *He* was looking at *me* like that.

But I couldn't get the air out to form words.

He looked at my mouth again, then slowly drew his gaze up to mine. He licked his lips. "I wouldn't say no," he whispered.

Steve's voice from the front of the van startled us both. "ETA, one minute. We're coming up to the stadium entrance now."

It was like a bucket of cold water, snapping us both out of whatever trance we were in.

Except his hand stayed on my thigh.

And when I dared risk a look at his face, he smiled.

Fuck.

CHAPTER FIVE

THE BOYS WENT STRAIGHT into rehearsals as soon as we arrived at the stadium. There were long lines of people outside already, and many had been there since late last night, apparently. Maddox never spared me another glance for a few hours, and I had to wonder if I'd imagined the whole incident in the car. But I swear I could still feel the burn of his hand on my thigh and see the shine of his dark eyes so close to mine . . .

I didn't imagine that.

But we got busy doing a hundred things, so I put it out of my mind and got to work. It was just hours before the concert, after all.

This was the final dress rehearsal to make sure jackets and pants were fine with the dance routines and not likely to split or tear on stage. They danced pretty hard—they were famous for it—and their clothes needed to stretch and move with their bodies accordingly. Of course, the wardrobe team had everything perfected.

And when I say perfect, I was referring to their pants in particular.

Made of some black latex denim worthy of a Spiderman suit, they looked like jeans but they fit . . . well, they fit like a second skin. They allowed the boys to move and dance, run and kick, flip and sit while looking like streetwear. They cost a fortune, of course, but they were worth every cent.

Those pants showed every thigh muscle, every curve, every line, every bulge.

Like I said. Perfection.

"I heard Maddox talking about his new guitar," Amber said, nodding to where the boys were now walking off the stage. I hadn't heard her come over. God, did she catch me staring again? Had I been staring?

"Yeah, he got the one he wanted. There were a few customs in store and one that suited him perfectly, so he got to take it today and he doesn't have to wait, so he was stoked. How did it go for you guys?"

"Good. We left before the crowd started to get too big."

I nodded. "How's Blake's knee?"

"Yeah, he said it feels good. But we'll see how long that lasts."

I checked my watch. It was two hours till showtime. "We better make sure these boys eat."

Catering always offered a range of carbs and proteins before a concert, and the boys knew by now how much to eat. But it was our job to make sure they wanted or needed nothing else before, during, and after a concert.

It was summer in the US. The tour was planned to optimize the good weather. But that meant we had to contend with heat. Even when the concerts were held at night, dehydration was a real concern. Not just for the boys on stage—who would come off stage drenched with sweat—but for the staff who ran themselves ragged behind the scenes.

So while the five boys ate and were supposed to rest

before the make-up and wardrobe teams moved in, Amber, Ryan, and I went through our lists twice to make sure we were good to go. "Water, energy gels, tubs of ice," I said, double-checking the supplies off the list. "Ice packs, towels, cans of oxygen."

We had last minute meetings with the security teams, with the sound teams and the stage crew. Everything was good to go. Everyone was pumped for the tour to officially begin. When the opening act went on, the noise of the crowd in the stadium was deafening, the excitement was contagious.

When we walked back into the main dressing room, they were all in various stages of undress. Maddox's shirt was undone, Blake wasn't wearing a shirt at all. Jeremy was pulling his pants up, thank God. And Wes had his pants and shirt on, no socks or shoes, and Luke was the only one who appeared fully dressed.

Wardrobe people fussed around them, trying to get them dressed, much like helpless parents with five toddlers. But the five of them were too busy looking at something on their phones, laughing and talking excitedly . . . and then they saw me.

"Here he is," Blake said, grinning. "The man of the hour."

"You trying to take Maddox's title?" Wes asked. "Well, he's no longer the sexiest man alive, and you're part of the band now, apparently."

"Can you even sing?" Jeremy joked.

"We should get him fitted for these pants," Luke said with a laugh.

"What the hell are you talking about?" I asked, not entirely sure I wanted to know. "And that's a definite no to both the singing and the pants, just so you know."

Maddox turned his phone around for me to see. There was a photo of me escorting him into the guitar shop under the title, *And the sexiest manager award goes to . . .*

The what?

"The sexiest manager?" I scoffed. "Is that some spoof newspaper? What's it called? *The Onion?*"

"Oh no," Blake said cheerfully. "You're on every website, and you're all over TikTok." He pointed his chin to the TV on the wall. "*Entertainment Tonight* even had footage."

What the actual fuck?

"Of me?"

Wes nodded. "The reporter wanted to know if you're related to the Hemsworths."

"Oh Christ," I grumbled. I took my phone out and found dozens of hits in half a second. Amber and Ryan had their phones out too, scrolling and reading.

This wasn't good.

"You know," Maddox said casually, "I don't mind one bit. It means they're leaving me alone."

I looked up at him then, to find he was buttoning up his shirt with a sexy-as-hell smirk on his face. But this wasn't funny. This was just another hassle we didn't have time to deal with.

I went back to my phone, scrolling through the pics. Someone had obviously taken photos of us when we were in the guitar store. It was after Maddox was told he could have the guitar and we went back out into the showroom. The crowd had begun to gather, and while they kept a respectable distance, they obviously took photos.

Everyone with a damn phone was a paparazzi these days.

The images were kinda grainy but clear enough to see

who it was. Maddox Kershaw inside the shop with me. With his hand on my arm, with him grinning, laughing. Me smiling back at him. Me standing beside him while he paid at the counter, us talking, his hand on my back . . .

Did he always touch me like that?

Did I really look at him like that?

Then there were photos of us leaving. Maddox was waving. I had my hand on his back, ushering him into the van and following close behind him.

The headlines were all variations of the same. *Maddox's hot manager. Manager or boyfriend? Sexiest men alive.*

The grab lines weren't much better.

Maddox Kershaw was seen at Iver Rigby's custom guitar store today ahead of their first LA concert looking very cozy with his manager.

Just who is Roscoe Hall, and how is he sexier than Maddox Kershaw?

I read the beginning of one article on an entertainment site.

Given he's six foot tall with sandy blond hair, rugged good looks, and has the body of Thor, you might be mistaken to think this is footage of Chris Hemsworth with superstar Maddox Kershaw today in LA. But long-time fans of the supergroup Atrous know him as Roscoe Hall, Maddox's personal manager . . .

Christ all-fucking-mighty.

"Wait, wait, this one's my favorite," Luke said, standing up and reading off his phone. "'The hottest bodyguard hall of fame just got another inductee.'"

They all laughed.

"Bodyguard?" Wes asked. "Does Steve know?"

I resisted the urge to swear. Barely. I'm glad they could laugh. I turned to Ryan. "Where's Ambrose?"

"He was with the concert director. Said he'll be back to see the boys before it was time."

"And we're trending on Twitter," Jeremy called out. "From what I can see, it's a mix of the concert, all of us going out in public this morning, and hashtag Roscoe."

"Pretty sure it's the polo shirt, Roscoe," Luke added. "It shows off your Thor body."

Maddox grinned right at me, broad and beautiful. "Hashtag Roscoe. I like it."

"It's not funny," I said.

"Mm," Amber said beside me. "Well, it is a little bit."

I stared at her like she'd lost her mind. "Until Ambrose decides it's not. Like he has time to deal with this right now."

"You've heard of 'all publicity is good publicity,' right?" Ryan said.

Yeah, well, I wasn't convinced.

Why was no one else concerned? Worst of all, why did they think it was funny?

Maddox came over to me. "You know, I honestly don't mind," he said. "If the world thinks you're sexier than me. They wouldn't be wrong."

Christ. Both Amber and Ryan heard that.

"It's not that," I replied, running my hand through my hair. "You're already a big enough target, and I just made that worse."

Maddox had an oh-shit moment before he frowned at me. "You didn't do anything. The media did it; the people with cameras and ridiculous headlines and tweets did this. Not you."

I withheld a sigh and remembered the time and place. He didn't need this right now. "You should finish getting ready," I said. "I'll go find Ambrose and we'll get this mess cleaned up. You just focus on you." I made a point of showing him my watch. "T minus thirty."

Thirty minutes until they walked on.

I left them and went in search of my boss. There were people running everywhere, talking into earpieces and walkie-talkies, and despite the concert chaos, I knew where to look. Ambrose would be in the thick of it.

Sure enough, he was under the stage surrounded by no less than five people, giving orders and instructions. His assistants, a stage crew manager and a logistics guy, and a stadium official were trying to talk over the sound of the opening act on the stage above us.

Ambrose saw me and gave me a nod, so I waited for him to finish. When he came over, we began the walk back to the main room where the boys were, hopefully, now ready to perform. Fully dressed would be a good start.

"What's up?" he asked as he walked. "Everything okay?"

He really was an organizational machine. The reason why he was the manager of the biggest boy band in the world was because he was incredibly good at it. He'd been with Atrous for five years, and his skills for managing them expanded with their fame.

"Yeah, everything's fine. There was some media hype this afternoon I wanted to give you a head's up about."

"The sexiest bodyguard bullshit?"

Of course he knew about it already.

"Yep."

"I saw it." He stopped walking as we got to the door. "Look, Roscoe. It's harmless hype at the moment, and quite frankly, getting the band on every entertainment site and social media platform two hours before kick-off wasn't a bad play at all."

"Ambrose," I began.

He put his hand up. "I know what you're thinking. I said it's harmless, *at the moment*. Let's just see what comes of it. You know how this industry is. It'll be about someone different tomorrow."

"And if it's not?"

"Then we deal with it."

I gave a nod. "Good."

"How's our boy, anyway?"

Our boy . . . God, I really hated how Maddox was singled out by everyone, from the media, his fans, to his own management.

"They're pumped," I said, including all five members of the band.

Ambrose was about to say something, but before he could, I said, "We've got twelve minutes." I opened the door and stood aside.

Ambrose walked in, all excitement and confidence, offering words of support and gratitude for everyone's hard work. The thing was, I liked Ambrose, and the boys respected him. They'd been together a long time, especially in this industry, and there was a deep level of trust.

There had to be.

And Ambrose worked hard, no one could dispute that. But at the end of the day, he was the right hand of Arlo Kim, the boss of Platinum Entertainment, and these five boys were a product of the company.

Did Arlo treat them well? Yes.

Did Atrous make Arlo Kim a fuckton of money? Yes. Did they put his company at the forefront of entertainment management on a global scale? Also yes.

It was a symbiotic relationship of sorts. Platinum Entertainment started small and moved heaven and earth to give Atrous the exposure they deserved. Atrous took the world by storm by putting in grueling hours and dedication, and in doing so, made Platinum Entertainment the success it was.

One couldn't have done it without the other. And Arlo Kim did respect the band. I knew that. But sometimes I just felt like these boys were the hamsters running the treadmill that made the whole hamster factory work. Platinum Entertainment *owned* these boys. They were just kids when they signed, with no idea of the success that lay before them. No one could have known.

They also couldn't have known how tied up their lives would be in those contracts. Were they happy ninety-nine percent of the time? Yes. Did the boys have creative control over their music? Mostly. Did Platinum Entertainment dictate their personal lives in the name of their public image? Yep.

But it wasn't just that.

Maybe I was cynical. Maybe I was biased. Maybe I saw Maddox work until he dropped all too often. I saw him stress. I saw him carry the burden of the whole band—and therefore the whole company—when no one else did. The reputation, the responsibility, the reason.

Maddox was the golden boy. Everything he wrote, everything he sang, everything he said turned to gold. Maddox bore the weight of Platinum Entertainment's expectations.

But at what cost?

So yeah, maybe I felt a little overprotective. And maybe

Ambrose calling him "our boy" rankled me more than it should because Maddox wasn't *his* boy.

Maddox was *mine*.

I was there with him, there *for* him, twenty-four hours a day, seven days a week, for years. My entire life revolved around him.

I understood him. Like very few people did.

We had something. A professional relationship, yes. But underneath that, there was friendship and empathy. And until very recently, I would have said what we had was a very platonic, very close professional rapport.

Until recently.

Until the hand-holding and the lingering looks, and the suggestive lip-licking and sultry smiles. The innuendos, his hands on my thigh, the way he said he wouldn't stop me if I kissed him . . .

That was all new. There had been a change in the last six months, and even now, knowing it would likely cost me my job, I just couldn't seem to stop myself.

So while Ambrose gave his epic spiel of encouragement, I watched Maddox. He was fully dressed now, his earpiece was fitted. His make-up and hair were perfection, and those pants . . . the way they fit him, hugged him in all the right places. Christ.

When I looked back up to his face, he was watching me, smiling. Actually, it was more of a smirk that told me he'd caught me checking him out.

I met his gaze and held it until Jeremy nudged him to get his attention. They did that thing they did at the beginning of every concert, where they stood in a circle, right hands in the center. "First concert of the tour," Jeremy said. "Let's give 'em their money's worth."

"Atrous," they all crowed in unison.

"Let's do this!"

We all clapped as they walked out, the stage director ushering them along. And it was only then that the whole room let out a collective sigh. Our job was done. The next two and a half hours were up to them.

We had a few moments to grab something quick to eat and begin packing up, and we knew the second the boys had walked out on stage because the whole stadium rumbled with applause and cheering.

We watched them on the live feed. We would meet them under the stage when they came off for a set break and outfit change, but for the first few songs, we got a front-row view.

They danced their asses off. They sang their hearts out. Choreography was perfect, the vocals were too. The veins in their necks stood out when they sang, and their sweat soaked hair and drenched shirts just added to their sex appeal.

The entire audience sang with them, cheered, danced, and screamed.

The huge screens to the sides of the stage showed close ups, the lights and laser shows were on point. They had the crowd sing with them, they involved them, they spoke to them, made them laugh. Twenty-six songs, three outfit changes, and an energy that was out of this world.

They held the audience of eighty-something thousand people in the palms of their hands.

It was a privilege to watch.

When they came off the stage for the last time that night, the five of them dragging, sweating, panting, they all but collapsed onto the couches. They barely had the fuel in their tanks to high five each other.

I didn't even mind the film crew catching this side of

them. Let the fans see what each performance took out of them.

But then the wardrobe crew moved in, pulling shirts off, leaving the five of them shirtless and very sweaty. They toweled off and we fed them more energy gels and water, and I did everything in my willpower to not stare at shirt-less-Maddox, or his muscular body, or his damn sleeve of tattoos . . .

And the film crew filmed that too.

When it came time to peel off those stage pants, I walked over to the film crew and put my clipboard in front of the camera. One of them looked ready to say something, but I cut her off. "If Ambrose has a problem with this, tell him to come find me."

That earned me a few smirks from the boys, but Maddox had his pants undone, fly open, still shirtless, so I made myself busy packing up shit that needed packing with my back turned. Sure, I'd seen them all undressed over the years—never fully naked, thank god—but this was different.

Now I wanted to look.

And that wasn't good. Maybe the lines could blur in the car or in a hotel room, but this was work. He'd done his job, now he needed me to do mine.

So I fetched him his bag and cleaned up all his mess, helping Amber and Ryan with anything that needed to be done. And before too long, we were in the van and heading back to the hotel.

Maddox slid into his seat, tired but happy.

"You guys killed it tonight," I said.

"It was good," he agreed. "Hit all my notes. Didn't fuck up any dance steps."

"You hungry?"

He nodded. "Yeah."

"Dinner's been ordered for all of you back at the hotel."

"Mm, dinner and a shower. Sounds great." He was quiet for a bit. I tried not to think of him in the shower, and I was grateful it was dark in the van. The passing street-lights were like a strobe effect, pulsing in time with my heart. "You can join me if you want."

"You boys always eat together after a concert—"

"I wasn't talking about dinner."

My gaze shot to his. He was sitting low in his seat, his legs spread wide, his hand resting on his belly, sliding lower . . .

Fucking hell.

"Maddox," I warned.

He laughed, as if he was just joking. But he wasn't, and we both knew it. He sat up straight, then leaned a little closer to me. "I saw you checking me out earlier," he whispered like it was all just some game.

I looked away because I sure as hell couldn't look at him when I lied. "No I wasn't."

He laughed again. "Oh, Roscoe." When it was clear I wasn't going to say anything, he changed topics. "So, what did Ambrose say about the sexiest bodyguard media frenzy?"

God, I'd almost forgotten about that.

"He wasn't too concerned," I replied. "Yet."

"I thought it was funny. I mean, I get why you didn't. When you said it made me a bigger target . . . Well, I didn't think of it like that."

I sighed. "You don't need anything to shine another spotlight on you, especially from me. I'm supposed to make your life easier, not harder."

"Hey."

I looked at him then.

"You do make my life easier. You make it bearable, Roscoe," he said gently. "They're just gonna write whatever they want, regardless of the truth or who they hurt in the process. You can't control it. You just have to let it go. Ignore it."

Wait up. "I make your life bearable?"

His jaw bulged and he looked out the window, narrowing his gaze at the passing city. "Yeah."

Christ.

"Maddox," I whispered.

It took him a second to look at me. When he did, his guard was up again. His eyes were black steel. I said nothing, just held out my hand, palm up.

He looked at it for a long second before he slid his hand into mine. We didn't speak again for the rest of the drive to the hotel, but his grip on my hand was a fraction too firm, as if he was scared I was going to let go.

Or just scared. I wasn't sure. So I held on just as tight.

———

MY PHONE BEEPED at 11:37 pm with a message from Maddox.

Can you come here please?

I was ready for bed. Everyone had gone to their rooms after a late meal. Concert nights were always late, but I'd had enough time to shower and change into my pajamas. We had to be up early in the morning . . .

I knocked on his door, and after a few seconds, it swung inwards. He stood there in some sleep shorts and an old T-shirt, his head down like he was embarrassed. I walked in, enough steps for him to close the door. "What's up?"

"I couldn't sleep," he murmured. "I'm so tired. Can you . . . can you stay for a bit?"

There was no playfulness now. There was no heat, no smirk.

Just sadness.

It made my heart ache. "Sure."

He lifted his gaze then, and he made a face when he saw the shirt I was wearing. "Really? Bruins? You're a Boston Bruins fan?"

"Shut up. You want me to stay or not?"

He gave me a tired smile and trudged over to the bed, climbed in, and pulled the blankets up. "I like the air conditioning on and lots of blankets," he mumbled and folded his arm up under the pillow. He patted the other side of the bed. "'S comfier than the chairs."

Fuck. Was I just supposed to occupy the same bed as him? To what? Sleep? How long was I supposed to stay for?

I sat on the farthest edge I could without falling off, sitting against the headboard, and shoved the pillow at my lower back. The TV was on, the volume barely audible. Some old western was playing, and I chuckled at the thought of him choosing this. But after watching five minutes of it, of the horse riding, the old saloon bars, the costumes, and the low-slung gun holsters and the corny lines, I had to admit, it was kinda cool.

"Never picked you for a John Wayne fan," I murmured.

But Maddox never replied. When I looked, he was fast asleep.

CHAPTER SIX

MADDOX COULD BARELY LOOK at me at breakfast time. Was he pissed off at me? Embarrassed? I had no clue. But we had an interview and a photo shoot before lunch, which meant a fair amount of alone time in the car to talk.

And I didn't waste a second. As soon as the van door was shut and we had some semblance of privacy, save our driver and Steve in the front, I tapped his boot with mine. "Maddox, talk to me."

There was no way I was letting something like miscommunication get between us. Not now. Shit was complicated enough without childish games.

He shot me a puzzled look. "About what?"

"About what's bothering you. You haven't said three words to me this morning."

"Nothing's bothering me."

I raised an eyebrow and waited . . . but not for long.

He scowled at me, then he turned to face the window. "You were gone this morning."

"Of course I was. I went back to my room at one o'clock," I said so only he could hear. "I'd left my phone in my room. And you weren't exactly clear on how long I should have stayed. You were sound asleep."

His annoyance became a frown. "I hate it."

"Hate what?"

"Not sleeping. I'm so tired but my mind goes all the time," he whispered. "It's better when I'm not alone."

"If you need something to help you sleep," I began, though I was pretty sure what his reaction was going to—

"No." He shook his head. "No drugs."

"It doesn't have to be drugs, Maddox. There are plenty of things on the market now that are natural or non-addictive. Or we can try meditation, or acupuncture, or massage, or anything. I don't know. There are a lot of alternative—"

"I don't want no wellness guru, hippy-loving crackpot—"

"Well, that's a broad generalization, possibly prejudiced—"

"I don't want anyone to know, Roscoe," he snapped.

Aaaand there it was.

"Just you," he added softly. He let out a shaky breath. "I trust you. And I hate that even you know. I hate feeling like a little kid or like I need adult supervision."

"You hate feeling vulnerable," I stated, and from the way his eyes shot to mine, I knew I was right. "I don't blame you," I added casually. "No one likes to feel that way. But for what it's worth, I'm glad you told me. If you need me to sit there and watch two John Wayne movies back-to-back, then I will."

That almost earned me a smile. "You watched two?"

I nodded. "They were actually pretty good. In a bad western kind of way."

The corner of his lip curled upward for a fleeting moment before it was gone. "Thank you. I thought this morning you'd think it was weird, and if I didn't look at you, I wouldn't see you not looking at me."

Oh, Maddox. "It's not weird."

"Can you not tell the others?" He winced. "I know I'm asking you to keep secrets and probably to lie at some point. But, Roscoe . . ." He chewed on his bottom lip and picked at the cuticle on his thumb. No more words were forthcoming.

"But Roscoe, what?"

"But I need you," he whispered. He took in a sharp breath. "In my corner. I need you to be on my side. I feel . . . I dunno, things have been weird and I don't know how I feel most days, but you make it . . . normal. Better. I dunno." He shrugged, his cheeks tinted pink. "I think it's because you've always been there. You've always been in the background and I know you'll be there. I trust you, and I can't say that about many people."

He grimaced as he inhaled, as though he was mad at himself for saying too much. He fidgeted his hands, opening and closing his fists, and when he met my gaze, his eyes were . . . fierce or scared. Or a mix of both?

"I am on your side," I said.

"I don't want the others to know. The guys, I mean. I don't want them to worry. And not Amber and Ryan either. Because then I'd have to ask them to keep secrets, and that's not fair. And then it's all too complicated."

"The guys won't mind, Maddox. They'd want to know if something's bothering you."

"They've got enough going on. We all do. And they don't need to be worrying about me on top of their own shit."

"You're not in this alone, Maddox. Jeremy adores you. They all do."

"Jeremy . . ." His eyes met mine again before he looked

back out the window. "Jeremy's my best friend, and I love him."

There was a but coming.

"I love all of them."

"But?"

He scrubbed his hands over his face and groaned. "Christ, Roscoe."

"But what?"

"But they're in the band. And I need someone who's not in the band. Someone who I can talk to and someone who'll just be with me for me. Someone who's comfortable in the silence and who doesn't expect anything from me."

It dawned then. "Me."

He nodded. "You."

Goddammit.

"I won't tell anyone. And honestly, I don't mind hanging out." I shrugged. "I get lonely too sometimes, so some company is nice."

He studied me for a long moment and eventually half a smile won out. "Nice? Spending time with me is *nice*?"

"Oh, fuck off," I whispered. "You don't get to play the 'but I'm Maddox Kershaw' card after telling me you like me because I treat you like a normal person."

He grinned. "That's a first. Have you ever told me to fuck off before? I don't think you have."

"Not out loud."

He laughed, and my god, it was a beautiful sound. "And I never said I like you because you treat me like a normal person."

"You kinda did."

"Pretty sure I'd remember. No, I like you because you're the hottest bodyguard in the world right now."

I groaned. "Christ. Is that still a thing?"

"Yep. Haven't you seen Twitter this morning?"

"No. I was kinda busy getting everything ready."

He took out his phone and tapped the screen a few times. "Well, things that were trending . . . our concert, my ass in those pants at our concert. Luke and Blake posted a shirtless selfie together in the dressing room. That was number one for a while. Made the Bluke fans happy. Oh, and here, look . . ." He turned the screen around to show me a photograph of me at the guitar store, and then he grinned as he read off some tweets. "Roscoe can guard my body any time. How do I sign up for him to manage me? How much heat do you think he's packing?" He shook his head. "Want me to read you the R-rated ones?"

"No. No, I don't." I ignored all mentions of me. "Do the fans know that Luke and Blake are the two straightest men in the band?"

Maddox's smile widened. "That's what makes it hot. I mean, they could have us." He waved his hand between us. "Two sexiest men on the planet—according to this tweet, anyway—who are both *very* gay. And we're always together. It really wouldn't be a huge leap to assume we fuck."

Jesus Christ.

Was it hot in the van?

He chuckled. "What do you think our couple name would be? Maddox and Roscoe . . . Mmm." He made a thinking face. "Doxcoe? Madscoe? Moscoe? They sound stupid."

"All couple names sound stupid," I said. "And why is your name first?"

Did I really just ask that?

He grinned, the kind of smile that stopped hearts all over the world. "Because I said it did."

"Oh, the 'but I'm Maddox Kershaw' thing again."

"It really is a double-edged sword."

I found myself smiling at him. This was him, this was the Maddox of old. Carefree, guard down, happy, funny, witty. Just Maddox.

"You know," he said, a wicked gleam in his eye. "We could break the internet. Right now."

"Break the internet?"

"Yep. One selfie." He grinned. "Of us."

"Oh no." I shook my head. "That's a bad idea."

He opened the camera on his phone. "It's a great idea."

"It's possibly the worst idea you've ever had."

Then, surprising the shit out of me, he climbed over and sat on my lap. He held his phone up at some magic selfie angle. "Smile."

"Maddox, this is a bad idea. And you should be in your own seat with your seatbelt on."

With his free hand, he took my arm and brought it around his waist. "You can be my seatbelt."

I ignored how he felt on my lap. I ignored how he felt against my chest. I ignored how he smelled. He, on the other hand, smiled the world's most beautiful smile and took some photos.

"Don't upload that," I said, trying to sound stern. "I mean it, Maddox."

"But if I do, then we don't have to decide our stupid couple name because the fans will decide for us."

"That's not funny."

Still sitting on my lap, he turned to face me. "What would be funny is if I put the caption something like 'You have no idea how good he smells,' and the internet will die."

"Maddox."

"Because you do smell really good," he whispered. "The world should know. It's a great injustice that they don't."

"The only thing that should happen is you sitting in your own seat."

"Well, I would," he murmured, his lips closer to my ear. "But your arm is still around me."

I looked at my traitorous arm and moved it. He chuckled and slid back over to his seat. Christ, this car ride had been dizzying. I needed to try to recoup some control.

"You can't post those photos," I said, my tone low. "Unless you want me on the first plane back to Vermont."

He shot me a look, alarmed and puzzled. "Why?"

"Because Ambrose would drive me to the airport himself. One, you not seated in your own seat. Two, no seat-belt. Three, on my lap. Four, fooling around. Five, in a moving vehicle. And six, because he can fire me anytime he wants."

"I told you before, no one's firing you."

I rolled my eyes. "It's not your decision."

He stared at me, amused and stubborn, and he smiled again. "It'd be interesting to see who holds the most power, me or Ambrose. Don't you think?"

"No. No, I do not think. That is a competition no one wins. No one."

"I mean, he can claim control and management, but if I walk away, what does he have? Pretty sure Arlo Kim would pick me."

This was a dangerous conversation. "What do you mean, walk away?"

Steve turned around in the front. "ETA, one minute."

Maddox sighed and fixed his cap, pulling it down tight.

I wasn't letting him not answer my question. "Hey. Do you think about walking away?"

He waited until the van slowed, then he shrugged. "Not really. I don't think I could." He gave me a smile that was all stage and performative. His public smile. "I don't know who I am without any of this."

The van door opened. I didn't want to drop this conversation but I had to. I grabbed my backpack and went out first. Maddox followed close behind, and security ushered us through the wall of photographers and fans.

And the madness began all over again.

One interview—live, on morning TV—and a photoshoot.

Madness and mayhem. Push and shove. Screaming crowds, the constant click of cameras, the call of names in a futile attempt to get a direct-eye-contact photograph or even for them to look in that general direction.

The boys would always be polite and wave if they could, but they mostly kept their heads down and kept moving. The majority of fans were just excited, which was great. But some . . . well, some were fucking crazy.

They screamed through the fencing, though, and the boys simply waved, and we followed the studio staff through the doors and into a large room where Bibi and the make-up and stylist teams were already waiting.

They were on a bit of a time crunch—traffic took longer than expected—but they swarmed in, did their magic in no time at all, and before we knew it, the boys were walking out onto the stage to a deafening applause.

They took their seats in formation opposite the hosts, and whereas their last TV appearance had been fun and showed the side of the band that was funny and loud, this interview was more serious.

"Your album *Beacon* shot to number one just about everywhere," the host said. "And for me, when I listened to this, I felt an undercurrent of hope, which I guess is what a beacon is. Tell us what the message is behind these songs."

Wes answered. "We all brought something to the table for this album. We wanted our fans to connect with each song for whatever they're going through. There's a journey in every album, I guess. Reasons to be mad, reasons to celebrate, to be grateful."

"Congratulations on kicking off your tour. Your concert last night was a huge success," the host said. I got the feeling she was a huge fan. "*Rolling Stone* called it an 'epic, cross-genre, multi-generational sensory experience.' How does that make you feel?"

Blake answered, saying it was surreal.

"If someone told you six years ago, when you were just a high school band with big dreams, that you'd be where you are now, what would you say?"

Luke answered with a laugh. "I'd have called them delusional. There's no way we'd have believed them."

"Which song on the *Beacon* album is your favorite? To sing, to perform?"

Jeremy put his hand to his heart as if he'd been wounded. "That's a tough question because we each wrote our own songs, or we co-wrote or produced. We had a hand in every song." He groaned. "But I'd have to say 'Fly.'"

"'Oceans,'" Maddox said quickly. It was the first time he'd spoken all interview.

"'Metronome,'" Luke answered.

"'Reflection,'" Blake said.

"'Puzzle,'" Wes said. "Because I wrote it, but 'Oceans' is beautiful." He smiled over at Maddox. "The melody and bridge combo is extraordinary. Maddox wrote it, and when he played it for us, we knew it was something special."

Of course this opened up a direct line of questioning to Maddox. "Can you explain what the song means to you?"

He smiled and shifted on his seat, nervous or uncomfortable. Or both. "'Oceans' . . . it's, uh, it's a personal thing. It's about power and depth, tumultuous and healing, the ebb and flow of life, I guess."

I watched from the wings, my pulse thumping oddly in my veins. The conversation with him in the car this morning had been a rollercoaster. He'd been everything from happy and flirty to vulnerable and scared.

And now to hear him talk about something personal in public just made my heart ache.

Jeremy commandeered the question, thankfully, and talked about the writing process, about what came first, the lyrics or the melody, and how a song is born.

Maddox was never excluded. He agreed and nodded and was involved, but the focus was off him, and I was relieved.

Until it was almost time to cut to a commercial. "Now, Maddox, I can't let you leave without asking you something that's been on everyone's mind since yesterday . . ."

She gestured to the screens behind them, and there was a photograph of me.

Fucking fuckity fucking fuuuuuck.

"Now, this is not your bodyguard, is it?" she pressed.

Maddox laughed. He actually fucking laughed. "No, that's my manager." Then, because he apparently couldn't help himself, he pointed at me standing off camera. "There he is. Roscoe, say hi."

Every camera swung around to face me.

I was going to kill him.

Amber and Ryan scattered like scolded cats, and all I could do was wave. Like an idiot.

"Roscoe, is it?" the host asked, grinning, because he'd just handed her the scoop of the fucking year.

"Yes, that's right," I replied.

"Now, you're sure you're not some long-lost Hemsworth brother?"

I couldn't help but smile at that, because that was ridiculous. One of the studio crew handed me a mic, which was also ridiculous. "Absolutely sure. Sorry."

"I have to ask," she said sweetly. "What's it like managing the biggest band in the world?"

"I'm part of a team, so it's not just me," I replied. "But I can say, confidently on behalf of the entire management team, it's like herding cats."

The five boys burst out laughing. Maddox laughed the loudest, and it was a genuine laugh too. He almost doubled over.

The director gave her the wind-up signal and she recovered quickly. "We'll be back after this commercial break with Atrous performing their hit song 'Fly.' Don't go anywhere."

The guys got off their stools and our sound crew quickly fitted them with their earpieces and mics, and they took their places on the dance floor. They played to the audience a little and when they went back on-air, the song was introduced and they sang.

Oh, they were great and Maddox was perfection.

But I was still going to kill him.

"I'll be in the green room," I said, not even waiting for the song to finish.

Amber gave a nod. "I'll herd the cats."

I grumbled all the way to the green room. The stylist teams were gone, already off to the photo shoot location. I began packing up all the mess, with probably more vigor than was completely necessary. I swear to god, they'd been in this room for less than thirty minutes. How did they make such a mess?

I heard them coming before I saw them, and when they bustled in through the door, they stopped when they saw me.

Jeremy meowed, and they all busted up laughing again.

"Pick up your shit. We leave in two minutes."

Jeremy, Luke, Blake, and Wes all stared at me. I'd probably never sworn at them before. Maddox pounced forward, his hands like claws. "Feisty kitty."

I sighed, letting the backpack I was holding drop so I just had the handle. I looked at the others, who were now trying not to smile. "Please collect your belongings. We're on a schedule."

I waited for them at the rear exit doors. The vans were lined up, and soon enough the guys filed out with their security, all of them with trying-not-to-smile smiles. Amber and Ryan gave me a nod as they walked past, Maddox was last, followed by Steve, and we walked in silence to our waiting van.

Steve slid the door shut behind me and Maddox watched as I took my seat. "I feel like I'm in trouble."

"You are."

"Like I've been sent to the principal's office."

"Put your seatbelt on."

"You put yours on."

He . . . he had a good point.

I put my seatbelt on and he smiled as he buckled his. "You know, I didn't bring the topic of you up in that interview. She asked me."

"You could have deflected the question."

"But you were right there. And you being all stern with your arms crossed was kinda hot."

Oh, for fuck's sake.

"And herding cats? I can't believe you said that."

I shifted in my seat. "Well, that was probably out of line. Sorry."

"Are you kidding? It was funny as hell. And I bet you anything you like . . ." He took his phone out, scrolled for all of two seconds, and nodded. "Yep. Herding cats is trending. And you. Soooo many pictures of you."

He turned his phone to show me the screen. And there I was. Standing next to a cameraman with my arms crossed and a none-too-pleased smile on my face.

Soooo many pictures of me.

"That is the exact thing I wanted to avoid."

Maddox looked at his phone again, scrolling. "Have you tried not being so hot?"

I sighed.

"Ooh, right click and save. This one's gonna be my screensaver." He scrolled some more. "And I found my lock screen pic."

He turned his phone long enough for me to see a zoomed in photo of me, again with my arms crossed. "Holy biceps," he mumbled. "And in a polo shirt. God, they're going to write fanfictions about you as a sports coach, or a preppy professor and I'll be the rogue student who needs a very firm lesson, if you know what I mean."

I didn't reply to that.

"You know they do that, right? Write fanfiction stories about all kinds of shit. We read some once. It was weird, and kinda hot, kinda gross."

"Yes, I know they do that."

"Have you read any?"

"No."

"I think you have and you're just too embarrassed to admit it."

"Can this conversation end now? Please."

He laughed. "Anyway, back to the herding-cats thing..."

My phone buzzed again, and needing the distraction, I checked the screen. It was Ambrose calling me. I showed Maddox the screen. "Oh, goodie. This conversation is gonna be so much fun."

I hit Answer. "Hall speaking."

"I saw the interview."

"Yeah, about that—"

"It's all over the internet."

"I know."

"The band has, in one way or another, held four out of the top ten trends on social media in the last twenty-four hours. Including you."

"I know. I tried to explain—"

"It's a good thing, Roscoe," he said. "It's keeping our PR team busy, that's for sure."

"It's hardly—"

"Anyway, we can discuss it later. I'm coming to the photoshoot. I have some news for the boys."

I contained my temper enough not to sigh. "Okay, see you there. We're on our way now."

I ended the call and took a deep breath as quietly as I could.

"So glad he let you finish one sentence," Maddox said, not looking up from his phone.

"He's coming to the photoshoot."

Maddox looked up then. "What for? If he reprimands you about the herding-cats thing, I'm gonna be pissed."

I scrubbed my hand over my face and decided it was just best to read my emails and messages.

After a few minutes silence between us, he tapped his boot to mine. "Hey," he said, waiting for me to look up before he continued. "I'm sorry about the interview. Next time I'll deflect the question."

"There won't be a next time," I replied. "I'll be staying in the green room from now on." *Where I should have stayed today.*

He chewed on the inside of his lip for a bit, then grimaced. He showed me his phone again, and this time it was a photo of us walking into the TV studio. I had my hand on his back, and he was smiling. "We have a couple name."

I rolled my eyes and sighed. For the love of fucking God. "Don't tell me what it is. I don't—"

"It's Moscoe."

I groaned and banged my head against the headrest a few times. After I sighed, again, I tried to stay composed. "Thank you for not telling me."

He grinned. "You're welcome."

CHAPTER SEVEN

THE PHOTOSHOOT for *Rolling Stone* was in an old, abandoned stage theater. The parking lot was fenced off with mesh-covered chain link, so our convoy was hidden from the street.

The venue itself was an amazing nod to Art Deco architecture and must have been magnificent in its prime. Now it was peeling paint, warped drywall, and sprung upholstery. Time and neglect hadn't been kind to the old-fashioned plaster molds and tin-pressed ceilings, wallpapers and drapery. It was creepy and eerie and would make an amazing horror movie set, but today it made a stunning location shoot.

There was more make-up, more hair stylists, and outfits and jewelry worth more than I made in a year. Amber, Ryan, and I kept everything in order, and Maddox handed everything off to me like he usually did. There was an interview to go with the photos, but the whole thing was really well done and a lot of fun.

"Last photo," the director called. He asked the five band members to show the tattoos on their right wrist. They each had a triangle inked there, each one a different section of the pentagon shape that together made up the Atrous logo. They gripped the forearm of the guy next to them, making a pentagon shape, and the photographer lay on the ground and snapped a pic from underneath. You could see the tattoos, but together they made their logo. It was a powerful photo.

He called it a cover-worthy shot.

The interviewer asked, "A pentagon for the five of you, obviously. Does it signify anything else?"

"No," Maddox answered. "A five-sided shape of equal parts. That's what we are. If one of us was gone, we could never be whole." He shrugged, somewhat nervously. "Like the saying goes, the whole is greater than the sum of its parts. On our own, we're just five ordinary guys. Together we conquered the world."

"None of you would ever consider a solo career?" he asked. "When and if the time ever comes?"

Maddox's expression was cool, if not a little offended. "God, no. Who the hell would I be without these guys? When I'm not with them, I feel like I've lost my phone or my keys. Five fingers, five senses, I dunno. Pick your analogy."

"I could totally go out on my own," Wes said, grinning.

Jeremy shoved him. "Fuck off. You can't even decide pizza toppings on your own."

They dissolved into laughter and more pushing and shoving, and I had to try to get the $20,000 diamond earrings off Maddox before they ended up falling down a crack in the floorboards.

I hadn't noticed Ambrose arrive—I'd actually forgotten he was coming—until he called out from the top of the auditorium. "Still herding cats, Roscoe?" he yelled out.

That brought about more laughter, and Ambrose made his way down the steps to the stage. He held up three fingers. "What does this symbolize?"

"Wes's IQ," Blake replied.

"How high Blake can count," Wes snapped back.

Ambrose's smile became a grin. "Three. Three symbolizes . . . Triple. Platinum. Boys, the album's just gone triple platinum!"

Holy shit.

There was a moment of stunned silence, then cheers and hell-yeahs, hugs and clapping.

"And I've booked a celebratory lunch at the Polo Lounge!" Ambrose said. "Let's go!"

Steve barely had time to blink before he was organizing his security team for a full public outing without warning. We packed everything up, checked that all the outfits and jewelry were accounted for and signed off on. We thanked the *Rolling Stone*'s crew, and after Amber, Ryan, and I made sure we had all our things, we filed back into the vans and were off again.

I only noticed the documentary film crew when they were leaving at the same time as us. They were either now avoiding me, or I no longer noticed them.

Maddox grinned at me from his seat in the van. "Triple platinum," he whispered. "Wow."

"You should be proud. You've all worked really hard. You deserve it." I opened the front pocket of my backpack and took out a velvet pouch. I slid Maddox's earrings into my palm and handed them to him, one by one.

He had four in each ear, and he preferred longer, dangling earrings that magazines had dubbed as pretty-punk. They were a hoop with attachments, some were chain, some were crosses, feathers, different lengths, different widths. All his jewelry was black, of course, to go with the all-black clothes he wore daily. But it suited him, matching his dark eyes and hair and his sleeve of black tattoos.

"Ugh," he said, fiddling with the last earring. "I can't get this one." He slid over, right up close to me. "Can you do it for me?"

He was too close, his face, his neck, the pale skin that disappeared under the collar of his shirt . . .

"Maybe if you did the ones at the back first," I suggested as I leaned in even closer, trying to see the back of the earring to clasp it. God, he smelled so good.

"But then I wouldn't need you to do it for me," he murmured, all rough and breathy. "And I'd have to come up with another excuse to get you this close."

I managed to clasp the earring and I pulled back, which was a mistake . . . because his face was right there.

His eyes went from mine to my mouth, and his lips parted.

Christ, he was going to kiss me.

My heart stopped.

Our faces were so close I could see his eyelashes and the galaxies in his eyes. But he smiled and leaned back and patted my thigh. "Roscoe, Roscoe, Roscoe," he murmured. "What am I going to do with you?"

"You're going to do nothing with me," I whispered in a rush. I glanced over to the front where I could see the back of Steve's head. He was busy on his phone and hadn't seemed to have heard us.

Maddox chuckled. "I don't know about that," he said, like he couldn't care who heard us. "You keep looking at me like that, and we'll be doing something."

Heat bloomed low in my belly, but I cleared my throat

and removed his hand from my leg. "You're playing a dangerous game," I breathed.

His smile was pouty, his lips pink and plump. He leaned in again, those dark eyes pinning me to the spot. "Am I? Because, while this is a lot of fun, I'm not quite sure I'm playing, Roscoe."

"ETA, thirty seconds," Steve called out.

Christ. That was the shortest drive ever.

Maddox sighed but he didn't move back to his seat. When the van slowed, I scooted forward, collected the backpack, and put it on. Maddox squeezed my bicep. "God, man. How much do you lift?"

I shot him a look over my shoulder.

He raised an eyebrow. "Think you could lift me? Wanna find out in my room tonight?"

Before I could answer, the van door slid open and it was game on. Getting into the Beverly Hills Hotel and the restaurant was without issue, and the meal itself was amazing. I sat with Amber and Ryan, both thankful and disappointed to put distance between Maddox and me. But all too soon it was time to go and there was quite a crowd gathered outside when we were leaving.

The usual screaming, cameras, photographers, all yelling for a split second of attention. Maddox kept his head down and I followed him into the van and pulled the door closed. "We're going straight to the stadium," I explained. "You can rest there."

Maddox groaned and slumped in his seat. He pulled his cap down low and closed his eyes, and honestly, it gave me time to get through some work messages and emails without worrying about Maddox being all hot and flirty.

Which wasn't exactly horrible. I just wasn't sure how much longer I could say no.

It was a decent drive to the stadium at Pasadena, and given Maddox still had his eyes closed, I risked a scroll through social media. Twitter, Instagram, TikTok . . . There was footage of me saying the herding-cats thing, which was now both memes and gifs, and there were already photos of us leaving the hotel at lunch. A lot of photos of the boys, mostly Maddox, but a lot of me too. Always by Maddox's side, or with my hand on his back, or following him into the van.

Roscoe herding cats again.

Moscoe pic alert!

Roscoe herds his favorite kitty!

For fuck's sake. Who the hell wrote those headlines?

I was used to being in the background, no problem. But being the focus made me feel uneasy. Especially any kind of romantic connotation or *ship* as it was called.

This wasn't about me.

But it did shine another spotlight on Maddox, and that put more pressure on everyone.

After the triple platinum announcement, the boys had forgotten about the whole herding-cats comment. They were stretching, practicing choreography, being fitted for something, having sound gear checked, eating, but very little resting. Amber, Ryan, and I were chasing one thing or another up until stage time.

Every song was perfection, every move was smooth. The whole production was state of the art, their vocals were flawless. They were charming, funny, sexy, and very talented.

The crowd roared like thunder, singing along to every word, screaming, chanting. The whole stadium pulsed with every beat.

When the show was over and they came off stage for the

last time, they were drenched in sweat. Their shirts clung to their torsos, their hair was stuck to their foreheads, and they were panting, breathless.

Grinning.

I helped Maddox and Luke out of their shirts and took their earpieces for the waiting sound guys, and I pretended not to notice when Maddox came back wearing only a pair of running shorts.

I didn't notice his lean body, muscular like a boxer and fit as hell, which wasn't fair because he worked out the least. His sleeve of tattoos ended at his shoulder, a mix of images —a dragon, a spray of stars, cherry blossoms—a work of art down to his wrist.

He put Michelangelo to shame.

He pulled on a black T-shirt and smiled at me, as though he knew damn well I'd been watching him. "We ready to go? I'm starving."

I gave a nod, wondering what flirty, sexual innuendos he was going to torture me with on the way back to the hotel.

"Hey, can I come with you?" Jeremy asked him. "Wes isn't ready. Julio, the PT, is torturing his shoulder for another ten minutes apparently."

Maddox froze for a second, then glanced at me. "Uh, yeah. That's all right, isn't it?"

So, no flirting with me then.

"Yeah, of course," I said. I held my hand out to Jeremy. "Pass me your bag." Then I called out to Ryan. "I've got Maddox and Jeremy. We're leaving now."

Steve motioned to Robbie, another security guy, to join us. "You're with us."

It was going to be a crowded van.

Robbie took the front seat, Maddox and Jeremy climbed

through to the backseat, and Steve and I took the seats near the door. I'd gotten so used to it just being me and Maddox over the years that it felt terribly crowded.

I missed the time to decompress. The silence, the comfortable ease of it just being him and me.

I missed him sitting next to me.

And I missed him being flirty and the playful daring in his eyes.

While Maddox and Jeremy talked about their performances, I took out my phone to see the response of tonight's concert, but there were still photos and bullshit articles on me. "Oh, for fuck's sake," I grumbled.

Steve grunted his agreement and he glanced at my phone. "Hm."

"You agree with me, right?" I asked him quietly. "This is not a good thing."

Steve rarely said much, but his words were usually well thought out. "I think it has the potential to become a problem."

"That's what I said. Ambrose and PR said it was fun, at the moment, and was good for publicity. Anything that keeps Atrous trending."

Steve scowled but kept his gaze ahead. "We may have to look at splitting your unit."

Splitting me and Maddox? That hit me out of nowhere. "Oh."

"It might be more efficient if you paired with one of the others instead."

"What are you guys talking about?" Maddox asked from behind us.

"Uh, nothing," I replied, giving him a smile.

Maddox looked outright surprised, then indignant, and it took me a second to realize what his expression meant.

Maddox knew I was lying.

"It's nothing." I turned back to my phone and decided to check emails instead. Maddox grunted, but Jeremy began a recount of the second set.

"Hm," Steve murmured after a while.

"Hm, what?" I asked.

"I won't suggest a change unless it's necessary. I know you two have a thing."

"A thing? What the hell does that mean?"

Steve still looked straight ahead. I think he shrugged, but he was so stoic it was hard to tell. "I won't suggest a change in units unless I think it's necessary." He looked at me then, serious. "And if I think it's necessary, I need you to agree with me."

Because if he thought it was necessary, it meant the security threat level had changed. That meant Maddox or the others could be in danger. "Yeah, of course."

"Because he will fight it," Steve murmured, staring straight ahead again.

"Who will fight it?" I whispered.

Steve gave the slightest nod, signaling toward Maddox. "He won't go with anyone but you."

Jeremy was still talking about one of their dance routines in the second set, so I was confident Maddox couldn't hear me. "He trusts me."

"Hm," Steve grunted again.

What did that mean?

"Anyway," I said, deciding to change the topic. "I'll be laying low at public meets for a while. Staying in the green rooms, that kind of thing. That way I can't be blindsided by nosey interviewers like with the herding-cats comment."

Steve nodded and that was the end of our conversation. I liked Steve. He ran a tight team, and he took no shit from anyone. I'd also seen his martial arts training, so I knew he was more than just talk. He was a good guy, exceptional at his job, and nothing got past him.

But did he think Maddox and I were a thing?

Had he worked with Maddox and me all this time, seen us talking, seen us interact with each other, and assumed we were . . . together? He said he knew Maddox and I "have a thing."

I didn't want to think about that. Or about the fact that maybe more people on the payroll thought the same thing. And I would absolutely not think about the fact that Maddox and I behaved like a couple.

The more I thought about it, the more I needed to know. I nudged Steve with my elbow. "What did you mean when you said we have a thing?"

He shot me a disbelieving look. "It's my job to follow behavioral patterns. And because I have eyes."

"Hey, boss," Robbie called out. "One block out."

"Thanks," Steve replied and undid his belt. He sat forward on his seat and told us the order of how we would get out of the van. As the van came to a stop, he met my gaze with a smile. "Watch."

Robbie opened the door for us. Steve jumped out, Maddox, then Jeremy, then me with their bags and my backpack. Steve had ushered them both from the van to the basement foyer where the elevator was, and Robbie would stay and wait for the others.

By the time I got inside, Jeremy had the elevator doors open and had stepped in. Steve stood, holding the doors open, but Maddox waited for me. Once I was just a few steps away and he was certain I'd be joining them, he got into the elevator. I followed, ignoring Steve's small smile as the doors closed us all in.

Did Maddox always wait for me?

The whole thing had been just a few seconds, and Maddox was really only just a few feet in front of me anyway . . .

But he had waited.

"I'm starving," Jeremy said, his head leaning back against the mirror behind him.

"Dinner's been delivered and should already be in the common room," I said.

"The second van is just a few minutes behind us," Steve added. "I think Wes and Ryan will be another ten or fifteen."

Maddox was staring at me from under his cap, as if he was trying to solve a puzzle, and I pretended not to know he was staring at me. Steve's smirk in the mirror was a little too told-you-so, and I also pretended it wasn't aimed at me.

When we got to our floor, Steve stepped out first. Seeing it was clear, he signaled to Jeremy and Maddox. I followed them out but stopped. "See you guys in there," I said. Maddox stopped, so I handed him his and Jeremy's bags. "Just be a sec."

Jeremy dragged Maddox with him because he was *starrrrrving* and Steve went with them. I went to my room, for no other reason than just to have two minutes peace and quiet without staring eyes or smug smiles.

I threw my backpack on the bed and splashed some cold water on my face in the bathroom. I just needed a few minutes for some deep breaths and head-clearing, that was all. I didn't want to look in the mirror right about then. I wasn't sure I'd like what I saw. So I sat on my bed, then lay back to stare at the ceiling for ten minutes.

I didn't think about how Maddox had me fix his earring,

how he looked at me, how he flirted, how he smelled up close . . .

"Get a fucking grip," I mumbled as I strode back out of my room.

This was an utter mind fuck I didn't need right now. We were on tour. Second concert done, twenty-one to go. There was no room for this mess.

The others were back when I walked in and I made a beeline for Ryan and Amber, parked my ass on the couch, and stuffed my face with takeout. They joked about me taking two of the boys in my van more often, and I joked right back saying I was happy to. I deliberately didn't look over toward where the boys were sitting. I could hear them talk and laugh and joke around, though I didn't hear Maddox much.

I very deliberately didn't look.

After we'd gone through our schedules for tomorrow, the boys had gone back to their rooms and we cleaned everything up, I headed to my room.

I was grateful that Maddox had gone to his room, and I was glad we didn't speak or make eye contact. It didn't particularly sit well with me, but maybe some distance would do us good. Two people had said that Maddox looked for me, or searched for me, in the last few days. First Amber and then Steve. And that had to mean others noticed it as well.

This had disaster written all over it.

A knock at my door startled me.

Shit. This can't be good.

I looked through the peephole and . . . a certain disaster stood there, all in black, cap pulled down low. He shuffled from foot to foot, keeping his head down, trying to look inconspicuous.

Christ.

My heart thumped, my stomach twisted. This wasn't good at all. Should I ignore him? Pretend I'm not here?

He raised his hand to knock again, and without thinking, I opened the door.

His gaze shot up, and he gritted his teeth. His nostrils flared. He was angry. He didn't wait for an invitation. He didn't say anything at all. He brushed past me, his body against mine, and walked into my room.

I closed the door and turned to face him, my adrenaline racing. Yep, he was pissed off. He was uneasy, like he didn't know what to do with his hands, and he was breathing hard. "What the hell's going on?"

"What?" I asked. "About what?"

"Don't play dumb, Roscoe. You know what. You and Steve being all chummy and whispering in the car."

"That was about something else."

He grimaced and gasped back a breath. "I heard my name. And I asked you what it was about, and you fucking lied to me."

I knew he saw through me. "Maddox . . ."

He pointed his finger toward the door. "I don't give a fuck what anyone else says or does or any of the bullshit they spin to me. I don't care. But you." He pointed at me and spoke through gritted teeth. "You don't lie to me."

I wasn't sure what to say to that, but he wasn't done.

"You lied to me, then you ignored me the rest of the night, and I won't fucking have it."

"I didn't ignore you," I said, lying again. It was pitiful and meek, and he saw through me again.

He shook his head. "Tell me what's going on."

"Nothing's going on."

"Bullshit."

"Maddox, it's not about you."

He stepped closer, really pissed off now. There was such betrayal in his eyes, but then he took a step back, and whatever he was about to say was gone. He shook his head. His breaths were short and shallow. "I thought I had you. In my corner. I thought we—" He stopped. "You know what? Fuck you. I don't need you. You wanna lie to me, then go right ahead. It doesn't matter." He waved his hand like he was done with me, made a move for the door.

"Maddox," I tried again. "Please don't."

He spun to face me. "Please don't what?"

"Keep your voice down," I whisper-hissed. "For fuck's sake."

"Please don't what?" he asked again. "And I don't give a fuck who hears me, Roscoe. Please don't what? Leave you? Lie to you?"

"Neither. Both." I didn't know what I was saying. "I don't know, Christ. What Steve and I were talking about was about me. Not you."

Okay, so that was not a direct lie. More like a half-truth.

"You really are a terrible liar," he said, his voice quiet now. "You told me you'd never keep anything from me. And now you can't even look at me."

If I look at you, I'll cross this floor, pull you into my arms, and kiss you . . .

I had to steel myself to meet his gaze. "Maddox, I am in your corner. I *am* on your side."

He stood there for a long second, searching my face, for what, I had no clue. He took a deep, shaky breath, then without another word, he turned on his heel and walked out. The door closed with a quiet snick and the sound took my breath away.

I wanted to follow him, but for what purpose? So I could lie to him some more?

I wasn't sure I could stomach that.

After about five minutes of just standing there, I took out my phone and sent him a text. *I am in your corner. We'll talk in the morning.*

He didn't reply. I didn't expect him to. The mood he was in, he'd be more inclined to knock on my door and throw his phone at me.

He didn't do that either.

So I had a steaming hot shower, climbed into bed, and stared at the ceiling for hours.

I THUMPED MY ALARM, cursing 5:30 am for the hell it was. After not near enough sleep, I sat up on the edge of my bed and checked to see if Maddox had replied.

He hadn't.

So I hit the hotel gym and tried jogging on the treadmill to see if that made me feel better. It didn't. Sprinting didn't either. Punching the shit out of the punching bag helped, but that hollow, heavy feeling in my chest didn't let up.

Steve and a few of the other security guys were in the gym too, but they kept their distance, and for that I was glad. I wasn't in the mood for any bullshit about how Maddox never took his eyes off me today.

There was no concert today, but our schedule was still full. Photoshoots, interviews, promotional shit all day long. But the boys got to sleep in . . . until eight thirty anyway. So after I'd showered, I met Amber and Ryan in the hotel restaurant for breakfast.

"Morning," I said, taking a seat at the table.

"You look like shit," Ryan said.

"Thank you. That's the look I was going for." I sipped my coffee. It was awful. "Ugh."

Amber stared at me. "You haven't seen it, have you." It wasn't a question.

"Seen what? I went to the gym, showered, came here." My stomach sank. "What did I miss?"

"What Maddox was doing at three o'clock this morning."

I almost choked on my coffee. "What he was doing? Where the fuck was he? He was supposed to be in his room. He was going back to his room." I had my phone out, trying to scroll through social media, looking for anything.

"He was in his room," Ryan answered.

I found it then. A hashtag of #whohurtMaddox was trending. He'd posted a video. I clicked on it, my heart in my throat.

The screen was very dark, he was clearly in his hotel room, on his bed. Leaning against the headboard, playing his new guitar. He wore his long sleep pants and a black T-shirt. His hair was kinda messy. He'd taken his earrings out, and his face was free of make-up.

This was going to hurt. I knew it.

I'd never heard the melody before. His voice was stripped down, soulful and raw.

Please don't ask me to choose between
Your lies or your leaving,
How can I decide
When my heart is breaking.
You're not on my side
my corner is bare,
So maybe I should go

No one would care.
I don't know how to leave you
Maybe you could stay, stay,
and lie to me a little longer.
Baby, a little longer.
Just one more day.
Tell me please,
How can I be enough to make you stay?

He posted it at 3:00 am.
You're not on my side. My corner is bare.
Was it about me? I was pretty sure it was.
Fuck.

The video he posted had almost two million likes, and the comments were . . . not surprising.

Maddox we love you. You're more than enough Maddox. Who hurt you, baby? Who broke your heart? You deserve better. Blah blah blah.

But there were some more concerning comments as well.

#WhohurtMaddox had been trending for a while, apparently. Usually followed by the ever so charming #Tellmewhohurtyou #Ijustwanttotalk and #Iwillkillwhoeverhurtyou.

"For fuck's sake," I whispered, shutting my phone off and leaving it screen down on the table. "I'll go talk to him."

I went to stand up, but Amber grabbed my arm. "Leave him for a bit. Considering he's had maybe two or three hours' sleep."

"I'm going to have to speak to Steve," I said. "There were some pretty aggressive comments."

"Probably a good idea." Ryan nodded. "Shall we try and guess what it's all about?"

"He's been having trouble sleeping," I admitted. "He didn't want anyone to worry."

Amber's expression was neutral, which usually meant something bad was coming. "What do you mean he was going back to his room?" she asked coolly. "Before, you said he was going back to his room."

Shit.

"He came to see me last night. After dinner. He stayed for maybe five or ten minutes, then went back to his room."

"What did he want?"

"To talk." Christ. I couldn't lie to them. "He was of the impression I was keeping something from him." I sighed. "In the van back to the hotel last night, Steve and I were talking about the possibility of changing some security measures, given that I seem to be popular right now, with that stupid interview and getting myself on camera. Having Maddox and I together seemed like a bigger target. Anyway, Steve wondered if it would be better if we split our unit and maybe one of you two took Maddox instead. Steve said Maddox won't go with anyone but me, so we'd need to keep it quiet until it happens—if it happens—and Maddox heard part of the conversation and questioned me, but I told him it was nothing. He can tell when I'm lying, apparently. He left my room upset. Or pissed off. Both. I don't know. I didn't go after him."

They both stared at me.

"Then I guess we're lucky he went back to his room," Ryan said. "And that he didn't leave the hotel."

I scrubbed a hand over my face. "Hotel security has to tell me if he does."

"If they see him leave." Ryan made a good point.

Amber pursed her lips together and tapped the table with her finger, thinking. "The song he sang in the video—"

"It's new. I haven't heard it before."

"He says something about lying," she continued. My eyes met hers and I knew what she was about to say. "It's about you, isn't it?"

I sighed, feeling a little sick to my stomach. "I think so. The line about not being on his side and in his corner . . . That's aimed at me. Well," I corrected, "I can't say for certain, but he accused me of that last night."

"Not being on his side?" Ryan clarified.

I nodded. "Because I lied to him. He said I was supposed to be in his corner." I pushed my still-full coffee away and stood up. "I need to go speak to him before Ambrose turns up."

They didn't object this time, either too stunned or they thought it was a good idea. Which I highly doubted. "Go easy on him," Amber murmured.

"Breakfast for them in one hour," Ryan said, checking his watch. "We leave in two."

I nodded and made my way up to our floor, a heavy lump of dread in my belly feeling greasier with every step.

I knocked on his door, not expecting an immediate response, given he'd only had about three hours' sleep. I knocked twice more, then sent him a text. *Open the door.* I waited another minute, then knocked again and yelled, "Maddox, don't make me get a hotel manager to open this goddamn door."

I heard him grumble before the door pulled inward.

He was still mostly asleep, his hair a mess, his sleep pants and T-shirt were crumpled, his eyes squinted and barely open. He snarled at me. "What?"

I did to him what he did to me last night. I brushed past him, our shoulders clipping, and I let myself into his room.

It was dark, the shades drawn, the bed rumpled.

"No, please come in," he mumbled, voice croaking. "Do whatever the fuck you want." He walked back to the bed, got in, and pulled the covers over his head.

I sighed. "Well, congratulations," I said, knowing he'd hear. "You broke Twitter again. Your little song was a hit."

No reaction, no reply.

"I'll be going to see Steve after I leave here. Given that a good few thousand of the comments on your post are threatening bodily harm to whoever it was who hurt you. So thanks for that. We really needed the security upgrade."

Still no reply.

"It's not just you in this band," I added, which was a low blow but not completely uncalled for. "You say you hate that the media and the fans make it all about you; then you go and do something like that. You just made it harder for everyone."

There was a long beat of silence. "Are you done?" his voice was muffled from under the covers.

"Not even fucking close. Christ, Maddox, Ambrose is gonna pitch a fit when he sees this."

He sat up on the bed and pulled the covers to his chest. He looked miserable. "I'm sorry."

I sighed, the anger in me dissipating when I saw the sadness that now clung to him. *Fucking hell.* I went to his side of the bed and sat down heavily.

"Are the others mad at me?" he whispered.

"I haven't seen them yet. Amber and Ryan are . . . concerned."

"About?"

"About you, Maddox. Every single person on this team cares about you."

He flinched and chewed on his bottom lip. "I'm sorry," he whispered again. "I was angry. And sad, I guess."

"I'm sorry too. About last night. I wasn't lying to you . . . I was trying to protect you."

"Protect me from what?"

I had to make myself answer. I wanted to say "nothing" and just leave, but I needed to be upfront. "Steve said it might be safer for everyone if you and I weren't a unit."

Maddox's eyes shot to mine. "What?"

"He said it might be best, but he doubted you'd agree with it. He, uh . . ." God, here goes. "He actually said he thinks we have a thing . . . together."

He stared. "A thing?"

"Yeah, like a *thing*. A romantic thing."

Maddox's eyes widened. "He said that?"

I nodded and swallowed hard. "He's actually not the first person to say that to me in the last few days."

He was quiet for a long moment. "Oh."

I shrugged. "Apparently we act couple-y. Like the internet needs any fuel for that fire. Anyway, Steve said if he did ever say our unit needed to split, he'd need me to agree with him because you wouldn't." I let out an unsteady breath. "You wanted to know this, so I'm telling you."

"But you think we should . . . not be together."

Christ, the way he said that.

"If it comes down to your safety, then yes. Whatever it takes, Maddox."

"I don't want that."

"I don't want that either."

He threw back the covers, got off the bed, and began to pace. "Roscoe . . ." He shook his head, and he was breathing like he'd just run around the block.

I stood up and grabbed his hand. "Hey."

He shook his head. "I don't want that."

As much as I didn't want that either, his reaction was a little more . . . concerning.

"I don't think you understand," he whispered.

"I don't think I do either." His breathing was a little shallow. Panicky almost. He'd probably still be pacing if I didn't have a hold of his hand. "Maddox, hey."

His eyes were wide, vulnerable. "Do you know what it's like to realize you're truly alone?"

I shook my head. He needed to speak so I let him.

"I have no one. I'm surrounded by hundreds of people and the world watches my every move, but I feel like I'm invisible. Everyone watches me but no one sees me. I have no one, Roscoe. No one who understands. No one who gets it. I thought I had you, but it was made very clear to me last night that's simply not true."

"You do have me."

"You lied to me."

"And you told me yesterday you lied to me every day, so how is this any different?"

"Because it is!" he cried. "Because it's you. And because you're all I've got."

His words hit me like a truck.

"What?"

"You looked me right in the eye and lied. And what do we have if we don't have the truth, Roscoe. That's all I ever asked from you. That was all I ever needed. And you looked me right in the goddamn eye, and you lied to me."

"I didn't mean to hurt you." He tried to pull his hand free but I kept a hold of him. I hated seeing him hurt like this. "You're not alone. I'm sorry if you feel you are, but I'm here. You have me. I do *see* you."

He shook his head. "I thought . . . I thought . . ."

"You thought what?" I whispered. I hadn't realized just how close we were, that I still had his hand in mine.

He squinted his eyes shut and put his head down, his chest rose and fell with his breaths, but no words came.

I put my other hand around his neck and pulled him against me, wrapping him up in a hug. He was tense at first and I wondered if I'd done the wrong thing, but then he sighed and melted against me. And he sighed again . . . until I realized he wasn't sighing at all.

It was as though he was breathing deep for the first time in forever. Like only now could he catch his breath.

I rubbed his back and he clung to me. "You okay?"

He nodded against my chest, but he didn't speak and he didn't try to move away. If anything, he held me a little tighter. But it wasn't just his tension and stress melting away. It was mine too.

I tried to remember the last time I'd hugged someone. Or been hugged in return. It had been . . . far too long.

"Can I ask you something?" I murmured.

He nodded, still clinging to me. He felt so good against me. After all these years of wanting this, more than anything, I was about to ask him something that would no doubt make him pull away.

"The song you sang in the middle of the night . . ."

I thought he might pull back or try to, at least. But no. He stayed right there, his forehead in the crook of my neck, his arms around my back. If anything, he held me tighter. "It was about you."

I was sure he could hear, or feel, my hammering heart. "Thought so."

"Please don't lie to me," he whispered. "I can't take it."

"Okay."

"Please don't leave me."

I squeezed him. "Okay."

I didn't know what this was or what was happening between us. But he needed me, and for some fucked-up reason, I liked that he did.

"Maddox," I said, pulling back so I could see his face. "If our security team says we need to change things up, then we will need to do that."

He tried to back up, so I cupped his face and held him right there. His eyes were wide, so dark and so beautiful. "I'm not going anywhere," I said firmly. "If you have to work with Ryan or Amber for a little while, that's okay. I'm still here. I'm not leaving you. Okay?"

He nodded. "'Kay."

"You're not alone," I whispered, glancing down at his mouth. "I see you, Maddox. I see you."

He leaned a little closer, sliding his tongue across his bottom lip like he was about to kiss me. And I thought, *fuck it*. He wanted me to kiss him. I wanted to kiss him. I wanted to fix this, I wanted to fix him, even if it broke me.

I tilted his face up, just a fraction. "Tell me to stop," I breathed.

His gaze dropped to my mouth, then drew back up to my eyes. "No."

So I ghosted my lips over his, the barest of touches. Lingering, longing, but not quite touching. Then I did it again, feather-light and his eyes rolled back, his eyelids fluttered closed.

And I pressed my lips to his a little harder, enough for him to gasp, and I pulled his bottom lip in between mine, just about to tilt his face and open his mouth to taste his tongue—

When there was a knock on the door.

We broke apart, both of us dazed.

"Hey, dickbag, open up."

Jeremy.

Fuck.

"Fuck."

"Maddox."

"Yeah, all right. Keep your pants on," Maddox replied and went to the door.

Trying to act casual, I leaned against the table just as he opened the door and Jeremy came in. He stopped when he saw me. "Oh."

"Yeah, I was just leaving," I said. "I've said everything I needed to say. Maddox, you need to be showered and ready for breakfast in twenty minutes. We leave at ten thirty."

I ignored the curious look Jeremy gave me and saw Maddox give a nod before I let myself out. I went as fast as I could into my room and had to lean against the back of the door. My heart was about to gallop out of my chest, my stomach was a giant knot, and my blood felt like I'd taken a 240-volt hit.

I'd kissed Maddox.

I kissed him.

And it was hot as hell.

I held his face. I held his body to mine. I felt him pressed to me. I felt his lips. Soft. So soft. His warmth.

I wasn't sorry.

He'd opened up to me about feeling alone, about feeling hurt by me, that the song he'd sung was about me. He'd shown me a piece of his heart, so I'd shown him mine in return.

Kissing him was the right thing to do.

Gathering my resolve, I found Amber and Ryan in the common room. Breakfast was being set up for the boys, so I grabbed a coffee and joined Amber and Ryan on the sofas. "How'd it go?" Amber asked.

"Yeah, good." I sipped my coffee. It was terrible, but I pretended it wasn't because it gave me something to focus on. "I left him with Jeremy and told him to be here for breakfast."

"Ambrose was in here looking for you," Ryan said.

I sighed. It was to be expected. "Where is he?"

"Said he'd be back in five."

"Was he pissed?"

They both stared at me like *what do you think.*

Great.

I took out my phone and spent ten minutes scrolling through entertainment sites, social media, and even news sites for any update on the damage. Not that there was much point. Ambrose's PR team would have been all over it for hours. I'm sure I was about to get told how bad it was.

Wes, Blake, and Luke came in and sat at the breakfast table, right on time. The last thing Maddox needed was to be late. He better get here before Ambrose.

And like he'd heard me, a few seconds later Maddox and Jeremy walked in. Maddox was freshly showered, his hair still wet. Black shirt, black jeans, black boots.

Sexy as hell.

He and Jeremy were smiling, which was a good sign. Maddox went straight over to the others but he didn't sit down. He stood, and shoving his hands in his pockets, he cleared his throat. "Uh, I just want to apologize," he said, awkward and genuine. "For posting shit online in the middle of the night. I didn't think, sorry. And I was duti-fully reminded"—he shot me a look—"that what I do affects everyone, and that we're a team and I didn't act like it."

Jeremy smiled at me, and Luke too.

"Anyway," Maddox said. "It was a dick thing to do, and I'm sorry. If there are ramifications or interview questions or whatever, I'll take those."

Wes stood up and hugged him, so Luke and Blake did too, and the five of them sat down to breakfast, smiling and laughing.

"Christ," Amber whispered, stunned. "Just what did you say to him?"

I smiled and sipped my coffee. "Apparently I told him exactly what he needed to hear."

AMBROSE RAN THROUGH ALL his notes and the itinerary, congratulated the boys on their hard work, thanked all the teams for their tireless efforts, then after wrapping it all up, he motioned to the door. "Maddox and Roscoe, a minute, please."

Fuck.

It wasn't *un*expected but it certainly wasn't going to be fun.

Maddox smiled at me but he rolled his eyes as though he'd been called out by the teacher. We followed Ambrose out to a quiet room, and although I stood with Maddox, I knew Ambrose expected me on his side.

"Maddox," he began cautiously. "Working on some new music this morning, I see."

It was a lighter way to broach the subject.

"Ah, yeah. If you're about to read me the riot act, Roscoe beat you to it already."

Ambrose's gaze went to me, then back to Maddox. "It wasn't ideal. The fan reaction has been . . . intense. To say the least." Then Ambrose looked at me. "Our guys are on that though, weeding out the threatening ones, that kind of thing."

"Sorry. I've already apologized to the guys. It wasn't my intention to upset people." He shrugged. "Should I pull it down?"

Ambrose shook his head. "That would only create more hype, and it's too late now." He went on for a bit on public image and not giving any more information than was necessary. Privacy was incredibly important—something he didn't need to remind Maddox of—and Atrous and Platinum Entertainment couldn't, and wouldn't, risk any reason for unsavory headlines. He chatted briefly about security, keeping the status quo for now, pending any new developments.

"But about the song," he went on. "There's been a lot of interest. In particular, Mr. Kim himself wanted to know if you'd be interested in talks, not now but perhaps after the tour, about some options for perhaps a single release."

"No," Maddox replied. He didn't flinch, he didn't blink. "No. No single anything. I've told you this before. I'm not doing anything without them."

"I figured you'd say as much," Ambrose replied.

"So stop asking me."

Ambrose narrowed his eyes but he finished with a smile. "We've got a long way to go. Best behavior, please."

Then he handed me some sheets of paper. "Questions and answers. Make sure everyone's familiar."

I nodded. "Sure."

Ambrose left and his assistants appeared out of nowhere to follow him. Maddox stood there for a long moment, clearly curbing his temper. Then his gaze fell on me, and he chewed on the inside of his lip. "So . . ." He smiled. "Interesting morning."

I barked out a quiet laugh. "Uh, yeah."

We stared at each other. His dark eyes were daring, his lips inviting. I let out a breath. "We, uh, we should go back inside. Before someone comes looking."

Maddox nodded slowly. "Just so I understood . . . He said the status quo remains unchanged. So that means it's just us in the car, right? No one else."

I tried not to smile but ended up laughing. I ignored his smug smile and held up the papers Ambrose had given me. "Work to do." I went back into the common room before I did something stupid like kiss him where anyone could see us.

Maddox went back to the band, and I walked directly over to Amber and Ryan to go through the brief from Ambrose about how best to field any questions or press about Maddox's 3:00 am upload.

Beneath it all, beneath the hype, the likes, the attention, was a man whose every action was scrutinized to the point where we had to be briefed. I hated that for him. I hated that he was subject to that.

Should he have uploaded a song at 3:00 am?

No.

But he was hurting and he needed to share that the only way he knew how. And that was through his music. Now everyone had to be told, prepared, and directed, falsely displaying his heartbreak on an international scale.

It was no wonder he hated his fame.

Not that he ever admitted that out loud, but it was a weight very few knew how to bear. I saw the struggle in him. We all did. The world didn't, though. They just kept pushing and pushing for more of him.

Part of me wondered how much he had left to give.

When it was time, we took our gear and headed down

to the waiting line of vans, and like always, Maddox climbed in before me. And as per usual, he sat on the backseat.

I took the seat nearest to the door, but he cleared his throat. "Uh, Roscoe?"

I looked at him over the back of the seat, ignoring the nerves, the butterflies, the anticipation. "Yes, Maddox?"

He grinned and patted the seat next to him. "We'd have more privacy if you sat here with me, but if you don't care, then I sure as hell don't," he said, getting up.

"No, wait," I said, quickly joining him in the backseat.

He chuckled and there was an awkward moment where neither of us spoke. Our convoy began to move out and Maddox cleared his throat. "So, this morning . . ."

My mouth was suddenly dry. "Yeah, about that . . ."

"What about it?"

"Did you want me to apologize and say it'll never happen again?"

"Hell, no. I mean, do you want it to never happen again?"

I looked at him, at his eyes, at his lips.

He smiled. "Yeah, that's what I thought." But then he looked at my mouth and his lips parted, his eyes seemed to lose focus for a split second, and he blinked back to his senses.

Then it was my turn to laugh. "You okay?"

He shook his head and wiped his hands on his thighs, embarrassed. "What the hell kind of kiss was that anyway?" he whispered. "It was like a not-kiss but possibly one of the best I've ever had."

"The best?" God, I couldn't believe we were having this conversation. "And what do you mean a not-kiss?"

He laughed and his cheeks flushed the most delicate

pink. He touched his lips ever so lightly with his fingertips. "It was . . . almost a kiss. I think we need to remedy the almost part."

I shot a look to the front of the van. If Steve could hear us from there, I had no clue. "Uh, I think that's something that should be kept behind closed doors. Don't you?"

"The van door is closed."

I rolled my eyes and tried to change the subject . . . somewhat. "And I'll have you know, there was no almost-kiss about it. It was absolutely a real kiss, and I'm beginning to wonder if you've ever been kissed properly."

His mouth fell open. "Oh, I sure have been."

"Not by me."

His eyes widened and he let out a breath, smiling. His gaze lingered on my mouth, and he whispered, "I want you to kiss me again."

I glanced to the front seat again, to the back of Steve's head. "I don't think that's a good idea. As much as I would like to." My chest felt far too tight.

He pouted. "But that's not a no, right? It's just a not in the van, or not where anyone could see us, or in front of other people thing, right?"

"Right. I think some ground rules should apply. If we want to . . . do what we did this morning, again."

"We want to, yes? I mean, I do." He put his hand to his chest. "A lot more . . . of what we did this morning. And honestly, I should thank you for kissing me first," he murmured. "I've wanted to do that for a while and just thought it'd never be a possibility."

I barked out a laugh. "You have, have you?"

"Yes, I have. Though I didn't think it was funny . . ."

I slid my hand over his and laced our fingers. "I'm not laughing at you, I promise. Thank you for being honest with me. About the song. About being hurt by me lying to you."

"Ah, yes, the lying thing. Glad you brought that up."

"Ugh, god."

He chuckled and brought our joined hands onto his lap, but his smile soon died and he studied the back of my hand, my fingers. "So, then," he said eventually. He was serious now, and I knew whatever he was about to say was important. "Tonight . . . will you come to my room?"

Christ.

"I, uh, I can, yes."

"I got about two hours sleep last night," he murmured. "I'll sleep better if you're there, that's all." He put his other hand over our already joined hands. "I'll even give you permission to kiss me again. If you want to, that is."

My stomach swooped, and I could barely speak. "I very much would like to."

"But?"

I chuckled. "But there need to be rules."

He sighed. "Can one part of my life not have rules?"

I squeezed his hand. "Some rules can be fun."

"Such as?"

"Well, rule number one could be keeping this"—I held up our joined hands—"a secret so I don't get fired."

He looked to the front of the van, his grip on my hand tightened. "No one's firing you. I've told you that before. A few times, I think. Maybe rule number two could be that you have to listen when I say shit like that."

I barked out a laugh. "Okay, sure. And like I've told you before, that's not your call to make. So maybe you should listen to me."

"Mmm, rule number three," he said. "Roscoe cannot argue with Maddox."

I snorted. "Rule number four. Roscoe will absolutely argue with Maddox."

He smiled. "And Maddox will absolutely argue with Roscoe."

"So we've established that some things won't change. That's good to know."

"I don't want things to change, between us, that is," he whispered. He looked at our hands on his thigh and smiled. "I just want this as well. I want us to be us, how we always have been, only better. Or more, I don't know. It's been so long since someone held my hand or kissed me because they liked me. Like the real me. Not just the name." He froze. "I mean, I'm not presuming you do, I just—"

I leaned over, cupped his cheek, and kissed him. I didn't care that Steve could probably see. I should have cared, but in that moment, I cared more about Maddox.

I pressed my lips to his, soft and sweet, and kissed him once, twice. Not pushing for more, not trying to deepen the kiss, but to let him know I heard him. I put my forehead to his. "I see the real you," I whispered.

He closed his eyes and his smile was so sad it damn near broke my heart.

"ETA, five minutes," Steve called out.

I sat up straight in my seat in time to see Steve turn his head back to the front. If he'd seen us, I couldn't tell. He thought Maddox and I were a thing before, so why should it matter? God, this was so confusing.

When I glanced back to Maddox, he was fixing his earring with an unreadable expression on his face. "Duty calls, huh?"

Ouch.

But I looked him right in the eye. "You know what? Yes, it does. If this"—I signaled between us—"is gonna be a thing, we need to deal with work us and private us. I mean it, Maddox."

He pouted. "Private you is so much more fun."

I glared at him until he rolled his eyes. I pulled my backpack onto my lap and took out the papers Ambrose had given me. "You need to read these. Everyone else has the same copies."

He took them and read the first few lines, then shot me a look. "Are you kidding me?"

"Ambrose," I said, by way of explanation.

"This is bullshit," he said, reading. He quoted the heading out loud. "'Proposed responses to possible questions regarding Maddox's video upload onto a social media outlet.'" His gaze went to mine. "He can't be serious."

I shrugged. "You know how he is. These interviews today are one after the other. Six in total. They're all going to ask, and you're going to be sick of hearing about it after the second interview. It's just to be prepared."

He read through the list, rolled his eyes a lot, and grumbled under his breath even more. He sighed when he was done. "Can you believe he wanted me to release the song as a single? After he berated me like a school kid for not being a team player and thinking of the band, then in the very next breath he wanted me to go solo."

"I think the reprimand was from him, the question about the solo song came from Arlo Kim." I shrugged. "Just my guess."

"Well, that shit pisses me off." He held up the papers. "And so does this."

"It's just PR bullshit," I offered.

The van slowed and I slung the backpack over my shoulder. "You ready?"

"Nope." He shoved the notes at my chest, and while my

hands were disposed, he took a hold of my face and kissed me. He half stood, bearing down on me, and shoved his tongue into my mouth. He kissed me for all he was worth. Demanding, hard, wanting.

He tasted sweet and warm, his tongue teased and claimed me, and I forgot where we were. I wanted so much to pull him onto my lap . . .

The van stopped and Maddox broke the kiss, his wet lips in a smug smile. "Now I'm ready."

The door slid open and he climbed out, and I had to tell myself to get my ass into gear. My mind was swimming, my legs were like Jell-O, and I all but fell out of the van behind him. The smug son of a bitch laughed.

The interviews were being held at the Grammy Museum, which was great for photos and an iconic back-drop for all the interviews.

The first was with *Billboard*, so after a quick stint with make-up and hair, they were soon taking their seats. Between arriving and now, the boys had been busy, we'd been busy, so there was no close interaction between us except for him handing me stuff to look after or me handing him whatever he needed. I found myself staring at Maddox laughing with Jeremy, thinking how those lips, that mouth, his tongue, had been on mine just a short while ago . . . It felt like a dream.

But then the interview started, and as there was no green room, per se, I stood at the back of the studio as far as I could. Where they couldn't involve me in any answers.

"How did Maddox take the prepared questions and answers?" Amber asked quietly.

"Yeah, fine. He rolled his eyes a lot."

After the interviewer had done the basic introductions and general hellos, he began with the most obvious question. "So, before we talk about the album or the tour," he began. "Maddox, I wanted to ask about the song you uploaded on social media this morning. Millions of hits across all forms of social media. That must feel good, right?"

Okay, so it wasn't so bad. There were a few prepared responses he could take from, and he did. The interview moved on, they did a photoshoot, and it all wrapped up nicely.

But the *Access Hollywood* interview that followed asked the same question. And he answered that from the scripted responses as well, just perhaps not as politely. There were more photos and more outfit changes, make-up and hair touch-ups.

Then the interviewer for *All Access LA* asked the same damn question. And then in the next interview, the *Hollywood Entertainer* asked about the song, and after that, then the interview with *LA Daily* did as well, and it was the final interview with *Music Central* that Maddox's patience had run out.

"I have to ask about the song you uploaded, Maddox."

"I bought a new guitar and was just playing around," he said, still being diplomatic and polite.

"But those lyrics were aimed at someone, right?" the interviewer pushed. "'Don't make me choose between your lying and your leaving,'" he quoted. "'How can I decide when it feels like my heart is breaking?'"

This time Maddox smiled. It wasn't his handsome, playful smile. It was his 'oh shit, what's he going to say' smile. "The lyrics speak for themselves," he said calmly. "They mean whatever the listener interprets them as. The beauty of art is that it can be interpreted however a person needs."

"That's very true. But I think I speak for the millions of folks on Twitter when I ask, 'Who hurt you?'"

Maddox's smile was gone. "You think there's a name behind those lyrics? Do you think I would tell you even if there was? Songwriters and artists just sometimes need to express something for no other reason than because they can. There doesn't need to be a story behind it, and it doesn't need to be public. We give enough of ourselves away without our personal lives being pulled apart for public consumption."

Aaaaaaaand there it was.

Maddox Kershaw and his damn mouth.

That damn beautiful mouth that kissed me earlier . . .

"Oh fuck," Ryan breathed beside me.

Maddox wasn't done. "I can appreciate the interest, the hype on social media, but the song was just a song. I uploaded it as a gift to the fans because I thought they'd get a kick out of it. But no one is entitled to make a headline out of someone else's trauma. Be it mine or anyone else's. No one's entitled to more than we freely give."

The interviewer stared for a second but he recovered eventually and the conversation moved on. He didn't ask Maddox anything else directly, and the other four guys carried on like nothing was out of the ordinary, answering questions and having a good time.

The interview wrapped up, and when it was over, ignoring all the interview staff, Maddox made a beeline for me and the other guys followed. They were over it and I didn't blame them. We were mostly packed up, so in no time at all we were making our way through the museum to the exit where our vans would be waiting. "Sorry, guys," Maddox said, talking to his bandmates. "But the 'who hurt me' comment was a red flag and that fucker knew it. There's already been crazy talk and death-threats online, and that shit ain't funny."

Jeremy gave Maddox's shoulder a squeeze. "We know."

"Look on the bright side," Wes said. "We've been doing this for what, six years? And in the last few years, you've said so much controversial shit in interviews that they stopped asking you about being gay."

Maddox paused for a second before he laughed. "That's really fucking true."

"Remember when that was the question everyone asked?" Blake said. "Every damn interview."

Luke snorted. "I really miss seeing the fear in an interviewer's eyes as they got themselves ripped a new asshole on a live broadcast."

Maddox's smile faded and he let out a sigh. "Next time I decide to drop an impromptu song, someone can rip me a new asshole."

"I would," Jeremy said, grinning. "But you'd like it too much."

Maddox shoved Jeremy into the wall, everyone laughed, and it was hard not to smile along with them when they joked around like that. Crude humor aside, when one of them was feeling bad, like Maddox was, they would comfort and joke until they felt better.

It was just how they were.

"Want me to ride with you again?" Jeremy asked Maddox as we were nearing the van.

"Nah, I'm good," he replied. "I'm gonna call Ambrose so none of you guys have to sit through that. It's the least I could do."

"Okay. See ya at the studio."

We climbed into the van and Maddox climbed through

to the back again. I followed him, and the door slid closed behind us.

"Did you really want to speak to Ambrose?" I asked, sitting next to him.

"Hell no." Maddox let his head fall back and he dug the heels of his hands into his eyes. "He's gonna kill me."

"No he won't," I said. "He might *want* to kill you, but he won't actually do it."

Maddox chuckled and dropped his head to my shoulder. "Thanks."

"I think they've come to expect a certain honesty from you. And part of me thinks Ambrose and Mr. Kim like it."

"It just pisses me off that interviewers think they can say whatever the hell they want, like I'm not a person. The band persona is one thing, but we're people too. I'm gonna call them out on that shit. Because if I don't, who will?"

I took his hand and he sighed, rubbing the side of his face on my shoulder. "Thank you."

"What for?" I asked.

"For just . . . being there, I guess."

I squeezed his hand. "Anytime."

He was quiet for a long moment. "I'm tired."

"How about you try sleeping tonight instead of singing songs to me on the internet?"

His laugh was quiet, breathy. "How about you stay in my room and I'll sing them to you in private."

I hummed, though it sounded more like a groan. "Sounds like things might get complicated."

"That wasn't a no."

I rested my cheek on his head. "No, it wasn't."

THE REST of the day passed in a bit of a blur. They had a session at a recording studio for an advertisement with Coca-Cola and then another interview, which was, thankfully, done back at the hotel.

Dinner was late and casual as we sat around the common room. The boys sat at the table; Amber, Ryan, and I sat at the opposite end of the room on the couches. I managed a few bites of food between fielding phone calls and emails and trying to keep an eye on the internet.

Sales were through the roof, charts were topped with no hint of slowing down, and the hype for Atrous was at an all-time high.

"*Music Central*'s interview just posted," Ryan said.

Great.

And within half an hour, Maddox's name was all over the internet, again, and his quotes, of course.

"We give enough of ourselves away without our personal lives being pulled apart for public consumption."

"No one is entitled to make a headline out of someone else's trauma."

"No one's entitled to more than we freely give."

The interview had been edited to make the interviewer appear sympathetic, and how that was spun was anyone's guess. It really was no wonder Maddox didn't trust them.

Maddox's face was plastered over every social media platform and every entertainment outlet around the freaking planet, it would seem.

"Well, on the bright side," Amber deadpanned, "at least your herding-cats comment is long forgotten."

I rubbed my temples. "God, wasn't that a year ago?"

She laughed. "Feels like it."

Maddox came over toward the door. "Roscoe, can we talk?"

"Um, sure," I said, getting to my feet. I gave Amber and Ryan a shrug, pretending that I didn't know what this was about. It was late and Maddox was tired. That was all I needed to know.

Maddox was waiting by the door, scrolling through his phone, and he looked up when I held the door for him. He didn't speak while we walked down the corridor, and without explanation, he stopped at his door, and held it open for me.

His room had been cleaned, his bed made. His guitar lay on the table, his new black coat hung over the back of a chair.

"Everything okay?" I asked.

He shook his head. "No." He threw his phone on the table and stepped in real close. "I keep thinking about how you were going to kiss me properly."

Oh god.

"Is that right?" I asked. I could barely speak.

He smiled victoriously, sultry, and his eyes shone like black fire. "Kiss me, Roscoe. No almost-kiss, no teasing. Kiss me like you fucking mean it."

CHAPTER EIGHT

I TOOK hold of Maddox's face in my hands and crushed my mouth to his. He wanted a proper kiss, so I gave it to him. Open lips, tongues, tasting and teasing. I tilted his head just so and kissed him deeper, harder.

He lifted his hands as if to touch me, maybe wrap around me, but they stopped mid-air and slowly fell to his sides. He melted into me and he let me claim his mouth, giving this perfect moment to me.

Him. Maddox freaking Kershaw was in my arms, his body against me, his mouth open for me. He was so warm, he tasted so sweet, like iced tea and mint gum. He smelled of citrus and desire, and he groaned into my mouth.

His hands found purchase on my back, my shoulders, my ass.

It wasn't enough.

So I walked him backward to the bed and he broke the kiss to smile, surprised. Heavy eyelids, plump and wet lips, messed up hair; he was the sexiest thing I'd ever seen.

I hitched his thigh around my hip and kneeled on the bed, laying him down. He chuckled until I pressed my weight onto his and claimed his mouth again. I swallowed down his moan and he let his legs fall open.

I could feel how hard he was. His erection pressed against mine through our jeans, and the friction drove sparks behind my eyelids. Then he gripped my hair and pulled, and I realized just how close I was to coming.

I pulled back, trying to catch my breath. Trying to find my senses.

"What's wrong?" he whispered, as breathless as me.

"Nothing, I just . . . need to slow down a bit."

He laughed and writhed underneath me, hooking one leg around mine, pulling our hips harder together. He ran a hand over my ass, gripping me and grinding against me, and my eyes rolled back in my head. "You're really fucking hot," he murmured. He writhed again, rolling his hips, needing more. "And I'm really fucking turned on. It feels so good to feel something, Roscoe. I want to feel everything. I want to . . ."

Christ, he was begging, pleading. Desperate, and wanting. And so sexy.

I slipped my hand between us, under the waistband of his jeans, and palmed his cock. He was so hard and so hot in my hand, I barely got my fingers wrapped around him before he arched with his head back, flexed like a bow strung too tight, and he pulsed in my hand.

His mouth fell open in a silent scream, the veins in his neck stood out, his face flush pink as he came.

And I thought he was beautiful before.

He jerked with an aftershock and groaned out a laugh. "Holy shit," he mumbled, his voice hoarse. "That hit me from nowhere."

"That was hot as hell," I whispered with a kiss to his jaw.

I let go of his still-hard dick and he winced, but he had a dreamy, smiley look on his face as he unbuttoned my jeans. "Your turn." I was going to say no, I meant to say no, but any hope of stopping him died when he gripped my shaft. "Fucking hell, Roscoe," he murmured as he pumped me. "You feel like heaven. Look at me."

I didn't realize I had my eyes shut. I met his gaze and he smirked. Maddox squeezed my cock, pumped and squeezed again, sliding and twisting his hold on me. "I want to see the look in your eyes when I make you come."

And that was all it took.

Pleasure detonated low in my belly as I thrust into his fist. I cried out, shuddering with the power of my orgasm, rocking into his hold, and he kissed me as I came back down to earth. Maybe that was why it felt like I was floating for so long.

His sweet, smiling kisses. Sleepy, sighing kisses.

I didn't want to come back down, ever.

"We need to shower," he murmured. "Come on. Up we get." He untangled us, rolled off the bed, and disappeared into the en suite.

"The room's still spinning," I replied.

His laughter echoed out from the bathroom before I heard the shower turn on. "Now, Mr. Hall. Your services are required."

I snorted and dragged myself off his bed, walked into the bathroom, and stopped mid-stride.

He was shirtless, sitting on a bench seat in his huge private bathroom, unlacing his boots. He grinned at me. "What?"

"Just . . . you." I waved my hand in his general direction. "Your bathroom's a lot nicer than mine. You got a bench seat?" The truth was, his whole room was twice the size of mine, as was his bathroom. And the shower.

He tossed his boot and began on the next one. "You're still very dressed."

"And you're wasting water." The shower was running, the room beginning to steam.

"I like it hot."

He pulled off his other boot, then his socks, and then he took off his jeans. Wearing nothing but a smirk, he walked into the shower. "You okay? You look a little stunned."

Holy fuck.

Sure, I'd seen him in various states of undress over the years but never fully naked. And those tight pants he wore on stage were all kinds of good, but naked? He was . . . he was a freaking vision. He was fit from hours of dance, lean, maybe even a little too thin. His sleeve of ink ended at his shoulder. His skin was flawless. He was muscled in all the right places, his ass was firm, his half-hard dick hung heavy and uncut.

I ripped my boots off, tossed my shirt, and couldn't get out of my jeans quick enough. I followed him into the shower, and with my hands on his hips, I kissed his shoulder, the nape of his neck.

Water ran off his body, hot and steaming. His hair was flattened. He put his head back, leaning against my collarbone, and he hummed.

"All those magazines and news polls that named you sexiest man," I murmured in his ear, "have no fucking idea how sexy you really are." I ran my hands down his arms, and holding his wrists, I put his hands on the wall in front of us, pressing myself against his back, his ass. "I want to do so many things to you."

He barked out a laugh and turned, leaning his back

against the tiles, his smile flirty and fun. "Never figured you for a dirty talker, Roscoe," he said, pulling me close. We were both semi-hard again, our cocks pressing against each other. Desire and testosterone swirled with the steam and made me dizzy. "I like it."

"I can tell how much you like it," I said, kissing him again.

It was a filthy wet kiss that had little to do with water running over us, and he broke away to smile. "I take back what I said earlier. About being kissed properly before. I thought I had. But you . . ."

"Told you it was because you hadn't been kissed by me."

"Now I have. And I do concur. You have quite the talented mouth. And hands." He looked down between us and went to palm my dick. "And—"

I gripped his wrist. "And we should get out of the shower. Someone's gonna come looking for one of us soon."

He tried to hitch his leg around my hip and I took a step back, shut the water off, and grabbed a towel. I threw it to him, then grabbed one for me. He grumbled as he dried off and tied the towel around his waist. He disappeared into his room and it occurred to me that my clothes were a mess.

Bloody hell.

After checking, my jeans were okay, but my shirt was not wearable. The jizz splatter was pretty obviously jizz. I pulled on my jeans, at least, and when I walked out to Maddox's room, he took one look at me holding my shirt in my hand and he laughed.

He was wearing his favorite sweats and a T-shirt, looking all kinds of relaxed and comfortable. And hot as hell. His hair was finger-combed back off his face, and he looked sleepy and happy.

"Need a shirt?" he asked. He pulled out one of his bigger, oversized shirts and threw it at me. "Try that."

It was long sleeve and black, of course, and it fit okay, if a bit tight around the arms. "Thanks."

"Throw your shirt with my dirty laundry in the bathroom," he said. "I'll put a laundry call in."

"I can take care of that for you," I said instinctively. It was my job, after all.

He lay on the bed and smiled at me. "You're not on the clock right now, are you?"

"Well, no. Not the last hour. But it's really no problem."

He rolled his eyes and patted the bed beside him. "Leave the shirt and come here."

"Hmm," I said, making a face. "How many shirts do you have that would fit me. If we make a mess of this one . . ."

He laughed. "I like the way you think, Roscoe. But I'm tired. Can you stay for a bit?"

I threw my dirty shirt toward the bathroom and climbed onto the bed. I lay down beside him, and he immediately snuggled into my side, his head on my chest.

It was so easy to put my arm around him, to hold him close. It was so easy to listen to him breathe, to sigh, to fall asleep.

It was all just so fucking easy.

It would have been easy to sleep beside him, to stay all night and wake up next to him in the morning. But that wasn't our reality.

I waited until he was in a deep sleep before I peeled myself away from him. I folded the cover over him because he said he liked lots of blankets. I put my socks and boots back on, and I bagged up his laundry. I put the call in, waited for the staff to come get it, and leaving Maddox well and truly asleep, I slipped out of his room.

It was late, and I didn't expect to see anyone. And if they saw me walking in the corridor, it didn't mean anything. I could have been at the gym or double-checking the common room was locked or getting some ice . . .

No one would know I'd been in Maddox's room. No one would know what we'd just done.

And I was almost back to my room. I had my key out and was just about to tap it to the door when Jeremy came around the corner with a packet of M&Ms in his hand. "Oh, hey. Needed something sweet," he said by way of explanation.

"Sounds good," I replied, trying to act cool. "Just heading to bed. Need anything before I turn in?"

"Nah." He smiled kind of awkwardly and looked down at my shirt.

No, not mine. He looked at Maddox's shirt. It was very obviously Maddox's shirt. He wore it all the time . . .

Shit.

Jeremy's eyes met mine, and without saying a word, he told me he knew.

Shit.

I opened my door, trying not to panic. "Okay then. If you're all good, I'll see you at breakfast," I said, disappearing into my room and closing the door behind me.

My heart was hammering, my mind was racing. This wasn't good. This wasn't good at all.

CHAPTER NINE

I HIT the hotel gym at 5:30 am. I hadn't slept well. My mind was filled with the look of recognition in Jeremy's eyes, wondering what was going to come of that. Though mostly my head was filled with Maddox. His body, his smile, his taste, his scent. The way he moved underneath me, the way he felt. How he leaned into me, how he responded to my touch, to my kiss. The look of desire in his eyes, the wanting, the need. His face when he came.

Yeah, my head was mostly filled with that.

So I did some weights, and when that didn't clear my head, I hit the treadmill.

Steve and some of his guys came in around six thirty, and that was my cue to leave. I was drenched in sweat by then anyway, though my head still wasn't right. A shower didn't fix me either. I considered jerking off, but that only brought visions of Maddox back when it was those mental images I was trying to get rid of.

I got dressed for the day, in jeans and one of my own shirts, and figured some iced coffees were in order. There was a Starbucks a few doors down. I'd been there before without incident, though this time photographers were snapping pics of me. More than usual. Typically, one or two were nothing new, but this was more than typical. This early in the morning? Christ.

And when I waited in Starbucks for my order—eight iced coffees took a few minutes—I noticed more papzz out the front of the store. And there were enough of them for it to be an issue. *Fucking hell.* With a long-suffering sigh, I shot a quick text to Steve, asking him to come get me. He and Robbie walked through the doors not more than sixty seconds later.

"Got yourself some fans, I see," Steve said.

"This is absurd," I replied. "I was just grabbing some coffee. I've done this a thousand times."

"We had to push through them." Robbie reassessed the view out the front. "Now they're blocking the sidewalk."

Once the order was done, it took Steve and Robbie to get me through the swarm of photographers. It didn't help that I had my hands full with two cup carriers, but this was ridiculous.

They called my name, "Roscoe, Roscoe, Roscoe," trying to get me to look at them, but like Maddox would do, I kept my head down and watched where I put my feet. They yelled questions about Maddox, about me, about the interviews yesterday, what Maddox had said, and what the band was doing for the final LA concert tonight. I ignored it all and followed Steve into the hotel lobby as Robbie followed close behind.

Hotel security kept the photographers and reporters out of the hotel, and the silence and room to move was very welcome. I didn't speak until we were alone in the elevator. "Thanks, guys."

"No problem," Steve replied.

"How the boys deal with that shit on the regular is beyond me," I grumbled.

"You deal with it too, right alongside them," Robbie said.

"But that's aimed at them, not me."

"Hmm," Steve said. "Might have to look at getting a runner to do your errands. Next stop is Vegas, and it's not gonna be much different than here."

I gave a nod as the elevator doors opened and we got out on our floor. I took the drinks to the common room where breakfast was being set up. Amber was there helping, and Ryan came in ten seconds later, and as I handed them their drinks, I told them both about the welcoming committee I had outside.

"The reaction to Maddox's interview has been interesting," Amber said.

Before I could reply—that I had no clue what she was talking about—the doors opened and Luke, Blake, Wes, and Jeremy walked in. I didn't make eye contact with Jeremy, still not prepared to face the wearing-Maddox's-shirt conversation. "Iced coffee, boys."

And before anyone could ask where Maddox was, he came in. Showered, hair wet, smiling. He went straight for his iced coffee and turned to give me a nod. "Thank you."

"You're welcome," I replied, making the quickest eye contact before looking away. Jeremy was watching, but he was focused more on Maddox than on me, thankfully. I took my drink and sat on the couch and went through the usual social media sites to see what Amber was referring to.

And yes, it was interesting indeed.

Not only were the fans supportive of Maddox saying their private lives were private and that they gave enough of themselves without it being used as a weapon against them for a quick headline, but other celebrities were speaking up too.

A lot of them.

Big names, famous people. Singers, actors, sports stars were all speaking up in support.

"Someone's trauma isn't a headline" was used a lot.

Wow.

Even Ambrose was happy with this turn in narrative, and Platinum Entertainment released a formal statement saying they supported Atrous and all other artists, jumping on the bandwagon to claim even celebrities had the right to be treated with respect.

Kinda hypocritical of a company that made many millions of dollars exploiting them, but whatever.

The boys had dance rehearsals all morning and we headed to the stadium early. They had to redo soundchecks and other stage checks, and I was looking forward to the car ride with Maddox.

Only Jeremy climbed in our van at the last minute.

"Is this okay?" he asked, looking at me.

"Yeah, absolutely," I answered, pretending not to care either way.

Maddox shoved him and laughed, but he could hardly say no, not when Jeremy was already climbing into the van. Maddox gave me a quick glance of frustration but followed Jeremy into the backseat. I took the seat near the door and did my best to damp down my disappointment.

It was a good reminder that I had a job to do and that Maddox's needs—and all the boys' needs—were my first priority. If Jeremy wanted to join us, he could.

I just wasn't looking forward to the possible interrogation I was certain was coming. I waited and waited for him to ask about me wearing Maddox's shirt, but he never did.

They talked and laughed, talked more bullshit, and laughed some more. Their conversation eventually came around to the new attention on social media as they scrolled through hashtags, reading comments and articles.

Maddox seemed . . . happy.

I replied to emails and messages, confirmed dates and locations, and sent copies to both Amber and Ryan's calendars. Just the usual daily stuff.

Until Maddox's phone appeared in front of my face as he dangled himself over the back of my chair. "What's this?"

The photo must have been taken this morning at the coffee shop. "Uh, that was this morning," I replied.

"It says you went in there alone but must have called security because you were escorted out," Maddox continued.

"Yeah, I had to call Steve and Robbie to come down to get me."

"Christ, Roscoe. You should have told me."

I switched my phone off and turned in my seat so I could see them both better. Maddox mostly. "I haven't had a minute with you," I replied. "When was I supposed to tell you?"

Maddox glared at me, then cast his eyes to the front of the van. "Steve?"

"Yes," Steve said, turning to look at us. "What's up?"

Maddox's jaw bulged. "Can you put a guy with Roscoe, please."

Steve glanced at me, then back to Maddox. "When?"

"All the time. Whenever he's in public."

I did my best not to roll my eyes or sigh. "Maddox, that's not necessary. It was no big deal, honestly. It's just that I had my hands full and—"

Ignoring me, Maddox looked around me to Steve. "Can you organize that or do I need to run it by Ambrose?"

Steve gave a nod and glanced at me before he turned back around to face the front. "I got it."

I sighed out loud this time but decided there wasn't any point in arguing.

Jeremy was scrolling through his phone. He was either oblivious to Maddox's *what the fuck* glare at me, or he chose to pretend not to notice. "That's actually a good photo," Jeremy said, turning his phone around to show me first, then Maddox. Then he laughed. "Oh my god, the headline. *Sexy Roscoe: herding cats pays off*." He chuckled as he read some more. "Uh, this article is pretty much all about your shoulders and biceps." He read on. "Oh, and your ass." He showed us the screen again. It was actually a photo zoomed in on my ass.

Oh, for fuck's sake.

Maddox snatched his phone and scrolled. "Hmm," he said, turning the phone sideways. "Well, they're not wrong."

I turned back to face the front. "Let me know if they decide to write anything worthwhile."

I ignored their chatter for a while and they were busy doing whatever on their phones, and soon enough we were at the stadium. They went straight into stage rehearsals and sound checks, while Amber, Ryan, and I spent our time in meetings with Ambrose going over our departure from LA to Vegas. We had two shows in Vegas, then one in San Francisco, one in Seattle, onto a single concert in Vancouver.

LA was busy with interviews and photoshoots, alongside three sold-out concerts, but we had a reprieve from interviews and other public appearances until one in Seattle and two in Vancouver. It was a relief, for me at least.

It would be a few days off from public scrutiny. Traveling was no picnic either, but at least there might be a day or two where Maddox wasn't a headline. Or me, for that matter.

I never got a spare minute with Maddox all afternoon. Not alone, anyway. There was always someone around: one of the boys, caterers, wardrobe, make-up, sound techs. But I caught him looking my way a few times, and he'd smile or smirk, maybe raise his eyebrow a little. It was like he was flirting without even trying.

And when they were on stage for the concert, we watched the live feed in the dressing room. The crowd was pumping, the mood in the stadium electric, and despite the warm night, the boys gave it everything they had. A hundred people ran tirelessly behind the scenes, yet I couldn't take my eyes off Maddox.

I'd seen him sing those songs dozens of times, from writing the lyrics to getting the melodies right, to studio recording and vocal practices. I'd seen every dance move so many times I could probably do the choreography in my sleep.

But watching him tonight was different.

In those pants and the way his sweaty shirt clung to his chest, I knew that body. His damp hair reminded me of him in the shower, when we'd been naked together. The way the veins protruded down his neck when he sang, the same way they did when he came.

I knew him differently now. And watching him on stage singing to eighty-something thousand people, all eyes on him, captivating them, enamoring them. They called his name, they sang his songs back to him, they chanted and cried.

They wanted him.

It was intoxicating to think he wanted me and that it was me who had been in bed with him last night.

It was hard to concentrate on much else.

When they came off stage for the last time that night, they were all exhausted, dripping with sweat but smiling.

We did our best to get them changed out of their stage gear, fed and hydrated, and they just about collapsed onto the couches in the dressing room. Though Maddox was dressed quicker than anyone else, which wasn't like him. We were normally the last to leave, but not tonight.

"See you guys back at the hotel," he said, then nodded to me and the door to leave.

Okay then.

We climbed into our van and had to wait a second for our driver and security detail. It was half a minute, tops. But Maddox wasted no time. He was sprawled on the seat, tired, sweaty, his legs spread wide, his hands resting on his crotch. His jeans bulged in a way that was sexy as hell. "Why are you looking at me like that?"

I let out a slow breath. We were alone so I could say what I wanted. "Because you're sex on a plate right now."

He chuckled and arched his back deliberately and ran his hand over his taut belly. "Mm, sex on a plate. Would prefer a bed or being bent over the back of the couch, but if you want to try a plate . . ."

I bit back a groan. "You shouldn't say things like that."

He met my gaze and didn't look away for a long time. "I missed you today."

"Missed me?"

"Yeah. You were gone from my bed this morning. Again. And then Jeremy rode in the car with us on the way here. I like it when it's just us."

The driver got in and so did Robbie. Steve would no

doubt be staying behind to make sure everything and everyone left safely.

I spoke quieter now so only Maddox could hear me. "Jeremy saw me last night. Wearing your shirt."

"So?"

"So he knew it was your shirt. He knew."

Maddox sat up and leaned against me, his head on my shoulder. "I don't care."

"I do."

"He won't care."

"Pretty sure that's why he rode with us today. I'm surprised he didn't say something." I shrugged. "He probably had every intention of riding with us tonight but you beat him to it."

"It's why I was ready first."

"Maddox—"

"Do you regret what we did?"

His direct question surprised me and he no doubt felt me freeze. "No. I don't. Do you?"

"Hell no." He put his hand on my thigh, now dangerously close to my crotch, so I covered his hand with mine to stop him from trying anything.

Then I decided to be completely honest with him. "I tried to regret it. I tried to convince myself that it should probably be just a one-time thing and we should keep this professional and not jeopardize anything, but that was the quickest ten-second thought I've ever had. I just can't . . . I don't want to stop," I whispered. "And even if I did want to, I'm still not sure I could."

He raised his head off my shoulder to look me in the eye, his face impossibly close. "I don't want to stop either," he murmured. Then he put his head back to my shoulder, snuggling in a little. "I like sitting with you like this. I've been alone for a long time. I got so used to the loneliness I forgot what it was like. To be with someone. To sit with someone and hold hands."

I squeezed his hand and risked a kiss to the top of his head, and we rode in comfortable silence back to the hotel. Robbie escorted us inside and into the elevator, and when Maddox put his head back on my shoulder and closed his eyes, Robbie smiled at us. "You gotta be beat, huh?" he said to Maddox. "The show tonight was jumping."

Maddox straightened, his eyes barely open, and he nodded. "Yeah, tonight was good, but I need some sleep."

"Did you have enough to eat?" I asked him. "I can order you something else if you want."

He shook his head. "Nah, I'm good."

The doors opened to our floor and Robbie held the door. "I'll head back down and wait for the others. You guys okay?"

"Yeah, we're good. Thanks," I replied, and we stepped out into the empty corridor. The doors closed and we were finally alone.

"We are so good," Maddox said, his voice hoarse. It wasn't a sore throat, it was his tired voice. He began walking toward his room. "But we're about to be a whole lot better."

"Uh, the others'll be here in about five minutes," I said.

He swiped his key and held his door open. "Then you better make it a very good five minutes, Mr. Hall."

I couldn't help it. I laughed and went inside. "Sure thing, Mr. Kershaw."

He chuckled as he followed me in and I turned and pulled him close. I slid my hands over his back and shoulders, down to his ass. "I'm all sweaty," he murmured.

"I don't mind," I replied, then I kissed him anyway. His hands found my face and we stood right there in his hotel room, kissing, for what must have been a few minutes. I wanted to do it for longer. All night if I could. With no push for anything more than to kiss him until he forgot his own name.

When I ended the kiss, it took him a few seconds to focus. He had a dopey smile on his face; he was kiss-drunk. I swiped my thumb across his bottom lip. It was plump and wet. "I could kiss you all night," I whispered.

"You should. All night. I want you to. Just like that, all night long."

I cupped his jaw, his long earrings at my fingertips. "The others will be here any second. We should go."

"I'm not staying long. I'm tired as hell."

He could barely keep his eyelids open as it was. It was cute, but he really needed to sleep. "I can tell."

He searched my eyes. "I want you to stay with me tonight. All night."

"Maddox," I breathed. "I wish I could."

"But?"

"But . . ." My job, his work, the band, his reputation, my reputation, the company, the fans. "Everything."

He pouted. "Come back for a little while. I'll leave the room early. You stay for another five or ten so no one thinks twice. By the time you get here, I'll be showered and not so gross. Though you didn't seem to mind it just now."

I chuckled. "You being all sweaty is the opposite of gross, just so you know."

"How about I get the concert sweat off me, then you make me a different kind of sweaty later on."

I laughed, then smacked another kiss on his perfect lips. "I'll leave when no one suspects anything."

So that's what we did.

We made our way to the common room, and just a few

seconds later the others arrived. It was mostly a quick congratulations on a successful concert and a run-through of what was happening tomorrow with us moving onto Vegas.

True to his word, when the business side of it was all done, he stood up. "Thank you to everyone for a successful opening," he said, nodding to the crew that was there. "And you four dickwads," he joked to Jeremy, Wes, Luke, and Blake. "Love you all, but I'm so freaking tired. I gotta crash."

He left with a final wave, and Amber's gaze cut to mine. Was she expecting Maddox to ask to speak to me again, for us to leave together again, or was it something else? I pretended not to notice and I stayed for another long, drawn-out fifteen minutes. Other staff called it a night before me, so it wasn't like it was obvious, but when I knocked quietly on Maddox's door, he opened it, pulled me inside, and quickly closed it behind me. He leaned his back against the door, pouting. "Thought you stood me up."

He was wearing lounge pants and a baggy gray T-shirt. His hair was wet, freshly showered. He'd taken his earrings out, though he still looked gorgeous, of course, but he was clearly tired. "You need some sleep."

He smirked and pushed off the door, putting his hand on my waist. "Wrong word choice. I need to be taken to bed, yes. Not to sleep."

He leaned his forehead on my chest and sighed, so I pulled him in for a hug. He fell into me willingly and was heavy in my arms. "You need to be taken to bed," I murmured against the side of his head.

He chuckled. "You're a quick learner."

I led him toward the bed and pushed him onto the mattress. I pulled off my boots and followed him, quickly pulling him back into my arms. I kissed him softly, sweetly, and he hummed, his eyes closed. We kissed like that for a long few minutes, never pushing for more. Just enjoying the sweetness, the intimacy.

It was easy to see he was too tired for much else, so I kissed his cheek, his closed eyelids, his forehead. I ran my fingers through his damp hair, brushing it back, and he was asleep in no time.

He used my arm as a pillow as his lips parted ever so slightly, his long eyelashes casting delicate shadows in the dim light. I traced the line of his eyebrow with my thumb. His cheekbone. His jawline.

He was devastatingly beautiful.

I wished I could have stayed all night with him, and I stayed there for as long as I dared. He felt so good in my arms—warm and muscular edges in all the right places—and he smelled like peaches and oranges. He tasted like heaven. But my eyelids were heavy and my blinks were getting longer, and if I let myself doze, I would sleep until morning and I just couldn't let that happen.

As much as I wanted to. I just couldn't.

So with a kiss to his temple, I peeled myself away from him and covered him with the quilt, pulled my boots on, and checked the peephole in the door. The hallway was clear, so I slipped outside and went to my room.

I showered and climbed into bed, wondering when the creeping feeling of regret would come. Or maybe the cold realization that this foolishness would need to end. Or maybe reality would snap its fingers and remind us of our jobs and that it was selfish of us to jeopardize everything.

But none of that came.

Instead, under my breastbone, a small ember of warmth glowed red. A tiny spark of something special caught aflame beneath my ribs. I put the heel of my hand against my sternum to see if I could feel the heat of it through my chest, which was absurd. I laughed at myself for being such an idiot.

But that little ember glowed some more. It burned a little brighter, warmer.

I wasn't brave enough to give it a name.

Not out loud, anyway.

So I rolled onto my side and closed my eyes, absolutely certain I could smell peaches and oranges on my skin.

***

THE NEXT MORNING WAS A RUSH. I hit the gym early, and when the band members came in for breakfast, Amber, Ryan, and I were busy organizing the move to Vegas. Even though we had logistics down to an art, it was always a pain in the ass and there was always additional stress.

Maddox said hello like he usually did, though there was a hint of a smile in his eyes. We didn't have any chance to talk or even share more than a passing glance until we were packed up and leaving the hotel for Van Nuys Airport.

"We're not going through LAX, right?" Maddox asked as we headed toward the van.

"Nope. Thank God."

The terminal for private charters was not out of the LAX departure terminal. I wasn't up for dealing with that shitshow. Maddox's thoughts must have followed the same train of thought as mine. "Sure as hell don't miss getting through the old check-in."

"Same."

Or, more to the point, I didn't miss the hundreds of fans screaming and pushing. We'd had a few close calls and I'd had to be more bodyguard than manager, but once we'd started flying private charter, my stress levels dropped considerably. As did everyone's.

And the private plane was a godsend too. We didn't have that last time and it was a logistical nightmare. We'd done tours on buses too, and that was too exhausting. This time we'd take one plane for all of us, and it was a huge relief for the whole crew.

With all our luggage taken care of, Maddox climbed into the backseat of our van, and as soon as I sat beside him and the door slid closed, he lifted my arm and slung it over his shoulder. He half leaned on me, making himself comfortable in the crook of my arm and playing with my fingers at his chest. "So I was thinking," he began, "that it'd be a terrible shame if we were a room or two short in Vegas and we had to share."

I snorted. "Is that right?"

"How does one go about incorrectly booking out a hotel?"

"I don't know."

"I woke up at two and you were gone," he whispered. Then he let out a long sigh. "I didn't go back to sleep."

I nudged the side of his head with my chin. Not a kiss but close enough. "You know why I can't stay."

"That's why we need to share a room."

"They'd put you with one of the boys before they put you with me."

"Not if we go last and they said, 'Oh, it looks like we only have one room left,' and we could say, 'Oh, that's a terrible shame, and there's only one bed? Whatever will we do?' and then it'd be fine."

I laughed. "Sounds nice."

"Oh, and I have your shirt."

"And I still have yours."

"You're not getting it back, just so you know. It's mine now."

"Everyone will know it's mine if you wear it."

"I don't care. You can leave the Bruins one too."

"You're not getting that."

"We'll see."

"Maddox," I murmured.

He sighed, and pulling on my arm around his shoulder, he pressed my hand to his chest. "So, tonight . . . will we have any time together?"

"I don't know. I'll try."

"I sleep better when you're there with me."

"I almost fell asleep in your bed last night. You were so warm and you smelled so good."

He turned then, sitting up a little and surprising me with a kiss. We were in the backseat and Steve and our driver couldn't see us unless they were actively looking, which they weren't. But still. This was risky.

I didn't care about that for too long though. He cupped my cheek, and his lips were soft and urgent.

"Stay with me tonight," he murmured. "Please."

Christ.

"I'll try. No promises though."

This time when he sat back, he leaned against the door and slung his leg over my thigh. Those black jeans with holes across the knees, tight across his muscular thighs . . . tight in all the right places. It'd be so easy to lean over him, lay my weight on him, and kiss him how I really wanted . . .

I swear he could read my mind. "You can if you want," he said with a delicious smirk.

"I can what?"

His smile became a grin. "You're looking at me like you

want to do very bad things to me." He pushed his leg up my thigh, a little closer to my crotch. "And I won't stop you."

I chuckled and squeezed his knee. "You're trying to kill me, aren't you?"

He laughed and pulled his leg back, ticklish. My gaze went to Steve, but he never turned around. I smacked Maddox's thigh. "You're gonna get us in trouble."

Maddox, now sitting up, took my hand. "I don't care."

But I did. It was easy for him to say he didn't care—there would be zero ramifications for him—but it could very well cost me my job. Even if he swore it wouldn't. Ultimately it wasn't his call.

"Have you read the reviews on last night's concert?" I asked instead.

"Nope. And I don't want to see it. The guys were reading a few this morning, laughing about it. It's all kinda crazy." He sighed. "It messes with your head if you read all the hype. You start believing it and . . . you know, it's not real. It's crazy-fame shit, talking about how I'm this and how I'm that, and then I log off and I'm just me. I'm not that guy they think I am or who they hype me up to be."

"True." I shrugged. "You're better in real life."

Maddox smiled and he nudged his knee to mine. "I did look for more Roscoe stuff though," he admitted. "You have fan clubs on social media now."

"Which is ridiculous."

He chuckled again. "I was going to make a fake account just to join so I could squeal with all the other fanboys and girls."

I snorted out a laugh. "God, please don't do that."

"Imagine the photos I could leak. I mean, if you'd let me take photos of you . . . of us."

I laughed again. "Then I *would* get fired."

He took his phone out and opened the camera, holding it out for a selfie of us. He dropped his head onto my shoulder, so I leaned my cheek against the top of his head, and we smiled for the photo. He studied the photo for a long while, then lightly touched the screen. "I like this," he murmured.

"You look great," I added. He looked great in every photo. "Me, on the other hand . . ."

"Are you kidding me?" He sat up, his expression disbelieving. He showed me the photo again. "Are you blind?"

"I hate photos of me."

He tapped the screen and brought up his last internet search. It was me. A lot of photos of me, mostly walking in public with him, by his side or one step behind. "Look at how fucking fine you are," he said. "And I hate to tell you, but the world is right. You are the sexiest manager."

"What were you just saying about all that hype being bullshit?"

"It's bullshit when it's about me. Not you."

I rolled my eyes. "Sure."

Steve turned around. "ETA, ten minutes."

Maddox sighed. "No more alone time," he mumbled.

"We've survived so far, haven't we?"

Maddox straightened up and met my eyes. He made a face and turned back to the front, clearly deciding not to say what he was about to say.

"What?" I prompted. Was he hurt by that? Offended?

"Are things not different now?" he asked. "With us?"

"Well, yeah. Kind of."

"Kind of."

"Behind closed doors, yes."

He nodded slowly but again, chose silence.

"Maddox, can't we just enjoy this? Whatever this is."
We really hadn't talked about what it was or, god forbid, put

a label on it. "It's new, and it's just ours. Can't we keep it that way? Without the complication of management, the band, the staff."

He chewed on his bottom lip for a few seconds. "Whatever this is," he repeated. "Whatever this is . . ."

"Well, what would you call it?" Christ. We'd known each other for years. I'd worked with him, *for* him, for four years. The hand-holding, the making out, and sexual side of this was just a few days old.

Maddox swallowed hard. His voice was quiet when he said, "I'd call it . . . good. That's what I'd call it. And I don't want it to end."

"So we need to protect it, right?"

"I don't like lying to the guys," he whispered. "I don't like hiding or having to censor myself. It's not who I am."

"I know. I don't like it either. But we need to look at the bigger picture here. We've just started a tour. We're down three shows out of twenty-three and we've got a long way to go. And this thing, this good thing," I used his words, "is still very new. Let's just test the waters before we go doing things that can't be undone."

"Is that common sense you're using against me?"

"I think so."

He pouted. "I know what you're saying, and I know it makes sense."

"But?" There was definitely a but.

"But if any of the guys ask, I won't lie to them."

I sighed. "Fair enough. Though Jeremy's already seen me wearing your shirt, so there's a good chance he suspects something."

Maddox sighed and leaned against me again, riding the rest of the trip in silence. We drove into the private terminal and our time alone together was coming to an end. Maddox lifted our joined hands and he kissed my knuckles. "You'll come to my room tonight if you can, yes?"

I nodded. "If I can."

The van slowed to a stop, and a second later, the door slid open. I climbed out first and waited for Maddox to get out. He had his cap pulled down low, his baggy black clothes hiding his body.

He could have worn a dirty potato sack and still been gorgeous.

Maddox put his hand on my back as we walked inside the terminal. He was swallowed up by the guys, talking and laughing, and I went to the service desk where Amber and Ryan were.

And we were both right. The day was beautiful, yes. I watched him practice, I watched him dance, I watched the way his body moved, I watched his throat when he sang. I watched him smile and laugh and pant for breath and lay on the stage when rehearsals were done. I could watch him forever.

But he and I barely spoke more than five words and were never alone until I knocked on his bedroom door at 10:00 pm.

He opened the door and smirked. The room was dark and he looked tired, but as soon as I brushed past him, he gripped my arm. The door closed and he pulled me in for a hug. "About time," he grumbled into my chest.

"Been a long day," I whispered. I rubbed his back and he moved under my touch much like a cat. "Need a massage?"

He chuckled and raked his hand down to my ass. "I need something."

I slid my hand along his jaw and brought him in for a kiss. It started sweet and soft, but as soon as our tongues touched, he groaned and deepened the kiss. He pawed at my shirt, trying to get it off me, breaking the kiss to laugh. He got mine off me and I made quick work of his T-shirt, pulling it over his head and tossing it toward the bed.

"On the bed, face down," I ordered.

His eyes went wide and he grinned. "You just gonna do me like that? No asking nicely . . ."

I laughed and turned him by his shoulders, push-walking him toward the bed. "Massage, Maddox. Nothing else."

"There better be something else," he groused as he kneeled on the bed. I could see how his track pants were tented.

I gripped his hips from behind and kissed his shoulder. "Do you want my mouth on you?"

"Fuck yes," he groaned.

"Lie down," I whispered. "Massage first."

I followed him onto the bed, kneeling astride his thighs. He put his hands up underneath the pillows, and his back stretched beautifully. He had a dancer's body. All those hours of hip hop and choreography had made him lithe and muscular. He was fit enough to sing and dance on stage for hours, and by god, he felt good under my hands.

I rolled the heels of my hands up his back, pressing my thumbs into the muscle. I had no massage oils, so I didn't push too hard, but I ironed out the knots in his shoulders. And if the moans coming out of Maddox were any clue, I'd say I did a pretty good job.

Kneeling over him though, straddling his ass, pushing against him, having him between my legs and touching him and having him moan like that, it was hard not to be turned on. Hearing him writhe and grunt didn't help either.

Then he widened his thighs and raised his ass up a

little. "Lie down on me," he whisper-moaned. "Wanna feel your weight on me."

But I did as he asked, aligning my cock with the crack of his ass, and I slowly pressed down on his back. I slid my hands up his arms and threaded our fingers while I kissed his shoulder, the nape of his neck, behind his ear. I rolled my hips, both loving and cursing my jeans for the friction. "Like how it feels?" I whispered into his ear.

He shivered and his breath caught. "Hell yes."

I ground against his ass again, my erection rubbing him in all the right places, and he tried to rise to meet my thrust. He wanted it . . . It would be so easy to undo my fly and pull his track pants down, just far enough . . .

I stilled and had to make myself rise up off his body. He whined, so I kissed his shoulder again. "Roll over," I urged him. "Time to do the front."

He twisted himself around so he was on his back. His torso rippled with the movement, his hand ran down his taut stomach to his dick, and he gave himself a squeeze through his sweatpants. He was fully hard now, his eyes were dark and heavy lidded, his smile sultry and delicious.

I slid one knee in between his thighs and positioned his legs until I was between them. I leaned over him and kissed his mouth, his jaw, his neck. I kissed all the way down to his stomach and palmed his erection. I pulled the elastic of his pants down and wrapped my fingers around his shaft. I nuzzled my nose into him, inhaling the very scent of him, then licked up the underside of his cock before taking him into my mouth.

"Oh, holy fuck," Maddox murmured, arching his back a little.

I took as much of him in as I could and sucked, swirled my tongue, and swallowed around him. He gripped my hair and tried to move his legs, but I held him still and sucked him harder.

"Roscoe," he groaned, a pained sound. A heavenly sound. "Gonna come so fast."

Oh fuck. *The way he said my name.*

He ran his hands over his chest, over his face, through his hair, trying to grasp on to some kind of control. He fisted the comforter at his sides and arched his back as he came, coming in spurts down my throat.

His body twitched, his thighs trembled, and he moaned indecipherable sounds that ended in a chuckle. I pulled his sweatpants up to cover him and he did a whole-body shudder and laughed again.

"Christ," he breathed, smiling that lazy post-orgasm smile, and he pulled me by my shirt until I was lying on top of him. He wrapped me up in his arms and snuggled into my neck . . . until he must have realized what was poking him in the belly. "You almost enjoyed it as much as me," he said, sliding his hand in between us to palm me.

"You said my name just before you came," I said, kissing up his jaw to his ear. "It almost ended me right then."

He rolled us over so I was on my back, and he grinned down at me and he purred my name. "Rossssscoe." He maneuvered himself between my legs, popped the button on my jeans, and slowly undid the fly. He ran his hands up my thighs, over my hips, digging his fingers in, then roughly pulled my jeans and briefs down. "Fucking hell," he whispered. "Such a beautiful sight."

I needed . . . something. So I gripped my base, hard enough to stem the orgasm that was lingering just under the surface.

Maddox batted my hand away. "Don't touch," he said before licking up the shaft. He tongued the slit and kissed the head. "This is mine." Then he proceeded to tease and taste, moan and murmur, pump me and please me . . . but not enough. Like he wanted to see how far he could push me, edge me.

I wanted to grip his hair and thrust into his throat. I wanted to come so bad. But of course I wouldn't do that to him . . . unless he wanted it. "Maddox," I warned. "No games. I need you to—"

He laughed, then proceeded to take every inch of me into his mouth. He finished me so fast, so intense and so fucking good, the room spun. He drank me, swallowing every drop, his tongue licking me clean. I saw stars, and I swear to god, my soul left my body.

He crawled up to kiss me softly, victorious and grinning, then proceeded to lie on top of me. "You have more self-control than I gave you credit for," he said casually.

I rolled us over, making him laugh, and he clung to me. I wrapped him up in a tight embrace, my leg over his hip, and he hummed happily. I was going to just lie like that for a little while, enjoy the moment, the sweetness and the closeness. I was eventually going to peel myself away and let him sleep, then go back to my room.

I just closed my eyes for a second.

The next thing I knew, my alarm went off. Maddox was in the bed next to me, sound asleep. His black hair was strewn across his forehead, his lips slightly parted. He grumbled at the noise of my alarm but didn't fully wake. "Turn it off," he groused, his voice thick with sleep.

I shot out of bed and found my phone, surprised to see I was still wearing undone jeans and socks. I found my shirt, pulled on my shoes, and glanced at Maddox. He was on his belly, his arms up under his pillow. Shirtless, wearing his sweatpants, sleep-rumpled, and absolutely beautiful.

Fuck it.

I leaned on the mattress and kissed his head. "It's morning," I said. "I gotta go."

He smiled, burying his face into a pillow. And I prayed no one saw me leave.

CHAPTER TEN

VEGAS, San Francisco, Seattle, Vancouver, Denver, Dallas.

They passed in a blur.

It was fitness training, dance rehearsals, meetings. Flights, traffic jams, sold-out concerts, a few interviews, a few TV appearances. Logistics, security, and keeping tight schedules. Late nights, stolen kisses, lingering touches, holding hands, snuggling in bed.

And since I'd slept that one night in his bed, Maddox couldn't see any problem in doing it every night. I sure as hell couldn't say no to him, even though I knew better. We were tempting fate every time, but I'd be lying if I said I didn't want to.

I *did* want to sleep in his bed every night. I wanted to hold him all night long. I wanted to wake up next to him. There was one time in Denver when the boys had something planned and it was late by the time we got back to the hotel. The boys wanted to have a few drinks afterward, and I had absolutely no problem leaving Maddox in Wes's room.

In my own room, I showered and tried to watch some

TV to dull my mind, but the bed was too big and empty without him. I missed his head on my chest as we watched the late, late movies. I missed his body against me. I missed his touch, his kiss, his taste. I missed the smell of his peach-and-orange body wash. I missed his smile, his laugh, the way he clung to me when he slept. I missed the sounds he made when he came.

One night. One freaking night apart and I missed him.

When Maddox surfaced the next morning, he was showered and dressed in his usual black from his cap to his boots, but he looked wrecked. I handed him his iced coffee. "Didn't sleep, huh?"

His tired eyes met mine. "And I wonder why. I waited for you."

What? "You were with the guys, set in for the long haul when I left." I would have been mad at his assumption, but he looked miserable. "You should have texted me."

He looked up at me from under his cap, tired and sad. "I wasn't sure if I could . . . or should. I didn't want to wake you."

"I missed you," I admitted.

His smile just about slayed me. "You did, huh?"

"Don't let it go to your head."

He sipped his drink through the straw just as Jeremy came over. "Hey, lovebirds. You ready?"

Maddox choked on his drink, and I felt the blood drain from my face. What the hell had he told him last night?

Before I could speak, Ryan called me over to give him a hand, and thirty seconds later we were on our way to the vans. If Jeremy was looking at me funny, I pretended not to notice. I half expected him to declare he was coming with us to the airport, but he didn't. I was relieved it was just

Maddox and me. As soon as the door slid closed, I turned to him. "What the hell did you tell Jeremy?"

"Nothing! He was joking. Except now, by the way we both reacted, he probably knows something." He sighed and his eyes found mine. "I hate lying to him."

"I know you do."

"I want to tell him."

"Maddox," I began. We'd been through this.

"I can't keep lying to him. I just can't. If he didn't suspect something before, I'm pretty sure he does now. And the other guys. They're not blind, Roscoe. And Vancouver was a close call."

"It was."

Blake and Wes had knocked on his door at late o'clock and we'd been lying in bed, all cuddled up. The TV was on and thankfully we were still mostly dressed. I planted myself at the far side of the table with my phone, a notepad, and pen, and Maddox picked up his guitar on his way to answer the door.

They were a bit surprised to see me there at that hour, but we passed it off as a late meeting regarding the trip to South America that was coming up, finalizing any last details. They didn't seem to care too much, more interested in Maddox's guitar. They also didn't seem to notice that my shirt was untucked or that I had to put my shoes on when I left.

If it had been Jeremy, or worse, Ryan or Amber, we'd have been found out for sure.

I sighed and Maddox lifted my arm so he could lean against my chest. "Jeremy won't care," he murmured, snuggling in the best he could in the backseat. "But he'll be really pissed if I hide it from him and keep lying to him.

Then he'll be pissed. And who knows . . . he might cover for us if we need him to."

I chuckled and kissed his cap. There was no point in trying to argue. He was right; he shouldn't lie to his best friend or to the rest of the band. Maybe not the others just yet, but starting with Jeremy would be okay. It would have to be, because Maddox wasn't asking.

He slept for the short ride to the airport. He boarded the plane with the guys, and Amber, Ryan, and I spent the almost three-hour flight to Miami in a meeting with Ambrose. It was actually convenient. There were few interruptions, and a private plane was spacious enough that we could sit and talk comfortably.

Ambrose had a lot on his plate, and I didn't envy him at all. While I just had to focus on Maddox, he had to worry about every member of the crew, staff, equipment, budgets, publicity, and about a hundred other things.

"Give me a rundown on the boys," Ambrose said.

"Blake's knee is holding up so far," Amber said. "But that's likely to change with every concert we do."

Ambrose was concerned. "Julio's been taping it?"

Ryan nodded. "Yep."

"And Luke and Blake want to see Recoleta in Buenos Aires," Amber added.

Ryan agreed. "Yep, and Jeremy mentioned a particular artist in Sao Paulo. I can't remember the name, but I'll get the details and let you know."

"Okay," Ambrose said. "And I'll see what I can do." Then he looked at me. "What about Maddox?"

"Ah, yeah, he's doing fine," I replied, which wasn't an overly helpful answer. I felt scrutinized and guilty for being secretive, for knowing more about Maddox than I should.

Not that I could tell them any of the things I'd learned about him in the two weeks.

"I thought he was looking happier this week," Amber said. "But then today he looked like shit."

"Yeah, he said he didn't sleep very well," I replied. "But he said he feels fine. I got him to laugh a few times this morning, so I'm sure he'll be fine after some decent sleep."

I wasn't telling the whole truth, but it wasn't like I could tell them he didn't sleep very well because I wasn't in bed with him.

Ambrose frowned at me. "Keep me updated. If he needs something to help him sleep, I can have Doctor Hardwick write him up a prescription for something."

Hardwick was the team doctor on tour with us.

"He wouldn't take it even if you did," I said. We all knew Maddox's stance on any kinds of drugs, but maybe Ambrose had some duty of care to suggest it, I wasn't sure. "He'll be fine. Concert's in two days. I'll make sure he gets some sleep."

Christ, Roscoe. Just say that shit out loud.

We talked about the media, about the photos all over the internet. Ambrose talked about my new popularity, though it had died down after the herding-cats comments, it spiked new interest every time some papzz or fan posted a picture of Maddox and me. Getting out of the car, walking into the hotel probably a little closer than we should, talking, smiling, me waiting for Maddox, Maddox waiting for me . . .

Seeing all those photos, one after the other, in front of Ambrose, Amber, and Ryan was a little uncomfortable. Not gonna lie.

Ambrose would never say directly that he approved of the Maddox and Roscoe shipping, but he liked the publicity. It kept the band trending, he said. It keeps the music streaming, he said. It was good for sales, he said.

And I knew then, firsthand and very personally, why Maddox hated being fodder for sales. Not for his music, not because he was a talented song writer and performer, but because of his personal life.

It wasn't a nice feeling.

We arrived in Miami at the same time as a heatwave. Which was less than ideal, to say the least. The concert was in two days and the heatwave was expected to last the week. Hot and humid, yes. But at least no hurricanes were predicted.

When we disembarked the plane and piled into our waiting vans at the private terminal, Maddox climbed into the backseat again, and I was quick to take the seat next to him.

He smiled but still looked tired. "Manage to sleep on the plane?" I asked.

He shook his head. "Nah. You?"

"Nope. It was a three-hour work meeting for me."

He scrunched his nose up. "At least I only had to listen to Wes and Luke whine about not getting laid often enough for two out of the three hours."

I snorted. "Only two?"

"Yeah, I told them to suck each other off in the bathroom and that shut them up."

I chuckled. "No takers?"

"Nope. So I told them to do it in their seats so I could watch."

"Take it that was a no too."

"Wes threw his pillow at me and told me to fuck off."

"Just another day, huh?"

"Hm."

"Did you, uh, did you get a chance to speak to Jeremy?"

Maddox shook his head. "Nope. I couldn't . . . not without the others hearing."

I should have been relieved. I expected to be. But for some strange reason I wasn't. Maybe some part of me wanted someone else to know? Even though it would possibly—likely—change how we worked together. Would they remove me from him? Separate us?

Probably.

He leaned forward and took his jacket off. "God, it's hot and humid."

I took his jacket from him and threw it over the seat in front of us. "Excuse me, driver," I called out. "Can we please have some A/C?"

Maddox sighed and took my hand. "You don't have to look after me all the time."

Technically, I did, but that wasn't the only reason. "I want to."

He scoffed. "Because it's your job."

"Because I want you to be happy."

He glanced over at me and squeezed my hand. "Sorry. I don't mean to imply that your job is . . . that you've been with me, you know, because of your job." Then he shot me another look, his hand frozen in mine. "Unless it is the reason you've been with me—"

"You know it's not. Maddox, you know it's not." I stared into his eyes and tightened my hold on his hand. "That's not what this is. You know that, right?"

He gave the smallest of nods, but I could see the relief on his face, in how his whole body relaxed. "And you know it's the same for me, right?" he murmured. "This isn't a work-only thing . . ." He shook his head, as if he couldn't get his words right. "It's complicated. But you're the one good thing that's happened to me in a long time. And I know that sounds weird and stupid because, look at me." He rolled his eyes. "I'm Maddox Kershaw, face of the biggest band in the world right now." He was quiet for a while and I let him gather his thoughts. In the end, he simply shrugged. "I feel guilty for complaining because compared to other people, I have no right. So I don't like to say anything."

"You can tell me," I whispered. "You've had a dark cloud hanging over you for a while now, Maddox. If you want to talk about it, talk to me."

"A dark cloud?" He made a face. "Is that what you call it?"

"What would you call it?"

"Poor little rich boy syndrome?"

"That's bullshit and you know it."

"That's how the outside world would see it."

"Financial status and popularity have no bearing on mental health. The richest person on the planet can have depression."

"Depression?"

"I'm not saying that about you. It was just an example. And sometimes fame and fortune bring with it a whole other level of problems. You've talked before about being lonely and isolated."

He was quiet again and eventually he put his head against my shoulder and sighed. "You know when we first signed with Platinum and we had that first taste of success, we made a pact. Don't get me wrong, Arlo Kim and the Platinum contract had us sewn up pretty tight with a lot of shit—and they still do. But we had a list. Just us, no legally binding shit, just a promise to each other. If we made it, we wouldn't drink alone and no drugs. How many bands before us were ruined because they turned to drugs and shit when the loneliness became too much?"

I kissed the top of his head and let him speak uninterrupted.

"But I get it now," he admitted quietly. "I understand why they look for some kind of escape."

"Oh, Maddox."

"If we hadn't made that pact, if we hadn't sworn to each other that day all those years ago, I don't know where I'd be right now."

I realized something.

"That night you texted me and said you couldn't sleep," I said, "the first night I came to your room, you were . . . you were tempted."

"I was scared, if I'm being honest. I was . . . I almost left the hotel. I could have found some shit-hole bar and got wasted or taken a hit of something to . . . to just forget. To pretend I was someone else."

I squeezed his hand. "Thank you for texting me. It was brave."

"If you hadda said no, I don't know what I would've done," he mumbled.

"I wouldn't have said no."

"Having you really helps. Just so you know."

Steve called out from the front. "Five minutes, ETA."

I could have groaned at the interruption. "Having you helps me too, Maddox," I whispered. "I know it's complicated and new, and we kinda feel up in the air right now with not knowing where we'll land. But I see the real you. I want you to know that."

He sat up and shifted in his seat, as though my admission of seeing the real him made him uncomfortable.

"I like what I see," I added.

"And what's that?"

"A complex man. A man whom the whole world knows but no one really knows at all."

His dark eyes shot to mine, and I knew I was right.

I decided to lighten the mood a bit. "He's also incredibly talented and funny. I don't think he has any idea as to how good-looking he is." I leaned in and whispered, "And he does things in bed that just about kill me, every time."

The corner of his lip curled upward, just a touch. "Is that right?"

"Hmm. So right."

He chuckled. "About that . . ." He glanced to the front of the van and lowered his voice even more. "We've done a lot of stuff, which I've enjoyed very much."

"I know you have. I was there."

He snorted, his cheeks flushing pink. "But I was wondering if there was any particular reason why we haven't . . . done more."

Oh, hell.

This conversation was either going to kill me with embarrassment or make me hard, so I figured it was best to just put it all out there. "Are you referring to penetrative sex, Maddox."

He chuckled. "Why yes I am, Roscoe."

"Is that something you might be interested in exploring, Mr. Kershaw?"

"Why yes, Mr. Hall, I do believe it is."

I grinned at him and shifted in my seat. "We probably shouldn't be talking about this. If I get out of the van with a boner, the press will have a field day."

He barked out a laugh, but then his dark gaze met mine and his hand slid dangerously up my inner thigh, his fingers brushing me. "We can't have that. Because no one gets to see this but me."

I leaned closer, our noses almost touching, staring into his eyes. "Talk like that and I *will* have a fucking hard-on."

He smirked, his eyes going from my eyes to my mouth back to my eyes. "Roscoe?"

"What?"

"Add condoms and lube to the list of things you need to get today."

The van began to slow. "Approaching the hotel," Steve called out. "And there's a crowd."

Fuck.

I sat back in my seat, trying to not concentrate on my dick. "Think of horrible things, gross and disgusting things." That did no good on killing my semi, so I readjusted my dick before grabbing our backpacks to hold in front of me.

Maddox was still laughing as the door slid open. He grinned as he waved to the screaming fans, and I tried to act inconspicuously to get inside unnoticed. When we filed into the elevator, I held the bags so they covered my crotch, and Maddox was still wearing that shit-eating grin.

"What's so funny?" Wes asked him.

"Nothing," I replied on Maddox's behalf. I was confident I wasn't sporting a raging hard-on anymore and that my backpack was enough, so I shoved Maddox's backpack into his chest. "Carry your own bag."

Maddox just laughed, and we scored a few interesting glances from the others. Steve, standing near the door, looked right at me and smiled.

It was the kind of smile that made me wonder just how much of Maddox's and my conversations he heard in the car. We were pretty well hidden in the backseat, so I don't know how much he could see . . . it wasn't like I paid a great deal of attention to anything but Maddox.

We were shown to our rooms, with reassurances our luggage would be brought up as soon as it arrived. While everyone took a quick break in their rooms, I asked if anyone needed anything, then armed with a list—and Steve and Ivan—I went shopping.

I, at least, had the foresight to change my shirt and put on a cap, not that it made much difference, but having two bodyguards made me hard to miss. Steve was more casual and relaxed, but Ivan was a huge guy that normally got noticed anywhere he went. The fact that he stood like a drill sergeant didn't help much either.

No paparazzi thankfully, but a few people looked twice. It was ridiculous. I was certain they were trying to figure out who I was. Important enough to have a security detail but not immediately recognizable. I was just really freaking grateful no one had noticed me buying condoms and lube.

If Steve noticed or even cared, he never let on. It certainly wasn't uncommon for me, or Amber or Ryan, to run to the nearest store and grab a whole list of things, especially on tour.

Hell, even in LA.

It was what we did for them.

Toothpaste, deodorant, face creams, lip balms, sunscreen, dental floss, ibuprofen, multivitamins, condoms . . . Five guys traveling around the world, someone was bound to forget something or run out of something.

We made it through the store and were almost out the door when two people came up to us. It was a guy and a girl. They looked kinda young, friendly enough. "Hey, you're with Atrous. Roscoe, Maddox's manager, right? Can we have a photo?"

Ivan stepped in. "No photos," he said, his voice deep and final. They barely came up to his shoulders.

I had both hands full. What did they want me to do? Put the bags down and pose with them? For fuck's sake.

"We just want a photo," the girl cried. Other people had stopped and were looking at us, and it was all happening in the doorway of the store.

Now Steve stepped in. There was something about him, the fact that he was shorter than most security, but there was a scary edge to him, and his gaze could cut glass. The young couple backed off and we managed to get into the van and leave without incident, even though I knew, without a doubt, there would be photos or footage somewhere.

Steve took the front seat, as per usual, and Ivan climbed into the back with me. I dumped the shopping bags onto the seat next to me. "Do you think they were a plant?"

Steve answered, "Probably."

A plant was someone or someones paid by a media outlet to cause a scene with a celebrity. A photographer lay in wait and took all the damning photos that earned them a shit ton of money. Basically, the kind of garbage you see sprayed all over cheap tabloid papers and websites.

Thank god it hadn't turned ugly.

Still, someone was going to be pissed when I got back to the hotel.

And I wasn't wrong.

"What do you mean a fucking plant?" Maddox said. "Someone tried to start something with you?" I'd been back at the hotel for all of twenty minutes and was in my room when Maddox had come banging on my door after overhearing Ivan telling someone about our trip.

"We don't know for sure. Probably. They were too aware, too perfect, ready-to-cry-victim type of people."

"Did they get to you? Touch you?" His eyes were wide and fierce. "If they fucking touched you . . ."

I put my hand to his cheek. "No. Ivan and Steve were with me. They didn't get near me." I kissed him softly, trying to calm him down. His concern for me was sweet and his want to protect me played a squeezy game with my heart. "I'm fine."

He growled, still not convinced. "I should have gone with you."

I snorted. "And made everything ten times worse."

He snarled and then pouted. "Fucking fuck."

"Oh. Speaking of that." I picked up the bag from the store that I'd kept aside and turned it over in my hand. "I believe you requested these."

A smile won out. "Do we have to go to that promo tonight? Can't we stay here? Alone. All night?" He took the box of condoms out of the bag. "With these?"

"We have to go. It's a corporate sponsorship thing. It's at some fancy upmarket place on the river. It used to be a warehouse. There's a gallery. There's expensive food, expensive booze. You and the boys can have a few drinks while the sponsors schmooze up to you. You like that kind of thing."

Maddox stared at me like I'd lost my mind. "No, I hate every single thing about that."

I grinned at him because I knew he'd hate every minute. "It'll be fun."

"It'd be much more fun if we stayed in."

I laughed. "True. But still, you're expected to be there."

He sighed, then tossed the condoms onto my suitcase, where I'd made some kind of attempt to unpack a few things. He ran both hands through his black hair, his long black earrings swaying with the movement. "I still can't believe you got harassed at a freaking store. That shit pisses me off."

"I'm fine. Though I must say, you being pissed off on my behalf is kinda hot."

"Fuck off," he said, but he smiled in the end. "And what the hell am I supposed to wear tonight?"

I shrugged as I walked to him. "Whatever's easy for me to get you out of. Keep the earrings though." I lifted his chin and kissed him. "Now go get cleaned up. We leave in forty-five minutes."

WE WERE all in the common room waiting for Maddox, of course. Everyone was standing around an iPad watching the footage of me leaving the store, how Ivan intervened and how Steve ended it. It was actually kinda funny to watch Steve step in and see the couple both take a step back.

"It was definitely a set up," Luke said. "Look at how well-positioned the guy with the camera is."

"And it was uploaded right after," Blake added.

It certainly seemed like it.

"Look at how quick they back up when Steve gets involved," Wes said with a laugh. "He must have given them the just-fucking-try-it eyes."

Jeremy laughed too. "Yep. The fuck-around-and-find-out eyes. My mother can stop people with that look."

"What are we watching?" Maddox asked. I hadn't noticed him walk in. But holy hell, I noticed him now.

He wore tight black jeans with more rips in them than denim, and a black V-neck T-shirt that looked so soft, I wanted to touch it. It was half-tucked in at the front, his belt buckle was black and shiny, matching his boots. He wore his usual black cap that was hotter than it had any right to be. He'd kept the long black earrings, four in each ear, just like I'd asked him to.

He was so fucking hot, all I could do was stare. Until Jeremy nudged me.

Fuck.

I shook my head and pretended my phone was the most important thing I'd ever seen.

"About time you showed up," Blake said, giving Maddox a shove.

He shoved him back with a laugh. "Fuck off. It takes time to look this good."

"Oh, please," Wes scoffed. "You wake up like that."

Jeremy was still staring at me.

He knew. I was certain of it.

I pretended not to notice. "Vehicles are waiting. Let's go."

Maddox was now staring at the iPad. He watched the footage, then he stared at me. I pretended not to notice that either.

Ryan walked in and clapped his hands. "Come on. Chariots are waiting."

I held the door as everyone filed out and made their way to the elevators. "You said it was nothing," Maddox said, apparently not caring who heard.

"Because it was nothing," I replied, cutting him a glance that told him to shut it.

"When I asked that you have your own detail, I thought it was precautionary. Not a necessity."

"Steve and Ivan had it handled," Jeremy said.

"So no one gives a shit that Roscoe now needs his own

security? What's next? Our families? Your ex-girlfriends? Grandparents? That'll be nice."

Jeremy, Wes, Blake, and Luke all looked at him, then at each other. He had a point, and when he put it like that, they knew it.

Steve, who had stood silently by the elevator doors, said, "I've already spoken to Mr. Ambrose." He looked at the boys. "Maddox is right."

The elevator doors opened and everyone piled in . . . except for Maddox. So I stopped, and so did Steve. "We'll take the next one," Maddox said as the doors slid closed.

The elevator next to it dinged and the doors opened. Steve held the doors and thankfully it was empty. I swiped my card and pressed the basement button before I turned to face him. "Maddox," I said calmly. "I said I was fine."

"This time," he said, his eyes full of fire. "You were fine this time. She was close enough to touch you, Roscoe. And close enough to touch you is close enough to hurt you. She could have had a gun or—"

The elevator came to a stop at a floor halfway down, and as the doors opened, Steve casually stepped in front of us. A middle-aged couple stepped in and gave us a smile, though Maddox pulled his cap down and stared at the floor.

Our conversation was over, for now. A conversation in front of Steve. A conversation between a band member and their manager.

Except it wasn't. We weren't just that anymore.

Maddox's anger at the situation was born from concern, which meant he cared. So, considering Steve had his back to us, I put my hand on Maddox's back and rubbed gentle circles. His shirt was as soft as it looked.

The elevator stopped at the lobby and the couple got out. Steve quickly hit the close-door button and he leaned against the wall. I didn't move my hand from Maddox's back . . . not fast enough, anyway. Somehow reassuring Maddox meant more than letting Steve see.

"We're increasing security," Steve said. "I'm meeting a team tomorrow to stay with us for the South American leg. The venue tonight has its own security. As part of the promotional deal, they have to secure the clientele."

Maddox gave a nod. "Thanks."

The doors opened to the basement, Steve ushered us into the last van and closed the door behind us, and the three cars rolled out. I understood Maddox's concern. I really did.

A few years before, in the middle of a red-carpet event, a celebrity was hit with a water bomb. It made the news all over the world for the simple fact that it could have so easily been not-water. What if it had been some kind of acid or a poison? Or some disgusting bodily fluid, or something that person was deadly allergic to? They'd been lucky . . . it had been water.

But it was a bit of a wake-up call. It changed a lot of security standards, for very good reason.

And Maddox was right. That couple at the store had got close enough to touch me, close enough to harm me. They could have hurt Ivan or Steve too. They were trained to know how to handle that, but I wasn't.

I never thought I'd have to deal with this shit.

"You okay?" I asked Maddox.

He nodded. Kind of. "Better, now that I know they're increasing security. Christ, Roscoe . . . seeing how close they got to you . . ."

I put my hand on his thigh. "I know. And I appreciate your concern. I do."

He slid his hand over mine and slung his leg over mine. "No one touches you but me."

I rubbed my hand up his leg. "Is that right?"

He smirked with an edge in his eye. "Yes."

"And this outfit you chose to wear tonight," I murmured. "Is it not a little sexy for a promotional photo event? Were you sewn into these jeans?"

His grin widened. "Consider it foreplay."

I laughed. "Foreplay?"

"Yep. You'll be thinking about taking me out of these jeans all night, so when we get back to the hotel, you won't want to do anything else."

Goddammit.

He chuckled. "You thinking about it already?"

I laughed and shifted in my seat. "You play a savage game."

He smirked, but not for long. "Is this a game for you, Roscoe?"

Well, shit.

"No. Is this a game to you, Maddox?"

"No." He played with my fingers that were resting on his thigh. "No, it's not."

Christ. Was this some kind of admission of his feelings?

"How long do we have to be here tonight?" he asked, changing the topic.

"It officially ends at ten."

"So we leave at ten, right?"

I chuckled. "You're the boss."

THE EVENT DRAGGED. Yes, the telecom company paid a fortune to have Atrous be the face of their product. Yes, it was a huge deal. Yes, this had been planned for almost a year. And yes, the food was lovely, the venue was gorgeous, the service was exceptional. Neil Ambrose worked the crowd and sponsors like the pied piper, and there really was no wonder why he was the one in charge.

But watching Maddox smile and laugh, pose for photo-shoots, watching him charm every man and woman in the place, watching people vying for his attention, his affection, made me want to walk up to him in front of *everyone*, take a hold of his beautiful face, and kiss him like I knew he liked.

And knowing it was very likely that when we got back to the hotel, I was going to take him to bed, that I would be inside him, made me want to leave.

I'd stayed with Amber and Ryan most of the night, making sure none of the boys needed anything, of course. But it was well managed. These sorts of functions were extremely well catered for, no one wanted for anything. They also had professional photographers who were the only ones allowed so we didn't need to run interference. Our own security stuck to the wings, and all in all it was a pleasant evening.

But by God, I wanted to take Maddox and leave. It was almost ten o'clock, but every minute felt like thirty.

"Hey," Jeremy said, bumping shoulders with me. I was leaning against the wall, staying out of the way with Ryan and Amber while keeping an eye on everyone. I hadn't seen him come over, and I hadn't noticed Ryan and Amber leave. They were talking to Wes and Luke, smiling about some-thing, and I'd been standing there watching Maddox talk to some exec.

"Oh, hey," I replied, giving Jeremy my full attention. "Wassup?"

"Was going to ask you the same thing."

I was confused for a second. "About what?"

"About what's going on between you and Maddox."

Oh.

I felt blood drain from my face. "What do you mean?"

Jeremy laughed quietly and turned to where Maddox stood. "I know my boy," he replied coolly. "And I know when he's getting some. Now tonight, he keeps searching the room for you and you can't take your eyes off him. It doesn't take Picasso to paint this picture, Roscoe."

I tried to swallow and couldn't.

"Jeremy, I—"

"Hey," Maddox interrupted us. He gave us a cautious smile. "What's going on here?"

Jeremy clapped his hand on Maddox's shoulder. "Roscoe here was just about to tell me how long you two have been a thing." He grinned at Maddox. "And then you're going to tell me why you never told me."

CHAPTER ELEVEN

MADDOX SHOT ME A WILD LOOK, shocked, then he looked at Jeremy and he sighed like he was relieved. "I'll tell you everything," he said. "But not here."

Considering where we were, that was a very good idea.

"So I'm right?" Jeremy asked.

Maddox's reply was quick and definite. "Yes."

"And you never told me because . . ."

"Because I asked him not to," I answered.

Jeremy met my eyes and nodded slowly. Someone walked past us and Jeremy gave them a bright, albeit fake, smile before turning back to Maddox. "So the others were just talking to Ryan and Amber about hitting a club. Steve's gonna flip his shit, but whatever. Don't suppose you want to join us?"

Maddox shook his head. "Jer, I'm peopled out."

Jeremy nodded. He knew three hours was about Maddox's quota of being his public persona. "Didn't think so."

"If you want me to go, I'll go," Maddox amended.

Jeremy sighed and put his hand on Maddox's arm.

"Nah, it's okay. I get it. But I'll tell you what," he said. "I'm riding with you and Roscoe to the nightclub. You can drop me off and it will give you fifteen minutes to tell me everything."

Maddox nodded. "Deal."

Jeremy clapped his hands together and grinned. "Good. I'll go let them know." And he wandered back to the others, leaving me alone with Maddox.

Maddox shrugged. "Well, I wanted to tell him."

So that was that.

Ten minutes later, after Steve had organized what needed organizing, the promotional evening was over and it was announced that Atrous was leaving. With security tight, we made our way from the gallery through the restaurant and bar to the waiting vans. The crowd was actually great, very respectful and polite. Though I doubted the nightclub would be the same.

We filed into the van. Maddox climbed straight into the backseat and Jeremy followed, sitting beside him. I sat near the door but turned to face them the best I could.

Jeremy waited for the door to close. He looked at both of us in turn. "You've got fifteen minutes."

"I wanted to tell you," Maddox began.

"How long?"

"Since this tour."

Jeremy nodded slowly. "I thought so. Something was different between you. There's been more staring than usual, more private conversations."

"It is different," Maddox answered quietly.

"And it's complicated," I added. "Obviously people can't know."

Jeremy stared at me like I was stupid. "Well, it might help if you don't spend every waking minute staring at him like it's the first time you've seen him. Because anyone in that room tonight could have seen it. Or earlier tonight when he first came into the common room and I had to nudge you to pick your tongue up off the floor. And, I might add, the way you've been looking at him isn't exactly PG."

I tried to respond to that, but what the hell could I say?

Maddox chuckled. "Mmm. How exactly have you been looking at me, Roscoe?"

I shot him a glare and Jeremy put his hands up. "Don't try being cute. I'm still pissed. Why didn't you tell me?"

"Because I'll probably be fired," I answered. "Or I'll be Platinum Entertainment's newest janitor."

Maddox glared right back at me. "And I told him I won't let that happen."

I was going to argue that point, again, but figured this wasn't the place or time.

"We had a deal," Jeremy said. "No secrets. That was the deal."

Maddox shook his head, his teeth gritted. "This is different."

"How is it?" Jeremy pressed. "Because it's you?"

"No." Maddox shook his head. "Because if Ambrose finds out, if they don't threaten to fire him, then they will sure as hell separate us. And I can't let that happen, Jeremy, because he's the one real thing in my life."

Holy fuck.

The one real thing.

Holy, *holy* fuck.

Maddox's face flashed in the passing streetlights. He was staring at Jeremy, pointing his finger at me. "He's a fucking light when everything else is dark, that's what he is. You know this!"

Jeremy stared.

"Maddox," I whispered.

"No, Roscoe," he shot back at me. "I know what you're going to say. You're going to defend the company, say you knew this would become an issue. We talked about this."

"And you dismissed my concerns."

"Because some things mean more. That's why. I don't give a fuck what Arlo Kim thinks, or Ambrose. Or the fans, or the media. I care what *you* think. And it'd be a whole lot nicer if you defended me on this. You're supposed to stand with me on this."

"I do. I am on your side." I wanted to touch him so badly, to hold him. "You know I am."

"And what about me?" Jeremy said. "What about the band?"

Maddox's eyes went to him. "What about you? Or the band. This doesn't change anything."

"Everything you do affects us. Christ, Maddox, haven't you learned that yet?" He was pissed and I understood. His best friend had basically lied to him for weeks, and me too, a manager he was supposed to be able to trust. But Maddox had spilled some of his heart here tonight, and that was not easy for him to do. Maybe Jeremy realized this because his tone was softer when he spoke again. "Everything you do affects us, Madz. And I know how long you've wanted this."

Maddox's gaze darted to me, ever so briefly before he looked out the window.

How long he'd wanted what, exactly? Just someone to be with? Or me in particular?

"What if it ends badly?" Jeremy asked quietly. "We're on tour. We have a fuckton of shows to do, a million miles to travel. We can't have fights or tension between you two if things go to shit."

"They won't," Maddox replied. He turned his face to me, then to Jeremy. "They won't."

Jeremy looked at me. "What about you?"

What about me? Christ. Wasn't it obvious? If things went to shit, I *would* be the newest janitor. But then I looked at Maddox, who was waiting for my answer. At his pale face in the dark, his big brown eyes, full of hope and fear. "I won't hurt him, if that's what you're asking."

"Two minutes, ETA," Steve called out from the front. There was a very good chance he'd heard this whole conversation.

A few long seconds passed by in silence. "Jeremy," Maddox said, his voice strained. "I need your support on this." His hands were clenched, his breathing shallow. "I can't have you fight me on this."

Jeremy sighed. "I'm happy that you're happy. I only ever want you to be happy. You know that. But it's not just you and me, and it's not just you and Roscoe. It's bigger than that, right? It's bigger than us."

Maddox frowned. "We're allowed to be happy, aren't we? We've given up so much of our lives, of ourselves, Jer. And yeah, we signed up for this, and this level of fame won't last forever. We should be grateful for the fame and fortune, blah, blah, blah. I've heard all that bullshit before. But what's the point to any of it if it's killing us?"

Oh, Maddox.

The vehicle slowed and we could see neon lights and crowds out the windows.

"Don't say anything to the others tonight," Maddox murmured. He looked defeated, and it broke my heart. "I'll tell them. Tomorrow, or something."

Jeremy patted Maddox's thigh. "I'm not gonna fight you on this, Madz. I'm just concerned, that's all. But at the end of the day, we stick together, right? If it's what you want, then that's all there is to it."

Maddox nodded, a little happier but not completely sold.

Jeremy looked to me then. "Roscoe, I'm gonna say this as his best friend and not as one of the band members. I probably expected more from you, not gonna lie. And if you do fuck him around, I'll request you to be *my* manager, and I'll make your life so miserable, you'll request that janitor's job."

"Jeremy," Maddox mumbled. "Christ."

Jeremy grinned. "I have to say shit like that. It's my call of duty as your best friend."

I chuckled as Steve opened the door. Bright lights, humid heat, and noise invaded the van, and Jeremy got to his feet. "Don't keep him up late. Busy day tomorrow." He grinned and patted my shoulder as he got out. "And don't wait up."

The door closed and Robbie got in the front. He turned to talk to us. "I'm to take you back to the hotel and come back. That all right with you?"

"Sounds great," I replied. Robbie gave the driver a nod and we began to move, so I quickly slid into the seat next to Maddox. "You okay?"

He nodded. "Yeah. I guess. He took it pretty well." He shrugged. "Except for the part where he threatened you."

I laughed quietly. "I'm glad he's looking out for you."

Maddox sighed and let his head fall back on the head-rest, still looking at me. He held out his hand, which I took and threaded our fingers. "I'm tired. Functions and publicity events are so draining. Three hours felt like an eternity."

"You were great tonight. All eyes were on you."

He smirked. "Apparently yours too. You looking at me was what tipped Jeremy off about us."

I laughed, not even caring that I blushed. "You have a . . . certain charm that I find attractive."

He slung his leg over mine again. "And by charm, you mean my ass in these jeans."

I brought my face in close to his. "Not just your ass. You have no idea of the power you hold when you walk into a room."

His gaze flickered down to my lips, then back to my eyes. "As soon as we get back to your room, I'm handing every ounce of power I have over to you," he murmured, voice low. "And you can do whatever you want to me."

Fucking hell.

"And Roscoe?"

"Yeah?"

"It better include your dick in my ass. Just sayin'."

I groaned at his words, the heat in his eyes, the heat in my balls.

"You're not too tired?"

He raised an unimpressed eyebrow.

It made me smirk. "I know how these nights wear you out. You can be on stage in front of eighty thousand people all night long, but three hours in a room of a few dozen people drains you."

"Being on stage is easy. There's a barrier, a performance. But up close and personal like tonight, those people are hard work. They all want something. They all want the famous me, on show, all the time. It's like a close-contact meet and greet. I've never been good with crowds of people up close like that. It's draining."

"I know."

"You *do* know. You're one of the few who do. And that's

why," he said slowly, "you're going to take me to bed. Make me forget the people, the responsibility, the rest of the world."

I lifted his hand to my lips and kissed his knuckles. "I can make you forget everything."

Maddox groaned. "Robbie?" he called out. "How far out are we?"

"Two minutes," came his reply.

"Can you hurry? I need to piss."

I nudged him. "You should have said."

He looked at me. "I don't need to piss. Jesus, Roscoe. The fuck you been? You just told me you're gonna fuck me and you think I need to piss?"

I chuckled. "Sorry."

"Mm, well, now you mention it, I kinda do need to piss, but that's not the reason I want to hurry."

The van had barely come to a stop before Robbie was out and had our door open. He ushered us into the elevator lobby and pressed the button. "I can take you two up to your floor," he said.

"Nah, it's okay. We've got it from here," Maddox said. "You better get back and make sure Wes isn't dancing on the bar half-naked."

The doors opened and we stepped inside. I waved my keycard and pressed our floor number, Robbie waved us off. "Wouldn't be the first time he's done that."

"No, it would not," I mumbled as the doors closed.

Maddox pulled me against him by the waistband of my jeans. "Speaking of first times . . ."

I kissed him then, pushed up against the mirror in the elevator. He opened his mouth for me, lifted his leg to hitch around my hip. I kissed him deep and he welcomed it. I ground my hips against him and he groaned.

The elevator doors opened and I shot back, not realizing we were on our floor already. Maddox laughed, grabbed my hand, and led me to my room.

He walked in first, tossed his hat, and pulled off his shirt before he disappeared into the bathroom. I heard the toilet seat go up and then the sound of him peeing. "Ugh. Do you know hard it is to piss with a semi?" he asked.

I laughed as I sat at the table and undid my boots. He appeared a minute later, his jeans undone. His sculptured body rippled in the dim light, his sleeve of tattoos, his long earrings, his pink lips . . .

He walked over and put his foot on my thigh. "Can you please help me with my boots?"

I did, of course, but this wasn't about his boots. This was about him standing over me, with his pants undone, and his crotch in my face. When I pulled off his second boot, he straddled my legs and sat on my lap, grinding and rocking. He smiled as he kissed me. "Make me forget," he murmured against my lips.

I gripped his hips and stood up, carrying him to the bed. I laid him on his back gently and he smiled. I pulled his jeans off and he watched, delighted, as I stripped off my clothes. His gaze raked down my body and he licked his lips. "Fuck yes."

I found the condoms and lube he'd thrown toward my suitcase earlier and I tossed them up onto the bed beside him. He ripped open the box, leaving some condoms and the lube within easy reach. He watched me roll one onto my cock while he stroked himself, then he turned over onto his belly, spread his thighs, and raised his ass.

Right, then.

He wanted to forget, he wanted to experience that place

where nothing exists but pleasure, and so help me God, I wanted to take him there.

I took care of him, massaging and gentle touches, teasing and tempting, and I kissed every inch of skin. I slicked him up and stretched him until he begged me, threatened me with "Please, please, please stop teasing and start fucking."

He gripped the comforter, rolling his hips. "Roscoe, I need more. I need you. I need you inside me. Give it to me, please."

I pulled my fingers out of him, added a lot more lube, then positioned myself over him. I pressed the blunt head of my cock to his hole and leaned over him, desperate to push in but holding back.

I kissed the back of his head, his neck, and sucked his ear into my mouth as I pushed inside him.

He was tight and hot, slick and welcoming. He felt so good it took every ounce of control for me not to ram into him. I kept my weight on my elbows, kissed his shoulder, his neck, giving him time. "Oh god, you feel so good."

Maddox whined and his breathing was rough. He pushed his forehead into the mattress, arching his back. "Fuck."

I stilled, half inside him, desperate for more. "Are you okay?" I breathed.

He moaned but I couldn't tell if it was good or bad, so I slowly pulled out. "What . . . what the fuck?" he cried.

I flipped him over and while he was still trying to find which way was up, and where to put his legs, I lifted one knee up to his chest and pinned one hand above his head. His mouth fell open, his pupils dilated. "Now I can see you," I murmured before kissing him, hard and deep.

He brought his other knee up and I pinned his free

hand above his head as I pushed back into him. His eyes rolled back in his head, his back arched, and he welcomed me inside his body.

I kissed him, my tongue finding his, and he groaned deep in his throat as I began to thrust slow and deep.

This was better. This was so much better.

I could see his face. I could watch his eyes, see every flicker of emotion, every ounce of pleasure. His cheeks flushed pink, strands of his black hair fell across his forehead, his neck corded with the strain . . .

I needed a better word than beautiful.

I let go of his hands and cupped his face, sweeping his cheekbone with a thumb. "God, you feel so good," I breathed, trying not to thrust too hard.

He brought his arms down and gripped my ass, pulling me in harder. "Fuck, Roscoe," he groaned, pushing his head back. "Right there. Oh, god. More."

So I gave him more. I drove into him, lifting his legs a little higher, and his eyes went wide, his mouth opened in surprise. He reached for his cock, pumping and sliding as I fucked him. His body jerked, his back arched, and he cried out as he came. His ass clamped around my cock as he painted stripes of come across his belly.

I didn't stop. I didn't give him a second to breathe. I kept fucking him through his orgasm, chasing my own pleasure until it became too much. He was too tight, too hot, too slick, too much, and I was so far inside him, buried to the hilt. I came so hard . . . so fucking hard.

"Oh my god," he gasped, bringing me in for a kiss. He thrust his tongue into my mouth and I convulsed as my orgasm ran its course. The room was spinning; every synapse buzzed and sizzled.

The only thing in the world in that moment was him.

He held me as tight as I held him, and we were a sweaty, sticky, panting mess, yet neither one of us moved. Reluctantly, I pulled out of him, took care of the condom, and quickly rolled us onto our sides and wrapped him up in my arms. I kissed the side of his head, nuzzling into his hair. "You okay?"

"Mmm," he hummed, sleepy and content.

I rubbed circles on his back. "We should shower."

"Mm-mm. More circles."

Smiling, I drew more patterns on his back, lightly scratching blunt fingernails in swirls and circles. I could have so easily fallen asleep right there, and I was pretty sure he was close to nodding off too. So I pulled back, cupped his face, and kissed him. Soft, with a hint of tongue. "Steaming hot shower?"

"Only if you wash me," he murmured into my neck. "And I think I'll stay here tonight."

"Oh, is that right?"

He opened his eyes, heavy lidded, smiling. "Gonna make fucking me again at three in the morning a whole lot easier if I'm still here."

I laughed and rolled off the bed, heading for the shower. Yes, I washed him, yes, I dried him, and yes, I went back to bed with him, held him in my arms, and drifted off to sleep.

And yes, I fucked him again at some ungodly time. He stayed on his front and I rolled on top of him, spread his legs, and buried myself in him, over and over. Over and over, again and again, and he writhed and rocked, murmured nonsensical things. He gripped the pillows and the sheets, he lost himself, gave himself over.

He wanted me to make him forget everything, and that was what I gave him. I took him to that place where nothing else matters. And when we were done, I took care of him, cleaned him up.

He smelled like me, and I smelled like him, and that pleased some primal part of me. He snuggled into me, clung to me, and I loved every second of it. I ignored the unfamiliar knock of my heart, the foolish butterflies in my belly, and closed my eyes.

———

ATROUS WAS in the news again the next morning. The promotional gig had been a hit. Approved photos were posted and the reviews were good. There were a few fan pics of us leaving the venue and getting into the vans but nothing that hadn't been seen a thousand times before.

The boys' night out at the club had been a highlight on local Miami TV channels, and social media, of course. Photos of them arriving at the club, photos of them inside, drinking and dancing, laughing, even though every article mentioned Maddox's noticeable absence—and mine— overall it was pretty good.

There was no mention or any photos of the boys bringing company back to the hotel, so that was a blessing. Given the lewd conversation at breakfast, the fact no one was photographed with them was clearly a testament to Amber and Ryan's management skills. There were smug smiles and knowing smirks pertaining to the action they got, and Maddox just laughed along with them. He made jokes and teased them, like it was any other day . . . like he hadn't had his brains fucked out twice.

Jeremy tried though. He shoved Maddox. "Shame you didn't get any last night," he said, his grin wide. "Plenty of hot guys there. You totally could have had your pick."

Maddox screwed his nose up. "And been rewarded with crabs. No thanks. Speaking of that." He looked over to Amber, Ryan, and I but waved his hand at his bandmates. "Can we get them deloused before tonight. Or fumigated or something. I have to share a dressing room with them."

They piled on him, literally. He ended up flat on the couch with the four of them piled on top of him, squashed and laughing, but it was funny. And at least it changed the subject.

We spent the day at the stadium doing stage rehearsals and sound checks, and after a group session in the gym, it was an early dinner and we called it a night. Miami was hot and humid, and after partying the night before and working hard all day, everyone was beat and turned in early.

I knocked on Maddox's door just after nine. He smiled like the cat just about to eat the canary as I entered, and he locked the door behind me. "I've been thinking about you all day," he purred. "Or, more to the point, what you did to me last night and what you can do to me again tonight."

I pulled a seat out at the table and sat down. "About that . . ."

He stopped; his smile faded. "What about it? Oh Christ, you're here to tell me you're done, aren't you?"

"I'm done?" I asked, quite frankly a little stunned. We'd had such a good day. "No. Why would you think that?"

"You have that apologetic look on your face. That look that says this is for your own benefit, even though it's not."

I stood up and took his face in my hands. "I'm not done with you, not by a long shot, okay?" He nodded, though there was a genuine vulnerability in his eyes that hurt to see. "Believe me, Maddox, last night was . . . special to me."

He smiled then, the kind that sparked light in his eyes. It didn't last long. "There's a but coming."

He really did know me. "But I don't think we should have a repeat of last night tonight, or any night before a concert."

He blinked. "What?"

"I don't want you to be sore when you're on stage. You give two hundred percent on that stage, and I don't want to risk you overexerting yourself. If you're a bit sore or whatever, then—"

"Oh my god, you're serious. Roscoe, I'm fine."

He was affronted and possibly a little offended, which was not what I wanted at all. I took his hand and sat on the dining chair, pulling him into my lap. He pouted a little, though he did put his arm around my neck. "Listen, please. I don't want you to be mad at me," I began. "But we need to be responsible. We can't give anyone a reason to suspect anything to begin with, but we also can't give anyone cause to separate us. And it'll just be the night before each concert, that's all. And that doesn't mean we can't do anything else, baby. I can think of a dozen different ways to get you off without fucking you into the mattress."

Maddox's smile was slow spreading. "Hold on, wait up." He wiggled his bony ass on my lap. "Two things. First one, I want to hear more about the dozen different ways to get me off. Honestly, you probably should have just led with that and saved us both some trouble. And second . . . you called me baby."

I laughed. "Did I? I don't remember that."

Keeping his arm around my shoulder, he straddled me and forced my face up so he could kiss me. "Are you taking it back?"

I smiled against his lips. "Not at all . . ."

He pinched my chin between his thumb and finger. "Say it again."

"Which part?"

He pinched my chin harder and rolled his hips, grinding himself on my crotch. "You know which part. Say it again."

I tried to kiss him but he pulled back just far enough so I couldn't, so I gripped his hips instead. "I can make you come a dozen different ways."

He snarled. "Wrong answer. I mean, it's not wrong, but it's not the answer I'm talking about and you know it. So maybe I'll decline your offer and you can leave." He went to stand up but I grabbed him and held him tight.

"Baby," I said, smiling up at him. "I can get you off in ways you've never imagined, baby. I could kiss you all night long, baby. I wanna sleep in your bed, in your arms, all night long, baby."

His smile was possibly the most beautiful, most genuine I'd seen on him in all the years I'd known him. He leaned down and kissed me. "You're lucky, Roscoe. Right answer."

"I tried."

He kissed me again. "Hmm. Now . . . what about this dozen ways to get me off that I've never imagined. I'm very interested in hearing about those."

I gripped his hips and stood up, carrying him. He laughed as I threw him onto the bed and crawled up his body. "Okay, so," I said, undoing his jeans. "This is number one."

IT WAS HOTTER the next day than it had been all week, and to make matters worse, it was concert day. There'd been measures put in place for the crowd, water stations and misters to name a few, and we'd made sure we had extra ice packs, water, and electrolyte pouches for the band and stage crew.

It was going to be brutal.

The dressing room and green room were all air conditioned, but directly backstage was not. It was a stadium so the stage was open to the elements, and even though it was an evening concert, it was still far too hot and humid.

The call was made not to run through a full dress rehearsal, and there were some last minute changes to the choreography. They needed to cut their exertion down. Those boys could, in a three-hour concert, dance and run the equivalent to an eight-mile race.

"Be careful tonight," I whispered to Maddox. They were all dressed and ready to go, we could hear the roar of the crowd, and I was helping him with his earpiece. "It's hotter than hell out there."

He gave me a nod. "Yes, Dad."

"If you want me to play daddy, that means I get to spank you," I murmured, and he barked out a laugh. "Don't overdo it. Pace yourself."

He grinned. "I'm sorry, what was that? You said the words daddy and spank, and I got sidetracked."

I sighed and went to help Wes with the cord on his earpiece. "Take it easy tonight," I said, aiming for them all to hear. I had to lift the back of Wes's shirt and feed the cord through. Why on earth he'd put his shirt on first, I'd never know. But Maddox was soon beside me, reaching up Wes's shirt and pulling the cord through. He shot me a very quick look that I couldn't read. Was he pissed off? Was he worried what others might think? I helped all the bandmates with their gear, with their outfit changes, with whatever they needed help with. It was my job.

I could feel someone's eyes on me, and when I looked

up, Jeremy was watching. He was kind of smirking, a bit surprised, maybe. Until Maddox shot him a glare too, and then Jeremy began to sing a not too familiar song. It certainly wasn't one of theirs. He danced all sexy-like and Luke hollered, "Sing it, queen," and Maddox shoved Jeremy so hard he almost fell. But they all laughed and were soon hyping each other up as they walked through the corridors to the stage entrance.

Amber, Ryan, and I followed, of course. Ryan was discussing something with the stage crew manager; Amber was giving the boys final instructions about the new set breaks.

I was trying to place that damn song . . . I couldn't really concentrate over the noise and the voices, and the damn heat back here was stifling. But the way Jeremy danced, the higher pitch, the catchy tune . . .

It took me a second.

It was "Jealous" by Beyonce.

Jealous.

Was Maddox jealous because I lifted Wes's shirt?

Holy shit.

The roar of the crowd got my attention, and I snapped out of my own head in enough time to watch the five of them take their place on the elevated platform to rise up through the stage. The crowd went off like a sonic boom.

"They're not going to take it easy," Amber yelled over the noise.

I shook my head. "No, they won't. Jeremy and Maddox in particular."

She made a less-than-impressed face, her brow beaded with sweat. It was hot back here. Too damn hot. They'd brought in industrial-sized fans that kept the air moving, but it was hardly enough. The stage crew were already red-faced and sweating; they ran, lifted, pushed, carried non-stop behind the scenes, and when the first set was done, they did it in triple time.

The boys came off stage for a change of shirts and much needed drinks, dripping with sweat like they'd been put under a hose. I handed them each an energy gel pouch. "Have these."

They washed them down with bottles of water in between getting wet shirts peeled off, patted dry, and fresh shirts put on. Wardrobe, hair, and make-up staff moved around them, maneuvered them like mannequins, and with the precision of a race car pit crew, they were back on stage.

Amber, Ryan, and I watched them on the live-feed screens for the whole next set. They still gave one hundred percent, they sang and danced, and despite the heat and humidity, the crowd roared and cheered.

But I could tell it was taking its toll. Jeremy bent over with his hands on his knees after one song, Blake was flat on his back, and Luke helped him to his feet and gave him a bit of a cuddle. All the Bluke fans screamed, but the truth was Blake was struggling.

And Maddox . . . well, he danced harder and sang harder than any of them, like he always did. He was flushed, his hair was drenched, his wet shirt clung to him, giving the entire stadium audience a pretty visual. The white fabric didn't leave much to the imagination.

The crowd fucking loved it.

They drank all their bottles of water, spraying the crowd as they continued to dance and sing, but at the end of the second set when they came off, all five of them almost collapsed. I passed out more of the energy gel pouches as they were wiped down. They looked like they'd all climbed out of a swimming pool, that's how wet they were.

We had ice packs on the backs of their necks, and the hair crew didn't even bother. Make-up was more of a clean-up at this point, and fresh T-shirts were pulled over their heads.

"You have to slow down," Ryan told them. "Forget the choreography. Just keep it calm. You've got five songs to go."

The five of them had their heads down, their shoulders heaved with ragged breaths. I grabbed a towel and patted down Maddox's hair and the back of his neck. "Take it easy," I said. I meant it for all of them, though for Maddox in particular. "Just sing. Slow it down."

"They came to see us perform," Maddox replied. "They didn't pay full price for half a show."

I dabbed a line of sweat rolling down from his temple. "They didn't pay to see you pass out."

"Professional performers know how to adapt to circumstances," Amber said.

I managed to half dab Wes's forehead when Maddox pulled the towel from my hand. He ran it over his face and stood up before he tossed it to Wes. "Five songs. We just gotta get through five songs. Come on, guys. Let's do this."

They each got to their feet and put their hands in the middle. "Atrous," they said in unison, though it was hardly a war cry.

Five songs may as well have been five hundred.

Of course, they didn't slow down, they didn't stop dancing. If anything, Maddox danced harder, sang louder, like he had something to prove. They gave one hundred percent and he gave 110.

But they got to the fifth song. The last song. I don't know how, but they did. Jeremy pulled his shirt off over his head to a massive roar and threw it into the crowd. They waved goodbye as the crowd cheered, they stood on the center elevator about to disappear into the stage. Like they always did, like they'd done a thousand times.

The stage lowered and the five of them were doubled over, resting hands on their knees. Jeremy fell to his ass, panting, sweating like I'd never seen. Maddox stood to his full height, turned, and swayed. Drenched and red-faced, he made eye contact with me. He reached for a pole, missed it completely, and crumpled to the floor.

I RAN to him and rolled him onto his back, and he groaned. His eyes were half closed, he was pale, his hair stuck to his face. "Maddox," I said, gently tapping his face. He stirred and moaned. Heat was radiating off him but his skin felt cool to the touch.

"I need water and ice," I yelled. "Now!"

I lifted him off the platform and laid him on the ground, right there, backstage in front of everyone. He was dead weight, offered no resistance. His head fell back, and his arms were limp. I tapped his face again. "Maddox."

Amber was there with ice packs and wet towels. She put an ice pack on his forehead, and I shoved one up under his shirt to lay it on his chest.

Maddox stirred and tried to sit up. I put my hand on his chest. "Stay there," I urged.

Jeremy was suddenly beside me. "Is he okay?"

"We need to cool him down," I said. Christ, it was hot back here. And there were too many people standing around watching, and there was no freaking air. "We need to get him into the air conditioning."

Without waiting, I picked him up and carried him through the crowd of worried onlookers.

I heard Amber yell, "Where is the fucking doctor?"

I don't know who she yelled at, but she was right. He was our team doctor and he was nowhere in sight.

Wes held the door open to the dressing room and I ran in, laying Maddox on the floor. It was so much cooler in here already, but we needed to get Maddox's core temperature down before this heat exhaustion became heat stroke.

"We need to get his boots and socks off," I said, and Blake and Luke made quick work of them. With my hand at the back of Maddox's neck, I half sat him up and pulled his sopping wet shirt up and over his head, feeding his arms through it like a parent does with a toddler. I gently laid him back down and put the ice pack back on his chest, and Ryan was there now with an ice pack on Maddox's forehead and one under his neck. I unbuttoned his pants about to pull them off when Hardwick raced in, coming to his knees beside me. He was a nice guy, about forty, and looked a bit like Denzel Washington.

But he should have been here already, and I was about to rip him a new asshole until I saw him. He looked like he'd been in the same swimming pool as Maddox.

"Sorry, we've got crew members down as well," he said, not taking his eyes off Maddox. He was feeling for a pulse. "Is he coherent? Has he been talking?"

"'M okay," Maddox mumbled. His breathing was still labored, like he couldn't get enough air.

"Should I call an ambulance?" I asked, assuming someone hadn't already. I looked around for anyone else. "Has someone called an amb—"

"No hospital," Maddox said, his voice quiet. He swallowed hard. "I'll be fine. Just need a second."

"Maddox," I said, aiming for calm. "You're not fine."

He opened his eyes and focused on me. "I said no hospital."

"He's okay," Wes joked. "He's arguing with Roscoe. He'll be fine."

"Maddox, I need you to drink this," Hardwick said, putting a bottle of electrolytes to his lips. He propped up Maddox's head to help him drink, and then Julio, the physical therapist, appeared on the other side of Maddox. He had a medic bag with him and I figured a few years at university studying human anatomy and biology made him more of an expert than me, so I got out of their way.

I stood up and moved to Maddox's feet, looking on for what felt like an eternity. Wes, Luke, and Blake were looking on too, as were Amber and Ryan. Jeremy stood beside me. He looked wrecked too: hot, drenched, and exhausted but concerned about his best mate. "Will he be okay?"

I met his gaze. "How about we get you guys cooled down too."

"I'm okay," he began to say.

Hardwick looked up at him, then pointed to the four bandmates. "Boots and socks off, shirts off," he barked. "Sit down, drink electrolytes, and sip water. Now, or you'll get a firsthand lesson about delayed onset."

Couldn't have said it better myself.

"Will he be okay?" Jeremy asked him.

Hardwick nodded. "He should be fine. Thanks to Roscoe's quick thinking."

Maddox lifted his hand up, barely. "Roscoe?"

I knelt beside him. "Yeah?"

He still held his hand up so I took it and his fingers latched onto mine with about all the strength I figured he had. "Stay with me."

"Yeah, of course," I replied, knowing full well that we were holding hands in front of everyone and trying not to care.

Julio went to check on Wes, Luke, Blake, and Jeremy. I put my other hand to Maddox's chest, his neck, and then his forehead. "He's not as hot now."

Maddox snorted, his voice weak. "I beg your fucking pardon."

The doctor laughed. "Not that kind of hot. Maddox, you almost cooked yourself. You're lucky Roscoe was here."

"You have no idea how true that is." Maddox smiled, though he was still obviously not back to himself. He lay there, slow breathing for another minute or two. "Hey, doc, um, I should probably have someone stay with me tonight, right?"

Hardwick completely missed Maddox's point. "You're going to need to take it easy, yes. But it wouldn't hurt to have someone on standby. Just in case. If you get headaches or dizziness, a rapid heart rate or blurred vision, you should call an ambulance."

"Roscoe will stay with me," Maddox said.

Hardwick looked to me and I rolled my eyes. "What about if he's more demanding than usual or argues too much? Can I call for an ambulance then? Have him taken away?"

"You're not funny," Maddox complained.

Hardwick smiled and took Maddox's blood pressure one more time. "Okay, you can try sitting up in a few minutes. Keep sipping those electrolytes," he said, patting Maddox's shoulder as he stood up to go check on the others.

It left just me and Maddox. He didn't appear to be letting go of my hand any time soon, so I sat on my ass beside him. "You scared the shit outta me," I whispered.

"Scared me too," he replied. "Felt like the air had a pulse. I just couldn't seem to breathe and I knew I was too hot."

"Feel better now?"

"Better. Except the receiver is sticking into my ass."

Each earpiece had a small black receiver, about the size of a wallet, that fit into their back pocket. It was hard plastic and couldn't have been comfortable. "Here," I said, gripping his hip and rolling him onto his side. I slid the receiver out of his pocket and gently rolled him back, making him smile. He was holding the ice pack from his chest, but he now had goosebumps. "You cold now?" It was probably nothing, given he was shirtless, barefoot, covered with ice packs.

"A little. I wanna sit up. I need to sit up."

He held his hand out again and I pulled him up into a sitting position. His knees were bent and he kinda slouched. He looked better but still exhausted. "Just give yourself a second to adjust," I said.

He nodded. "I'm okay. I wanna go sit with the boys."

Jeremy, Wes, Luke, and Blake were sitting on the couches. From what I could tell, Hardwick and Julio were about done with them. "Okay, then let's get you up. You sure you feel okay?"

He smiled at me with something in his eyes that made my heart thump. "Thank you. For looking after me."

God, I almost caressed his face. "Anytime."

I stood up and pulled Maddox to his feet. I held onto him for a second, making sure he didn't get dizzy or sway, and with my arm around his waist, I helped him over to the couch and sat him next to Jeremy.

I thought they might have ribbed him for being dramatic or something, but they were only concerned, asking him how he felt and how they'd never seen someone hit the ground so hard. I handed Maddox the bottle of electrolytes he hadn't finished. "Sip this."

"It tastes terrible," he griped.

I was just about to tell him I didn't care how it tasted when the doors banged open and Ambrose walked in. "How is he?"

Maddox gave a half-attempt at a wave. "He's here. He's fine."

Ambrose crossed the room in long strides, concerned. He asked them all how they were feeling and declared in the future they'd be canceling any concert if the heat was too much. I'd believe that when I saw it.

But apparently his most important piece of news was that apparently the whole world already knew Jeremy and Maddox had collapsed, and Ambrose was preparing to give a brief press release in a few minutes.

"I didn't collapse," Jeremy said. "I just fell onto my ass."

"How did they know?" Luke asked. "We were backstage?"

"But not completely out of view. When the platform lowered down, they saw you two fall," Ambrose said, looking at Jeremy and Maddox. "You can see it on the footage. Jeremy kinda drops, but Maddox sways and falls. It's all over social media. There are a lot of upset fans right now so I need to let them know you're okay."

Maddox went to stand up. "If you need me to show face—"

"No," Jeremy and I said in unison. That earned me a few strange looks, but I didn't care. "Maddox, let him worry about that. You were told to rest."

"Yeah," Jeremy added. "The last thing you wanna do is go live all pale and shit or pass out mid-interview. Christ, could you imagine?"

"Yeah, they're right," Ambrose said quickly. Though I was pretty sure he'd have loved for Maddox to join him on camera. "You let me worry about it. I'm just glad you're okay. That everyone's okay. We've got a few of the stage crew and sound crew who are being tended to as well. But I'll go set the record straight to the public and put some worried minds to rest." Then he looked directly at me. "Roscoe, a word . . ."

I followed him out to the corridor, out of the air conditioning to where the air was hot and thick. "I heard your quick actions with Maddox made all the difference tonight. I just wanted to thank you."

"Everyone did their part," I replied, playing it down. "But can you do me a favor?"

He cocked his head. "Sure."

"Don't mention me in any of your damage-control reports to the media. Don't say it was me who carried him or half-stripped him or saved him or whatever. Please. We don't need any more hype around him or me, and I'm sure security would agree." He probably didn't like me telling him how to do his job, but I held his gaze. "Maddox certainly doesn't need any more stress right now."

Ambrose gave a nod, but whether he agreed with me or not, I couldn't tell. What he was going to say to the public was anyone's damn guess. "Oh," I added, "the doc said it was probably best Maddox not be left alone tonight, in case he gets dizzy or begins to feel sick. Maddox volunteered me."

"You?"

"He'd rather have me in his room than someone he doesn't know."

"Fair enough." He nodded with a serious expression. "He wasn't in good shape, I heard."

I shook my head. "It wasn't good. They were all ragged, and it's only because Maddox goes the hardest on stage that he was the one to actually collapse. Jeremy wasn't far behind him. There really needs to be a contingency plan put into place for days like today. I was about ready to put him in an ambulance, and I don't need to tell you how that would look."

Ambrose nodded again.

"We fly out for Buenos Aires the day after tomorrow," I reminded him, though I was certain I didn't have to. "And I'm assuming that's only if the doc gives Maddox a green light."

"I've spoken to Hardwick already," Ambrose replied. "He said he should be fine to fly in thirty-six hours. Next concert is in five days. Rest day tomorrow should help him recover. But the doctor will explain all that to him."

I nodded at that. Of course Ambrose would have asked about the next concert. Though I could hardly blame him because Maddox would be on that stage in Argentina if it killed him. "I better get back in there. Good luck with your press release."

As soon as our conversation was over, his assistant swooped in with a clipboard of notes and a make-up technician began dabbing at his face. I went back inside to find the boys still on the sofas, eating around a coffee table. Maddox saw me, acknowledged I was back in the room, and went back to his plate. He was now wearing a shirt and I was glad he was eating something; that was a good sign, surely.

Ryan waved me over to where he and Amber were standing by the far table. There was a plate of food piled high. "Catering left it for you," Ryan said.

"Thank you." I hadn't realized how hungry I was.

Amber nodded toward the door. "What did Ambrose want?"

I shrugged and had to finish chewing my first mouthful. "Same old. He's holding a press conference. He's in damage-control mode." I told them what was said in the corridor in between shoving food in my face. "I haven't looked online. Has everyone gone mad with the rumors?"

"Pretty much," Ryan said.

"Well, I'm not looking at that bullshit tonight. I'm getting him back to the hotel and pretending none of it exists until I've had at least five hours sleep."

They chuckled, because they understood the media craziness.

"Oh," I added. "And I'm in with Maddox tonight. To keep an eye on him. Doctor's orders and Ambrose approved it. If you need me and you're wondering where I am. I'll be lucky to get five hours sleep on that couch in his room."

Amber side-eyed me, guessing damn well I wasn't taking the couch. She didn't say anything, thankfully, and before Ryan could swallow down his mouthful to speak, Maddox called me over. I took one last bite before discarding my plate on my way over to him. "Can we go?" he asked. "I need to go."

"I think the doc wanted to see you first," I said, taking his hand and pulling him to his feet. "I'll go find him. Have you had enough to eat?"

He nodded, and I could see his plate was half empty. "I really need to piss," he said.

"Thanks for that," I deadpanned, and Jeremy and Wes laughed.

The doctor was in the corridor talking to some of the stage crew, and he quickly wrapped up their conversation when he saw me. "How is he?"

"Better, I think. He's eaten, not much, but that's nothing new. He wants to leave. He's just using the bathroom."

"Good. If he pees, he can go."

"Pardon?"

"Dehydration and heat exhaustion. I need to know if he has any problems with urination. It means his kidneys—"

"Oh. Uh, sure. Of course."

We went back into the room and waited until Maddox came out of the restrooms looking rather pained. *Oh hell.* "Oh my god, are you okay?"

"I went in there without shoes on. Of course I'm not okay. Christ." He lifted his foot up, looking at the sole with disgust.

I laughed, relieved. I went in search of wet wipes while he tried to smear his feet on Blake and Luke.

He was clearly feeling much better.

I packed up his gear, and by the time he had his boots back on, we were ready to go. The other boys were packing up and wouldn't be far behind us, but Maddox looked utterly beat. He almost fell asleep on me in the van on the way back to the hotel. I put my arm around his shoulder and he leaned against me, and we both just reveled in the silence.

I showered with him, scrubbing him clean, kissing him softly on his lips, his eyelids, his cheek, his shoulder. I dried him off and we climbed into bed, naked.

There would be no sex tonight, but it was warm and intimate, and everything Maddox seemed to need.

I needed it too.

There in the dark, the outline of his face lined in silver light, his dark eyes on mine. I thumbed his eyebrow. "You scared me tonight," I whispered. "When you fell. Scared the life out of me."

"Scared me too."

"You were so pale and hot. You were all floppy and the heat coming off you was . . . frightening."

"I overworked myself."

"I told you not to go so hard on stage tonight. It was too hot, and you give too much of yourself."

"I don't want anyone to be disappointed. The fans. They come a long way and spend a lot of money to come see us. I don't want to let anyone down."

"Even if it kills you?"

He frowned. "I'll know next time when to pull back a bit."

"Just a bit?"

He almost smiled. "If I don't pass out, then you can't be my hero and save me and take care of me."

I kissed him chastely and brushed his hair back from his face. "I'll save you and take care of you anytime. You don't need to almost kill yourself to get me to do that."

He smiled sadly. "I'm sorry I scared you. But thank you for being with me."

"I wouldn't be anywhere else."

"What do you think Ambrose said in his press release?"

I shook my head. "Let's not worry about that tonight." I was sure the internet was a disaster zone right now, but I couldn't bring myself to care. "There are more important things tonight."

He snuggled into his spot in the crook of my arm, his head on my chest with my arms wrapped tight around him. "Go to sleep, baby."

"Hmm," he murmured, quickly drifting off.

I kissed the side of his head, breathed in the smell of him, and closed my eyes.

THE NEXT MORNING, I checked the social media fallout while Maddox showered. There was a lot of noise about Maddox, and yes, he was trending and the footage of them had gone viral. But Ambrose's little press release was effective; the hysteria died down, and posts of concern became posts of well-wishes.

Thankfully Ambrose hadn't mentioned me and I was relieved not to see my name tangled with Maddox's for once.

Maddox came out dressed in his usual black outfit. "Did you see Twitter?" he asked. "And TikTok?"

I nodded. "I was expecting worse."

He half-smiled. "Same." Then he patted his belly. "I'm so hungry."

I stood up and planted a kiss on his mouth. "Then let's get you fed."

We went to the common room where breakfast was laid out. It was technically a free day, so there really wasn't anyone buzzing around too much. Amber and Ryan had the morning off, but Wes, Luke, Blake, and Jeremy were already there, though from their wet hair and half-full plates of food, I deduced they hadn't been there long.

But I knew something was off. The way the boys were acting, the sidelong looks, the glances, the silences. Maddox took his iced coffee and plate of fruit and sat next to Luke on the couch. I pretended not to be watching, but then Jeremy called me over. "Roscoe, got a sec?"

Shit.

This wasn't going to be good.

I sipped my coffee, aiming for casual. "Sure, what's up?"

Jeremy looked at Blake, then Wes and Luke as if giving

them the floor to speak. Maddox sighed and put his plate on the coffee table. Clearly he knew something was wrong too. "Just say it."

There was a long beat of silence, and when no one else spoke, it was Jeremy who broke it. "They know about you and Roscoe. I didn't tell them, but I won't lie to them either. They need to hear it from you."

CHAPTER TWELVE

MADDOX'S GAZE shot straight to mine, wide with uncertainty and fear, before he turned back to Jeremy. "If you didn't tell them, how'd they know?" Maddox asked.

"Because we're not blind," Luke said.

"And we know you, Maddox," Blake offered. "We'd wondered if something was up with you two, and last night kinda sealed it."

"Last night?" I asked. God, which part? My mind raced . . .

Wes looked over at me. "Roscoe, you called him baby. In front of everyone."

Holy fuck. I could feel the color drain from my face; my stomach felt like ice. "I did?"

Wes nodded. "When he was passed out on his back. You lifted him half off the floor, pulled his shirt off, and said, 'Come on, baby,' clear as a bell."

I didn't want to believe it but the four of them nodded. "You did," Jeremy said. "I didn't say anything last night, but after you left, Wes asked me if I heard you say it."

Luke gave a pointed glare at Jeremy. "And I asked what he knew and he wouldn't say any more."

He put his hands up. "It was not my place to say."

All eyes eventually fell on Maddox. He looked at me and shrugged. "Roscoe and I are . . . together. I dunno. Seeing each other. With each other. I dunno what to call it." He met my gaze and winced. "Together?"

I nodded, it was all I could do to offer a show of solidarity. It made my heart do crazy things to hear him say that out loud. "We are." I swallowed my nerves and looked at Maddox's bandmates, at his best friends. "What he said. I don't know what to call it either. We're just . . . together."

Maddox smiled at me, just briefly. Jeremy watched Maddox; the others all nodded slowly. "How long?" Blake asked.

Maddox put his hands about nine inches apart. "About that long."

Christ.

Wes shoved his shoulder. "Not his dick size, asshole."

Maddox laughed. "What? Too soon?"

Resisting the urge to bury my face in my hands, I pinched the bridge of my nose instead. "Way too soon."

They laughed and Jeremy put his hands up. "And I've known for all of two days. So don't blame me."

Maddox sighed and crossed his boots at the ankles. "A few weeks. Just this tour. We didn't want to tell anyone because Roscoe could lose his job. Or they'd separate us or some stupid shit. It wasn't a deliberate secret. It was just . . . it was just nice to have something good in my life, ya know?" He ran his hand through his hair. "I'm sorry for not saying something."

None of them said anything for a while.

Maddox chewed on his bottom lip, his face a mask of

sadness. "I can't fight with you guys over this. I know we always said we'd never do anything to jeopardize the band. And that's still true. Nothing's different, nothing's changed."

"You're different," Blake said quietly. "We noticed it. I mean, how could we not?"

"How have I changed?" Maddox asked, on the defensive.

"You're happier," Blake replied.

Oh god.

"And it's not even that you're less stressed because you're finally getting some," Wes said. "You're less . . . nervous. Or something."

Bloody hell.

"We all know how long you've been wanting him," Luke said, smiling.

Wait, what?

Maddox looked around for something to throw at Luke. He did a double take at the iced coffee in his hand. "Shut up. Don't make me throw this at you."

Luke and Blake both turned to me. "Oh, you didn't know," Blake said, now smiling. He shook his head at Maddox. "You're banging him but didn't tell him you've been pining over him for two years?"

Two years? Holy shit.

Maddox's cheeks went red and he shot Blake a daggers-glare. "Wow. Okay. You can shut up now too, please, if you wouldn't mind."

"Did you tell him about 'Oceans'?" Luke asked.

Oceans . . . my mind was spinning too much to follow. "Wait . . . the song?" "Oceans" was a song on their latest album. Maddox wrote it; he said it was his favorite. "What about it?"

Wes barked out a laugh. "You never told him?"

"Can everyone just shut up?" Maddox cried, his hand to his forehead. "Look. I don't want you guys to be mad at me, and I'd also appreciate it if you didn't embarrass me anymore than you already have. Thanks. But with me and Roscoe . . ." He shook his head and clenched and unclenched his fists, a nervous trait he had. He took a deep breath, then another. "I don't want you guys to tell me to choose. Please don't make me choose. My priority is the band and you assholes. Always. But I need this as well. And I know that sounds selfish, and I'm sorry. I know I ask a lot of you guys already, with all the shit that goes on. But I . . . I need this for me."

No one said anything, and I wasn't sure it was my place to speak. These were his best friends, his bandmates. They didn't need me inserting myself in between them, but I hated seeing Maddox singled out, for which I was mostly responsible. "Don't blame him," I said. "He wanted to tell you all from the beginning but I asked him not to. So if you wanna be pissed off"—I looked them all in the eye, settling on Maddox—"it's on me, not him."

"I'm not pissed off," Luke said. "I just wish we'd been told."

"Can you understand why we didn't say anything?" Maddox asked him. "Can you imagine what Ambrose is gonna do? It means things will change, and I don't want anything to be different."

Blake studied me for a bit. "Do Amber and Ryan know?"

I shrugged. "I haven't told them, but if they know or assume, I can only guess. I think Amber suspects something." God, just saying that out loud to them made me feel like shit. "I'll tell them."

"Roscoe," Maddox began.

"I can't ask these guys to lie to their managers or ask them to cover for me." This was going to end badly, I just knew it. "I'll tell them today."

"Jesus Christ," he mumbled. He ran his hand through his hair and his gaze fell on me. "Now I know why you didn't want to tell anyone." He pulled at his shirt collar, fanning it for air.

"That's not fair," Wes said.

"Fair?" Maddox stared at him. "What's not fair is this thing"—he waved between himself and me—"is barely a few weeks old. We don't even know what to call it, if we can call it anything, I don't fucking know, yet we need to declare it to the whole fucking management team like it's some financial transaction. We're not getting married. We're not initiating peace talks with North Korea. It's not that big of a deal."

"No," Luke said. "But the way this company is run is a big deal. The rules, the contracts, they're a big deal, Maddox. Now, I'm not against you two, honestly. You know I like Roscoe. He's a part of the Atrous family. And it's good to see you happy. I mean that. But things could get really complicated, really fast, if things get ugly. And that fallout will affect us all."

Maddox shook his head, his jaw bulged. "We won't let that happen."

"You say that now," Blake said. "But things *get* complicated, Madz."

Maddox stood up. "You know what's funny? Is that you all think I'm asking permission. Well, I'm not. But believe me, when one of you finally finds someone you want to bring into the 'Atrous family'"—he used finger quotes—"I'll remember this conversation. And we'll see how fair it is then." He pulled at his shirt again. Like he was too hot, and he was breathing too heavy.

"Maddox?" I asked. "Are you okay?"

The doors opened and Hardwick came in, all smiles. "Ah, Maddox. Just the man I wanted to see. Check-up time from yesterday." The mood in the room only then seemed to dawn on him. "Oh, I can come back if now's not a good time."

"Now's the perfect time," Maddox said, stomping out.

I was left, very awkwardly, with Wes, Blake, Luke, and Jeremy. "So that went well," Jeremy said, letting out a huge sigh.

I inhaled deeply, trying to sound calm. "Look. I don't know what I can say to make any of you feel better or reassured in any way. But he's . . . he means a lot to me. And we've talked about the what-ifs and it's pretty obvious what happens if things turn to shit." I shrugged. "I'll be transferred or fired. Nothing for you guys will change."

"Roscoe," Wes said gently. "We don't want that. That's the exact thing we don't want."

"Is it worth risking your job over?" Blake asked me.

"He is, yeah." I nodded. "He is worth it. And I offered to change units, to swap with Amber or Ryan, but he said no."

"He's been happier these last few weeks than he has been in a long time," Jeremy added, resigned. "We can all see that."

Luke ran his hand over his face. "I don't want to sound like the prick, but our concerns are valid."

"They are," I agreed. "And so are his. He's been . . . God. I shouldn't say anything else."

"He's been struggling," Jeremy offered. "We know."

Blake met my gaze. "He denies it every time we ask if he's okay."

"He doesn't want to burden you with it," I told them. "He says you guys, like him, are dealing with enough. But he talks to me. He tells me how he feels, the loneliness, the isolation, the pressure, the fear of not being enough. He talks to me. Finally. And you guys can think it's just us banging—pretty sure that was the word someone used—but this whole thing between us started because he was scared to be alone, and he wanted someone to hold his hand. Literally. I held his fucking hand. So think of us what you will, but it's not just some meaningless sex thing." I sighed. "Not for me, anyway."

A staffer came in and made her way over. "Uh, Roscoe? The doctor wants to see you? It's about Maddox."

Oh god.

I ran to the door, not knowing where to go. "Second door on your right," she called out behind me.

Second door . . . I pushed the door open. "Is he . . . ?"

Maddox was sitting up on a foldaway table. "I'm fine."

"He's not fine," the doctor said, as if it wasn't his first time. "His blood pressure is far too high, and after yesterday, with the heat exhaustion and dehydration, he—"

"I'm not going to the fucking hospital," Maddox said.

I went to him and rubbed his back just as Jeremy, Luke, Blake, and Wes came in the door.

"Oh goodie," Maddox deadpanned. "Everyone's here." He stood up from the table. "Doc, I said I'm fine. Just been a stressful morning arguing with these dickbags." He thumbed to his four best friends. "Come and take another reading in an hour and I'll be fine."

The doc looked at me. "He's on bedrest for the day. No public appearances, no gym session."

"That's a shame," Maddox mumbled as he took a step toward the door.

"No exercise of any kind, including sex or dance practice. No alcohol," the doc added. "If his blood pressure doesn't come down, I'll need to reassess his travel tomorrow and whether he'll be going to South America at all. I'll need to speak to Ambrose."

Everyone stared. No one breathed.

Maddox rocked back on his heels and he took a sharp inhale as if he couldn't quite catch his breath. "Like fucking hell," he breathed, his voice tight. "I'm getting on that plane tomorrow."

"Okay," I said, putting my hand on his arm, trying to defuse the situation. "Maddox is on bedrest. From now on." Then I glared at the doctor. "Telling him that the tour is in jeopardy is not going to lower his blood pressure anytime soon."

The doctor shrugged. "He needs to know."

Maddox thumped his chest. "*He*'s in the fucking room."

I met his gaze. He was pale and his breaths were short and sharp. "I'm sorry. Maddox, I—"

"You know what?" he said, pulling his arm free. "This whole day can go to fucking hell." He stormed out, bumping shoulders with Jeremy as he went. "And anyone who wants to go with it."

Goddammit.

I chased after him and caught up before he reached his room. He swiped his card and pushed his door open, and I followed him in. He threw his key on the table and snatched a hoodie off the back of a chair just to rage-throw it across the room. "Fuck!"

I grabbed his arm and swung him around, pulling him straight into a tight embrace. He was tense at first and resisted a moment. His breaths were hard and fast. Too hard, too fast. "Breathe for me," I murmured, holding him until he calmed down.

"Roscoe," he mumbled into my chest. "I'm really fucking mad. You might wanna—"

I pulled back, took his face in my hands, and kissed him. Hard. Tongue, teeth, lips, hands, frantic and demanding. His shock gave way to welcome and he began kissing me back, and once I felt his body surrender to me, when the fight and anger in him was gone, I slowed the kiss.

I still had him pulled against me, he wasn't going anywhere. We kissed for I don't know how long . . . until nothing else mattered. He hitched one leg around my hip and I hoisted him up and carried him to the bed. I laid him down and settled my weight on his.

"You cheated," he said, smiling now. "The master of distraction."

"It worked though, did it not? You're not so mad now. Do you feel okay?" I ran my hand over his chest. "You were pretty worked up."

"I feel much better." He spread his legs wide and wrapped them around me. "You better finish what you started, or I'll be mad all over again."

I chuckled and kissed him, slow and lovely. I slid my hands up under his shirt, aiming to get it off him, when I remembered. I quickly pulled his shirt back down. "The doctor said no."

"Fuck the doctor."

"No thanks. He's really not my type."

Maddox stared for a minute before he conceded a smile. "I'm glad to hear that."

I rolled us onto our sides, keeping him close, our legs tangled, my hand on his cheek. He was looking into my eyes in ways that both thrilled and scared me. It was so honest, so real. My heart squeezed. There was so much I wanted to say, so much, and I had no clue where to begin.

"I'm sorry you fought with the guys about us."

He made a face. "They'll get over it. I'm not giving in. I compromise everything else. But not this."

"I don't want you to fight with them. Not over me. They're like your brothers, and I don't want to get in the middle of that."

"But it's not you I'm fighting over. It's me. I'm fighting for me. I need this."

"Is it just you though? If I didn't work with you, it might be different. But I am part of the team, and that makes it different. What happens between us does affect the others. If we fight or if things end between us, there is a fallout. But if I was some random person, it wouldn't change anything if we . . . broke up. I don't know if that's the right word."

He smiled and sighed. "Break up. That implies we're a couple, does it not?"

God. "Well, I don't know . . . we both said this morning we didn't know what to call us. Just that we're kinda together or seeing each other. I don't know what that makes us."

His cheeks flushed pink and he smiled into the palm of my hand. "I dunno, Roscoe. We're seeing each other. And I'm not seeing anyone else. I don't want to see anyone else. Do you want to see other people?"

I shook my head. "No."

"We're seeing each other most nights, we're exclusive." He smiled. "I think we're dating, Roscoe."

I laughed. "I think we might be."

He made a face, nervous or uncomfortable. "I've never . . .

I've never had a boyfriend or dated anyone. I'm twenty-three, so that's pretty lame." He let out a quiet laugh and ducked his head. "Just so you know. I'm probably not very good at it."

Holy shit.

I lifted his chin and kissed him softly. "I'm not very good at it either. My last relationship ended because my entire life revolved around a certain singer in a band."

He grimaced. "Sorry about that."

He didn't look sorry. "I'm not. I wouldn't change a thing."

He smiled then. "Can't say I was actually sorry about it either. I was just being polite."

I barked out a laugh. "Thanks." That was years ago though, and it reminded me of something he'd said to Jeremy. "Can I ask you something?"

He looked worried. "Uh, okay?"

"It was two things, actually."

"Oh, that's worse. Just remember we're supposed to be lowering my blood pressure."

I chuckled. "It was something you said to Jeremy the other day, and something the guys said earlier."

He groaned out a laugh. "Yeah."

I stroked my thumb across his cheekbone. "You said to Jeremy that you'd wanted this for a long time, and today Luke said you'd wanted me for years. Then Blake said you'd pined after me for two years."

He closed his eyes and pressed his forehead to my chin. "Christ, Roscoe. Don't make me say it."

"Don't be embarrassed," I whispered. "I've had . . . thoughts . . . about you for about the same time."

His eyes met mine. "You have?"

I nodded, smiling at the hope in his face. "Probably

longer. I told myself it was impossible. That it could never happen."

He frowned. "Impossible? It's not *im*possible."

"I know that now." I kissed him soft and sweet. "It's not easy. But it's not impossible."

"I've liked you since the day you started," he murmured, his dark eyes searching mine. "You walked into the dance studio and Ambrose introduced you, remember? You were the hottest thing I'd ever seen. I thought you were straight at first. Then I found out you were gay and I was like, oh my god, yes, aaaaand then I found out you had a boyfriend. Which sucked." He smiled sadly. "Not that it mattered because I never thought it was possible either, to be honest. I told myself I couldn't have that. I couldn't have someone in my life. Not while I was in Atrous. I couldn't have both."

I thumbed his cheek and kissed him softly. "Yes you can. You're allowed to be happy. You deserve to be happy." I sighed. "But that brings me to the second thing . . ."

"Oh god."

I chuckled. "The song 'Oceans.'"

He groaned. "You were never supposed to know."

"You wrote it for me?"

He searched my eyes for the longest time, and then he sang in a near whisper, melodic and haunting.

I am lost
in oceans of blue

endless waves
that pull me under
depths I've never known

oceans of blue

in a storm of you
may the stars above guide us,
may your lighthouse bring me home

"Maddox," I murmured. I damn near could have cried.

"You have the bluest eyes," he said. "I dreamed of getting lost in your eyes. I dreamed that one day you'd look at me like you're looking at me right now."

I brought his lips to mine, kissing him. It was sweet and tender. My heart was in it. God, my heart was in it.

He sighed and scanned my face as if he were taking in every detail. Eventually he smiled. "You called me baby in front of them. That's how they all knew something was up."

"I have no actual memory of saying that. In my defense, I was stressed and panicking because you were passed out and I needed to get your core temperature down, and that included picking you up and peeling your shirt off you."

He smiled. "I like that you were so worried about me." His cheeks were pink. "And you can call me baby anytime."

I ran my fingers through his hair. "Hey, baby," I whispered.

He looked at me, those dark eyes wide and bright. He was smiling that real smile, the one he rarely showed anyone. "Yeah, baby?"

I shook my head, disbelieving that he was in my arms, looking at me like that, calling me that. "You're so fucking beautiful."

He pecked his lips to mine, smiling. He studied my eyes for a long moment. "I don't know why the others don't want me to have this. This, right here, being happy with you. I don't know why they don't understand. I've never had this. I've never had anyone . . . and now I have you."

I held him a little tighter. "They said they realized how

much happier you are. They want that for you, they really do. They're just worried about everything else. And that's fine. Let them worry about that stuff."

"I don't want to be a problem. I don't want this to be a problem. I wanted them to be happy for me."

"Give them time."

He sighed. "Are you still going to tell Amber and Ryan?"

"Do you want me to?"

He seemed to consider this. "I thought I did, but now I don't know. I don't want anything to change, but I don't want any secrets. If we tell them, then let the chips fall where they may, but at least we won't have to hide anything."

"Wait up . . . just how public are you talking?"

He laughed. "Just when it's us. In the hotel or in a car or on a plane. Not in public. I don't think I want to offer you up for a public sacrifice just yet."

"Sacrifice?"

"Yeah. The fans. You know, the slightly obsessed ones who for some strange reason think I'm going to marry them? Well, they probably won't like the idea of us being together too much."

"But we have a couple name already. They started it."

He laughed but he soon fell quiet. "You know that gives me an idea . . ."

"What's that?"

"We should tell Amber and Ryan, and Ambrose too. But we'll give them a list of terms and conditions. Like no public displays of affection when we're working, no public making-out sessions, no hand-holding in front of fans or papzz. Or the documentary crew. I don't even notice them anymore." He sighed. "But when we're here or in the common room with the staff, or if we're just hanging out, if I want to sit with you, I can. That kind of thing."

That made me smile. "Good idea."

"That way they can't be the ones to dictate anything. Or tell us no. Ambrose'll know we've thought this through."

"I love that idea, but just don't get your hopes up. Ambrose will always have conditions of his own."

Which could have me unemployed. But I didn't say that out loud.

He nodded. "I'm okay with that. I'm just done hiding. We're officially dating now. You even said so."

I chuckled. "I'm dating Maddox Kershaw. Maddox fucking Kershaw. And not the Maddox the world thinks he is." I brushed my thumb along his jaw. "But the real you. The Maddox only I get to see."

He searched my eyes. "Christ, Roscoe." He took my hand and put it to his heart. A raw vulnerability pooled in the depth of his gaze. "My heart. You probably shouldn't say shit like that if you want to lower my blood pressure."

I laughed. "God. Sorry."

He cupped my jaw and drew me in for a kiss with just a hint of tongue. The kind of kiss that started something more, and I was just about to pull him on top of me when someone knocked on the door.

"Hey, dickwad, it's me. Open up."

Jeremy.

Maddox groaned and pulled away. "Christ."

"You want to see him?"

Maddox nodded, so I rolled off the bed. I readjusted my crotch and patted down my hair before I opened the door. Maddox laughed behind me, and Jeremy gave me a nod. "Hey," he said. "The dickwad was meant for him, not you."

I nodded. "Yeah, I got that, thanks."

I stood aside and let him in. Maddox was now sitting up, leaning against the headboard, holding a pillow against his chest. It looked casual enough, though the bed was all messed up and I was sure Jeremy could probably tell what we'd been doing.

"Excuse me for not getting up," Maddox said. "I'm on doctor-ordered bedrest, and I have a raging hard-on."

I gasped, audibly. Loud enough to make them both look at me. *Christ.*

Maddox laughed and Jeremy snorted. "Thank you for that grand piece of information that I did not need to know."

Maddox's smile began to fade. "Wassup?"

"How are you feeling?"

"I'm fine. Just need to chill for a bit."

Jeremy pulled out a seat from the table and faced Maddox. "We didn't mean to stress you out. We're on your side, just so you know. I know it probably didn't feel like it back there, but we've got your back. Always. You know that. We might argue and bitch about shit, but when it comes down to it, we support each other. It's what we do."

"It didn't feel like it," Maddox said. "Kinda felt very one-sided to me."

Jeremy shrugged. "Probably because we've never argued over anything so personal before. Normally we disagree on choreography or lyrics, or whose bridge composition we go with, or whose turn it is to clean up. We've never had to discuss serious relationships before." Jeremy gave me a smile. It was almost a little sad, but it was genuine. "For what it's worth, Roscoe, I'm glad it's you."

"I'm glad it's him too," Maddox added.

I wasn't sure what to say to that. "Uh, same."

Jeremy sighed but he seemed relieved, happier now that

he'd said his piece. "Anyway, they're looking at taking a trip to Bal Harbour."

Maddox grimaced and Jeremy nodded. "I told them that'd be your reaction."

"Are Amber and Ryan good to take you?" I asked.

Jeremy nodded and smiled. "Yeah, and Steve and the boys are on it."

Maddox looked at me. "Did you want to go? You can go if you want. I'll happily just stay here."

I looked at him like he'd lost his mind. "Shopping? Not if I can avoid it."

Jeremy chuckled and he ended with a sigh. He looked at Maddox. "Are we good, Madz? I just want you to know that we've got you, man. No matter what."

"Yeah, we're good."

"The others wanted to come see you but we figured with the blood pressure thing . . ." He grimaced. "That's new and kinda worrying. Not gonna lie."

"I'm fine, honestly."

"Bedrest," Jeremy said.

"That's what we were doing when you interrupted us," Maddox replied.

I sighed. "We weren't really. Christ, Maddox, don't tell him that."

Jeremy studied my face. "Are you blushing?"

"No."

Maddox laughed. "Okay, Jer, leave him alone. Leave us alone. He was about to lower my blood pressure."

Oh, for fuck's sake.

I held the door for Jeremy but couldn't look him in the eye. He laughed as he walked out. I shut the door and glared at Maddox. "Did you have to tell him that?"

"We've always talked like that. It's how we are. You've heard us talk like that for years."

"Yeah, but it was never about me."

He moved the pillow and began to rub himself through his pants. "Come over here," he purred.

And of course, there was another knock at the door.

"It's Doctor Hardwick."

"Fuuuuuck," Maddox grumbled.

"I'll get it."

I opened the door. "Is Maddox here? It's been an hour," the doc said.

An hour already? Jeez. I welcomed him in and Maddox was still on the bed, still leaning against the headboard with one knee bent. It hid the semi he was sporting. Maddox smiled at the doc. "Bed rest. Just like you said."

"Uh, I'll leave you to it," I said. "I'm just gonna go see Ryan and Amber before they leave."

Maddox shot me a curious look, but I ducked out the door and found Ryan and Amber in the common room.

"How's Maddox?" Amber asked.

"Good. The doc's just doing another blood pressure check now."

"Okay, well, let us know how it goes," Ryan added.

"Will do."

"Has he had high blood pressure before?" Ryan asked.

I shook my head. "No. But he's been under a lot of stress, and then maybe with yesterday and him passing out . . ." I shrugged. "Um, so there's something I want to tell you before you go," I began. "If you've got a second."

I had their undivided attention.

God, here went nothing. I took a deep breath and let it out slowly. "Maddox and I . . . we're, um . . ."

"Together?" Amber asked. "We know."

"We gathered," Ryan said. "But thanks for telling us."

Okay, I wasn't expecting that. "Well, yeah. We've just decided to make it official. I guess. After yesterday. The guys noticed . . . well, Jeremy already knew, so that's not exactly true. But the others noticed."

"When you called Maddox *baby*," Amber said. *Was she smiling? Was this funny?*

"Uh, yeah. Apparently I did. Though I have no recollection of that."

"The truth comes out when you're in a high-stress situation," Ryan said. "We all heard it. We all saw how worried you were. How you looked after him." He shrugged. "We kinda assumed you wouldn't be leaving him today."

I shook my head again. "No, probably not. He says he feels fine, but he needs to have a rest day for sure."

"We won't have the boys out late today," Amber said. "We've got an early start tomorrow."

"If Maddox is okay to fly," Ryan added.

"He'll be on that plane," I said. "You know, wild horses and all that."

Amber smiled at me. "Thanks for being up front. You know I've seen how you two have been watching each other. I pointed it out to you." She nodded her chin at Ryan. "Ryan had no idea but I caught him up."

I smiled, embarrassed. "It's still all new. And for the record, Amber, when you asked me a few weeks back, nothing had happened at that point so I wasn't lying. But now . . . well, now it has happened, and we don't want secrets. Anyway," I continued. "The boys are probably going to be talking about it today, and it's not fair if they have to hide it in the cars or whatever. So you can tell them, you know."

"And Ambrose?"

"I'll ask to meet with him today."

Amber nodded slowly. "And if he says it's a deal breaker?"

My stomach knotted. "I . . . I don't know. I guess we'll cross that bridge when we get to it. Anyway, I should get back. We have an eight-hour flight tomorrow. If you want to chat, or discuss any concerns, I'm happy to talk."

Amber gave me a smile and Ryan nodded, and I walked out feeling oddly relieved. I still had to speak to Ambrose and I didn't know if Amber and Ryan were on my side yet, but they seemed okay with it.

Maybe.

I let myself back into Maddox's room to find Doctor Hardwick still there, which surprised me. "Oh, everything okay?"

"Yes, yes," the doc said. "Just wrapping up."

I went to the fridge and got a bottle of water while the doctor packed away his blood pressure cuff.

"The doc said I'm fine," Maddox said.

"Hm, well," Doctor Hardwick replied, picking up his bag. "His blood pressure has come down, but it's still not where I'd like it." He gave a pointed look at Maddox. "Continued bed rest for the day. I'll do another reading in two hours and again tonight."

"But I'm getting on that plane tomorrow."

"If it stays down and within the recommended guidelines." The doctor made his way over toward the door. "Any questions?"

"Can I at least jerk off?"

I choked on my water and the doc shot me a look before turning back to Maddox. "Uh . . ."

"You said no sex," Maddox added, smiling. "By which I

assume you mean nothing to elevate the heart rate too much for a prolonged period of time, like a vigorous—"

"Yes, that's what I meant," the doctor clarified. "Nothing vigorous. My suggestion is to just watch a movie, read a book, take a nap."

Maddox grinned. "But that wasn't a no."

The doctor sighed on his way to the door. "If your blood pressure is elevated when I come back in two hours . . ."

I saw the doctor out, and when I came back, Maddox's grin had widened. "You have two hours to have me sated and sedated, Roscoe." He tossed the pillow he had resting in his lap and palmed his dick. He began to unbutton his pants. "You better get busy."

"Sedated?"

"Yeah. So thoroughly wrung out I can't move."

I put the bottle of water on the table and walked over to the bed. I kneeled on the mattress and crawled up his body. I held myself off him, looking down. "I told Amber and Ryan."

His eyes went wide. "You did?"

I nodded. "They were spending the day with the guys. I didn't want them to have to lie or keep secrets for us."

"How'd they take it?"

"Pretty good. I think."

He pulled me by my shirt so my weight settled on him. His legs spread, as did his smile. "You know a day of bedrest doesn't sound too bad. Now that the doc said sex was okay."

"He didn't say that."

"He said nothing too vigorous." Maddox rolled his hips and ran his hands down over my ass. "So take your time, Roscoe. Go slow. You've got two hours. Make it last."

WE SPENT the day in bed. It wasn't all sex; there was a lot of touching, a lot of cuddling, and snoozing. We ordered room service; we watched some TV. We looked online at what the world was saying about the concert, about Maddox, about him passing out. Now that the hype of all that was mostly over, pictures of Jeremy taking his shirt off on stage were the hot topic. There were a thousand pictures of him, drenched with sweat, muscled torso gleaming under the lights, launching his shirt into the crowd.

Maddox was more than happy to have the spotlight on someone else.

It was mid-afternoon and I was sitting at the table checking my emails and messages. I'd organized a meeting with Ambrose for later this evening. The boys were back at the hotel, and after another visit from Doctor Hardwick, Maddox's blood pressure was back to normal.

It wasn't even that we'd had a relaxing day. We'd had a peaceful day . . . a wonderful day.

Maddox sat on his bed, leaning against the headboard like he did, writing in his notebook or strumming on his guitar, then scribbling down chords and words.

The way the sunlight caught his smile, the way he moved his fingers, the way his hair fell down his forehead, how his earrings swayed in time with his music . . .

He was poetry in motion.

"What are you smiling at?" he asked.

"You." I ignored the heat in my cheeks, the hammering of my heart. He looked happy. Happier than he'd been in a long time. "I wish . . . I wish you could see yourself through my eyes."

He smiled, obviously surprised by my honesty and the depth of my words. He plucked a chord on his guitar. "And how do you see me?"

"Right now, you're unguarded. Relaxed. Happy."

He stared, and maybe I imagined that he gripped his guitar a little harder. "Maybe I am. Happy, that is."

"I'm glad."

"I forgot what this felt like," he admitted, playing a few chords on his guitar. "Just to be me."

The way he said that hurt my heart.

"I mean," he shrugged. "I don't even know who I am anymore. Not really. But when I'm with you . . ." He laughed and strummed his guitar. "I think I feel like me when I'm with you."

I went over to him and took his guitar, leaning it gently against the bedside table. I sat next to him, took his face in my hands, and kissed him. "I just want you to be happy. Whatever it takes."

He kissed my palm. "What do you think Ambrose will say?"

I sighed. "The truth? I bet his concerns will be legal and contractual. He's not going to see the personal side of it. It's just a business development that he'll deal with like he deals with everything else."

Maddox flinched. "We're not a business development."

"I know that. I doubt he'll see it differently." I shrugged. "He's a doer and a fixer. He manages everything efficiently and effectively, like a production line. It's what makes him so good at what he does."

"You know what would be nice?" he asked. "If people said, 'Hey, you two are a thing? That's cool, congrats, man,' instead of us being a bullet point on a crisis management list."

I leaned in and kissed him again. "We still have a few hours before we meet with him. Let's not worry about it until then."

Except we didn't have a few hours because there was a knock on the door. I handed Maddox back his guitar. "I'll go see who it is." I half expected to see Jeremy through the peephole, but it wasn't. It was Ambrose. *Shit.* I opened the door. "Neil," I said, hoping Maddox would have fair warning. We were both fully dressed, thankfully; me in jeans and a polo, and Maddox was wearing some long lounge pants and a T-shirt.

Ambrose gave me a nod and walked into the room. There were no niceties or greetings. "Thought you'd be here," he said to me.

Right, then.

Maddox put his guitar down and got off the bed. "I'm supposed to be on bedrest."

Ambrose nodded. "I know. The doctor said you were much better this afternoon."

"Yeah."

"Good. That's good." His gaze went from Maddox to me. "Look, something's come up with the concert production team and there are some logistics issues; I can't make our meeting tonight. I'm supposed to be on my way to see them now, so I don't have time to chat. I know what's going on between you and I'm aware you've discussed this with the band members and the other managers."

Of course he knew.

Of course he did.

"So I brought these." He put some papers on the table. "One for each of you. Read through them and we can discuss this on the plane tomorrow if you need. I've instructed legal you may have questions, and they're to help in any way possible."

Maddox and I were speechless.

"I really do apologize for my bluntness. Make a list of

anything you want to ask. We will have lunch, just the three of us, when we arrive in Buenos Aires. I'll make time, I promise." He walked to the door and turned to face us. "I want you to know Platinum Entertainment supports you."

He was gone then, leaving us still just standing there, stunned. Well, I was stunned. Maddox was holding the papers Ambrose left with us.

He read the heading on the first page. "Oh, you've got to be fucking kidding me."

CHAPTER THIRTEEN

"IT'S A NON-DISCLOSURE AGREEMENT," I explained, trying to reassure Maddox for the nth time. He was sitting on the bed and I was kneeling in front of him, holding his hands. "I've signed a dozen of these over my time with the company. Whoever comes into contact with the band or the office premises or the studio has to sign these. You know that."

He shook his head. "But not for this. This is different."

"It is. But it's not. He's looking out for everyone's best interests."

Maddox's was basically an NDA to prohibit exposure and possible defamation. Mine was more of an employee agreement, much like all the others I'd signed. Only this one now included Personal Proprietary clauses. That was kind of humiliating, but I couldn't say I was surprised.

"They're not looking out for *our* best interests, Roscoe. This is to protect the company. No one else."

I couldn't defend that because he was right.

"We knew there'd be stipulations," I tried.

"God, I hate this." He shook his head. "It's not just rules

and stipulations. It's my life. They own every part of me. They control every part of me. And now they own you too. I'm so sorry."

I leaned up and took his face in my hands. "Don't apologize. It's not so bad. We're still both here, together, and we'll see each other every day."

"And every night."

I smiled. "And every night." I sat back on my haunches and sighed. "We're supposed to be having dinner with everyone."

Maddox rolled his eyes, his face etched with sadness. "My whole life is a contract. Be here, wear this, say that, smile."

"Did you want me to tell them you're not up for it? I mean, a day of rest is a *full* day. They'll understand."

He shook his head. "Nah. We should go. It's our first team dinner as . . . well, as us. And I'm hungry."

He looked miserable. I stood up, and taking his hands, I pulled him to his feet and wrapped him up in a big hug. I held him tight and rubbed his back. "It'll be okay, baby. We'll get through it. It doesn't matter what happens out there, because when that door closes, it's just you and me."

He nodded against my neck. "I wish the world out there would disappear sometimes."

I didn't want to say it, but that wasn't going to happen any time soon.

Dinner was an organized team thing. We did that every now and then on tour, on a free day, and sometimes before flying to a different country. We always held these things in the common room of the hotel we stayed at, where we did everything.

Everyone was in good spirits; chatter and laughter ran along both sides of the long table. Maddox sat on one side of me, Amber on the other, Ryan across from me. I mostly chatted with them while Maddox talked with the guys.

This formation wasn't new. We'd sat together like that a thousand times at these kinds of things, but it did feel a bit different. At one point, Maddox put his arm around the back of my chair, and it felt like everyone stopped and stared.

Of course they didn't, but I was hyperaware of his every touch, his every glance. This was our first time being in front of them all as a couple. They knew about us. And now we were parading it.

It was strangely both exhilarating and embarrassing.

"No, Ambrose is in some logistics meeting," Maddox said, and it snapped me out of my head. "He paid us a little visit before he had to leave."

"He did?" Jeremy asked. "What'd he say?"

Maddox put his fork down. "Not much. Just played the NDA fairy and dropped off two confidentiality contracts."

"Holy shit," Luke said.

"Oh god," Amber said, grimacing.

Wes acted all cute. "How romantic!"

Jeremy's eyes flashed to mine as if he wanted my take on it. "It wasn't that bad," I said. "They're fairly standard."

Maddox sighed. "Well, I used to think being gagged and bound sounded like it would be fun, but it's really not."

Christ.

Everyone laughed. "NDAs are standard for everything," Jeremy said. "Everyone from our hairstylists to our house cleaners has to sign them, so don't worry too much about it."

"We had to hand out a few at the club the other night," Blake added. "Well, I dunno about you losers, but I needed two."

There was more laughter and more trash-talking, and I

knew they were only saying that stuff to make Maddox feel better. I also knew it didn't work.

"But we're not some random hook-up in a club," Maddox said when we were back in his room. He was still mad about the whole NDA thing. "You're not gonna run off to the media and sell a story or a photo. If I didn't trust you, I wouldn't be with you. Hell, you're the one person in the world I can trust."

I cupped his face, his long earrings dangling over my fingers. "I would never hurt you." I kissed him. "Not ever."

He basked in that for a second.

"Forget about the contracts," I urged him. Then I nudged his nose with mine, ghosting a kiss across his lips. "Put it out of your mind. I'm sure we can find other things to do."

ALL MY ASSURANCES didn't mean shit the next day. We'd been in the air for all of thirty minutes when Ambrose called Maddox and me over for a chat. Ambrose's section of the plane was considerably nicer than ours. Maddox was already sitting on the leather seat across from Ambrose, so I sat next to him, our thighs touching.

Ambrose smiled at us. "You've had a chance to read the revised confidentiality agreements?"

We nodded. "Yep."

"Any questions about those?"

I shook my head. "No."

Maddox nodded. "Uh, yeah. Just one. Do you think it's really necessary?"

Ambrose didn't even blink. "Yes."

Maddox stared right back. "It's insulting."

I resisted the urge to sigh.

"How long have you been with us?" Maddox asked him. "Five years?"

Ambrose nodded.

Maddox raised his chin. "And have I ever, *ever* asked for anything?"

Ambrose flinched. "Maddox—"

"No. Spare me the condescending bullshit. This is not to protect me. This is to protect the brand, the company."

"I hate to be the one to tell you," Ambrose replied. "You *are* the brand."

Maddox laughed. It was not a happy sound. "I'm sure the others will be happy to hear that." He sat forward in his seat and held up five fingers. "There are five of us. Always. Not one. Five."

Ambrose sighed. "I know that. That's not what I meant."

Maddox aimed a cold, steely gaze at Ambrose. "I signed it, though, if that's what you're concerned about. Your precious contract. But not for you, and not for the company. I did it for Roscoe and I did it for the band. Those four guys back there . . . I did it for them. To protect them."

Ambrose took a moment to let the mood settle. "Maddox, I understand your concerns, but we have contracts in place for a reason. Contracts, I might add, that specifically state that band members are to refrain from interpersonal relations with staff. The company has already expressed leniency because it involves you."

Maddox's jaw bulged, his nostrils flared. His voice was quiet and cold. "Is that a threat, Ambrose?"

"Okay, look," I interrupted, trying to keep the peace. I put my hand on Maddox's thigh. "No one's threatening anyone. We signed the papers, it's done."

Maddox's expression softened when he met my gaze. "You know why I have a problem with this."

"I know," I replied gently. God, we'd talked about this late into the night and the morning. For Maddox it was about control, which I understood; his entire life was wrapped up in contracts. But what was the alternative? If we didn't sign, they'd deem our working relationship to be outside their professional parameters and I'd be on the first plane home. He'd argued that, if it ever came down to it, he'd win in a pissing contest with Ambrose, and I'd argued that no one on this tour needed that kind of stress.

We could discuss long-term rules and whatever after the tour. We just had to get through the next few weeks and see where we stood.

Maddox took a deep breath and his hand slid over mine, threading our fingers. In front of Ambrose, and that was a pretty ballsy move. "Okay, Ambrose, here it is. I have my job to do, Roscoe has his job to do. That won't change. What we do in our own time is no one else's business, and we're not asking for special treatment. The public gets told nothing. I won't have us used as a marketing ploy to spin for ratings. We travel as we always have; during the day, Roscoe's with me. On a plane, like now, Roscoe's with Ryan and Amber, and I'm with the guys, like we always do. But in hotels, wherever we are, Roscoe and I share a room."

Ambrose stared at him, then shifted in his seat. "About that . . ."

"It's not negotiable," Maddox replied flatly.

"We think it might be for the best if Roscoe moves to a different unit." Ambrose then looked to me. "You can take Jeremy and Wes. Ryan can take Maddox. That way there's no conflict of interest and no safety concerns."

"Safety?" I asked.

"No," Maddox said at the same time.

"Security has expressed concerns," Ambrose continued, looking at me. "That the two of you together pose a bigger security risk . . ."

"Oh, so, when it was good for ratings, you didn't care," Maddox said sardonically. "But now that you can use it against us, you're all ears. How terribly convenient." His grip on my hand was getting a little bone-crushy.

I pulled my hand free and patted his quickly. "Is that the only stipulation?" I asked Ambrose.

"Roscoe," Maddox cried, giving me a disbelieving glare. "What the hell?"

"Maddox," I whispered. "Riding in a separate car is better than not sharing a room, don't you think?"

"We shouldn't have to choose!"

I sighed. This was going nowhere. It wasn't going to go anywhere. I understood both sides. The business/management side, but my heart sided with Maddox. I squeezed his hand. "It'll be fine. We'll just get through this tour first."

Maddox's jaw was clenched shut. "I'm really sick of being a pawn in this game." He pulled his hand from mine and stood. "And I'm really fucking sick of having my own life dictated to me." And with that, he stormed through the door to his section of the plane.

I sighed. "Jesus Christ."

Ambrose's expression was stoic, though his nostrils flared just a fraction. If that was any indication, he was slightly ruffled. "Thank you for seeing my point of view," he said.

His point of view?

"Let's just make one thing clear," I said, my voice low. "I'm on his side. Every time. And I'm telling you, as his manager, he's not coping with stress right now. He doesn't sleep unless I'm there. He has trouble breathing sometimes, and his blood pressure went through the roof the other day. So don't fucking push him, because like you said, *he's* the brand. If he can't go on stage or if he refuses, the others won't go on without him and this whole tour gets canceled." He stared and I stared right the fuck back. "I'm on his side. I always have been. And I'm telling you not to fucking push him."

I was about to say more until I noticed Jeremy standing by the door. I don't know how much he heard. Enough by the looks of it.

"Jeremy?"

"Uh," he looked between us. "Just checking everything's okay? Maddox is pissed, and you've seen that movie where they talked about not putting the Hulk in a flying tin can . . ."

I stood up, giving Ambrose one last glare as I walked out.

When I got up to Maddox's section, he was standing at his seat, fighting with the blanket and pillow. "Hey."

He didn't turn around. "Fuck him."

"No thanks. He's really not my type."

Wes, in the seat behind, laughed. Maddox turned then and his shoulders sagged. "Don't try being funny. I am *pissed* off."

I sat on Jeremy's seat. "It won't be so bad."

"How can you be so calm?"

"Because he didn't fire me." Though after my parting words, that could change. I didn't say that out loud.

Maddox sighed at the ceiling. "Fuck."

Jeremy came back in and stopped when he saw me in his seat, though he did smile. "Hey, Roscoe, is there a mile-high club for ripping your boss a new asshole at thirty-thousand feet? Because you just gave Ambrose a one-way membership."

I snorted and Maddox shot me a look. "You did what?"

I shrugged. "I don't know about ripping him a new asshole, but he knows where I stand."

"Speaking of standing," Jeremy said, ushering me out of his seat.

I stood up and gave Maddox a smile. "Try and get some sleep." Though that was very unlikely now.

I went back to my section, knowing Jeremy would tell Maddox what he heard me say, and I was glad. I wanted Maddox to know I would defend him, and it didn't hurt that the guys knew it either.

Amber's eyes met mine as I took my seat. "What happened?"

"Well, he didn't fire me," I replied. "Yet."

BUENOS AIRES WAS A BEAUTIFUL CITY. Our security was about tenfold, but the massive crowds were respectful and polite, mostly. They lined the streets, cheering and waving, so we had a full police escort to the hotel.

Getting into a vehicle with Jeremy and Wes and watching Ryan take Maddox was an odd feeling.

"This is new," Wes said as I took my seat. "We got Roscoe the cat herder."

"I bet Maddox is such a happy kitten right now," Jeremy said. "I bet Ryan's day just got a whole lot worse too. A moody Maddox is not fun."

"Leave him alone," I muttered.

Jeremy laughed. "I'm just kidding." And he *was*

kidding, I could tell by his eyes. Did he like me more now after he'd heard me defend Maddox to Ambrose? Possibly. Then he took out his phone and called Maddox. "Hey, Madz. Just wanted to let you know that Roscoe is as miserable as I bet you are."

I couldn't hear what Maddox replied but from the way Jeremy laughed, I could only assume it was colorful. Then he checked the screen. "He hung up on me."

"I'm not saying this with one hundred percent certainty," I said, "but there is a very good chance you deserved that."

Jeremy laughed at that. "So how long have we got you for?"

I shrugged. "For the remainder of the tour, I think."

He sighed, his smile fading. "It's such bullshit. I mean, I can understand why Ambrose did it. I guess. Or why he thought it was a good idea, at least. But changing how we operate halfway through a tour is bullshit, and does he honestly think Maddox is gonna put up with it?" He shrugged. "It accomplishes nothing. If anything, it makes it worse."

"We'll be fine," I replied. "It just is what it is. We adapt and roll with it."

Wes squinted at me. "You've met Maddox, right? I mean, you *do know* him. So you know that he adapts to change like a . . . like a Rubik's Cube dropped off the top of a building."

Jeremy made a face at him, then he tilted his head. "Well, that's a weird analogy, but it's kinda true."

"Yeah," Wes added. "He can know the ground's coming at him and he can see it getting closer and he can tell himself he's gonna be okay, but when it hits, he's in a thousand broken pieces before you know it."

I didn't like that analogy at all.

"The ground is the change," Wes clarified. "And Madz is the Rubik's Cube. In case you didn't get that."

"Yeah I got it, thanks," I murmured. "But he's not broken."

No one spoke for a while as we weaved our way through the streets to our hotel.

Wes shivered. "I wasn't expecting it to be so cold."

We'd given them a weather rundown before we left, but apparently he hadn't listened. I called out to the security in the front seat. "Hey, Robbie, can we get some heat back here please."

I could feel Jeremy staring at me, and I eventually risked a glance at him. There was something about his expression. Was it understanding? Or acknowledgment? Empathy, maybe? "He'll be okay."

I nodded and went back to reading emails and checking my newly updated schedule, which now revolved around Jeremy and Wes and not Maddox. It made my heart hurt.

When we arrived at the hotel, we were taken to our floor and into what would be the common room for our five days here, so we could sort out rooms and keys. We arrived first, Luke and Blake with Amber were next, and it was a few very long minutes before Maddox and Ryan came in.

Maddox searched the room until he saw me. My relief and smile were instantaneous; the butterflies and heart-skips were too. But there wasn't time for anything else, because the hotel manager was soon calling out our names and keys were distributed.

Luke. Jeremy. Wes. Blake. They each took their key in turn.

"Maddox and Roscoe."

Maddox grinned and took the key. Jeremy nudged me

and I had to bite the inside of my lip to stop myself from smiling. We slipped out of the common room and walked down the hall without a word. Maddox stopped at our room, opened the door, and held it for me.

It felt . . . exciting, somehow. That we were now officially sharing a room. It almost made up for us being separated.

Almost.

The room was huge, with spectacular views to downtown. There was a very large, very soft-looking bed, a couch, a table with chairs. I slid my backpack onto the table and I had barely turned around before Maddox slammed into me, his arms around me, his face pressed into my neck.

"I missed you," he mumbled.

"I missed you too."

He pulled back. "We get to share a room."

"Ambrose is a fast learner."

He smiled. "Jeremy told me what you said to him."

I kissed him, soft and lingering. "Maddox, we have one hour before we're supposed to be back out there and I really don't want to spend it thinking about anyone but you."

He hoisted himself up onto me, wrapped his legs around my waist, and grinned, sultry and dark. "Shower?"

Hell yes.

I walked, carrying him like that, into the huge marble bathroom. "Shower."

THE NEXT THREE days were busy. My days were spent mostly with Jeremy and Wes, driving with them to the stadium for rehearsals and fittings. There was choreography practice and a shopping trip—which Maddox actually went to, only to spend time with me—and it was weird being around him but not with him. I was fine with helping Jeremy and Wes and going from one band member to two, but I hated the fact that Ryan got to spend all that time with Maddox when it should have been me.

The nights made up for it though.

Sharing a room with Maddox was as easy as breathing. Sharing a bed without fear of being caught was even better. If someone knocked on the door, there were no excuses, no pretending.

He'd play his guitar if I had work to do, and he'd jot things down in his notebook when the urge took him. Waking up next to him was my most favorite thing. I hit the gym and left him sleeping and would come back to the room to find him on my side of the bed, dozing.

Then we would shower together and go for breakfast with the team. He held my hand once and put his arm around my waist. I even slung my arm around his shoulder one time. It was thrilling.

It was just peaceful and easy. So fucking easy.

Concert day was hectic, our schedules full. We were at the stadium by early afternoon for final dress rehearsals, and the crowd had been lining up since before dawn. Thousands of people were outside the stadium buying merch, and we could hear them singing and chanting Atrous songs hours before the boys were to take the stage.

It was a beautiful thing.

"He hates it," Ryan said next to me.

I glanced from the guys on stage to him. "He hates what?"

"Having me instead of you." Ryan shrugged. "Gotta say, I thought managing one guy would be so much easier than having two. But I get it now."

I wasn't following. "Get what now?"

"The crowds, the photographers, the cameras." Ryan shook his head and frowned. "I mean, they scream for the others too, but it's different with him."

I nodded. "It is."

"It's scarier."

"I know."

"Steve seems more on edge too."

"Steve? Why? Did something happen?" Why would the head of security be on edge?

"I think he knows Maddox isn't comfortable with me. It makes him . . . distracted." Ryan grimaced. "Have you seen the pictures?"

"No." What fucking pictures? I had my phone out in a heartbeat. And there it was, all over social media.

Pictures of Maddox getting out of the van at the stadium. Grainy photos taken from a distance but easy enough to make out the details. And a video. Maddox exiting the van after Ryan and looking around, looking for someone, until Steve grabbed him and led him into the door.

Along with a multitude of headlines all hedging around the same thing.

Why is Maddox not with Roscoe?

What happened to Moscoe?

Did they break up? Are they fighting?

Look how miserable Maddox is!

Did Moscoe split?

Jesus fucking Christ.

"The media doesn't let up on him, do they?" Ryan asked.

I shook my head. "Nope."

Ryan watched the guys practice on stage for a bit. "He doesn't trust me."

"It's not that he doesn't trust you," I replied gently. "It's nothing against you specifically. It's that he's been with me for years. We have a . . . cohesion." I wasn't sure that was the right word. "We know how to move around each other without having to say it. Like you with Jeremy and Wes. You know how to manage them, you know how they think, how they act, but I'm still learning. Maddox doesn't trust easily. And for good reason." I held up my phone. "You see how he gets treated."

"Do you really think that's all it is?"

Probably not. "Maybe. He'll need some time to adjust. He doesn't take to change very well."

Wes's description of a dropped Rubik's Cube came to mind.

"I think we should change back," Ryan said.

"Honestly, Ryan, I do too. Nothing would make me happier. But Ambrose won't have it."

"Well, I'm gonna say something to him." Ryan nodded to my phone. "Just do me a favor."

"What's that?"

"Don't read the comments on any of those posts."

I sighed, and he clapped my shoulder as he walked off. Goddammit.

Only I didn't have to read them . . . because when the guys were supposed to be eating and resting before the concert, I'd gone to check on a wardrobe issue for Wes, and when I came back, Maddox was talking to Steve.

Well, talking, yes, but it looked a lot more like hushed-yelling. Maddox was holding his phone and Steve was nodding. It wasn't a happy exchange, and Maddox sighed visibly when he saw me.

I went straight over. "Hey," I said, holding up Wes's

boot as if it explained anything. "I just had to get some tape. What's going on?"

Maddox's eyes were black daggers, wild and dangerous. "Have you seen this? What they're saying about you?"

Me?

Oh, the comments.

"I read some headlines and figured none of it warranted reading. And Ryan suggested I do myself a favor and not read them, actually."

Maddox gripped his phone so hard his knuckles went white. "They can say what they want about me, I don't give a fuck. But you're not fair game. Absolutely fucking not." He turned his ire to Steve. "More security on him from now on." Maddox stormed off and all but kicked the door open as he went through it. "Where the fuck is Ambrose?"

I let out a low breath and offered Steve an apologetic smile. "I'll talk to him."

Jeremy, Wes, Luke, and Blake were all staring at us, stunned. "What the hell was that about?" Luke asked.

"Some threats were made online," Steve answered. "Against Roscoe."

All eyes went to me. "I'm fine," I said, walking toward the door. "I better go calm him down."

I found him talking to the stage crew. I caught the end of their conversation; they hadn't seen Ambrose either. Maddox shot me an angry glare. "No one's seen him. Typical." He thumbed his phone screen and I heard Ambrose's voicemail click in. "And he's not answering."

I slipped my hand into his. "Walk with me."

We walked further along the corridors. River Plate Stadium was huge and oval in shape. The corridors seemed to go forever. I stopped at a set of steps and leaned against the handrail, pulling him against me. "We can't control what people say or the way they behave online."

He inhaled deeply, I assumed to get a hold of his temper. "Roscoe, please don't be passive about this. This is not okay. What they said is not okay." He was shaking and breathing hard. "I am not okay."

"Oh, baby."

I held him tighter, and I steadied my breaths until his were synced with mine. Inhale, exhale, calmer, resigned.

"You didn't sign up for this," he whispered.

"Yes I did," I murmured. "When I fell for you."

Wait.

What?

Where the hell had that come from?

I froze, and so did he. He pulled back to look me in the eye. "What?"

My mouth fell open and my cheeks felt as though they were on fire. "Um . . . I'm not quite sure why I said that, like that, to you. I mean, it's true. If I'm being honest. It has been for a while. But I don't know if I was supposed to say it out loud or if you were ready to hear it. Christ. Maddox, can we just forget I said that?" I palmed my forehead. "Sorry. On a concert day of all days. You have a lot on your mind. I don't expect you to say anything back to me."

He smiled.

He fucking smiled.

"You know what?" I added. "I'm not sorry I said it. You should know it. You deserve to know how I feel. Smile all you want, I don't care. Yes, I've fallen in love with you. Probably about three years ago, for what it's worth. But these last few weeks kinda sealed it for me. So let the world say what they want about me, I don't give a fuck. I signed up for it when I started working with you, and I would do it all over again. Because if that's what it means to be with you, then I'm okay with that."

His eyes sparkled. "Are you done?"

"I think so. I'm not sure."

His grin widened and he put his hands to my face. "Can we just back up a little to the part where you said you've fallen in love with me?"

I sighed and tried to gather as much courage as I could. "It's true. I love you, and I didn't mean to say it like that but I want you to know."

"I love you too," he whispered. "God, for the longest time. And now you look at me and I know you see me, and it fills me with something in here." He put my hand to his chest. "Roscoe—"

I crushed my mouth to his and he kissed me, eager and leaning into me, giving himself to me. It would have been so easy to push him against a wall. Or to find an empty room.

A sound down the corridor pulled us apart. Maddox was smiling at me, fisting the front of my shirt, love in his eyes. "Did you do this to distract me?"

I laughed. "No."

"Well, it worked."

His phone buzzed and he fished it out of his pocket. Ambrose's name flashed across the screen. He hit Answer and put him on speaker. "Maddox," Ambrose began. "Yes, I've seen the comments and the articles. Yes, I've got legal on it. And yes, I've spoken to Steve. He said you were . . . angry. Though I could tell from the four voice messages you left."

"Damn right I am," Maddox answered. "I want this dealt with, and I want you to promise me Roscoe's safe. I'm not playing, Ambrose. I walk on stage in less than two hours. You fix this, or I will."

Maddox hung up, smiled at me, and let out a breath. "I feel much better now."

I chuckled. "I think Ambrose just sprouted some gray hair, but okay."

He shrugged. "He better do something, or I will walk on that stage and end a whole bunch of careers, starting with his."

I took a deep breath and threw my arms around him. "Calm down, Rocky. I'm sure he's doing all he can. Now, if you're done being overprotective and wonderful, we need to get you fed and rested. You have a show to do, and there's about a hundred thousand people out there waiting for you. Opening act starts in forty-five minutes."

He pulled back and frowned. "Overprotective?"

"And wonderful." I turned him around to face the way we came and slung my arm around his shoulder, walking us back to the dressing room. "Let's just get through tonight's show."

He put his arm around my waist. "You know how to calm me down."

I stopped walking just outside the dressing room door and looked into his eyes. There were a gazillion people running around getting last minute things ready, but I didn't care. I needed him to know. "I meant what I said. It wasn't some distraction."

He smiled, a full, just-for-me smile. "I know. And I meant it too."

"I know. We can talk about it later tonight, after the concert."

"Yes, we will." He strode into the room and made his way to the guys, who were clearly happy to see him. And obviously surprised at his change of mood.

"You okay?" Jeremy asked.

Maddox nodded. "Yep, never better."

Luke grinned. "Must have been the quickest blow—"

Maddox shoved him, and they joked and laughed a bit before settling down and focusing on their set lists and last minute choreography. Ryan shoved a plate of food into Maddox's hands. "Eat."

Maddox growled at him and I chuckled, earning an odd look from Ryan and a grin from Maddox.

"Everything okay?" Amber asked me.

"Yeah. He's all right now. Though he was pretty direct with Ambrose, so no doubt that's gonna leave a mark."

"Not with Maddox," she clarified. "With you."

"Me?"

"You've seen social media, right? Hell, it even made the news in some places."

"I didn't look specifically. I saw a few headlines. It doesn't matter." I took a deep breath. "Like I told Maddox, we can't control what the public thinks. But getting him all hell-bent out of shape before he walks on stage doesn't do anyone any good. Ambrose said he's fixing it, and I have to trust that." I sighed. "I mean, Christ. So Maddox and I get photographed separately and half the world blames me for dumping him, and the threats roll in. It's ridiculous, right? They have no clue what our reality is or that we're even actually together, or if we're not. They make up bullshit fantasies in their heads and think they can say shit online without consequence."

The muted rumble of the crowd in the stadium reverberated through the room. "Opening act is about to go on," Ryan said. "Time to move."

Everyone flew into motion. Final touches on hair and make-up, and audio pieces were fitted before shirts went on. I didn't think anything of it, I just swept in and helped

Jeremy and Wes. I was their manager now; it was my job. I taped the earpiece wire to Jeremy's back—exactly like we did every time—and just when I was fixing the last piece of tape, a hand came out and stopped me.

A familiar hand. Maddox's hand. Tight around my wrist.

He looked a mix of anguished and livid. "No."

"No, what?" I asked.

"I'll do it," he mumbled and flattened the tape on Jeremy's back. He patted him. "You're all good."

Jeremy turned and pulled his shirt on, giving Maddox an inquisitive look. Then he leaned in and inspected his face. "You have a little bit of . . ." He reached up as if to wipe his cheek. "A smear of jealousy, right there."

Maddox batted his hand away. "Fuck off. I can't . . ." His eyes met mine and he mumbled, "I don't like it."

I stared right back at him. "Well, that is something else we can talk about after the show because this is my job."

Before he could reply, Bibi spun Maddox around. "Hold still," she ordered, Q-tip in hand. "Close your eyes. You smudged my work."

He made a disgruntled noise but obeyed. He wouldn't dare not do as Bibi said, so while he was distracted, I helped Wes with his boots and then it was time for them to go. Maddox was focused now, huddled together with the guys, giving each other a pep talk like they always did.

They put their hands out in the middle, one atop the other. "Atrous!"

"Let's give 'em what they came for," Luke said, and they cheered and clapped, psyching themselves up.

On the whole tour, this would be the biggest concert. One hundred thousand people, sold out in record time. The numbers were mindboggling. It was five ordinary guys doing extraordinary things. Well, they weren't ordinary. But they were humble and gracious, and they came from working-class families. Five normal guys who worked their asses off, tirelessly, endlessly. Their success was not overnight. It was seven years of a constant, hard slog. It was countless hours in the recording studio until they were hoarse, and even more hours in a dance studio until they dropped.

No one in the industry could say they didn't deserve their success. I couldn't help the pride I felt watching them before they walked on stage. It was one of my favorite things.

I'd almost forgotten about Ambrose and Maddox's request for him to "fix it" before he walked on stage, and I hoped Maddox had forgotten about it too. We got busy and there were a thousand things to keep my mind occupied.

The roar of the crowd was deafening. The whole place shook and thrummed with the energy, with the music and dancing. The crowd was a sea of people, moving and swaying, singing with the boys. Every word, every beat.

It was incredible.

Thankfully the weather was cool for the huge crowd and no one passed out. It even got a little chilly backstage once we'd stopped running around after the first set. I had a godawful feeling that Maddox was going to say something to the crowd and to the hundred thousand cameras about the online bullshit, but thankfully, he never did.

And truth be told, by the end of the night, after the last song was sung and they'd come off stage, I hadn't given that whole mess another thought. We were flat-out busy, the boys were on a high—totally exhausted, sweating and laughing—and after winding everything down, packing everything up, we were good to leave.

Just like always, the vans were lined up and our security

escorted us out. The plan was Amber would be with Luke and Blake in the first vehicle, I would be with Jeremy and Wes heading in the second, and Maddox and Ryan would take the third.

We could hear throes of the crowd at the security fencing, waving their phone flashlights in the air as they sang, yelled, screamed their names. And before I could get halfway to the van, Maddox zipped in, linking his arm with mine and leading me to the second van and climbing in.

Steve yelled at Robbie to usher Ryan, Jeremy, and Wes into the third van, and Steve quickly followed us. And that was all I heard before Maddox slid the door shut behind us.

I fell into the back seat and stared at him, wide-eyed. "What the hell was that?"

He grinned and fell into his seat beside me. "That was me fixing the social media problem that Ambrose couldn't fix."

The van began to drive and Steve stuck his head over the front seat. "Everyone good back there?"

"We are great back here," Maddox replied.

"A bit of notice'd be good next time," Steve said. He didn't sound too happy.

Maddox, on the other hand, was far too cheerful. "Affirmative, boss."

Steve gave a short grunt as he turned back to the front, and Maddox grinned.

He took my hand and he was almost sitting on my lap. Which I didn't mind at all, really. "You all right there?" I asked.

He chuckled, edging in a little closer. "Much better with you in here with me. Ryan is nice and all, but he tries to talk to me."

"The audacity of him actually talking to you."

Maddox nudged me. "Shut up. You know when not to talk to me."

"Because I've been with you for years. Give him some time."

He was quiet for a few seconds. "The show tonight felt good. The crowd was amazing. Argentina is always so much fun."

"It was. The concert tonight was one of the best I've seen. You were all on point tonight."

"When the crowd sings like that, it's the best feeling in the world." He was clearly still riding the high of such a great concert, but the adrenaline would wear off soon and the exhaustion would kick in. He must have danced, run, jumped, and sang his way through at least ten miles. At least it wasn't steaming hot like it had been in Miami.

And of course, right then he shivered. "You cold?"

"A little."

"Steve," I called out. "Can we have some heat, please?" I began to peel off my coat.

"Keep yours on," Maddox said. "I'm not that cold. Just cooling down, I guess."

I ignored him and finished taking my coat off and put it over him like a blanket. I tucked it under his chin. "Is that better?"

"Yes," he murmured, all smiley. "Thank you."

I tilted his chin toward me and pressed my lips to his. His mood was contagious and I found myself smiling. "You're so cute."

He grinned. "You dropped an 'I love you' on me today. It's possibly the best day ever."

"You dropped one right back on me, so we're even," I replied, my cheeks hot.

"No one's ever told me that before," he said, so casually

it took a second for me to put it together.

"What?"

"It's true." He ducked his head, his cheeks pink. Then when he looked up and met my gaze, I saw only honesty. "I mean, people tell me all the time. Fans scream it all the time and write it on social media and whatever, but that's not real. And I know the guys love me, but it's not the same. I mean that no one's ever told me that before and meant it like how you meant it today. I've never been with anyone like that." He shrugged. "I've been a part of Atrous since I was sixteen. There's been men, yes. But no one that ever meant anything. Until you." He laughed, embarrassed. "So when I say no one's ever told me that, that you were the first, it's true."

Holy shit.

I palmed the back of his head and pulled him in for a kiss, not giving one single fuck if Steve or the driver saw. "Thank you."

"For what?"

"For telling me."

He made a pained face as if he were mad at himself. "I get jealous."

"I know. I saw."

He chewed on his lip for a bit. "I know it's not funny. And I know I'm doing it, but I can't stop it. I know you don't think of Jeremy or Wes like that, and I do trust you. It's not that I don't." His eyebrows knitted. "And I know it's just your job, but I still don't like it. I can't stand it, if I'm being honest. You touching Jeremy's back today, just . . . I saw red."

"I would never look at or touch another man that way," I whispered.

"I know. It's just . . . I've never had someone." His eyes

met mine, anxious and vulnerable. "I've never had anyone in my life. Anyone permanent, that is. If you know what I mean. And now I do. Finally. And I'll be fucking damned if I'm gonna let someone take that away from me."

There was a lot to unpack in that, and I wasn't sure where to begin. "Okay, see, here's the thing. No one's taking anyone from anyone, least of all taking me from you."

He let his head rest on the back of the seat, his tiredness beginning to kick in. "I've never had anyone," he whispered. "Anyone that meant anything to me, anyway. Not like you. It's my first taste of real life, Roscoe. You're the only real thing in my life. And I know, rationally, if I try to keep too tight a hold on you, it will push you away, but at the same time, I'm too scared to let go."

I put my arm around his shoulder and pulled him closer. "I'm not going anywhere. And even if there are times when we can't be together, I'm still yours, okay?"

He smiled that slow, tired smile. He reached his hand out from underneath my coat, took my hand, and put it to his chest, over his heart. "I've had a lot of important days in my life," he murmured. "A lot of days that some bands and some singers can only dream of. I've won awards, sold-out stadiums around the world, smashed sales records. But today you told me you loved me . . . and that wins."

I leaned in and kissed him. "I love you," I whispered before kissing him again, soft and sweet.

"The real me."

God, it sounded like a question. The quietest, saddest question I think he'd ever asked me.

"The real you. The you that grew up in the suburbs. The you that hates crowds, despite being in front of a hundred thousand people tonight. The you that doesn't like tofu but eats it when your grandmother cooks it because she thinks you like it and you don't want to upset her. The you that leaves your crap all over the bathroom floor, that hogs the bed, that loves animal wildlife documentaries."

He looked at me and smiled.

"The you that needs silence and solitude because you find people exhausting," I added. "The you that writes a song a day, but your lyrics are more like poetry. You compose a lot of music that you never show anyone. The you that loves the rain and that likes to hold hands. That's the you I love. The real you."

His eyes became glassy and he nodded. "Christ, Roscoe." He wiped his eye on his sleeve and let out a half groan, half scoff. "I'm really gonna need you to take me straight to bed when we get to the hotel. I don't want to meet with the others. I want you to show me how much you love me."

"Steve?" I called out. "How far out are we?"

"Three minutes," he replied.

Maddox smiled and raised an eyebrow. "Eager, are you?"

I took my coat that he'd been using as a blanket. "Put this on."

"Why?"

"You'll see."

The thing was, that coat was huge on him. It was one of those puffer jackets that even looked big on me, so it made him look tiny. I pulled the collar up to hide most of his face. Then, as the van slowed, I moved to the seat next to the door. "Hey, Steve? Maddox isn't feeling too good. He can't get warm. I'm gonna take him straight up to the room."

"Okay, sure thing," Steve said.

Maddox gave me a sly smile. He whispered, "Roscoe, that's naughty."

"Act miserable."

When the door opened, I took our bags, stepped out, and held Maddox's arm as he climbed down. I heard the click of cameras as I escorted him inside. But then, of course, Luke and Blake were ahead of us and were waiting for the elevator with Amber, so Maddox needed to play along a little longer. "Nice coat," Luke joked as we all stepped into the elevator. "It's a bit big on you. Might wanna try something from the kids' section next time."

"Very funny, asshole," Maddox said, his voice quiet.

"He's not feeling too good," I said. "He can't get warm."

Amber grew worried. "He needs to be in isolation. I'll send the doctor to your room."

Isolation, when someone was sick on tour, was standard procedure and—after Maddox's heat exhaustion episode last week and now this—I was beginning to think this was not my brightest idea.

Maddox shook his head. "I just need a hot shower, some honey lemon tea, and a decent night's sleep. That's all. No one needs to panic. Roscoe already made me wear his coat like I'm five years old. I'm fine, really."

The doors opened and we walked out onto our floor. "Tell the others we'll see them at breakfast," I said as we walked off to our room.

Maddox opened the door. I slung the do-not-disturb tag over the handle and locked it behind me. Maddox laughed. "Don't take up acting," he said, taking the coat off. "You're a terrible liar." Then he pulled off his boots. "Amber was about to call an ambulance, but Blake and Luke totally know what we're doing." He unzipped his jeans and peeled off his shirt, rubbing his hand slowly over his abs and pecs. "How do you want to fuck me, Roscoe?"

I went to him and pulled his hips against mine.

"There'll be no fucking tonight."

He was about to protest, so I cupped his jaw in one hand and began to walk him backward toward the huge bed. "I'm gonna make love to you. Slow, so slow. I'm gonna take you to the edge and keep you there until your body can't take it anymore."

"Holy fuck," he breathed, his pupils dilated, his skin broke out in goosebumps.

I slid my hands under the waistband of his jeans and pushed them down over his ass. "Get on the bed."

I followed him onto the mattress. I worshiped his body, every inch of his skin. He wanted to know what love felt like, so I showed him. With my body, my hands, my mouth, and finally my cock. I held him so tight as I moved inside him, and he clung to me, fingers digging into my back as he writhed with pleasure.

I kissed him, deep and unforgiving, as he came. He was so wrung out, so boneless and emotional and exhausted that he fell asleep holding onto me. A tear rolled down his cheek, tracking to the hair at his temple. I wanted to ask if he was okay, but he was already asleep.

So I kissed his forehead instead, whispered, "I love you," hoping that even his sleeping mind heard me, and closed my eyes.

———

"TOLD YOU IT WOULD WORK," Maddox said, smiling. We were sitting in the common room having breakfast. We were side by side, our knees touching, our feet tangled. Other staff were buzzing in and out but we didn't have to hide here. We were the first ones there, which was also a first. I'd already been to the gym and when I'd gotten back to our room, Maddox was showered and ordered me to hurry up because he was starving.

He wore his usual black jeans, black hoodie, and black military boots. His long, dangly black earrings swayed as he laughed, and he looked . . . happy.

Maddox Kershaw hadn't looked genuinely happy for a long time, and I couldn't help but cherish knowing it was partly because of me.

Between sips of coffee, bites of cut fruit and thick-cut toast and eggs, he was scrolling the internet on his phone. He wanted to see what the reaction had been to him pulling me into the van after the concert; his ploy to show fans that we weren't apart or miserable or whatever else they thought. And it had worked.

"All the fans love you again," Maddox said. "Even the crazy ones. And they love the fact that I got out of the van wearing your coat, holding your arm."

There were also a few retractions and apologies from some entertainment channels, so Ambrose's apparent method of fixing the online threats toward me had been threats to sue them into oblivion. I couldn't even be mad about it.

Those retractions and apologies had garnered some traction, with fans claiming that Platinum Entertainment truly protected its employees, blah blah blah. If only they knew that Maddox had had to yell for Platinum Entertainment to respond as such . . .

"Are you feeling better?" Amber asked. I hadn't heard her come in. I almost sat up straight, removing my foot from around Maddox's, but I stopped myself. *We didn't need to hide anymore.*

"Oh yes, much," Maddox replied smoothly. "Thanks. Hot shower, hot tea. Fixed me right up."

"Good, I'm glad to hear that," she said, making her way over to the breakfast buffet.

Maddox leaned over to me and whispered, "And when I say hot shower and hot tea, I mean a hot dick in my ass and coming so hard, I went to an alternate reality."

I snorted and nudged him. "Don't get me thinking about it."

He laughed. "Are you picturing it right now?"

Luke walked in, followed by Blake. "Oh, I see someone's feeling miraculously better," Luke said, putting his hands on Maddox's shoulders.

Maddox shot me a humored glance. "Yep. Hot tea, hot shower. Fixed me."

"Is that what they're calling it these days?" Blake asked. He readjusted his dick. "I need to get me some hot tea and hot showers."

Luke laughed and shoved Blake toward the food. "You need to start taking cold showers."

Jeremy came in next and Wes not long after, and once they were all seated with Maddox, I went in search of Ryan. He was coming down the corridor on his way to the common room. "Got a sec?" I asked.

"Uh, sure." He looked toward the doors to where breakfast was, which I understood.

"I won't keep you. I know we've got a big day and you must be hungry . . ." I let out a breath. "I just wanted to apologize for last night. When Maddox grabbed me to ride with him in the van. I didn't know he was going to do that. If I did, I would've given you a heads up."

"It's fine," Ryan replied. "No harm, no foul. We were in a secure location. But maybe tell him if we're in an open crowd, maybe it's not a good idea."

I nodded, relieved. "I already told him that."

Ryan sighed. "For what it's worth, I asked Ambrose to switch us back. I told him that separating you would only cause more problems, and what happened last night is a prime example."

"What did he say?"

"He said no."

I resisted rolling my eyes. "Thanks anyway."

"Is he, uh, is he feeling better?" Ryan asked. "Amber said he wasn't feeling too good last night?"

I felt guilty that they were concerned. "Yeah, he's fine, thanks." I looked down the corridor to the elevators. "Is Ambrose still here?"

"Nah. He's gone with production."

I nodded. The stage production crew would be tearing down the stage and equipment getting it ready to fly out to Brazil tomorrow. "Yeah, of course."

"He said he'd catch up with you later."

"Oh yay."

Ryan laughed. "Something to look forward to."

I clapped his upper arm. "I better let you go eat."

"Yeah, busy day," he said, and I followed him back into the common room.

Maddox and the guys were laughing about something, so I refilled my coffee and stuck by Amber and Ryan. We went through the day's schedule: a live radio interview, then a photoshoot in La Boca, and the guys wanted to see Recoleta and Palermo Soho, and finally an organized late dinner at some fancy place at the Puerto Madero waterfront.

And at exactly 8:57 am, we were in the elevator on our way down to the parking garage. Steve gave Maddox a stern glare. "No funny business today, if you don't mind."

Maddox grinned at him and gave him the Scout's salute. "On my honor, I will do my best . . ."

I couldn't help but smile. It didn't help that I found him ridiculously cute, and his happiness was contagious. He was definitely the kind whose mood affected those around him. Seeing him in such a good mood put a smile on everyone's face.

But, like a good employee, I took Wes and Jeremy into the second van and Maddox linked his arm through Ryan's and pulled him to the last van.

Maddox was grinning and even Ryan was smiling as they climbed in, and the photographers through the security fencing click, click, clicked away.

I got a text message before I even had my seatbelt on. Of course it was from Maddox. *That should keep them guessing.*

I felt Jeremy's eyes on me, and when I looked up, I realized I was smiling. I tried to stop.

"That hot tea and hot shower last night must have sure been something," Jeremy said, seemingly amused.

I rolled my eyes. "Any discussions pertaining to said hot tea or hot shower are strictly off limits."

Wes laughed. "You probably should have told Maddox that before he was gloating at breakfast." I shot him a look and he laughed some more. "Just kidding. But your face just told us everything we needed to know."

I groaned. "Ooh, I know," I said, pretending to be excited. "How about the three of us play a little game of shut the fuck up? Let's see who wins."

Jeremy burst out laughing and he shoved Wes. But then he gave me a nod, still smiling. "I can see why you and Maddox get along."

And the rest of the day went exactly according to plan. The radio interview went well—mostly in English but also with some help from some translators—the sightseeing and touristy things were fun despite the need for SWAT-like security.

The people were friendly and polite, and the boys even posed for a few photos with some locals after their photoshoot. The food was amazing, the atmosphere of the city was welcoming. And what I was most thankful for, it wasn't like a sauna, given it was winter.

I mostly stuck with Wes and Jeremy but there were a few times when I found Maddox by my side. Just walking along the street or standing in line at a market stall or food kiosk, and we sat next to each other at the restaurant, our thighs touching under the table. We talked and laughed as a whole group, all of us, and for a few fleeting moments, I imagined what it might be like if we lived a normal life.

And by normal, I meant no SWAT-like security, no clearances before we entered anywhere, no paparazzi, no cameras.

Maybe we'd never know, but I saw glimpses of what life with Maddox could be like. And so help me God, I wanted it. Part of my heart ached for it.

How was it even possible to long for something you've never known?

That normality that Maddox longed for, fought for . . . I understood now.

THE NEXT MORNING was another early start. We were flying to Brazil, which was only a short flight, but logistically the distance didn't matter. We had to be at the private terminal by eleven, which is why I was surprised when Ambrose had asked to see us at 8:00 am in his hotel room. I thought he'd have been gone for hours already.

I also didn't know what to expect in his room. I was secretly hoping there wasn't an open suitcase on display or his underwear lying around, but what I wasn't expecting was a room set up like a government tactical headquarters.

He had two laptops, iPads, clipboards, and his bed looked like he hadn't ever slept in it. There was no suitcase at all that I could see. God, did he sleep at all?

"Take a seat," he said. "Sorry I didn't catch you yesterday."

He was clearly very busy.

"I didn't have a second to spare," he continued. "Rave reviews about the concert, I must say. Five-star performance by everyone involved, so thank you for that." He smiled at Maddox. "But then I did spend some time, which I couldn't afford, dealing with this."

He turned one of the laptops around. It was a picture from after the concert. Maddox grabbing my arm, a grin a mile wide, and pulling me into the van with him. There were headlines and comments that had been exactly what Maddox had predicted.

Back together.

All smiles in Argentina.

Maddox looks so happy!

Moscoe are back together—were they ever apart? Moscoe forever!

Not that any of that meant much to Ambrose, because he was pissed. "This change in manager units was to better the security around you two. Then you go and pull a stunt like that."

"I asked you to fix it, and you didn't," Maddox shot back.

"I was handling it," Ambrose replied.

"I handled it better!" Maddox said a little too loud. "I

will not stand by when one of us is threatened."

"Social media can be a dangerous tool," Ambrose tried. "Weaponizing your fans—"

"They were already weaponized. They threatened to kill him." Maddox put his hand on my arm. "Actually fucking kill him, and you think for one second that I *wouldn't* do anything about it? You're damn lucky I didn't walk out on that stage and tell the world what I thought."

Ambrose took a deep breath and exhaled slowly.

"I know you were only trying to help, but it is not your job to *fix* anything, Maddox. You jeopardized your lead security by changing vans at the last minute. These things are planned for a reason. And that's to make sure all five of you are escorted safely into your vehicles with minimum exposure outside, from the building to the vehicle. You've seen the footage. You saw Jeremy and Wes left alone for a split second, you saw Ryan have to hurry to get them into the car, and Robbie had to double back. This is not just about you, Maddox."

Maddox frowned. "I'm confused. The other day you called me the whole brand. Am I the brand or not?"

The sarcasm was a bit much. I groaned. "Maddox."

Maddox hadn't taken his eyes of Ambrose. "Yeah, I'm sorry I caused a split second of confusion. But I wanted the situation with Roscoe fixed, so I fixed it."

"I was fixing it." Ambrose was not happy. "We sent injunctions to all the social media sites requesting the removal of any accounts who had threatened harm to any one on our team and forwarded their IP addresses to the authorities. We requested official apologies and retractions from any site that posted anything pertaining to further harm. There are procedures in place for this, Maddox. Legal procedures."

"Do you think anyone hell-bent on hurting someone gives a shit about legal procedures, Neil?" Maddox asked.

Ambrose's nostrils flared but he managed to keep his calm. "Legal procedures are the first step in this process. Things have to be done by procedure so if anything goes to court, every box is checked. You know that. Let us deal with this. As for now, the units remain unchanged. Roscoe, you're with Jeremy and Wes. Maddox, you're with Ryan. Steve's been advised."

"What?" Maddox cried.

Ambrose's tired eyes turned hard. He'd had enough arguing. "Not negotiable. Especially after you were both photographed around the city together yesterday, looking very cozy with each other—which is enough to keep the PR team busy for a week—the best security measures are to keep the two main targets separate."

I finally felt it was my turn to say something. "Ryan asked for the units to be changed back," I said.

Ambrose pursed his lips. "And I told him no."

"Then you know that no one is happy with this arrangement," I added. "Not me, not Ryan, not Maddox, Jeremy or Wes, not Steve. No one."

"I don't do these things for approval ratings or Girl Scout cookies, Roscoe," Ambrose replied. "I put these measures in place to keep you and everyone else safe."

Maddox stood up. "Look, Ambrose. I appreciate what you do. I know this"—he gestured to the laptops and paperwork—"can't be easy. I get that. But what I do isn't easy, and what Roscoe does isn't easy either. It's all various shades of shit for everyone. And we didn't set out to purposefully make your job more difficult, just like I can assume you didn't make ours more difficult on purpose either. It is what it is. You've expressed your concerns, we've expressed ours, and it's pretty clear nothing will change." He opened and closed his fists, and his voice was way too passive for my liking. His breaths were short and sharp. "You obviously have a lot of shit to get done, and quite frankly, I'm done with this conversation. So let's just leave it at that. I need to go."

Maddox walked toward the door, which was my cue to follow, so I stood up. "I told you not to push him," I whispered. Ambrose heard me just fine. And I followed Maddox out. I had to chase him halfway down the hall. "Hey, wait up."

He shook his head and kept walking, faster now, quickly swiped his key card to get into our room, and he pushed the door open, hard, and all but fell inside. "Hey," I tried again, grabbing his arm.

He spun around to face me, his face pale and pained. He was trying to inhale but couldn't quite manage it.

I put my hand to the side of his neck. "Hey," I whispered. "Breathe for me. Breathe."

Then, like a switch, his lungs kicked in and he gasped in some air.

"That's it," I murmured. "Breathe in, breathe out."

He did as I asked, his chest rising and falling with measured breaths, his eyes wide with fear and shame. When he was breathing okay, he let his head fall forward and his shoulders sagged, and I pulled him in for a hug.

"You're okay," I offered gently, holding him tight while rubbing his back.

He was heavy against me, as if he'd been totally zapped of energy. "Sorry."

"You have nothing to be sorry for."

He got heavier like my words weighed too much.

"Come and sit down," I said, urging him to the bed. I

knelt between his legs, held his hands, and peered up into his eyes. "Maddox, baby, you're okay. I've got you."

He became teary but he blinked them back and swallowed hard. "I have . . . I have some trouble catching my breath sometimes."

I nodded, because this wasn't the first time I'd seen him like this. It was the worst, but not the first. "Okay."

"Not for a while though. And that was a bad one." He let out a shaky breath and practiced his breathing for a bit. "I just got worked up and I wanted to fucking yell, but then I thought he was gonna send you home or something, and god, I had to leave . . ." He let out another shaky breath. "Fuck, Roscoe."

I leaned up and cupped his face. "Hey, I'm not going anywhere. I love you. I'm not going anywhere."

He nodded, though his breathing was still a little rough. "Kinda feels like I'm losing my grip."

"Your grip on what?"

"Control. No matter how crazy or how bad it got, I could always handle it. All the fame and the loneliness . . . I could . . . I could handle it. It was awful but I had a hold of it." He shook his head. "And now I have you and I'm so happy, but it feels like I'm just waiting for someone to rip it away from me. Because if they split us up . . . if they use it against me . . ." His eyes were black with fear. "I don't know if I will come back from that."

"Oh, Maddox," I breathed. "I'm staying with you."

He let out a long, unsteady breath. "I'm sorry for freaking out." He barked out a laugh. "It sounds crazy, and I swear, I'm not. I've just never really said any of this out loud before."

I pulled him to his feet so I could hug him properly. "Thank you for telling me now."

He tightened his hold on me. "You make everything better."

I pulled back and held his face. "You tell me if you start to feel like it's getting too much, okay?"

He nodded, resigned. "Don't tell the guys. They don't need to be worrying about me, and it's no big deal. It just comes out of the blue sometimes. Like my lungs don't work. But I'm fine once I catch my breath."

"Okay." I kissed him softly. "Are you ready to be around everyone. We need to get organized to get to the airport."

He smiled. "Yeah. I'm fine. Much better now that I talked to you."

I kissed him again. "I'm glad you're feeling okay."

He sighed, smiling, though it didn't quite meet his eyes. But he wanted to hang out with Jeremy and the boys in the common room for a bit—to prove to me that he was fine? I could only guess—while I had some work to do with Amber and Ryan going through our checklists.

Soon enough we were boarding the plane. Maddox was with the boys, like always, and I was further down the plane in our separate section with Amber and Ryan, like we always were. I shoved my coat in the overhead compartment and was about to take my seat when I saw Doctor Hardwick sitting a few rows back by himself.

I hesitated. Did I say something? Should I? As a manager or as a boyfriend . . .

Christ. Maddox would kill me if he found out, but I had to know . . .

I slid into the seat next to him and he pulled his earbuds out. "Hey, doc, got a sec?"

He straightened in his seat. "Yeah, sure."

I met his gaze. "Hypothetically, if someone was having panic attacks, how would I help them?"

CHAPTER FOURTEEN

HARDWICK STARED AT ME.

"Hypothetically," I repeated. "If a personal friend of mine was having some anxiety issues."

"I can't offer medical advice—"

"If they were having trouble breathing sometimes, hypothetically," I added, speaking over him. "Is there some information I should know? Perhaps maybe something online I could read?"

He pursed his lips. "That would be a good start."

I swallowed hard. We were treading a fine line here and I needed him to know how sincere I was. "I care about this person," I admitted quietly. "A lot. And I worry about them."

He nodded slowly, still not saying anything.

"I spend a lot of time with them and need to know what I should do if they have a panic attack when they're with me. Hypothetically, of course."

He still didn't look like he was going to speak any time soon.

"Do I just sit with them, help them breathe, that kind of thing?"

Hardwick sighed quietly. "Reading some credible medical websites would be helpful, but yes, what you suggested is a good starting point."

I nodded. "It's hard because they don't want anyone else to know. This hypothetical person. But asking them to reduce stress and not to argue with their boss is like pissing in the wind."

Hardwick almost smiled. "Reducing stress and not arguing about anything would be recommended."

Okay, so that's about all I could say and about all he could answer. But now he knew. He knew that I knew, and he knew we were on the same page.

Hypothetically.

The cabin crew came through and noticed my empty seat. "You better go take your seat," Hardwick said.

I gave the crew member a nod and stood up. We were taxiing out to the runway so the look she gave me was polite but curt. "Thank you, sir. I'll need you to take your seat immediately."

I turned back to Hardwick. "Thanks."

He smiled and put his earbuds back in, and I went back to my seat. I searched up some medical websites and began to read.

SAO PAULO, Brazil, passed in a blur. The concert, the day of sightseeing, the media, the photos, the fans . . . it was over in a blink, and before we knew it, we were heading back to the States.

We had a sold-out show in Atlanta and then Nashville, intense rehearsals, stage checks, tightened security, screaming fans outside the hotel at all hours, a late show television interview, and a day doing an unplugged session at the Grand Old Opry, which would be released later in the year.

It was crazy.

But we stuck with Ambrose's instructions: me with Wes and Jeremy, Maddox with Ryan. The trade-off was Maddox and I still shared a hotel room, and once that door was shut, the only two people in the world who mattered were us. We made love, we snuggled in bed, we showered together, we watched TV. We still ate breakfast and dinners together with everyone else, but any time we were in a common room or a dressing room, he basically stuck to me.

The concerts were flawless, the reviews were all outstanding. The TV interview was fun, and like they always were, the boys were fun and charming. Maddox was at the back, Jeremy did the most talking, and while they were *all* involved and joked and laughed, Maddox barely said two things.

Seeing him now, not wanting to be in the spotlight or the main focus all the time, hit me different knowing he was dealing with anxiety. I realized now, him asking to change the interview format so he wasn't the center of attention was a sign I should have seen. And it was also incredibly brave of him to ask.

I was watching his every breath, waiting for that panicked glazed look in his eyes or for him to become breathless or pull at his collar.

But he didn't. He didn't seem to smile as much, though, and I often saw Doctor Hardwick lurking in the background, watching.

Washington DC and Philly passed in a blink, and then

Chicago and Detroit. All concerts were sold out, media hype was huge, with fans lining up from before dawn the morning of the concert. Merch stalls were crowded. Fans cheered and sang loud enough that we could hear them in the dressing rooms.

By Detroit, Blake had his knee iced and taped every day, Wes had his shoulder taped up, and Maddox had to use the throat spray. "My throat's scratchy," he'd said, swallowing a few times. He'd tried drinking ice water, hot lemon water, but nothing worked. The doc gave a few squirts of the anti-inflammatory forte stuff and he got through the concert.

But when they came off the stage . . .

All five of them were on the floor in the dressing room, sweaty and exhausted. Blake had his knee up and iced, Julio was working on Wes's shoulder . . . and Maddox could barely speak.

The next morning, he couldn't speak at all.

His voice was nothing but a hoarse, abrasive bark. He sat on the couch in the common room while everyone else ate their breakfast, miserably sipping honey tea, hoodie pulled up, leaning heavily against me, and I had my arm around him.

This was probably our first public display of affection in front of everyone. But it wasn't cute or romantic. Maddox was miserable.

Hardwick worked around him, checking his throat and ears, taking his temperature, his blood pressure, all while Maddox never moved. He stayed against me the whole time. "Fever, pharyngitis, and laryngitis. Your throat looks like the Eye of Mordor," he mumbled. Maddox nodded because he'd expected as much. "It's been sore for a few days, hasn't it?"

Maddox nodded again.

Goddammit.

"Maddox," I whispered. "You should have said something."

The doc patted Maddox's knee, stood up, and tossed the little plastic cover from the thermometer. Everyone waited for his verdict . . .

"Next rehearsal?" he asked.

"Four days," I answered. "Toronto concert is five days."

Hardwick frowned. "Absolute voice rest for four days. Silence. No singing, no talking, no whispering. Tylenol, corticosteroids, vitamin C, fluids, bed rest when you can. Steamy bathrooms will help your respiratory. Flying today won't help, but we can't do much about that."

"Will he be able to sing in Toronto?" Jeremy asked, concerned.

"We won't know for two or three days," the doc replied. "Everyone needs to wear a mask in communal areas, on the plane, in a car. Sitting here. Roscoe, you especially. He's not contagious right now, but that could change. I'll just go grab my bag and I'll be back."

Jeremy leaned in from a distance and patted Maddox's shoulder. "On the bright side, we get four days silence from Maddox! Roscoe, you gotta be relieved."

He was joking, clearly, but Maddox pulled out his phone and sent a quick text to Jeremy, which I could read.

Fuck you

Jeremy's phone pinged. He read the screen and laughed, but then he crouched down to be on eye level with him. "Want more tea? Or a Sprite? Mom used to always give me flat Sprite when I was sick. I can get you some."

Maddox shook his head but he still didn't move from his spot. I felt his forehead, which was still clammy, like it was both hot and cold at the same time. Poor thing. I gave him a squeeze and he sagged against me, his head on my chest.

Jeremy took Maddox's cup of tea before it could spill, and stood up. "Aaaaand he's out."

"Is he asleep?" I whispered.

Jeremy nodded. "He looks terrible," Blake mumbled. "I mean, terrible for him. He still looks better than any of us."

Luke came over and inspected Maddox's face. "We could shave his eyebrow. Just one."

"He'd kill you," Jeremy said. "But we could totally draw a dick on his face."

"No one's touching him," I growled, tightening my arm around him.

Wes sighed. "Oh, Roscoe. Don't be such a party-pooper."

Hardwick and Ambrose came walking in together. The doc had his bag with him. Ambrose had an iPad, a look of concern on his face, and two assistants on his heel. "He's on total vocal rest for four days," Hardwick explained. "We'll see how he's feeling before rehearsals."

Jeremy and Blake both put their fingers to their lips at the same time. "Shh. He's asleep," Jeremy whispered.

The doctor knelt in front of Maddox and pulled his hood back. "Some Tylenol should help with his fever. Maddox, wake up for me." He gave his shoulder a bit of a shake.

Maddox stirred but put his head back on me, so I shuffled him to a seated position. "Hey, baby, you need to take some medicine."

Maddox opened his eyes, barely, and gave me a filthy glare. The guys all laughed so he shot them the same look, and when the doctor held up a paper cup of pills, Maddox bestowed the same look on him.

"You want to go to the hospital to have these administered?" Hardwick said, no nonsense.

Maddox pouted, rather cutely, and took the cup. The guys all laughed again and Maddox summoned the energy to give them a middle finger. Hardwick handed over a bottle of water but looked at me. "He needs to stay hydrated." Then, he stood up and turned to Wes, Luke, Blake, and Jeremy, holding up a bottle of pills. "All of you, vitamin C and zinc. Now."

While they all whined and carried on, Ambrose stood watching Maddox and me. Maddox was leaning on me again, his feet tucked up underneath him, his head on my shoulder, my arm around him. He looked small and he was still miserable, and if Ambrose didn't like that he was laying all over me, I did not care.

"Will he be all right to fly?" Ambrose asked quietly.

I nodded. "Of course." I was going to add that he'd never let anyone down yet but decided to keep that to myself. "I'll sit with him on the plane. He shouldn't be with the band in case he becomes contagious."

"It's not likely to be," the doc said. "Unless his throat becomes infected, then yes, he'll need to be isolated. It's better to be safe than sorry though." He looked at Ambrose. "Whatever you have planned in Toronto for the next three days won't include Maddox."

Maddox lifted his head and groaned his dissent. It was more of a croaky whine. They were supposed to be doing a morning TV show interview and song in Toronto.

"Complete vocal rest means no groaning," Hardwick said, pointing a hard glare at Maddox.

Wes laughed. "No groaning? Well, shit, no sex either. Roscoe—"

Jeremy shoved him, and I pretended not to notice

Ambrose's reaction. Meanwhile Maddox found his phone and sent a quick text. Wes's phone beeped and he read the message and laughed some more. "Maddox, oh my. That's very explicit. I'm telling your mom you used that word."

Maddox began texting something else and I took his phone. "Pills now. Tell him to fuck off later."

Thankfully Amber intervened. "Guys, go finish packing. We're leaving here in one hour. And Blake, you're supposed to be resting that knee. At least you're wearing the brace." Then she gave Maddox a sad smile. "I'll get you some vitamin water. There was some in the vending machine."

Maddox nodded and reluctantly took his pills, grimacing as he swallowed them. He frowned at me, the most pitifully sad face. He clearly didn't handle being sick very well at all.

"You'll feel better soon," I said gently. "How about you lie in bed while I pack up our room?"

He nodded again and I helped him to his feet, but he was quick to grab ahold of me. I took his arm and led him toward the door. "Text me if you need anything," I said to Ryan. "And thanks, Doc."

Amber caught us in the hall. She handed me the vitamin water. "Thank you so much," I said. "Let me know if you need me or if anything changes."

"Will do."

I finally got Maddox back into bed and he let out a low groan. "You're not supposed to make any noises," I said, sitting beside him and brushing his hair off his forehead. "The Tylenol will kick in soon and bring your temperature down. Close your eyes and rest, baby."

He smiled, kind of. Then he signaled with his hands

that he wanted to write something. I grabbed the hotel notepad and pen.

Thank you.

"You're welcome," I replied.

He scribbled something else. *Never had anyone to look after me before.*

I leaned down and kissed his forehead. "Well, now you do."

He smiled, and his blink was slow. I took the notepad and wrote something down for him.

I love you.

He read it and smiled, but he hugged the notepad to his chest and closed his eyes.

THE FLIGHT to Toronto was short, thankfully. Maddox's temperature had come down, and as soon as we got to the hotel, Hardwick knocked on our door to give him more meds. It was only Tylenol and whatever that steroid was, but he was looking a little brighter. Still tired though, and he was happy to lie in bed and watch TV or doze off to music.

And I'd be lying if three days in isolation with Maddox was a bad thing. Even if he was sick. I fed him honey and lemon tea and made sure he drank lots of water. On the second day, he wanted a bowl of mashed potatoes and more vitamin water, and on the third day, he wanted KFC mashed potatoes and gravy, fries, and nuggets. For breakfast.

He was clearly feeling much better.

He still hadn't used his voice, and we found writing notes to each other was a lot of fun and flirty. Or just downright dirty.

He handed me his notepad and I read his scrawl. *Blowjob?*

I quickly wrote out my reply. *Not good for your throat.*

Good for yours.

I laughed. "Think you can get through it without groaning? Or whimpering?"

Nodding, he pulled the front of his sweatpants down and gripped his half-hard dick. He stroked himself nice and slow.

Damn.

When I didn't move fast enough, apparently, he pushed me down on the bed, straddled my chest and tapped my lips with the head of his cock. Oh hell, yes. I flattened my tongue and opened wide, and he leaned forward, slipping into my mouth.

The only sound he made was a low growl that rumbled low in his chest as he came. I finished him off, without mercy, and left him a boneless, sated, and sleepy lump in bed.

I went in search of Amber and Ryan, asking if there was anything I needed to do to help, but not before I left a message in Maddox's notepad. *I love all of you, Mr. Kershaw.*

ON THE THIRD MORNING, the boys did the morning show interview without him. They had to leave the hotel at 6:00 am, and Maddox wanted to see them off. It was the first time he'd seen them since we arrived in Canada. He wore his black hoodie, gray sweats and socks, and a face mask, which did little to hide how hard he found it to watch them get ready without him.

"You sure you're okay?" Jeremy asked.

Maddox nodded, barely. He took out his notepad. *I should be going with you.*

Jeremy gave him a sad face. "How are you feeling?"

Maddox shrugged.

Jeremy gave him a hug. "We need you better for tomorrow and the day after. Don't worry about this interview. We got you."

Luke joined in on the hug, then Blake and Wes, and it made my heart full to see it. They'd missed him, and seeing him now, I realized just how much he'd missed them. When they let him go, he wrote in his notepad for them. *Don't have too much fun without me.*

Wes took his notepad and drew a huge dick on it with a smiley face. Maddox chuckled, reached into his hoodie, and pulled out his middle finger.

And then it was time for us to go.

Yes, I'd be leaving Maddox at the hotel. Doctor Hardwick was staying, other staff were around, and even some security would stay behind. If Maddox needed anything, anything at all, all he had to do was text. The boys doing a media event in the city was a priority, and so it was all managers on deck. Which was fine, it was my job, but it didn't make leaving Maddox any easier.

"You sure you're okay?" I asked, both hands on the sides of his neck. We were in the common room but I didn't care.

He nodded.

"You text me if you need me," I whispered. "We'll be right back, okay?"

Once upon a time, Maddox having alone time was the norm. Now he looked a little panicked at the thought.

"Get some rest," I murmured, then pulled him in for a hug and whispered in his ear so only he could hear. "If the doc gives you the all-clear, I'm working you over tonight."

I left him smiling and joined the others on our way to the waiting vans. It felt odd to leave him.

"Feels wrong," Jeremy said. "To leave him."

Wes nodded. "Not having the five of us. Feels weird."

It pulled at my heartstrings, though I tried to smile. "Was just thinking that."

The interview went well. Of course, the big news was that Maddox wasn't there. "He's on voice rest before the concert," Blake had said. The interviewers were excited because this was *news*, and they got to ask a line of questions that would no doubt be replayed all over the internet, and it was good for ratings.

Kinda pissed me off, to be honest.

But the boys handled it like pros. They made a few jokes about how nice it was that Maddox wasn't allowed to speak, and it was the quietest he'd ever been in his life, and how they didn't have to hear his lame jokes, and the interviewers laughed. The guys all looked at the camera then, told Maddox they loved him, and they quickly moved on talking about the tour and the album.

And then it was time to perform.

Without Maddox.

"So we're gonna do things a little differently today," Jeremy said into a mic as they took their seats. Four stools stood in front of a guitarist and a pianist, microphones in the front. "We were going to do our normal performance for this song but it didn't look right with it just being the four of us." He looked at the camera. "Maddox, I know you're watching, brother."

And then they did a totally stripped-down version of "Fly."

They each took turns singing Maddox's lines. It was beautiful and it hit so different when it was slowed right down and sung like that.

I knew it would have broken Maddox's heart. His guilt at not being there, his guilt at letting the boys down, at letting his fans down. I could just imagine him lying in bed, the covers all pulled up over his head, feeling like utter shit.

I really wanted to get back to him. Like right now.

I took out my phone and shot him a text. *You okay?*

No reply.

Fuck.

I sent another one. *Maddox baby, you okay?*

His text bubble came up on screen and my relief was immediate. But then the bubble disappeared, reappeared, and disappeared again before his reply came through. *Sure.*

Sure. Hmm, right. I was one hundred percent certain he was not okay. I wanted to call him so he could hear my voice, but I was in a studio standing a few feet from the camera crew filming the band sing. I sent another text instead. *Will be home soon. Will bring KFC.*

His reply took a while to come through. *Thx. ILY.*

I love you too. All of you.

"Everything okay?" Amber mouthed to me.

I shrugged and she frowned, but the song ended and the producer called for commercial break. The guys went and thanked the hosts, said a round of goodbyes, and security ushered us into our vans. The crowd was big and closing in, screaming and yelling, cameras trained on our every step, and the silence when the doors closed was a relief.

There was no way we could go through a fast-food drive thru. "Maddox wanted KFC. I told him I'd get him some. Anyone else?" I asked Jeremy and Wes. And after a call to the other van, I put in a call to have our orders delivered to the hotel.

"How is he?" Jeremy asked. "Really?"

I met his eyes. "He's okay. Apart from the feelings of failure and guilt for letting you guys down. If the doctor says he can't perform . . . then I don't know what he'll do."

Jeremy nodded slowly. "He'll perform anyway."

"And risk permanent larynx damage," Wes added.

I sighed. "I'm sure he'll be fine."

He had to be.

He just had to be.

MADDOX ATE HIS MASHED POTATOES, half a chicken nugget, and a few fries while the others ate and chatted. He didn't grimace when he swallowed, though, so I guessed his throat felt okay . . . but his smile was gone. He didn't speak—not that he was supposed to—but his silence was somehow louder now than it had ever been.

We had a few minutes before Hardwick wanted to see Maddox, but I needed to talk to him first. I tapped my watch and he nodded, so I stood up, mumbled our excuses, and we went back to our room.

I pulled out two chairs at the table, sat in one, and waited for him to sit in the other. I scooted closer until our knees bumped and I took his hands. "I know you must be feeling like crap," I said. "I just want you to know that it's okay to feel that way." He opened his mouth but I put my hand up. "No talking."

Maddox sighed.

"Baby, I know watching them play without you must have been hard."

He sucked on his bottom lip and he got a little teary.

"You wanna know what Jeremy said in the car? That it felt wrong without you. That something was missing. They didn't want to perform without you."

He tilted his head, anguished. "It was the first time," he whispered.

"Hey, no talking."

He shook his head; his voice was a little rough. "The band played without me."

I cupped his cheek. "No, baby."

"But it means they can. If they had to. Atrous would be okay."

What the hell?

"Maddox, what are you saying?"

"All these years it was us five. We couldn't be anything but five. We always said if one of us—" He swallowed hard. "If one of us couldn't, or wouldn't or didn't want to . . ."

"Baby."

"They'd be okay." He let out a shaky breath. His chin wobbled. "I don't know how long I can keep doing this, Roscoe. I don't know how much I have in me. I'm so tired. I'm so fucking tired. But then I can't be anything else. This is all I am. I don't know who I am without this, without them. I don't even know who I am *with* this."

I held his face and kissed his forehead, his cheeks, his lips. "Oh, Maddox."

"They could be Atrous without me."

I shook my head because, no, I didn't think they could be. But that was the problem. The whole band's existence, the lives and professions of his four best friends was on Maddox's shoulders. That responsibility, that pressure was what weighed him down.

He let out another shaky breath, then inhaled sharply,

and again, and again. His breathing became jagged and shallow, and he put the heel of his hand to his sternum and he shook his head.

I cupped his face and made him look at me. "Breathe, Maddox. In." I inhaled. "And out."

So I breathed with him, slow and steady, in and out, until the fear in his eyes subsided.

Then there was a knock at the door. "It's Doctor Hardwick."

Goddammit.

I let out an almighty sigh, then looked up into Maddox's eyes. "You up for this?"

He practiced his breathing, in and out, nice and slow, and nodded. I stood up, kissed him softly, and opened the door. As soon as the doc walked in, he could clearly tell something was up.

"Everything okay?"

Maddox nodded. "Yeah."

"You're not supposed to be talking."

"First time just now. In three days."

"That's true, doc," I said. "He hasn't said a word in three days until just now."

"How does your throat feel?"

"Better. The spray and the lozenges help."

"Good."

I put my hand on Maddox's shoulder. "Want me to duck out for a bit?"

He shook his head. "Please stay."

I sat on the bed while the doctor checked Maddox's throat, looked in his ears, took his temperature. He was happy with his recovery. "Dance rehearsal this afternoon should be fine. Take it easy, though. And I want you to run through some light voice work this evening. Full stage rehearsal tomorrow should be okay, but don't overdo it. No straining, no high notes. Okay?"

Maddox smiled. "Okay."

I thought Hardwick might have been done or made some small talk before leaving, but he didn't. He pulled out the chair next to Maddox and sat down. "You seemed a little stressed when I first came in."

Maddox shook his head. "Nah. I'm fine. I'll be better once I get back to work."

"How are you feeling about the concert in two days?"

"Looking forward to it."

"Being worried about your voice is no different than a pro football player worrying about their first game after an arm or a leg injury."

"I'm not worried about being on stage, doc. Roscoe and I were just talking about—" Then he changed tack. "Actually, can you please tell him I now have the green light for a *lot* of sex?"

I barked out a laugh. "That is not what we were talking about!"

Hardwick's smile ended with a sigh. "How many more concerts to go?"

I answered. "Five."

The doc looked squarely at Maddox. "Okay. Five is doable. How's the breathing?"

Breathing . . . because calling it what it was—anxiety, panic attacks, stress—was apparently off limits.

Maddox gave a small dismissive nod. "It's fine."

I raised my eyebrow, which Hardwick caught. He pursed his lips. "Maddox."

"Roscoe helps me," he said quickly. "If I can't catch my breath."

"And if Roscoe's not around?" Hardwick asked gently.

He had his hand on Maddox's knee. "Maddox, it's okay. You know what to do when you start to feel like you can't get enough air. You can do it on your own if you have to."

Maddox looked like he was about to protest, but the doc put his hand up. "I know you don't want to hear it, but we are going to talk about it and we're going to set up some appointments. After this tour. When we get back to LA. No more excuses."

Maddox studied the table for a long second. "So, I wasn't joking about the sex thing. It's a go for launch, right? Because Roscoe is all about the rules. What the doctor says goes, so if you could just give him a nod, that'd be great. Or even if you don't think it's a good idea, if you could still just nod, I'd really appreciate that."

I couldn't help but laugh. "Christ, Maddox."

The poor doc sighed and got to his feet. "You are medically fit to engage in whatever consensual activities you choose. As long as it's not too strenuous. Oh, and no taking anything into the throat."

Oh my god.

Maddox chuckled. "Believe me, it's not going in my throat, doc."

"Maddox! Jesus." I couldn't believe it.

"On that note, I shall leave you to it." Hardwick picked up his bag just as there was a rather loud, obnoxious knock on the door.

"Hey, dickbag. Open the door."

Maddox smiled. "Jeremy."

"I'll let him in, and I'll go notify Ambrose that you're good to go," Hardwick said as he walked to the door, and two seconds later, Jeremy walked in.

"So, what's the verdict?"

Maddox smiled. "He said the test results show, without doubt, that *you're* the dickbag."

Jeremy's smile became a grin. "You can talk, which means you can sing?" Maddox nodded and Jeremy pulled him into a bear hug, his feet off the ground. "Thank fuck."

Maddox laughed. I swear it made my heart squeeze to see him happy. "He has to take it easy today at dance rehearsal," I said. "No pushing himself."

Jeremy put his arm around Maddox's shoulder. "Your dad is such a drag."

Maddox shoved him, smiling. "Fuck you."

"No thanks. We've been through this, Madz," Jeremy joked. "I don't swing that way."

Maddox grabbed him by the back of the neck and they play-shoved for a bit, but Jeremy was soon pulling him to the door. "Come on, the boys are out there waiting to hear."

Maddox spared me a glance over his shoulder as Jeremy led him out, but I already had my laptop in hand and was following them out. I had a lot of work to do, already feeling bad that Ryan and Amber had carried more than their share of our workload.

I followed Maddox and Jeremy into the common room and made my way over to the table where Ryan and Amber were sitting. They saw Maddox, saw how happy Jeremy was, and quickly deduced that he'd been given the all-clear to perform.

"Oh god, that's a relief," Amber said, giving me a warm smile. "I mean, I'm glad he's okay, but the whole Plan B thing was getting a little daunting."

I opened my laptop. "Plan B?"

"Yeah, what to do if he was out for this concert, for the rest of the tour," Ryan answered, then he shrugged. "His position affects everyone: center choreography, main vocals."

I tried to keep my expression neutral, but it wasn't easy. "Yeah, I get it. But the boys did really well without him today. Changing the song to suit the circumstance was smart."

My morning with Maddox replayed through my mind. Him wondering how long he could do this, how long he wanted to. The pressure put on him to stay, the people he'd disappoint if he didn't. His anxiety about it all.

I considered my wording carefully. "I gotta say, maybe we should use this as a learning curve for what happens when one of them is ruled out. Not if. But when. I mean, it's bound to happen, right? It's *going* to happen. Knees, shoulders, voices, stress." I shrugged, trying not to give too much away. "I think we need to consider putting contingency plans on the table after this tour. We just expect them to bounce back, to endure it. It's not just Maddox. Wes and Blake are held together by athletic tape right now."

Ryan nodded. "I agree. But you know how Platinum is," he said, keeping his voice low. He rolled his eyes and mimicked Arlo Kim. "Gotta make hay while the sun shines."

"Yeah well, you can't make hay if the horse pulling the plow can't take another step," I replied.

Amber never took her eyes off me, studying, scrutinizing in that way that made her very good at her job. "There's something you're not telling us." She wasn't mad or snide. If anything, she was concerned. "Is he okay?"

Fuck.

Of course she was asking about Maddox. I met her gaze. "Between us three," I whispered, "I don't think so. I mean, his throat is better . . . Ryan, you should know . . . and so help me god, do not repeat this to anyone. Don't let him know that you know. I'm only telling you because he's supposed to ride with you now, but he's been experiencing some . . . breathing issues."

They both stared. I didn't like doing this behind Maddox's back, but if Ryan was to be spending time alone with him, he should know. This wasn't a boyfriend thing; this was a professional responsibility thing.

I looked over to where the boys were still talking, laughing, not paying us any attention at all. I turned back to Ryan. "It's like he can't get a full breath, so he just needs you to breathe with him, nice and slow, hold his hand, stay with him and stay calm, and it should pass."

Amber stared. "You're talking about panic attacks."

I met her gaze. I didn't deny or confirm it. I didn't have to.

"Holy shit," Ryan murmured. Then he shook his head. "You know what? He should ride with you. Honestly. Fuck Ambrose's bullshit rule. And it's not just because I don't want to deal with this; it's because when he's with me, he spends the whole time looking for you. He's relaxed when he's with you. Why add stress when we don't have to?"

I made a face. "Ambrose was pretty clear."

Amber leaned forward, her eyes narrowed. "But who is our first concern? Them?" She nodded toward the guys. "Or Ambrose?"

Well, Ambrose was technically our boss. But the truth was the five members of the band were our top priority. Always.

In the end, I nodded. "Okay. Thanks. But please, don't say anything. He'd never forgive me if he knew I told you. He hasn't even told the boys."

"I'm assuming the doctor knows?" Amber asked.

"Yep."

"And Ambrose?"

I grimaced. "Not exactly. He thinks it's a blood pressure thing. Maddox doesn't want him to know. He says it will put more pressure on the others, and that just makes him feel worse. But I have told Ambrose that Maddox shouldn't be pushed right now." I shrugged again. "He just thinks I said that so he wouldn't separate us. Which isn't his fault. Because he doesn't know what's going on, so how could he know?" I let out a long slow breath and admitted something I'd known for a while. "Maddox should tell him."

They both agreed without saying it out loud. Their faces said enough.

"I think Hardwick wants him to see a therapist after the tour." We had five concerts to go. And that felt doable. "Ten days. We just have to get through the next ten days."

DANCE PRACTICE WENT OKAY. Maddox was pissed at himself for missing a few steps, for being a bit out of sync. He was distracted and frustrated, and I had to remind him to take it easy.

He knew these dances. He knew the moves, every beat, every motion. He *knew* them.

"Stop overthinking it," the choreographer told him before he made them start at the beginning.

"Stop overthinking it," Maddox repeated sarcastically when we got back to the hotel. He was sweaty and tired, still frustrated. "Jeez. Why didn't I think of that? Such an easy solution. Has he considered telling a diabetic to produce a little more insulin? Because if I could stop over-thinking shit, I would."

I rubbed his thigh. "How does your throat feel? Not sore at all?"

He looked annoyed at me for asking but he sighed. "It's fine."

I could tell he was tired and stressed. "Good. Because you're supposed to do some light vocal sessions tonight, and I was thinking you could do some groaning and begging."

A hint of a smile pulled at his lips. "Begging?"

I leaned in and whispered, my lips brushing his ear. "Yep. After a steaming hot shower, I'm going to rim you until you beg me to fuck you."

His breath caught. "Fuck."

"Yes, I intend to."

He shifted in his seat and glanced around the common room. "You better not be teasing me."

I laughed, not giving a shit who saw us, and tilted his chin toward me for a kiss. "It's a promise, Mr. Kershaw."

His dark eyes gleamed with desire. "You better deliver, Mr. Hall."

And deliver, I did.

Was it an attempt to distract him, clear his mind so he thought of nothing else but what I was doing to his body? Yes. Was it an attempt to flood his body with endorphins, to make him feel good, to help him sleep? Yes. Was it hotter than hell, near perfect love-making? Did his body react to every touch, every kiss, did he writhe and moan, beg and groan when I gave him what he so desperately wanted? Also yes.

But I woke up to a noise at a bit after three in the morning to find Maddox out of bed. He was sitting on the sofa by the window, the blinds open, watching the city lights below. He had his guitar in his lap but he wasn't playing it. His notepad sat beside him, open, pen at the ready.

"Baby," I murmured, my voice croaking with sleep. "Whatcha doing?"

"Did I wake you? Sorry. I was trying to be quiet."

I moaned and stretched my arm out to his side of the bed. "Come back to bed."

"Can't sleep."

"What can I do to help?"

He smiled. "Nothing. You just being here is enough." He lightly plucked the guitar string, coaxing the sweetest chords into the air. "This song is about you."

"It is?"

He nodded and played another chord, ever so gently. "I always wondered what possessed Elton John to sing a song like 'Your Song,'" he mused. "I think maybe now I know." He turned in his seat and looked at me, the hint of a smile on his lips. "He could have given his man anything in the world, but somehow a song . . ." His words trailed off. "A song *about* you is easy. I could write a thousand. But a song *for* you? To put into words . . ."

I lifted the blankets on his side of the bed. "Come here, baby."

He seemed to hesitate for a split second, but he put his guitar down and slid back into bed. I folded him up in my arms and rubbed his back. He nuzzled into my chest. "I love you, Maddox. 'For every day I have lived, for every beat of my heart.'"

He froze, then pulled back to see my face. Even in the dark I could see his smile. "That's one of our songs. Off our first album."

I chuckled and pulled him back in to where it was warm. "What can I say, I'm a fan. Want me to sing it?"

"No, please don't. I've heard you sing."

So of course I did. "'For every day I have lived . . .'"

He laughed and pinched my ass. "You're butchering one of our songs. Pretty sure that's a crime."

"I'm not that bad."

He chuckled quietly and I could feel him smile against my chest. "I was sixteen when I wrote that. I had no idea what love was. I thought I knew. I knew what I wanted it to be."

"Was falling in love with me everything you wanted it to be?"

He squeezed me, snuggled in, and sighed. "And so much more. I don't know how I survived before you."

I kissed the side of his head. "I love you so much, Maddox."

"Love you, too."

"Get some sleep, baby."

"'I want to dream of you,'" he whispered. "'Where the world can't touch us, where time can't betray me. Where your smile lives on forever. That's where I'll be.'"

It was one of their songs from their last album. I finished it for him. "'Where love still lingers, I want to dream of you and me.'"

WE'D JUST HAD breakfast and were getting organized for the full dress, full stage production rehearsal. It was a busy day. We were literally five minutes away from leaving, everyone was in good spirits . . . until Ambrose walked in for a quick briefing.

He gave us a bulleted rundown on all the usual particulars. What to expect at the stadium, what last minute minor details had been changed, what times we needed to be done.

"Unit teams are as follows," he said. I knew it was coming . . . I just knew it. "Luke and Blake with Amber, Wes and Jeremy with Roscoe, Maddox with Ryan."

Ryan and I both moved to object, but Ambrose declared the meeting over, turned on his heel, and walked out.

"I'll go speak to him," Ryan said.

I stopped him. "Don't worry about it. He clearly saw the pictures from yesterday."

Maddox and I had been photographed leaving the dance studio complex; the photos were everywhere. Us side by side, my hand on his back. And obviously Ambrose didn't like us not following his rules.

"Are you sure?" Ryan asked.

I nodded. The truth was, Maddox could handle riding with Ryan just fine. What wouldn't have gone down well was another reprimand or a caution or an official warning of breach of my employment contract. "I think it's best if we just keep our heads down and get through the last five concerts."

Ryan gave a nod, and although Maddox was pissed, he more or less agreed with me.

He just wanted this tour to be over.

The rehearsal went fine. Maddox's throat and voice held up well, though he didn't push it too hard. He rested when he should, he drank honey tea, lots of water, and took his pills like a good boy. He didn't sleep much that night, and like the night before, I woke to find him writing in his notebook sometime after three. He was frowning at the paper, his knee bouncing, like his mind couldn't settle.

He was tired the next morning, though of course he never complained. He was quiet though.

The Toronto concert went well, and Maddox's voice was strong. Wes was rolling his shoulder, grimacing. Blake limped off the stage.

The Ottawa concert was much the same though everything was beginning to take a toll. It wasn't unusual to find them asleep in the dressing room or barely able to keep their eyes open during hair and make-up.

The Montreal concert went off like a firecracker. The Olympic Stadium was packed with sixty-five thousand screaming fans, and it really felt like they were part of the show. They roared with each song, they danced and sang every word, and the guys left absolutely nothing behind on that stage. For over two hours, they gave every single thing they had.

When they came off after the last song, they were breathless, sweating, exhausted. Wes's shoulder would need more PT, and Blake's knee would likely need another injection, at the very minimum. Maddox's throat was sore again, though not inflamed or swollen like it had been. Jeremy was sucking on an oxygen can and Luke was flat on the floor.

They were happy, yes. The concert had been great, the crowds were awesome, but there was no bounce in their steps as we left the stadium. There was no hyped-up excitement, no laughing as we bundled into the vans and drove back to the hotel.

Maddox didn't sleep too well. He hadn't slept well for over a week. Even after the concert, the hot shower, and a belly full of food. He was utterly exhausted but slept fitfully at best. I'd pulled him in for a hug, rubbing his back and holding him tight, and he sighed and leaned heavily into me.

"Two more concerts to go, baby," I whispered. "Just two."

Leaving Montreal for Boston, Hardwick put Maddox on another twenty-four-hour voice rest, which to be honest, I think he was thankful for. We spent the day traveling anyway, but Maddox was happy to pull his hoodie up, hunker down in his seat, and stare out the window.

Boston was always one of my favorite cities, but not even being back in the States helped Maddox's state of mind too much.

We were almost at the finish line. We were so close we could almost see it, but I was beginning to wonder if we'd ever get there.

The Boston concert was at the Gillette Stadium, which felt impossibly large. We'd played in bigger, but for some reason it felt vast and never-ending. It felt like a chore. The rehearsals, even the actual concert. The crowds were amazing, the fans always were. Mostly. But god, I just wanted it all to be over.

Everyone was tired: the boys, the stage crew, the production crew, the make-up and wardrobe teams. The smiles and the energy from the beginning of the tour were long gone, as I knew they would be by now.

When we finally got to New York City, the guys wanted to do a thank you video to their fans. The tour was almost over and this would be their personalized send off. It was just an impromptu and candid thing, filmed on Luke's phone set up on a tripod in front of them. They sat in the common room at the hotel, with Maddox, Jeremy, and Blake on a sofa, Luke and Wes sitting between their legs on the floor. "Hello!" They all waved at the camera.

"Maddox is back on voice rest," Jeremy announced. Maddox waved again and managed half a smile. Jeremy took Maddox's small notepad and held it up for the camera. "He's supposed to write down what he wants to say, but it's basically just rude words and obscene pictures." Maddox snatched back his notepad and shoved Jeremy. He quickly scribbled something down and Jeremy gasped. "Mom! Maddox said a rude word!"

It was all in good fun, and they were joking and hilarious and charming, just like always. They thanked everyone for the amazing tour, and how they loved all the fans, and how the whole team behind the scenes had worked really hard, and how they were in New York City for the final show of the tour. It was short and sweet, but they wanted their fans to know how much they appreciated their support.

But when the interview was over, when they all got up from the couch, Maddox came straight over to me and into my arms. He was so tired, so over everything. I kissed the side of his head. "Wanna go to our room?" I asked. He nodded against my chest, so I took his hand and led him out.

I didn't give it another thought. We ordered some room service and put some movie on the TV, Maddox strummed on his guitar for a bit, and I answered emails.

But then Jeremy called Maddox's phone. He hit Answer but he still wasn't supposed to be talking, so he put it on speaker.

"You're on speaker," I called out.

"Guys, you better come here. To the common room," he said, his voice low. "Uh, now."

Well, shit, that didn't sound good at all . . .

So we went.

They'd uploaded the video onto their social media platforms, as was the plan, and sure enough, within an hour, they were trending.

The power they held, the driving force of their fans. It was pure madness.

But I hadn't checked my phone, I hadn't looked at social media. And there on the TV screen on the wall in the common room was a photo. Just a usual photo of Luke laughing, clearly taken just after the video they'd done, but there behind him . . . it was kinda blurry but distinguishable enough.

"I didn't notice before I uploaded it," Luke said, pale and horrified. "I'm so sorry."

He'd taken some photos after the video had stopped filming. They'd all been mucking around with their phones. In the background of the photo was Maddox and me. My arms around him, his arms around me, his face against my neck, his eyes closed, my lips at his ear. It was a lover's embrace, no doubt about it.

"We were gonna take down the photos, but we didn't know if that'd make it worse," Jeremy said. "But Madz . . ." He shook his head. "It's too late. They're everywhere. This photo of you and Roscoe has gone viral."

CHAPTER FIFTEEN

VIRAL WAS AN UNDERSTATEMENT.

It was trending on every social media platform, along with variations of *Roscoe and Maddox, Moscoe is real, Raddox in love,* blah blah blah. It was on every news entertainment site, every music site; it was everywhere.

Not only was there the photo of Maddox and I hugging, but now every photo of us together *ever* was being posted. Photos that were years old, photos from yesterday. Us smiling, us in Buenos Aires, in Miami, him waiting for me, him dragging me into the van, him wearing my coat, my hand on his back, me carrying his stuff . . .

So many photos.

It was . . . well, it wasn't fucking good.

Then Ambrose walked in, eyes narrowed, iPad in hand, and one of his assistants behind him appeared a little bewildered as though she'd just witnessed him lose his shit. He looked at us all together, noticed the screen with the photo on it, and sighed as if he was clinging to his last thread of sanity.

Luke stood up. "It was my fault. I took the photo, I

uploaded it without noticing what was going on in the background. I know better, but I'm so used to seeing them together, I guess I just didn't even notice. I don't know." He turned to us again. "I'm really sorry."

Ambrose was flustered and angry, though he let out a slow breath. "What's done is done. It can't be removed, it's everywhere. But there will be no more private uploads until this tour is over. From anyone. I have no idea how PR will spin this."

"Spin this? If there is an apology," Maddox said, his voice a little gruff. He cleared his throat and tried again. "If an apology is released because head office believes two guys hugging is something to be sorry for, I will lose my fucking shit."

Ambrose stared at him, so I tapped Maddox's knee. "Babe, you're not supposed to be talking." Then I looked at Ambrose. "What he means is that if there is any kind of press release about this, *at all*, he will lose his shit. And I'll be right there with him."

Maddox smiled at me, then turned back to Ambrose. "Tell them nothing," he said, his voice still low and rough. "Don't lie about us, don't make excuses, and absolutely, under no circumstance should you apologize. I give them enough of me without letting them post shit about my personal life. Let them talk, let them post whatever they think. I don't care. I will absolutely not apologize to the fans or the public for being gay. There is no spin to this. Tell them nothing. Business as usual, and fuck anyone who thinks I don't deserve to be happy." He stood up and stepped over to Luke and he held out his fist for a bump. "'S all cool, man. You know what? I'm glad it's out there. Leave the photos up. If they're taken down it will look like we're backtracking, and now if I wanna hold Roscoe's hand in public, I fucking will. If we're done here, I'm going back to bed."

Maddox headed toward the door, so I stood up to go with him, giving the guys a smile over my shoulder as we walked out. I was so proud of Maddox for saying all of what he just said, and from the expressions on their faces, the guys were too.

And Maddox wasn't kidding when he said he was going back to bed. He crawled under the covers, pulled them up over his head, and stayed there. I joined him for a bit, checked on him every so often, made him more honey and lemon tea, and gave him cuddles and forehead-kisses.

He read, he watched some TV, he stared at the wall. He didn't sleep, he didn't talk, but he rested his body, which was better than nothing. His mind didn't seem to slow down at all though. He wrote in his notebook for a bit, still bundled up on the bed, and then he ripped out a piece of paper and handed it to me.

I should have asked if you wanted that photo taken down. Sorry.

I shook my head. "Nope. Leave it up." I brushed his hair back so I could see his eyes better. "Are you worried about what people think?"

He shook his head, but then he shrugged. It was hard to have an important conversation when he wasn't supposed to talk. He took the piece of paper back and wrote a quick line. *Worried you didn't want that.*

"Baby, don't worry about me. I just want to be with you. I agreed with everything you said to Ambrose, and if you want to hold my hand in public, I'd be okay with that."

He smiled but it didn't last long. He took back the piece of paper and scribbled something else down before handing it to me. *What happens after tour?*

I put my hand to his cheek. "Well, I think we should take it one day at a time. We'll find a way to make it work, Maddox."

He shook his head. "No. Me in LA, you here."

Oh shit. That's right . . . I was going to see my parents. Which I hadn't forgotten about, I just didn't realize it was coming up so soon. I was staying here for a week . . . A week without Maddox. God. The idea felt like a lump in my gut. "It's just for a week," I said, aiming for conviction. "We'll be fine. I haven't seen my folks in ages and they're just a few hours from here, so it makes sense to see them now. Plus, we have a break after the tour." The truth was, he would need a week's rest when he returned to LA, and I'd be back before he needed to see any doctors. But man, even the thought of him being alone . . . "You know, I could always come back and see my folks after, if you need me to go back to LA with you."

"Or I could come with you?" he whispered in a rush. Then he let out a shaky breath. "I mean, if you want me to. Or not. I mean, if you don't want me to, I'll understand. I can just go home." He tried to inhale but it was stilted and he made a small gasping noise. His hands were trembling. *Jesus Christ.* "I shouldn't have said anything, sorry."

I pulled him in close and held him. "Breathe with me," I murmured, taking some deep breaths in and out. I waited until he was in sync with me before I spoke. It didn't take long, so I pulled back and kissed his lips. "You want to come with me to meet my folks?"

He squinted his eyes shut. "I'm just not ready to not have you around, that's all. I didn't really think of it as a meeting-the-parents thing. God."

I chuckled. "I would love for you to come with me." I

kissed him again and put my hand to his cheek. "Is that what you were so nervous about?"

He made a face. "I wasn't sure . . . Roscoe, I don't . . ." He shrugged.

I kissed his forehead, his cheek. "You don't what, baby?"

"I don't want to be alone. I don't want to go back to my house alone," he murmured. "And there's nobody I'd rather be with than you."

"Look at me," I whispered. I waited for his eyes to meet mine. "There's nobody I'd rather be with either. I love you, and I'd love you to come back to meet my folks. And I know you don't want to talk about it, but when we get back to LA, we're going to make some appointments to see some doctors. About your throat and about your anxiety." His whole body flinched at that, so I tightened my hold him. "Listen, baby, please." I took a few deep breaths, knowing he'd do the same with me. "I'm not going anywhere. And whatever the doctors say, whatever we have to do, we'll get through that together too. Okay?"

He was silent and still, so I rubbed his back and kissed the side of his head. "You're not alone, Maddox. You don't have to fight these battles on your own anymore."

He let out a shuddery breath, and he clung to me, trembling until eventually he couldn't fight it anymore and he began to cry. I held him in my arms as he sobbed. I rubbed his back, I kissed his head, I wrapped him up in my arms, and by the time he'd cried himself out, he was asleep.

I wasn't a therapist. I wasn't anything even close. As big as this felt, I knew this wasn't a breakthrough. This was nothing more than a crack in the wall, a small hole to relieve some pressure.

The dam was yet to break.

It was coming, though. I could feel it.

THE NEXT MORNING we were due at the recording studio in Lower Manhattan. Between the photo of Maddox and me in each other's arms and the video the guys uploaded, and the final concert of the tour, Atrous was hot news.

We got to the recording studio just fine. We spent four hours there, the boys worked hard and had a lot of fun. Maddox was kinda quiet in the morning. He'd taken some Tylenol for a headache, but his voice was fine. I'd been so swept up in them singing, I'd almost forgotten about the outside world.

Until we tried to leave.

Word had traveled fast. We were filmed going into the recording studio, apparently, which meant we had to come out at some point, and a sea of people greeted us. The police were trying to get the street cleared, traffic was at a standstill —our vans were stuck half a block up—and to make matters worse, there was scaffolding along the front of the building entrance.

It was a mess.

Our security was tight and I had every faith in Steve and his team, but there were news reporters and cameras, paparazzi, and an absurd number of fans.

Steve gave us the rundown. "When the first van pulls up, Amber you'll be ready to move out. Blake and Luke, heads down, watch your feet, keep your hands down. Don't wave, don't stop. Move together, and do whatever security tells you to do."

Fucking hell.

"Ryan and Maddox, you're next. With me." Steve looked at Robbie. "You and Roscoe will be in the third van with Jeremy and Wes, same drill. Heads down, move fast but watch your feet. There will be local security and the police. We should be fine."

I felt better knowing Maddox was going before me and that Steve was with him.

"Okay, okay," Steve said, talking into his walkie-talkie. "We're on the move. First van approaching now."

Amber, along with Luke and Blake and their security, went out the door. Amber could handle herself just fine, she didn't take a backward step, not for anything.

Steve pointed to Ryan and Maddox. "We're up."

Steve went to the front, Maddox held the back of Steve's shirt, and Ryan covered the back. The crowd swelled and surged, and the noise was absurd. The police were there now, trying to keep people back, and our van pulled in.

"Okay, we're up," Robbie said. He went first, Jeremy and Wes close behind, and me behind them. We were ushered from the front of the building toward the vehicles, which was no great distance, but the crowd pushed and shoved and closed in like a wave.

My only priority was to protect Jeremy and Wes and get them to the van. The screaming and the yelling from the crowd were almost deafening, the click-click-click of cameras, and the swarm of people was disorienting, but I could hear my name being yelled above the others.

"Roscoe, are you and Maddox together?"

"Roscoe, look over here!"

"Roscoe, how long have you and Maddox . . ."

Christ almighty.

It was scary as hell, and I realized that maybe Ambrose had a point. Maybe separating me and Maddox was a good idea.

We were about halfway through, almost there, when the yelling got louder, deeper, and closer. It was a frantic noise, a commotion, and it was aimed at me. I was shoved hard from the side . . . then everything happened in slow motion.

I was falling, and I knew I was falling, but I was still trying to protect Wes and Jeremy. There was a swarm of people like hornets, jostling, shoving, yelling, pushing. My head hit something really fucking hard as I went down, and my vision swam, my head spun, darkness ebbed at the edges . . .

But then hands grabbed me, pulled me up to my feet, and threw me into the van. Outside the van was utter chaos. Inside the van, I was sprawled on the first seat, my pulse pounded in my ears, blood ran down my face . . . but a familiar face, beautiful and terrified, stood over me, and he screamed at the driver. "Drive, drive, drive!"

CHAPTER SIXTEEN

I SAT in the common room, surrounded by a whole lot of stark expressions, while the doc fussed over my face and Maddox paced. I had a bump on my right temple and my right eyebrow was swollen and split, but it had stopped bleeding. The corner of my eye had a red blotch, I already had some bruising, and a headache was shaping up nicely.

But I was okay.

"You're lucky it wasn't worse," Hardwick said quietly. "You don't need stitches or glue. You didn't lose consciousness?"

I shook my head. "Nah, I saw a few stars, but that's it."

Maddox, who was still pacing, made a growling sound.

"I'd be happier if you went to the hospital," the doc added. "Have some scans done."

"Honestly, I'm fine. I've had worse playing high school hockey." I put the ice pack back to my eye and gave a pointed nod toward Maddox and murmured, "It's not me I'm worried about."

"Hmm," he said, getting his bag. He pulled out a seat

away from the rest of us, near where Maddox was wearing a line in the carpet. "Maddox, take a seat for me."

Maddox stopped and looked at the doc holding his blood pressure machine like he'd never seen either of them before. To everyone else, it would look like he was checking his blood pressure, which technically, that's what he was doing. But he was also getting him to sit and take some deep breaths and hopefully calm down.

"This is major news," Ryan said. He handed me his phone. It wasn't just on social media; it was on every news broadcasting station across the country. Probably the world. The footage was surreal to watch. So much had happened in just a few short seconds.

Steve, Maddox, and Ryan got through to their van despite the crowd and the pushing and shoving. Then Robbie, Jeremy, Wes, and I came into view. The crowd lurched like a wave, Robbie stood aside to give Jeremy and Wes clear access to the open door of the van, but a man came over the top, pushing the whole crowd and bursting through, and I got hit and shoved directly into a very sturdy scaffolding pole.

Robbie got Jeremy and Wes into the van and went for the man who had done the damage, but then from the bottom of the screen, through all the people and the commotion came two figures dressed in black. One wore a hoodie, though his black hair could be seen, along with his long, black earrings. The other wore a black security shirt and fury in his eyes.

Maddox, with Steve right behind him.

Maddox shoved someone away and picked me up by the shirt like I weighed nothing. He all but threw me into the van and came in after me, the door sliding closed behind us, and the van pulled out.

The footage played a few more seconds of the commotion. Steve and Robbie were still there, but there were cops everywhere by then and the recording ended.

"Wild scenes today as fans and photographers clashed when the world-famous band Atrous were leaving a recording studio in Manhattan," the reporter said. I turned it off and handed Ryan back his phone. I'd already seen some photographs and the headlines . . . I didn't need to see any more.

"Are Robbie and Steve back?" I asked.

Amber nodded. "Yeah. They're fine."

"Holy shit," Luke said, they were all crowded around, looking at his phone. They'd watched it a dozen times already. "Maddox just yeets that guy." They were obviously up to the part where Maddox threw that man to the side so he could get to me.

The four of them all stopped and stared at Maddox, who was still with the doctor at the other end of the room. Hardwick was now on the chair beside him and they were talking. Well, Hardwick was speaking. Maddox was nodding.

Jeremy got up and pulled the ice pack off my face. He inspected my eye. "You're still pretty."

"Thanks," I mumbled. "You okay?"

He nodded. They were all a bit shaken up, understandably, but they were physically unharmed. Then he glanced down toward Maddox. "Don't think someone else is, though. I think he wants to punch the shit out of something, or someone."

Then, with the worst possible timing, Ambrose walked in. He had his business face on, and it looked like he'd aged a decade since yesterday. He came straight over to me. "How are you holding up?"

"I'm fine," I replied.

Maddox intervened then, slipping in between us and planting himself on my lap. Not beside me on the sofa, but on my lap. If Ambrose was surprised, he didn't show it. Maddox, on the other hand, had that I-fucking-dare-you-to-say-something look in his eyes that went well with his back-away-from-my-man vibe he was emanating.

I didn't mind. I actually kind of liked it. His protective nature, particularly of me, literally saved me from god knew what today. Being trampled? Maybe. Being hurt a lot worse? Definitely. As soon as he saw me in trouble, he ran to save me, without hesitation and without any regard for his own safety, and no doubt to the utter dismay of Steve.

I put my arm around Maddox's waist and he frowned at my sore eye. "I'm so sorry," he whispered.

"If you could all gather around," Ambrose began. "I'll update you on what I know."

Jeremy sat next to me, and when Maddox shot him a glare, Jeremy reached over and took his hand. Luke sat next to Jeremy, Blake sat on their laps, which made Maddox sitting on mine less of a big deal, and Wes stood by the armrest next to me and put his arm around Maddox's shoulder.

Ambrose took a deep breath and looked at everyone. "Three people have been charged over the incident. Further charges are expected as the investigation moves forward. They've brought in more people for questioning."

"More people?" Jeremy asked.

He gave a nod. "The police believe the men who began the altercation were paid."

"What the fuck?" Blake asked. "Paid? By who? For what?"

"We believe a photographer might have paid two local men of no fixed address to start an altercation."

What the fuck?

Same as the couple in the grocery store. Paid by someone to start something and be ever so conveniently right there to catch the whole thing on camera. I never imagined it would happen to us. To me.

Ambrose swallowed hard. "We also believe that Maddox may have been the intended target."

I tightened my arm around Maddox's waist. "Pardon?"

"The two men were told to target the man who came out last. He always traveled in the third vehicle. That's usually Maddox, but today it wasn't."

I put my other arm around him too, and I noticed Wes's arm went around Maddox's neck and Jeremy pulled Maddox's hand toward him.

"And the photographer?" Luke asked.

"Is being questioned by police. The two men identified him from all the photographers that were there, and those who were in the position to benefit. They said he offered them five hundred dollars each." Ambrose shrugged. "The investigation is on-going and I've asked to be kept updated. Our legal team is dealing with it and no one here will be involved at any further stage."

"What about the guy Maddox threw?" Jeremy said.

Ambrose gave a tight smile. "Like I said. Our legal team is taking care of it. From my understanding, the guy is a fan and was just glad no one was seriously hurt."

Blake scoffed. "That'll change when he realizes there's money involved."

"Probably," Ambrose replied. "But we'll let legal worry about that. That's what we pay them for."

"And the two homeless men?" Maddox asked quietly. "Are they okay?"

"They were detained," Ambrose began.

"It wasn't their fault," Maddox said. "If by 'no fixed address' you mean living on the street, they were offered a lot of money. More money than they've seen in a while, no doubt. If it was a choice between having food in your belly or not, it's not really a choice, is it?"

I leaned my head against him and gave him a squeeze. It was so typical of him to think that, to worry for them.

"But the photographer," Maddox said, his voice still low and melodic. "I want him charged with everything that'll stick and sued into oblivion. And whoever he sold the pictures to and the footage, wherever money changed hands, sue them too. If any media site or tabloid contracted him to do it, take their whole fucking company down."

Okay then.

Maddox folded himself against me then, his head in the crook of my neck. His bony ass was sticking into my thigh but I didn't care.

Ambrose sighed. "Tonight's stage rehearsal is off."

"What?" Wes, Luke, and Blake asked in unison.

"I think you've had enough excitement for one day," Ambrose said. "I need to discuss changes with security and we're re-evaluating—"

"Roscoe rides with me," Maddox said. His voice was still calm, but too calm, too even. It was somehow more unnerving than his yelling voice.

Ambrose made a face. "Maddox, I think we can discuss this in private—"

"There's nothing to discuss. I'm not asking, I'm telling."

Ambrose ran his hand through his hair, exasperated. "You would be safer—"

Maddox unfolded himself from me and stood up in one fluid step. "How safe were we today? How fucking safe were we today? Look at his face." Maddox gestured to me. "They touched him, Ambrose. They touched him. And what did you tell me before? Close enough to touch, close enough to hurt. What if they'd had a better shot at him. What if they'd had a gun?"

Wes reached out for him. "Hey Madz, calm down."

"I won't fucking calm down," he said, looking at everyone. "Do you know how close we came today? It could have easily been one of us. It was *supposed* to be one of us. Don't tell me to calm down." He put his hand to his chest like it hurt, then turned back to Ambrose. "Roscoe's with me. I don't care what you have to do to make it happen. We tried it your way. Now we do it my way." He grimaced, breathing hard and sharp, and he pulled at the collar of his hoodie. "Christ, why is it so hot in here?"

I stood up. "Okay, let's go get some air."

"No!" Maddox shot back, pulling his arm free from my hold. "I'm sick of being a trained circus monkey that's been punished for wanting something outside the cage. Well, you know what? I'm done being nothing but a commodity in this goddamn trade-off. What I want is not *something* to be fucking bargained for! Christ, Roscoe, I will not fight with you over this. Anyone, but not you."

"I'm on your side, Maddox," I said calmly.

He pulled at his hair, his chest heaving. "Then listen to me! No one fucking listens to me!" he spat. Then he turned back to Ambrose, his voice cracking. "I can't do this without him. I can't breathe. I swear to fucking god, if you take him away from me again, I'll go public. Interviews, on stage, social media. I'll scream it out the car fucking window if I have to. I will tell the world how no one in this company listens to me." He gasped for air, short and harsh, like his lungs weren't working at all. He spun to face me, panicked, his hands in awkward fists. "I can't . . . can't . . . breathe . . . Roscoe—"

Doctor Hardwick swooped in and grabbed Maddox, all but carrying him back to the sofa they'd been sitting on before. "Everyone out," Hardwick said, kneeling in front of Maddox. Then he stood, grabbed his bag, and turned to where everyone was standing, wide-eyed, horrified. "I said everyone out! Now. Out."

Ryan and Amber began to usher everyone out, not that they wanted to go, clearly.

I sat next to Maddox and Hardwick handed me an aerosol of oxygen like they used backstage. I put the mouth-piece in front of Maddox's mouth and nose and rubbed his back. "Breathe in, baby. Nice and slow. That's it."

I looked up to find Ambrose still standing there. He looked . . . lost. Hardwick, who was kneeling in front of Maddox again, fingers on Maddox's wrist, followed my line of sight. "Neil, I've asked you to leave," the doc said. He was absolutely no nonsense, no bullshit, and I liked that about him.

"Maddox," I said smoothly, keeping eye contact with him. "Breathe with me."

Ambrose did leave, thankfully, and Hardwick went back to checking Maddox's pulse. It felt like it lasted forever, but his breaths were getting deeper and more measured, and after a little while, Hardwick uncurled Maddox's fingers, patted his knee, then sat on the other side of him. "That was a big one," he said.

Maddox nodded and he pushed the oxygen can away, then sagged against me. I put my arm around his shoulder and he felt so small. So vulnerable. He wiped his sleeve on his face and sniffled before he started to cry, so I pulled him closer and held him. His breathing was still off but he had a handle on it.

Once my own heart rate simmered down, my head began to throb, the cut on my eyebrow and the bump on my temple making themselves known. God, had that whole debacle with the crowd and the photographers been just this morning?

What a fucking day.

"I'll need to go tell the others you're okay," Hardwick said gently. "No doubt they're all on the other side of that door waiting."

"I can't face them," Maddox mumbled through his tears. His hands were tucked into the sleeves of his hoodie, and he put them to his face. "It's embarrassing."

I held him a little tighter. "You don't need to face them right now. But they'll be worried."

Maddox cried some more. "I'm sorry."

"Don't apologize," I murmured. "You have nothing to apologize for."

The doc looked at me over the top of Maddox's head. "I'll call them into the meeting room. It'll clear the hallway. Go to your room, get some rest."

Maddox would probably sleep now anyway. He was always so worn out afterwards.

"Maddox," the doc said. "I'll come and see you in a little while. We can't let this go on any longer. We're gonna have to get you some help."

Maddox never replied but he heard it, and for now, that was enough. Maddox had tried to deal with this on his own, but that was no longer an option.

He needed help.

I held him tight for a minute or two after Hardwick left,

giving him plenty of time to get everyone into the meeting room so the hallway was clear. "Come on, baby," I said, peeling Maddox off me.

He was still heavy and reluctant to move, so I helped him to his feet. "Let's go to our room. We can watch a movie, order waffles and ice cream, have a nap."

Maddox sighed, and though he had his head down, he nodded. I tucked him into my side and we walked out. I was prepared to shield him from anyone who might still be lurking in the hall, but it was all clear.

He crawled into bed. I kicked off my boots and joined him. He looked so exhausted, and so unbelievably sad. "I'm sorry," he said again as he studied my swollen eyebrow. "Your beautiful face."

"This face was never beautiful," I said, aiming for funny.

He reached up and ever so lightly traced my eyebrow and my temple. "Does it hurt?"

"Nope. Well, it would if I accidently banged it, but just like this, no."

His eyes flickered between mine. "I feel responsible. I am responsible. If it weren't—"

I thumbed his cheek, his eyebrow, his lip. "You're not responsible. It was not your fault. Actually, you saved me, remember? I saw the footage. You literally flew in and grabbed me and got me to safety. So if it weren't for you, it'd be a lot worse."

"But if it weren't for me, you wouldn't have a target on your back."

"Okay, Maddox, my love," I said firmly. "Listen to me. We're not playing this game. You're not to blame. Saying I wouldn't have been hurt if we weren't together just makes me feel bad. We *are* together, and no fucked-up photographer looking for pay-dirt is gonna change that. Please don't feel guilt over this. This is not on you."

He closed his eyes and was quiet for a while. "I freaked out in front of everyone today." His chin wobbled again. "Fucking hell, Roscoe. They all saw me. I was holding it together so well, and then Ambrose came in and I knew he was gonna separate us—"

I kissed him softly to stop him from getting worked up again. "No one is going to separate us."

"If you'd been with me today, you wouldn't have been hurt."

"We don't know that. Maybe it would have been worse. We don't know that either. There's no point in stressing over what-ifs, baby." That probably wasn't the best thing to say to someone with a panic disorder. I had to reassure him. "Maddox, I promise you, everyone in that room who saw you just now loves you. They don't think anything bad about you, I promise."

"You don't know that either."

"I do know it. They love you. They'll just be worried, that's all. It probably just scared them a little to see you like that. And that's okay." I swiped my thumb along his jaw.

He became teary. "They're gonna think I'm crazy, treat me different—"

"No, they won't. They love you. And you're not crazy." I brushed my fingers through his hair. "Jeremy's gonna knock on that door any minute and yell, 'hey, dickbag,' just like he always does."

He almost smiled.

"It's the one thing I am absolutely sure of in this world," I added. "Is that those four guys love you like a brother. They'll do whatever needs to be done, okay? Just like you would do anything for them."

He closed his eyes and I stroked his hair until he drifted off to sleep. He was so freaking tired. He had shadows under his eyes and his usually beautiful skin was a touch pallid. And watching him as he slept, taking in every detail, every line, I knew right then that I would do anything for him, whatever he needed, because I loved him. More than anything I'd ever loved.

I kissed his forehead, and even knowing he wouldn't hear, I whispered anyway, "Love all of you."

———

MADDOX DOZED FOR A WHILE, got up and showered, we ordered the waffles and ice cream I'd suggested, and sure enough, Doctor Hardwick came by to check on him.

"What did you tell them?" Maddox asked.

"I told them what I could," he said. "That I knew physical and emotional burnout when I saw it. And it isn't just you. It's all of them. That years of constant pressure for perfection on the world stage and high levels of stress from every angle has taken its toll, on the whole team, Maddox. I told them I was surprised it took this long, that even the strongest steel will buckle eventually."

I squeezed Maddox's hand and he nodded quickly, swallowing back his emotions.

Hardwick continued, "The boys wanted to see you, naturally. I asked them to give you a few hours to rest. They were all very concerned, as you could imagine. They care a great deal for you."

Maddox chewed on his bottom lip and nodded again.

"We have a decision to make about the last concert," Hardwick added.

Maddox's head shot up. "What about it?"

"Whether you would be up for performing, or if we should cancel it." Hardwick shrugged. "I know which I'd prefer, but I also know what you're going to say."

"We can't cancel," Maddox said quickly. "People have paid a lot of money for tickets, and they've traveled or taken time off work and school. We can't cancel the day before. I won't let them down like that."

Hardwick nodded. "That's what I said you'd say."

I rubbed Maddox's back. "You wouldn't be letting anyone down. If we have to cancel, we cancel. Your fans will understand."

Maddox shook his head. "I'll be fine. On stage is fine. It's my happy place. And it's just one concert. One. Then it's all over and we can do whatever you need me to do. Roscoe and I were going to see his family for a few days while we're on the East Coast, but I promise as soon as I get back to LA I'll see whoever you want me to see." He wiped his hands on his thighs. "But I have to do this last concert." He turned to me, eyes wide. "I have to. I have to do this."

As much as I probably wished otherwise, I knew that'd be his answer as well. So I nodded. "Then we'll get through it. We can start working on a plan or whatever it is we should do. Like for breathing and relaxation." I'd tried reading all I could about panic attacks, but it was hard to follow. "And we'll get through it."

Hardwick nodded and got to his feet. "Let me make some calls."

He'd only been gone for about twenty minutes when there was a knock on the door. "Hey dickbag, open up."

I chuckled because I knew Jeremy would never treat him any different.

I opened the door to find all four of them waiting, so I

stood aside and let them in. Maddox was lying in bed and they all piled on top of him. There was swearing and muffled laughter, but mostly laughing, and the five of them wrestled for the best spot on the bed.

"Are you watching *Rick and Morty*?" Wes asked.

"Shut the fuck up, it's funny," Maddox replied. Pretty sure he was underneath Luke.

"Oh my god, it's the 'Pickle Rick' episode," Blake cried.

I laughed, and knowing he was in good company—and knowing he needed some time alone to talk to his friends—I figured it was a good time to duck out. "Maddox, I'll be back in ten."

I needed to speak to Ambrose and I found him and Doctor Hardwick in the meeting room. I knocked and stuck my head in. "Oh, is Maddox okay?" Hardwick asked.

"Yeah, he's okay. All the guys just joined him in our room so I thought I'd come make peace," I replied, looking at Ambrose.

"How's your eye?" he asked.

I lightly touched the bump on my eyebrow and then my temple. "I'll live."

"We were just discussing the concert tomorrow," Hardwick said.

"Maddox wants it to go ahead," I replied. "If it's canceled, I think he'd feel worse. He already feels enough guilt. Ambrose, I know you're in a difficult spot. You want to keep everyone happy and you answer to the company, and the band is just a small part of what you manage. I get that. And I appreciate the work you do . . ."

"But things need to change." Ambrose sighed. "I think we need to take a look at a lot of things. Workload for one, taking some pressure off the boys, off Maddox in particular. I told Arlo Kim what Maddox said about being a commodity and a circus monkey in a cage. How he makes all the money, all the sacrifices, but no one listens to him. And he's not wrong. He was always pushed harder than the others, and what he said today hit home. I told Mr. Kim that things needed to change."

"They need a vacation," Hardwick said. "Time off. Time to disengage and to energize. They could all use a recharge."

I nodded. "They need time to be themselves, to be twenty-three. The isolation is rough on them." I sighed. "Anyway, I'm sure we'll have time to discuss plans moving forward. I just wanted to check that I still have a job, I guess."

Ambrose damn near smiled. "Of course you do. Maybe I should be asking if I still have mine?"

I snorted. Maybe all the shit that went down today reminded Ambrose, and Arlo Kim, that Maddox was more valuable to the company than how he'd been treated. Platinum Entertainment might have owned Atrous, but without Atrous, Platinum Entertainment was nothing. "You might wanna give Maddox some time before you ask him that question."

His smile was rueful. "I never meant to hurt him. I was just doing what I was told, based on information and recommendations given to me."

"I know that; I understand. And he will too, one day. Right now, he just thinks you want to separate us, and the thought of not having me around scares the hell out of him. I can calm him down when he feels panicky. He trusts me."

Ambrose's eyebrows knitted together. "If I'd've known how serious it was, with his breathing like that, I wouldn't have split your unit."

"He couldn't have admitted it to you," Hardwick said,

"when he couldn't even admit it to himself. Not that I could have told you on his behalf either, with patient confidentiality. He forbade me to tell anyone. Like I told you before, he was adamant no one else find out. He was very persuasive."

"You mean stubborn and threatening," I said with a smile.

"Oh, I know how stubborn he can be," Ambrose said, smiling now. "But regardless, Roscoe, you were very good with him earlier. You knew what to do, and he turned directly to you for help." He nodded slowly. "It really is in his best interest if you stay with him. Everyone told me that and I should have listened."

"Everyone?"

"Both of you, Maddox, Ryan, Steve. Even Jeremy asked if I was sure." Ambrose sighed. "I think this has been a wake-up call for me. I was so busy listening to so-called experts and protocol models about security, and I should have been listening to those who were in the middle of it."

"You didn't know how bad it was," I allowed. "But yes, maybe listen next time."

We were all quiet for a moment. "So, the final concert?" Ambrose asked. "Do we pull the plug, or do we go ahead. To be honest, after today I'm not sure what to do."

I clapped his arm. "We listen to the guys in the middle of it."

Ambrose met my eyes and nodded. "Yeah, of course. I didn't learn much in the last minute, did I?"

I laughed. "I'll go find Ryan and Amber."

A few minutes later I opened the door to our room. "You guys decent?" I called out before walking in.

They were all still there. Maddox was sitting up now, leaning against the headboard. Jeremy was beside him, Blake was laying across the foot of the bed, and Luke and

Wes were now on chairs with their feet on Jeremy. They were still watching *Rick and Morty*.

They all straightened up when they saw who I had with me. The room was now kinda crowded. "Hey, guys," I said, smiling at Maddox. He brought his legs up and hugged his knees like a shield. "It's okay," I said. "Everything's okay. We just wanted to ask you all a question while you're together."

Ambrose stood beside me. "We have one concert to go. It's a big one. Did you want to go ahead with it or cancel? Postpone?"

"You're asking us?" Wes asked.

Ambrose nodded. "One hundred percent your call. I'll go with whatever you decide. You don't have to answer right now. But I'm doing a press release at three o'clock. If I have something to tell them, that'd be great. If not, then no problem. We make an announcement when you're ready."

The five of them stared at him, and Maddox's eyes went to mine. "I want to do it."

Jeremy, Wes, Luke, and Blake all turned to Maddox. "You sure?" Jeremy asked. "Madz, if you need—"

"I need to do this," he said quickly. "For me. To prove that I can. And for the fans. But for me." He swallowed hard. "So the anxiety doesn't win. Which is probably fucked up. No one tell Hardwick I said that." He let out a shaky breath and gave me a smile.

No one else could have possibly known, but that was the first time he'd used the word anxiety. First time I'd heard him say it, anyway.

Jeremy clapped his hands. "Well then, there's your answer. Thunderbirds are go."

"Hell yes!" Blake crowed and the others cheered.

"And while we're all here," Maddox said. "Just so you

know, I'm not going back to LA with you guys. I'm staying on the East Coast with Roscoe, just for a week, before we head home." He glanced at Jeremy and chewed his bottom lip. "Staying with his parents."

Jeremy's eyes almost popped out of his head. "You're meeting his parents, fucking wow."

"Holy shit," Wes said.

I felt Ryan and Amber's eyes boring holes in the side of my head, but I never took my eyes off Maddox. I smiled at him and his cheeks tinted pink.

"Okay, everyone out," Amber said. She was trying not to grin, and she winked at me as she shoved the boys out the door.

The room was deafeningly quiet when they'd gone.

"Should I have told them that?" Maddox asked. He was still sitting against the headboard, still holding the pillow, still devastatingly beautiful.

I nodded. "Absolutely." I knelt on the bed and crawled up, wrapped my hand around his ankle, and pulled him so he was lying down. Then I prowled up his body and kissed him soundly on the mouth. "Yes."

He put his hand to the side of my face, to my sore eye and temple. "Does this hurt?" He frowned. "I hate that someone hurt you."

I settled my weight on him and he spread his legs for me. I brushed his hair from his forehead and searched his eyes. I could have lied to save him from further guilt, but if I expected him to be honest with me about his pain, I needed to be upfront about mine. "It's not so bad. Bit tender."

He turned my chin so he could kiss my eyebrow first, then my temple, ever so lightly. "I love you, Roscoe. I don't know why you're still here, why you're not running for the hills. But I'm grateful."

"I'm here because I love you. Because I've been in love with you for years. Because I see the real you." I kissed him, pulling his bottom lip between mine. "Life's not always going to be this crazy."

He searched my eyes. "Will you still love me when there's no more band, no more touring, no more screaming fans? When I can't sing or dance?"

"Baby," I whispered. "I will love you no matter what."

He stared, seemingly holding onto that moment for the longest time, his eyes like glimmering onyx.

"Do you believe me?" I whispered. "Please say you believe me."

He nodded. "I believe you."

I kissed him then, slow and deep, and began to take his shirt off. "Tomorrow's a concert day," he said, smiling. "I thought that was against your rules."

I laughed and kissed down his neck. "If you want me to stop . . ."

He groaned and rolled his hips, grinding his erection into mine. He dragged his hands over my ass and pulled me hard against him. "Does it feel like I want you to stop?"

No. No it doesn't.

WE HAD a full police escort to the stadium the next day. Metlife Stadium was huge, but once we were inside the grounds, we were free from fans and media.

The media, press, paparazzi, and anyone with a camera wanted any piece of us they could get their hands on. The news had been horrendous. The footage of me getting hit, of Maddox grabbing me and pulling me into the van, was on every channel, on every social media site, on every station. Maddox and I were trending, again. The footage, the headlines, the photos, the fans' outrage and sympathy . . .

And Ambrose's press release had gone well. He was very clear, cut and dry; anyone who even looked wrong at any of his staff would be buried by our legal team. He was in full-boss mode, and his eyes could have cut glass.

I liked it.

But we'd all agreed to avoid whatever was online. It wasn't good for anyone's mental health, and we had enough to concentrate on.

Maddox hadn't slept well. But he swore he was okay. We just had one show to get through.

And once we were at the stadium, they were all business. Sound checks, rehearsals, stage checks, last minute set changes . . .

And the crowd began to roll in. The hype began to charge the air backstage and the nerves kicked in. Maddox didn't eat much, but he seemed in good spirits. He was smiling, chatting, though I caught his knee bouncing more than usual.

"How are you feeling?" I asked him, trying to keep it upbeat.

"Yeah, good," he said.

I wasn't convinced, and I found myself taking deep breaths with slow releases without even meaning to. It wasn't until I noticed him copying me that I even realized I was doing it.

"I'm okay," he said quietly. To me or himself, I wasn't sure.

But he kept his head down as though he couldn't look me in the eye. And maybe seeing my blatant concern made him feel bad, maybe he needed to shut it all out for a while so he could get in the zone. Maybe me asking him if he was okay every ten minutes was making him worse.

So I made myself stop asking him.

One more performance.

One more concert.

That's all we had to get through. It'd all be over in three hours.

It felt like I was waiting for the ax to fall. Maybe I was more nervous than him. I helped him with his earpiece, then with his shirt. When they were ready to go on stage, they stood around in a circle, like they did every time, with their hands joined in the middle.

"Atrous forever," they cried in unison.

And I stood behind them as they waited for their introduction. Maddox took some deep breaths, his shoulders rising and falling. His hands were fists at his sides. I wanted to take him aside and run him through some deep breathing exercises, but I had to believe him when he said he was okay. Part of me knew he wasn't, part of me hoped he could get through this.

Part of me knew this was too much and he should have said no to this concert. He should have put himself first. Instead he put everyone else before him. The expectations of his best friends, of eighty thousand screaming fans, was a cruel and unbearable weight to bear.

He carried it through the first set.

Though he missed a few steps in his choreography, and he was breathless when he sang. When he came off the stage, he threw his water bottle at the wall. "I can't keep time," he growled, his rage directed only inward.

"Hey," Jeremy said, trying to soothe him. "Don't sweat it, man. I miss shit all the time."

"I never miss," Maddox shot back. "I never fucking miss."

I intervened, pulling him aside. "Take a breath for me," I whispered. "You're doing great out there."

His eyes were dark fire. "Don't patronize me, Roscoe. If I'm shit, tell me I'm shit."

I ignored that. "You've got a full set to get through. You know these moves, you know the songs. Forget everything else and just go by feel. Just remember to breathe, Maddox."

A pained look crossed his features before he shook his head. "I need to go," he mumbled before joining the boys and heading back on stage without a moment to spare. They launched straight into another song. The crowd went crazy and we could feel the whole stadium boom and shake with the power of it.

And Maddox did well for the first few songs of the second set. He belted out notes and danced his heart out. But then he mistimed a dance move, and in the next song he missed one move altogether. In the next song he mistimed his line in the bridge, and in the song after that he missed a whole line.

Jeremy stood beside him, his arm around his shoulder and sang with him.

But it was too late.

A thread had been pulled, plucked a long time ago. He'd held it together for months, years maybe. But he was beginning to unravel.

The next song started, the music blared, and the intro began . . . but Maddox didn't sing. Blake quickly covered for him and Maddox leaned over, his hand on his knee, trying to breathe.

"Is his mic not working?" the stage tech beside us asked.

He screamed into his walkie-talkie. "Someone get a check on mic one!"

It wasn't his mic.

Maddox spun to look in our direction, looking for me, his hand to his chest, his mic fell to the stage. And without thinking, without a single thought about the eighty thousand witnesses, before someone could stop me, I took the steps two at a time and raced out onto the stage.

CHAPTER SEVENTEEN

I SAW NOTHING BUT MADDOX, and the absolute panic—the sheer terror—in his eyes. I scooped my arm around his back, under his arm and hauled him off the stage and down the steps. Hardwick met me at the bottom with a can of oxygen and he put the mouthpiece directly on Maddox's face.

We couldn't stay here. The stage crew and the production team were all standing, staring at him.

"Let's get him into the dressing room," I said, still with my arm around his back, and I half-carried him. He was heavy, listless.

"Can we clear the room, please," I yelled, and the few wardrobe people quickly disappeared.

I lowered Maddox onto the couch and he lay down, the doc still holding the oxygen to his mouth. A tear rolled toward his temple, his chest heaved.

Oh, baby.

I took his hand and squeezed. "It's okay, Maddox. We've got you."

There was a monitor showing a live feed of the stage,

like there always was, and Jeremy's voice rang out. "He's okay!" I hadn't even realized the music had stopped out there. "He's had some voice issues on this tour and he really wanted to sing for you guys. He's gonna be upset that he let you down, so I'm gonna need you guys to do Maddox a real big favor, okay? We're gonna need you guys to sing all his lines, okay? Can you do that for him?"

The crowd roared, louder than any concert I'd heard. I could feel the rumble through the floor.

The music started and we could hear the crowd sing, singing for him. Maddox pushed the aerosol of oxygen away, he held his hands to his face, and he cried.

And he didn't seem able to stop.

Every line the crowd sang, the more he cried.

Hardwick sagged beside me, his face drawn. He shook his head sadly, and I nodded.

This wasn't good. This was *all* bad.

Me running out on stage and taking Maddox off would already be online, by eighty thousand different cameras. Maddox missing his lines, pulling at his shirt collar, that'd all be out there for the world to see.

And you know what? I didn't care. None of that mattered.

The only thing I cared about, the only thing in the world that mattered to me was Maddox.

The doc had the good sense to turn the monitor off, though it didn't matter much. We could hear the crowd belt out the chorus.

"I should be out there," Maddox sobbed, his voice cracking. He still covered his face with his hands, but then they were fists and he became angry. "I should be out there!"

"Maddox, I want you to breathe for me," Hardwick said gently.

Maddox pushed up to a half-sitting position, tears spilled down his cheeks. "How can I? I freaked out on stage, in front of everyone, the whole world watching and I couldn't fucking breathe because I'm broken."

"You're not broken," I said. "Maddox—"

He shot up off the couch and stepped past us. "I'm fucking broken," he said, then picked up the monitor and threw it against the wall. Then when that wasn't enough, he kicked a table, shoving it into another table, and when he turned to see what else he could smash, I wrapped him up in my arms.

He tried to pull away but I held him, but he struggled against me so I relented my hold. He broke free the second I let him go, and he swiped his arm through a row of full water bottles on a table, sending them flying. Then he kicked a chair over, and I went to go to him again but Hardwick's hand on my arm stopped me.

Maddox screamed as he pulled at his hair. He upended another table, but then he lost his footing and he fell against the wall. With no fight left in him, he slid down, his head in his hands, and sobbed, gasping for air. He tried to speak but no sounds came out, his face a mask of pain and sadness.

Unsure of what else to do, I knelt in front of him and put my hands on his head, his jaw, his shoulders. "You're not broken," I whispered.

"I need to go out there, on stage, Roscoe," he rasped. "But I can't. I can't." He gulped back some air. "I can't do this. This is all I know. This is all I am. I love it, but it's killing me." He sobbed again. "It's killing me."

I turned to Hardwick. "Can you get Steve for me?" He frowned, but he dashed out the door. I put my hand to Maddox's cheek. "Maddox, baby, I'm gonna take you out of here, okay?"

He nodded with a fresh wave of tears, and I realized then that he was fisting the front of my shirt. "I'm not leaving you," I told him. "I'm gonna take you somewhere, just you and me, somewhere you can breathe."

He nodded, just as Hardwick and Steve came through the door. I looked up at them. "We need to leave," I said. "Not just the stadium. We're leaving New York City, and we're leaving tonight. I need to get him out of here."

I could see the doc had a dozen questions he wanted to ask, but Steve took one look at Maddox and nodded. "Come with me."

An hour later, I had a rental car, our bags packed in the trunk, a sleeping Maddox in the front seat, and we were on I-87 headed north.

CHAPTER EIGHTEEN

MADDOX SLEPT FOR SEVENTEEN HOURS.

He appeared on the cabin deck, disheveled, and confused about where we were. Our laughter must have woken him. I ran up the embankment, cleared the two steps onto the deck, and collected him in a crushing hug. He was all warm from being in bed.

"Hey, beautiful," I murmured.

He sighed in my arms. "What time is it?"

"Two o'clock."

"Did you give me something that made me sleep?"

I shook my head. "No. You were exhausted." I could hardly rouse him to get him out of the car at three this morning when we'd arrived, and he'd curled up in bed and gone straight back to sleep.

"Hey, dickbag!" Jeremy called out as he walked toward us from the woodpile.

Maddox pulled back, squinted at the afternoon sun. "Where am I?"

"Manchester," I replied.

He looked at me, then looked out at the view. It was

rolling green pastures, hills, cattle, a barn. "Uh, I've been to Manchester and it doesn't look like this."

I laughed. "Manchester, Vermont."

Jeremy climbed the steps and collected Maddox in a tight embrace. "I just got here an hour ago. The boys wanted to come, but then all the security would have to come and it would have been a big deal. As it was, Steve wouldn't let me come up by myself." He pointed back down to where he'd come from, and there was Steve behind the woodpile. Steve waved at us. Jeremy laughed. "I was chopping wood. And that's not a euphemism."

"He was trying to chop wood," Steve yelled. "He didn't even know which end of the ax to hold."

Jeremy snorted. "Not entirely true."

Maddox scratched his head and shot me an odd look. "Is this your parent's place? Why are we here?"

"This is my aunt and uncle's ranch, just outside of Manchester. My parents will be here tomorrow."

Maddox made a face. "Oh good."

Jeremy snorted, and I rubbed Maddox's arm. "They'll like you."

He ran his hand through his hair and looked out to the mountains at the horizon. "It's nice here."

"Thought you might prefer some open space and not another hotel room." I gestured to the other cabin past the woodpile. "My aunt and uncle used to run those ranch stays, but the insurance made it hard. There's three cabins, and the main house is up over the rise."

"I'm in the next cabin, Steve's in the far one," Jeremy said. "How freaking cool is it here? There are some horses we can ride. We were gonna light a fire later on and cook out."

Maddox breathed in deep and closed his eyes. "The concert . . ."

"The concert went just fine," Jeremy replied. "We got the crowd to sing the last few songs with us and the media loved it. The whole stadium sang. It was kinda magical."

Maddox gave him a sad smile. "I'm sorry."

"I know you are," Jeremy replied. "But there's no need to be. We got through it. Just glad you're okay."

Maddox was quiet for a few long seconds. "Did Ambrose flip his shit?"

I shook my head. "No. He understood."

"He's actually been pretty good," Jeremy said. "He put out a presser this morning. He said the band was taking a well-deserved break after the tour, which we were gonna do anyway. You could imagine the questions they yelled at him about you, but he shot that shit down pretty quick. He was kinda savage."

Maddox nodded slowly. "And everyone else went back to LA?"

"Everyone," I replied. "It's just us."

"And you wanna know the best part?" Jeremy asked, his grin wide. "There's no Wi-Fi here. At all. If you wanna use your phone, you need to walk up the hill. We're completely cut off from everything, like it's the olden days."

I laughed. Jeremy'd been here for maybe two hours. I doubt he'd think it was so great in a few days . . .

"Jeremy!" Steve called out. He was holding the ax out. "You wanted to do this."

Jeremy grimaced and trudged back down the steps. "Before I knew how hard it was."

Maddox chuckled, and when I held my arm out, he walked right into a hug. He breathed in deep and clung to me. "Thank you."

"For what?"

"For bringing me here. For knowing what I need when I don't. For taking care of me."

I squeezed him and rubbed his back. "You hungry?"

He nodded. "Yeah."

"My aunt dropped off some food. There's fresh bread and some deli meat, fresh eggs, and tomatoes. They grow all kinds of things."

I led him inside to the small kitchenette. The cabin itself was very humble. It was old, consisted of one bedroom, a tiny bathroom, a small living area with a wood fire, a couch, and a small kitchenette. And that was it. It was a very far cry from the five-star hotels we'd been used to. Or Maddox's mansion, for that matter.

"I like this," he said with the hint of a smile. There was no sarcasm or jokes. "It's cozy and warm. It feels . . . good. Kinda homey." He leaned against the counter while I threw together a sandwich for him. "Did I really sleep all night and half the day? I don't even remember getting here. Did you carry me in?"

"Almost. You were exhausted, and honestly, I think you could probably sleep for a week."

He scrubbed his hands over his face. His hair still had product in it from the concert last night and he still wore his dangling earrings. He wore his usual outfit—gray sweat-pants and a black hoodie—and he still took my breath away.

I handed him a plate with his sandwich. "Thank you," he whispered.

I kissed the side of his head. "You're welcome. Let's sit out on the deck and watch Jeremy make a dick of himself."

"I'm glad he's here," Maddox said. "I mean, time alone with you is great. But it's nice that he came too."

"He was coming here whether I wanted him to or not," I

admitted. "He loves you, and he was worried. He also said if I didn't give him the address, he'd tell the police I kidnapped you and he could just follow the FBI helicopters."

Maddox chuckled. "Sounds about right."

"And Steve refused to let him drive by himself," I added. "He got everyone to the airport this morning and made sure Robbie had the latest brief, and they drove straight here."

We sat in the two chairs on the deck and laughed as we watched Jeremy and Steve try to do the Captain America thing, where he splits the wood with his bare hands. Maddox finished his sandwich and pulled his chair closer to mine, put his leg over my thigh, and when that wasn't close enough, apparently, he sat on my lap. Just curled up, with his arms around my neck, his head on my shoulder.

"Your aunt and uncle don't mind us being here?" he asked.

"Not at all. It's good to see them. And I told my uncle I'd help him around the ranch while I'm here. I used to spend the summers here when I was a kid, helping out."

"Will you tell me everything," he murmured.

"Everything about what?"

"Everything about you. You know every single thing about me. I knew you grew up in Vermont, but I never pictured it like this."

"I grew up in Bennington. It's about twenty-five miles from here. My parents still live there, and my dad's brother owns this ranch. But my parents sold the house I grew up in and bought a condo, so their new place doesn't really feel like home to me."

"Do you miss being here on the East Coast? Do you miss seeing your family?"

"Not really. Well, I didn't. Until I needed to take you somewhere safe and the one place I thought of was here. I knew if I could get you here, you'd be okay. It's private but it's all open spaces. There's room to breathe here, and the outside world may as well be a million miles away."

He sighed. "It's perfect. We could stay here forever."

"Well, we could . . . until winter. The one thing I absolutely do not miss from here is the snow in winter and the freezing cold. But mostly the snow."

"Oh, yeah. I'm not a fan. But maybe one time, if you teach me how to ski and if there's log fires to fall asleep in front of."

I rubbed his back. "That actually sounds pretty good. And speaking of family, you should call your mom. She was worried." She'd seen the footage, obviously, and all the news updates. "We'll need to walk up the hill."

"Okay. Can I just stay here for a second first?"

"Of course." I gave him a squeeze and kissed the side of his head.

After a while, Maddox eventually sighed, peeled himself off me, and went in search of his boots. I waited on the deck and we walked up to the top of the rise. We could see the main house from here and the view on the other side was just as vast and just as green. I hit Redial on his mom's number and handed him my phone.

"Roscoe?" I heard her say.

"No, Mom. It's me."

"Oh, Maddox, I've been so worried!"

I took a few paces away so he could have some privacy, but I could still hear what he said. "I'm okay. ... Yeah, he took care of me. ... Yes, he is. ... Well, about that . . . Mom, it's still kinda new. ... We'll talk about it when I get home. ... Next week. I just need a few days to decompress, Mom. ... I just wanted to let you know I'm okay. ... Yeah, of course. ... Love you too."

I gave him a smile and he gave me back my phone. "I think I just told my mom about us." He made a strangled laughing sound. "God. There's no getting out of it now. She knows, there's no going back."

I laughed and threw my arm around his shoulder as we began walking back down the hill. "That's okay with me."

"Hey, Madz," Jeremy called out. "Come and help me start the campfire. And I can show you my cabin."

Maddox groaned but he smiled as he walked off toward Jeremy. Steve came up and joined me on the deck. I fell into one chair, he sat in the other. "Gotta say, this is a helluva spot."

"Nice, huh? But I'll ask you that in a few days when you'd kill for decent coffee and a halfway reliable internet connection."

Steve chuckled and we watched as Maddox and Jeremy walked over to the next cabin. It was maybe fifty yards away, and they were talking. "How is he today?" Steve asked.

"He's still tired, but now that the tour's over he seems calmer, relieved. I don't know. Maybe that's just because he's here and he managed to get some sleep. Time will tell, I guess." I shrugged. "He and Jeremy have a lot of things to talk about."

"Do you think he's done with the band?"

"Who, Maddox?" I shook my head. "No. I think he needs a break. A break from everything for a good while. But he loves music and the four guys. They have stuff to work through, don't get me wrong, but they're like brothers. And I think how they work as a band, going forward, will be different. How Atrous comes through this will be different than how they've gotten through everything else."

"It has to be," Steve said. "They've had too much pressure on them for too long. Maddox especially. They were just kids when they started. Do Arlo Kim and Platinum Entertainment know how lucky they are that it's *those* five guys? Those five guys together, in particular. They don't have week-long benders, they don't touch drugs, they don't trash hotel rooms, they don't wreck sports cars for fun or do interviews when they're drunk. They're good kids, they're humble and respectful, mostly, and they've handled everything better than most ever could." He shook his head. "What Maddox said about being a circus monkey in a cage was right on. I get why he feels that way, and I don't know how Maddox lasted as long as he did, to be honest. Humans aren't meant to be tested for tensile strength."

I smiled at him. I liked that analogy. "No, they're not. But I think he knows there isn't some magic fix for this. He's on a long road, and it's not gonna be easy. But he'll be okay."

Steve nodded slowly. "I'm glad you two finally figured it out, too."

"Figured what out?"

He laughed. "That you had a thing. You both spent two years trying to not check each other out, looking when the other one wasn't."

I nodded, not even embarrassed. "I'm glad we figured it out too."

Steve looked over to where Maddox and Jeremy had disappeared. "We should go and see what they're doing. They shouldn't be left unsupervised, especially if they're trying to light the fire pit."

I chuckled. "That's a very good point."

As evening became night, we sat around the fire grilling

some steaks and burgers—the fire that Steven and I fixed, not Maddox and Jeremy, after their disastrous attempt. My aunt and uncle came down from the house and met Maddox, and they'd made enough sides and fresh bread to feed an army. We ate, we talked, we had a few beers, and we laughed.

But the night turned cold, and after Maddox had yawned for the fifth time, I pulled him to his feet. "That's our cue," I declared. "It's been . . . actually, it's been lovely. But Maddox is falling asleep." And he yawned again, just to prove my point. We said our rounds of goodnights and headed back to our cabin.

"I smell like a campfire," Maddox said, sniffing his hoodie. "Even my hair smells. I need to shower."

"Okay. Want me to fix you some hot tea or something?"

"No, I want you to shower with me."

I snorted. "That shower cubicle is tiny. I barely fit in there by myself."

Maddox's smile disappeared under his hoodie as he pulled it over his head. He tossed it onto the couch. "Then we better stand *really* close together."

He kicked off his boots and his eyes never left mine as he pulled his sweatpants down.

Fucking hell.

We really didn't fit in the shower, and we probably splashed more water outside the cubicle than in it, but neither of us cared. We did manage to shampoo his hair and half-scrub each other before we took it to the bedroom.

"God, Roscoe," he moaned as I lubed his ass, fingering and stretching. "I need you to make this good. Fuck me so hard. Please."

I didn't need telling twice; my already aching dick longed to be inside him. I pushed him onto his belly and bit the back of his neck. "You keep talking like that and this will be over before it begins."

He laugh-groaned into the mattress, arching his back and spreading his legs. I rolled on a condom, added more lube, then pushed into him in one long, deep thrust. He cried out, a guttural sound, fisting the pillows above his head. But he backed his ass onto me, wanting more.

So I gave it to him.

Just like he wanted. Hard, deep, over and over, again and again. He felt so damn good, so hot and tight. I gripped his hips, nailing him, and when I hit that spot, that sweet spot inside him, he unraveled underneath me. I held his hips still while he came, fucking him harder still, filling the condom inside him, and he groaned like I'd never heard.

Pain, pleasure, both, all at once. And even when I held him afterwards, his whole body jerked and twitched, making him laugh every time. "What the fuck did you do to me?" he asked, chuckling, groaning.

I kissed the side of his head. "I did what you asked me to do."

He snuggled into me, warm and sleepy. "Promise me you'll do that again."

I held him tighter, drifting off to sleep with him. "Certainly gonna try."

He chuckled and sighed, his breathing evened out and I smiled into his hair, and I fell asleep wondering if this was the beginning of our new normal. Would we get to have this —having nights with family and friends, making love, sleeping in each other's arms without a care in the world?

I wanted that with him. I wanted that *for* him. Sure, we had a long road ahead of us, with Maddox's panic disorder; doctor appointments, therapy, whatever it took. They had to figure out the path Atrous would take from here, but I had no doubt they'd be okay.

Maddox *would be* okay.

He knew now that everyone around him loved him and supported him. And they now knew that he'd struggled for too long, that he'd tried to be strong for everyone else and it almost broke him.

It was all in the open now, and they could begin to move forward. Whichever direction they took, whatever they decided, they'd be okay.

So yeah, that night for the first time in far too long, sleep came easy.

———

MY PARENTS ARRIVED the next morning to find me laughing my ass off watching Steve trying to teach Maddox and Jeremy how to roundhouse kick a haybale. Dad hugged me and Mom fussed over my eyebrow and temple, which was now a nice yellowing purple, but at least it gave time for Maddox to walk over while Jeremy laughed at him in the background.

He was clearly nervous, wiping his hands on his jeans. "Mom, Dad, this is Maddox Kershaw," I said, putting my arm around his shoulder. "Maddox, this is Allison and Derrick Hall, my parents."

Dad shook his hand. "Nice to finally meet you, son."

Maddox's cheeks flushed. "Likewise."

Mom took Maddox's hand in both of hers. "Oh, you're even more handsome in real life."

Oh god.

"I've seen you on television and in all the papers," Mom kept on. "And of course Roscoe has told me all about you."

"Mom," I tried.

"He has?" Maddox asked, slightly amused, slightly horrified.

Mom patted his hand. "All good things, I promise. He's always talking about how wonderful you are. For years, actually."

Oh, dear god.

"Mom, I don't think we'll play the 'let's embarrass Roscoe' game today. Please?"

"Yes, let's play that!" Jeremy said, grinning as he walked over. "Tell me everything!"

Of course my mother would find Jeremy adorable, and for the rest of the day my parents told them all embarrassing stories of me growing up. My awkward teenage years were a particular highlight, which Jeremy found hilarious. But it put Maddox at ease so I didn't mind too much.

We ate a lot of food and talked half the day away. It was so good to see them, and maybe I had missed them more than I'd realized. Maddox and Jeremy decided to drag Steve along for a walk through the fields, giving me some time alone with my folks.

"You look tired, love," Mom said. "And your eye. I saw it on the news, where that man pushed you into the pole. It was terrible."

"I'm fine. Better now the tour's over, that's for sure."

"Until the next one," Dad chimed in. "You're always traveling off to somewhere."

I nodded. "It's been pretty crazy." I wasn't telling them that things would be different now, maybe slower, because I honestly didn't know if they would. "We have a break in our schedule now for a while. Still busy but not so much travel-ing." I smiled at them. "Maddox mentioned wanting to come back here to spend some more time, maybe in winter. So that might be something we can plan."

"Would it be just you two this time?" Mom asked, hinting.

"Maybe." I felt my cheeks heat. "Then again, he's one of five. Maybe the guys will come with us. Usually where there's one, there's one more, or four, not too far away."

"That can't be easy," Mom said.

"Sure it is," I replied. "I knew what I was getting into, and I wouldn't want it any other way. He needs those guys as much as they need him." I sighed. "It's a different life, Mom. It's a different world. It's not all glitz and glamour like the papers say it is. It's empty hotel rooms and exhaustion, it's isolation and loneliness because they can't go anywhere. They can't even go to a grocery store without it being a full security issue. They have no normal. Nothing in their life is normal."

She nodded, though I doubted she really understood. "Well, I'm glad he has you."

"I'm glad he has me too."

"He really is more beautiful close up than the pictures show."

I laughed. "I know. Believe me, Mom. I know."

"Not sure how I feel about all those long earrings though," Dad added.

I shook my head, still laughing. "Oh, Dad, they're one of my favorite things."

He shrugged, resigned. "Must be a gay thing."

I rolled my eyes and laughed again. "Must be."

FIVE DAYS LATER, we packed up the cabins and got ready to leave. Maddox was nervous about going back to LA. It meant going back to real life and facing his mental health head on. We'd had an amazing week at my uncle's ranch. A week removed from the hype, the media, and the noise of all the bullshit that went with it.

But we couldn't stay here forever.

Maddox hadn't had another panic episode, though last night he practiced some deep breathing when he was talking about flying back to LA. He'd started to feel anxious and antsy knowing he had to deal with his reality again, and he recognized it for what it was and countered it with his breathing exercises. It was a tiny step in the grand scheme of things, but it felt so much bigger.

Maddox and Jeremy had talked a lot over the five days, and their friendship seemed even stronger now. Or maybe it was just restored back to what it had been, how they used to be. I didn't get involved in their conversations about the future of Atrous because at the end of the day, I just wanted Maddox to be happy. Whatever he decided was fine with me. But if Maddox had had any doubt about what he'd face back in LA, if he'd be facing it alone, it was gone. Because whatever Atrous decided, they would face it together. Maddox knew that now, and I swear some of that weight he'd carried for so long was lifted.

Ambrose had organized a jet for us to catch at the Bennington airport. Given there were four of the team, including Maddox and Jeremy, it warranted the effort. An airport that size probably hadn't seen too many private jets in its time, and Steve was very happy with the isolated, rural setting rather than going into Boston.

"We'll be home by dinner time," I said, lifting my suitcase into the trunk.

Maddox slid his guitar into the backseat and chewed on his bottom lip. He met my gaze, a little nervous. "Uh, about that . . ."

"What's up? You feeling okay?"

He laughed. "Yeah, I'm fine. I just don't want to go home alone. I don't want to be there alone. It's a pretty big house."

I know. I've seen it.

"And it's not even that I don't want to be alone, Roscoe," he added. "I don't want to be away from you. I'm not ready to leave you just yet. I dunno if I ever will be." He took my hand. "Stay with me. At my house. It's big enough. You can have your own room if you want. There's like eight to pick from. But what we had here was good, right? Staying here together. And I know it won't be like this all the time, but I want it anyway."

I put his hand to my heart. "You want me to stay with you?"

"Yes. Live with me. Every day. We can cook and argue about laundry like normal couples. Or whatever they argue about. I'm sure we'll find out."

I laughed. "Well, when you put it like that . . ."

Maddox kissed me with smiling lips. "Is that a yes?"

I nodded, my heart two sizes too big for my chest. "That's a resounding yes, Mr. Kershaw."

Jeremy tossed his bag into their rental car. "Hey, dick-bag, you ready to go back to the real world?"

Maddox sighed, though he was still smiling. Was he ready to go back and face everything? He looked at me and nodded. "Yeah, I'm ready."

"WE'VE GOT A VERY special guest tonight. It's been two years and the world has been waiting so please join me in giving a very warm welcome to Maddox Kershaw!"

Maddox walked out on stage to a huge round of applause. He wore tight black jeans with my old Bruins shirt under a dark gray blazer. He wore his hair a little longer now, tucked behind one ear, his long black earrings swaying with each step. He smiled, waved at the audience, and met the *Late Show* host with a hug.

He'd been nervous before tonight. But it was time. He was ready.

He took his seat and took a few deep breaths while he waited for the crowd to quiet down. "Maddox, welcome back!"

"Thank you, it's good to be here."

"Now, you've been on a bit of a break, out of the public eye for a little while, but that doesn't mean you haven't been busy. There was the online concert you guys did last year, and the release of the unplugged session Atrous did at the Old Opry, but you guys have managed to have a break."

"The break's been good, actually. Like a full battery recharge." Maddox nodded. This was his first public appearance, his first interview in a long time. "But somehow still busy, just in a good way."

"Before we get into all of that, first I want to talk about the documentary that Platinum Entertainment released last year. It was called *Under the Spotlight*, and it was filmed completely candidly behind the scenes on Atrous' last tour. It showed some pretty harrowing insights of band life, the absolutely crazy schedules, the physical and emotional toll it put on all of you, and it was very personal."

Maddox nodded. "The filming was kinda weird at first. I mean, we're very used to cameras and having an audience wherever we go. But this was a film crew who were to follow us around all the time, which I thought I'd hate. And for the first few days, I did. But then after a while, I forgot they were there. I got used to them, they just blended in, and that was when they got to film the real us." He took a slow breath.

"We actually debated whether we should release the documentary. We all watched it together, and I'll admit it wasn't easy to see. I got to see myself spiral, basically, from the beginning of the tour until the end. And I got to see how that affected everyone around me, which was hard, but it helped me appreciate everyone a bit more. And it showed just how many people it takes to put on a stadium tour. The crowd sees five guys on a stage, but there are literally a hundred and fifty people you don't see." He let out a slow breath. "In the end we decided we needed to be honest with our fans, and the documentary should be released so people can see just what it takes."

"There were arguments, tears, laughter, food, jokes, stress," the host said. "Times when you guys would need help walking to the dressing rooms, you'd need oxygen, laying on the floor. It was compelling to get a glimpse of that."

Maddox nodded again. "That's what happens on tour. You're under immense pressure, emotionally, physically."

"It was very personal, for all of you. Fans got a front-row view of not just your backstage life," the host said, "but we also got to see how fans, paparazzi, and photographers would harass you, to the point of physical assault. I think for me, that was the most disturbing thing. The measures you would need to take just to leave a hotel or a store."

Maddox took a deep breath and nodded. "We'd hoped that the documentary would help people see us as humans. I know that sounds weird, but we're just people. And we come to expect a certain amount of excitement from fans, because we understand people *are* excited. They connect with our music, which is amazing. But then we began to see a level of entitlement that wasn't good for us; not just from fans but from photographers as well. We hoped that the documentary would highlight those issues and people could see how harmful it was for us."

"And your management company, Platinum Entertainment, takes it very seriously now too," the host said. "After the New York incident."

Maddox smiled. "They sure do."

The truth was, Platinum Entertainment set new industry standard safety measures when it came to the press and fans and how they interacted with celebrities. It didn't hurt that they had a juggernaut legal power to bury anyone —and I do mean anyone—who looked at any of us the wrong way. Maddox had put it to Ambrose, and Ambrose delivered.

When Ambrose said things needed to change, it wasn't just talk.

"Now," the host continued, "let's talk about your anxiety and panic disorder, which we got to see glimpses of in the documentary. You've been very open and upfront about what you went through during that time. That can't have been easy."

Maddox let out a slow breath. He knew this question was coming. He'd approved it. "No, it hasn't been easy. It's taken a long time, actually, and a lot of therapy and coping techniques. It's something I still live with, but I'm on top of it now. Removing a lot of unnecessary stress helped, but learning how to cope was the key for me. And again, for me it was about the honesty. I *should* talk about this. It's not something to be ashamed of. It took me a while to figure that out too. I think the hardest part for me was accepting it. I had everything: money, fame, traveling the world, doing what I loved. How could I complain, right? To complain about getting everything you ever wanted would be ungrateful. And I didn't want people to think I was ungrateful. Because I am really thankful."

"But you worked hard for that success. Countless hours. Thousands of hours. Since you were sixteen."

Maddox nodded again. "Sure. And the work was tough. But with that level of fame comes isolation. You can't leave your house or your hotel room. Eventually your phone stops ringing because you can't do anything or go anywhere. You can't make new friends because how do you know if people like you for the real you or if they just want a piece of the fame and money, you know? And suddenly the walls are closing in and the guilt, and the pressure to do better, be better, be more." He shook his head and sighed. "And there was a stopping point. A point where my mind just said no more. I had nothing left to give."

"When was your stopping point?" the host asked gently.

"I've thought about that a lot," he replied. "There was a point that I can see now, with the gift of hindsight, that I would call the tipping point for me. When I knew that things really weren't good. I hadn't been coping for some time. We'd begun the tour for the new album and I wasn't in a good headspace, really, at all. And we were in the car, going to a rehearsal or to a photoshoot, I can't even remember, but I felt like I was losing my mind. In my head, I knew things weren't good. Nothing felt real, just a hollow blur. But I had to keep it together, right? My chest was all tight, and I was trying to just breathe air like a normal person when Roscoe held out his hand for me to hold."

The audience ooooh'd and awww'd, the cameras panned to show people in the crowd put their hands to their mouths. Even the host frowned. "That's sweet, but Maddox, that's also kind of sad."

Maddox laughed, embarrassed. "It is sad. I was so lonely, so deprived of human contact. I was a mess. But that touch . . . wow, you know human touch is a helluva drug. I was so starved of just the simplest things like holding hands that it honestly grounded me. He held my hand and I could breathe. I hadn't truly realized just how much it felt like I was being held underwater until I broke the surface and could breath. That's when I knew that things weren't good for me." He tucked his hands under his legs, his cheeks pink. "He was a literal lifeline. In the end, I had to want to save myself but he showed me I was worth saving."

The audience awww'd again and applauded. "Now, speaking of Roscoe," the host said. "He's here tonight."

The cameras panned over to the wings of the stage

where I stood. I waved and the crowd clapped and cheered. Maddox grinned at me. "Yes, he's here tonight."

The host was excited now. "And some very exciting news for you both last year . . ."

Maddox nodded slowly, trying not to smile. "Yes. I asked him to marry me and he said yes."

The crowd erupted into cheers and applause. One camera trained in on me, one on Maddox. I couldn't help but smile, but I stayed where I was. I wasn't joining Maddox on stage.

"And no, Mom," Maddox said down the camera, "there's still no wedding plans yet. We're just happy where we're at."

"Tell us about the proposal," the host said. "Was it romantic?"

Maddox laughed. "Uh, no. We were arguing about which way the driveway should go, you know, up to the building site—"

"You were arguing?"

Maddox laughed and nodded. "Yep. He's never let me get away with anything. And I thought, you know what? I want to argue with him every day of the rest of my life." He smiled. "And so I asked him."

The host laughed and looked over to me. "Is that really how it went?"

I nodded. "Exactly like that."

"And who was right about the driveway?" the host asked. "If you were arguing . . ."

Maddox cleared his throat and shifted in his seat. "We don't need to talk about that."

Everyone laughed, the host included. "Now you mentioned a building site? Are you building a new home?"

Maddox's smile widened. "I bought a property outside

of LA. Sixty acres with an old barn and nothing else. I had some cabins added."

"Some cabins? Like log cabins?"

Maddox laughed. "Not quite. More like little houses." He held up his hand. "Five little houses, each with a deck and a porch; one for each of the boys, and we converted the barn into a recording studio. There's a communal barbecue area with a fire pit, and we just go there to chill out, have a jam session, record some stuff. We got the idea from Roscoe's family ranch in Vermont. We took all the guys there last year and stayed for two weeks, and we loved it so much that we replicated it back here."

The host leaned in, excited. "So you have been recording some stuff? Because there was talk of disbanding at one point. Talk us through that."

Maddox let out a long breath. "It was an option, yeah. We'd been through a lot. You know, we were thrown onto the world stage at sixteen, and it got to a point where I didn't even know what normal was supposed to be. Blake needed surgery to fix his knee. Wes's shoulder needed PT and time to heal. We were just at a breaking point, as a team, we were exhausted. But I actually broke, which the whole world saw, pretty much." He took a second to breathe. "So we took time off. And we talked a lot about what we wanted, as a group and what we wanted as individuals, professionally and personally. It wasn't easy, because we'd always said it would be the five of us or none of us. That was how it worked. If one of us pulled the pin, we'd all walk away. We made that pact when we were sixteen."

"But so much happened since then," the host offered. "So much has changed."

"True. Almost everything was different," Maddox replied. "But not that. Not us. We were still us. Just five ordinary guys who loved to sing and make music. That would never change. So we asked ourselves what that meant for Atrous, as musicians and creative artists, where did we go from there. What would it mean for our fans who loved and supported us so much?" Maddox smiled and let out a slow breath. "Our manager, Neil Ambrose, and Arlo Kim, the boss of Platinum Entertainment, told us to write whatever music we wanted. To be the band *we* wanted. They sat us down and reminded us that we put our souls into every album, every song, every performance. It was what made our fans connect with us on such a personal level. So this should be no different. No matter what music we produced moving forward, if we did it with honesty and put our hearts into it, then our fans would know. They'd feel it. And they reminded us of why we do this. They basically gave us full creative control over what we produce. Moving forward, anything Atrous produces comes from us."

"So you decided Atrous would stay together . . ."

"We did."

The audience burst into cheers and clapping, and Maddox just beamed. I was so proud of him.

The host side-eyed him. "Now, you know the internet is always full of rumors, most of which we just scroll right on by. But there have been whispers in certain circles about the possibility of a comeback, possibly a song. Is there anything you can tell us?"

Maddox's smile was slow spreading. "Maybe . . ."

The audience went crazy and Maddox had to wait for them to be quiet so he could finish. "I can tell you there is an album and a song. But it's a two-for-one deal because it's actually the title track, so you get both the name of the album *and* the song . . ."

The host waited and waited.

Maddox leaned back in his seat and put his hand on the host's desk like he owned it. He was relaxed and knowing it was genuine now made me so happy. Maddox grinned. "Actually, if it's okay with you, I brought some friends along. I thought we could sing it for you."

Jeremy, Wes, Luke, and Blake walked out on stage to gasps of surprise, excited squeals, and a standing ovation of applause. The host's face was priceless.

It wasn't easy to pull off this kind of surprise, but we'd managed it. Ambrose had pulled some strings and made it possible. Jeremy handed Maddox his guitar.

The five of them sat on some stools with a mic stand in front. No dancing, no band. Just five magical voices and Maddox's guitar. "This song is called 'Code Red,'" Maddox said. "I wrote it a few years back, one night in a hotel room. We were on tour and it was late, and Roscoe's gonna kill me for saying this," he laughed, embarrassed. "Anyway, he was asleep and I was watching him with this really terrible, godawful feeling that I was falling in love."

The audience laughed.

Maddox shot me a timid smile. Yes, I was going to kill him.

"Anyway," Maddox continued. "This is it. 'Code Red.' I hope you like it."

A hush fell over the audience, the spotlights shone on the five of them, Maddox strummed his guitar, and began to sing.

THE END

MADDOX'S NOTEBOOK

→ Code Red ←

i don't know how to tell you
i don't know the words
i don't know what you see in me
i don't know what you heard

the sirens cut the night
all the birds take flight
all the world stops turning
can you, can you feel me burning

(somebody call it)
code red
i'm falling
code red
i'm falling
in love with you

When the lights are too bright
When the night is too dark
when you look at me like that
you start a wildfire with just one, just one spark

(baby, baby)
the sirens cut the night
and i'm losing the fight
you hold my hand
and everything is alright

i need you to believe me
i need you to see me
no one knows me like you do
no one knows how
you saved me
you saved me

(somebody call it, somebody please)
code red
i'm falling
code red
i'm falling
in love with you

Oceans

(intro – humming)   Luke

i am lost
in oceans of blue

Blake

endless waves
pulling me under
depths i've never known

oceans of blue   Maddox
in a storm of you
may the stars above guide us,
may this lighthouse bring us home

i am lost
in oceans of blue   luke and Blake
i am so lost
in oceans of you

Wesley → [Rap verse]

Let the current take me
i want to drown in the blue
Jeremy → where there is nothing but silence
and visions of you

may the stars above guide us,   Maddox
may this lighthouse bring us home

repeat chorus x 2 ← all

(humming to fade)

Beacon

close your eyes
feel my touch
close your eyes
when it all becomes too much

surrender to the passion
feel me, want me, love

my heart burns for you
a fire inside me
a beacon to shine
a light in the dark
my heart is the beacon
baby, be mine

open your mouth
taste my touch
open your eyes
can you get enough

surrender to me
feel me, want me, love

my heart burns for you
a fire inside me
a beacon to shine
a light in the dark
my heart is the beacon
say you'll be mine

Puzzle

when you long for a place you've never been
when you miss a person you've never  seen
when you want to walk away
to find a dream you've never dreamed
in a place that has no name

~~[scribbled out]~~

the person i miss is me

none of the pieces of me fit anymore
this impossible puzzle
this impossible puzzle of me

When home feels like a stranger
when days all bleed into one
When the only thing you long for
to feel things you've never felt
to feel anything at all

because none of the pieces fit anymore
this impossible puzzle
this impossible puzzle of me

the person i miss is me

Reflection

you knew these eyes once
a distant memory
something far away
a familiarity flickers
but you can't place it
you can't quite place it

the eyes that once looked back you
not so long ago
where possibilities once shined
where light and glitter once stared back at you
is gone

When was it lost
when did those eyes change
a familiarity flickers
but you can't place it
you can't quite place it

A stranger stares back you
the face looks familiar
but the eyes
you don't recognise the eyes
where light and glitter that once stared back at you
is gone

 jisei

the fire that burns in each of us
a passion
a dream
for which we live

a fire that always burns
a low ember
or a raging wall of flame
my only gift to give

behind the ribs it burns
it fuels and feeds us.
sustains us and defeats us

To live without it is to not live
my only gift to give
take my voice and you take my will
my mind
my life

to let the embers fade to black
is my first death

to ask me to walk away
to silence me
is the cruelest way to die

behind the ribs it burns
the fire the keeps me alive
this first death
is the cruelest way to die

Wonder

i wonder sometimes
if you stare at the moon
like i do

if the silver outlines your face
like it used to

if the moonlight touches you
like it used to

baby i wonder
i wonder about you

i wonder sometimes
if you find peace in the night
like you used to

if you sit under the stars
and wonder about the universe
like we used to

i wonder sometimes
if you think of me
like you used to

i wonder sometimes
if you stare at the moon and wonder
like i still do

baby i wonder
if you only knew
all the times
i wonder about you

ABOUT THE AUTHOR

N.R. Walker is an Australian author, who loves her genre of gay romance. She loves writing and spends far too much time doing it, but wouldn't have it any other way.

She is many things: a mother, a wife, a sister, a writer. She has pretty, pretty boys who live in her head, who don't let her sleep at night unless she gives them life with words.

She likes it when they do dirty, dirty things... but likes it even more when they fall in love.

She used to think having people in her head talking to her was weird, until one day she happened across other writers who told her it was normal.

She's been writing ever since...

ALSO BY N.R. WALKER

Lacuna

Bossy

Free Reads:

Sixty Five Hours

Learning to Feel

His Grandfather's Watch (And The Story of Billy and Hale)

The Twelfth of Never (Blind Faith 3.5)

Twelve Days of Christmas (Sixty Five Hours Christmas)

Best of Both Worlds

Translated Titles:

Italian

Fiducia Cieca (Blind Faith)

Attraverso Questi Occhi (Through These Eyes)

Preso alla Sprovvista (Blindside)

Il giorno del Mai (Blind Faith 3.5)

Cuore di Terra Rossa (Red Dirt Heart)

Cuore di Terra Rossa 2 (Red Dirt Heart 2)

Cuore di Terra Rossa 3 (Red Dirt Heart 3)

Cuore di Terra Rossa 4 (Red Dirt Heart 4)

Natale di terra rossa (Red dirt Christmas)

Intervento di Retrofit (Elements of Retrofit)

A Chiare Linee (Clarity of Lines)

Senso D'appartenenza (Sense of Place)

Spencer Cohen 1 Serie: Spencer Cohen

Spencer Cohen 2 Serie: Spencer Cohen

Spencer Cohen 3 Serie: Spencer Cohen

Spencer Cohen 4 Serie: Yanni's Story

Punto di non Ritorno (Point of No Return)

Punto di Rottura (Breaking Point)

Punto di Partenza (Starting Point)

Imago (Imago)

Il desiderio di un soldato (A Soldier's Wish)

Scambiato (Switched)

Galassie e Oceani (Galaxies and Oceans)

French

Confiance Aveugle (Blind Faith)

A travers ces yeux: Confiance Aveugle 2 (Through These Eyes)

Aveugle: Confiance Aveugle 3 (Blindside)

À Jamais (Blind Faith 3.5)

Cronin's Key

Cronin's Key II

Au Coeur de Sutton Station (Red Dirt Heart)

Partir ou rester (Red Dirt Heart 2)

Faire Face (Red Dirt Heart 3)

Trouver sa Place (Red Dirt Heart 4)

Le Poids de Sentiments (The Weight of It All)

Un Noël à la sauce Henry (A Very Henry Christmas)

Une vie à Refaire (Switched)

German

Flammende Erde (Red Dirt Heart)

Lodernde Erde (Red Dirt Heart 2)

Sengende Erde (Red Dirt Heart 3)

Ungezähmte Erde (Red Dirt Heart 4)

Vier Pfoten und ein bisschen Zufall (Finders Keepers)

Ein Kleines bisschen Versuchung (The Weight of It All)

Ein Kleines Bisschen Fur Immer (A Very Henry Christmas)

Weil Leibe uns immer Bliebt (Switched)

Drei Herzen eine Leibe (Three's Company)

Über uns die Sterne, zwischen uns die Liebe (Galaxies and Oceans)

Unnahbares Herz (Blind Faith 1)

Sehendes Herz (Blind Faith 2)

Thai

Sixty Five Hours (Thai translation)

Finders Keepers (Thai translation)

Lightning Source UK Ltd.
Milton Keynes UK
UKHW010812260122
397682UK00011B/99

9 781925 886634